STORM
GLASS

ALSO BY JEFF WHEELER

The Kingfountain Series

The Legends of Muirwood Trilogy

The Covenant of Muirwood Trilogy

Whispers from Mirrowen Trilogy

Landmoor Series

STORM GLASS

the HARBINGER SERIES

JEFF WHEELER

47N⬤RTH

Published by 47North, Seattle

www.apub.com

Amazon, the Amazon logo, and 47North are trademarks of Amazon.com, Inc., or its affiliates.

ISBN-13: 9781503902329
ISBN-10: 1503902323

Cover design by Mike Heath | Magnus Creative

Printed in the United States of America

To Jennifer

There are many worlds. Yet we constantly separate ourselves, by degrees, from the others. We create arbitrary distinctions to set ourselves apart. But let me speak first of the two main worlds that orbit each other. There are those who live in estates and cities that have mastered the clouds and sit on their perch of air to overlook the vast landscapes below. That is the upper world. The world of the wealthy. The world of the gifted. The world where the Mysteries hold sway. The other world is darker. There are neighborhoods of extreme poverty. Winding alleys and street urchins and gangs. This is a world of fog. It is a world of coughing, sickness, and pestilence. It is a world where industry beckons the ambitious to risk their all—and where the mighty and rich descend in shame after their fortunes have been ruined by games of chance and power. These are very different worlds. And yet, they are much the same.

—Lady Corinne of Pavenham Sky

CETTIE

CHAPTER ONE

THE GIRL WHO CAN SEE THEM

Cettie of the Fells. That was what people called her. She had small glimpses of memory of the time before, but they were so far back that, try as she might, she could wring no details from them. One of the memories was of an officer in his regimentals, so she had always fancied that her birth father was a captain of a sky brigade. She had the vague impression of a long brown mustache and sideburns, of thick wavy hair the color of chestnuts, and of eyes the color of clouds. It was a brooding face, a sad face. He'd given her up to another, however, and when she was three or four, her new guardian died. The rent collector found her not long after, half starving, determined not to go outside and ask for help for fear she'd be taken away. And for good reason. The magistrate promptly delivered her to a cruel woman who only accepted Cettie's deed for the payment she'd receive in exchange. That first woman had given way to another and then another and then her current guardian, Miss Charlotte, but they were all the same—they made the children they took in work, and they punished them. Everything since had been a blur of misery. It had all brought Cettie to this moment, darting through the streets of the Fells, searching for a glimpse of her missing friend.

Cettie and Joses were Miss Charlotte's eldest wards, and, together, they took care of the younger children in the household. They were rarely given food by their guardian, so Joses stole to feed them. He'd never been caught before, but he'd been away for much too long this time. What if the authorities had found him?

The streets were chaotic and crowded. The Fells brimmed with businesses of every shape and sort—smelters, glass makers, linen weavers—as well as factories that made sugar, factories that hewed wood, and factories that hacked animals into bits. Some of the meat fed the factory workers, who in turn fed the factories with their wits and brawn. The rest was crated and boxed and hefted aboard sky ships to ascend to the manors in the clouds, where cooks would prepare it in feasts to be hewed and slurped by the rich.

Cettie had heard people whisper tales that the Fells had once been a thriving industrial center with happy inhabitants, but she only knew it as a smoky, crowded series of mismatched tenements—a place where everything was part prey and part predator. After the sun went down, even the officers were afraid to walk the streets.

And the dark was coming, but she still hadn't found Joses.

A gnawing feeling of dread and desperation overpowered the hunger in her hollow ribs as she tramped through the streets, searching for a sign of her friend's dark hair, for the subtle swagger she'd recognize in an instant.

A shadow passed overhead, and she looked up quickly. It wasn't a cloud blotting the light; it was a sky ship—a zephyr, the smallest kind. Nimble and quick, they were notorious for their use by agents of Law, but they were also sometimes used to transport people or letters from one end of the Fells to the other. As this one passed, she craned her neck to watch it go by. She had no idea how the wooden hull, the spars, and the side sails managed to float through the air. It was a magic of sorts. One of the Mysteries.

A heavy body slammed into her and knocked her to the ground. The impact stunned her, but she hastily came to her feet before someone stepped on her fingers, tore her tattered dress, or collided with her again.

"Watch yerself!" scolded a worker angrily. She retreated from him, lest he take a swing at her. Even so, as soon as she was a good distance from him, her gaze found the zephyr again. It was one of her dreams to steal aboard a sky ship and be taken to one of the floating manors. Though none of them were located directly above the Fells, she'd heard people from the City speak about what it was like to live underneath the upper class's hulking sky manors. They hovered over the City in an interconnected maze, leaving the area below in shadow come noonday. There was a risk that whatever magic upheld the manors might fail and those living below would be crushed, yet people still swarmed to live in the City, willing to take that risk in the hopes of a better life.

Cettie had never set foot outside of the Fells, but she dreamed of leaving. If she proved herself capable and useful and a hard worker, she hoped to one day qualify for the lottery and earn a position at one of the floating manors.

The slant of the sun on the street warned her that time was running out. Maybe Joses was already back at Miss Charlotte's? Could they have missed each other? Cettie hated being away from the younger children for so long. No doubt some of the littlest ones were already crying for want of food, and if their guardian awoke from her drunken stupor, there would be beatings. If she didn't make it back, what would happen to them? That settled things in her mind. She whirled around in the middle of the street, starting back through the throng. It was hard to soothe hungry children, and even as she walked, she scanned the cobbles for a dirty farthing. But there was nothing to be found, and she already knew there wasn't a scrap of food in Miss Charlotte's dwelling.

She glanced back once more to look for Joses, only to discover a boy following her. He was probably sixteen, and he was much taller than her. He had the look of a gang member—feral eyes, grimy coat and cap, and a dangerous air. She had nothing to steal, but gangs were always looking for novices. Others who could be trained to take the risks while they reaped the rewards. She hastened her steps, her breath coming fast and hard.

She lived in a busy area, and the noise and commotion made her ears ache. After several blocks, she risked another backward glance. The young man was still trailing her. He met her gaze this time, a sort of acknowledgment to her that he was indeed following her, seeing where she'd lead him. Well, Cettie had no doubt that Miss Charlotte could thrash a sixteen-year-old boy well enough. She'd not want to lose any of the income the children's deeds brought her.

She almost stopped midstride when she saw a zephyr hovering over the row of tenements. Was it the same one she'd seen overhead earlier?

A crowd had gathered in the street to gawk at it. A few people pointed fingers. Some hurled curses. The law was not respected in certain places within the Fells. Yes, the lawyers and tradesmen within the city center thought highly of it—after all, the law upheld their rights and protected their wealth—but in the tenements the officers could be brutal and cruel. A sick feeling replaced the nervous one.

The zephyr was hovering over Miss Charlotte's.

Cettie heard shouting the moment she opened the door. Miss Charlotte was in hysterics. The men speaking with her were trying to be civil, but it was clear they were losing patience.

"If you don't produce the deeds, ma'am, then you cannot prove your words. Stop wailing and fetch them."

"When my husban' gets back, he'll not stand for this! Can't you wait till he gets back?"

"We cannot wait. It will be dark soon." A sigh of exasperation. Cettie heard the crying children through the holes in the walls. No doubt they were terrified by the fuss, especially if Joses had not returned to comfort them.

Cettie approached the stairs carefully, trying to keep her ripped shoes from making a sound. Miss Charlotte snuffled and devolved into tears again, her words garbled by her emotion. Cettie peeked around the corner and saw several officers of the law gathered around the sofa, wearing their dark jackets with gold stripes and gray cloaks. Their boots were high and glossy.

One of the officers turned and saw her. "There's another one!"

She did not run. Instead, she walked into the room, trying to stand up straight even though she was starting to tremble. She had never encountered an officer before. They were tall and strong, and they'd come in a zephyr!

"How old are you, lass?" one of them asked. He had sandy-brown hair and a mustache.

"I don't know. Twelve, I think," Cettie answered. She took pride in using proper words. She knew she would need to speak well if she hoped to work for one of the wealthy households.

"You live here?" he pressed.

She nodded. "What is the problem, sir?"

"At least *you're* not hysterical," the officer grumbled. "Did you come from the street just now?"

"I did," she answered simply.

"Let me see your hands. Are you hiding anything behind your back?"

Cettie hadn't realized her hands were behind her back. She unclenched her fingers and displayed her dirty palms.

He frowned. "Do you have any pockets? Any money?"

"I have nothing," Cettie said. "Why are you here?"

"Don't be impertinent," another officer snapped impatiently.

"Easy on her," said the first. "At least she's sober. So you live here? You know this woman?"

Cettie nodded. "She's my guardian."

"Don't listen to her!" Miss Charlotte snarled. "Send her up to quiet the little uns. That's all she's good for. I'm the mistress of this house. You wait until my husband gets back. I don't know where the lad went. I can't afford no advocate. You can't—"

"Shut it!" the officer with the mustache said, turning and yelling at her. "You get the deeds. Bring them to me right now, or I'll arrest you and take you to the Ministry of Law, so help me. Do it!"

Miss Charlotte cowered and started sobbing again, but she crept back toward her rooms to do the man's bidding.

"I will go quiet the children, if you please," Cettie said gently, hoping he wouldn't yell at her next.

"Hold," the mustached officer said. He held up a black-gloved hand and gave her a serious look. "A boy was caught stealing. Said he did it because you had no food here. Not a crust. Is that true?"

Joses. Cettie's knees were knocking, and her throat was too thick to speak. She felt like crying. They'd caught Joses. That meant she'd never see him again. But she would be truthful. Maybe the officers would bring the children food. Maybe they'd even take pity on her friend.

She nodded.

The man frowned again, and she feared another outburst. "The lad's name?"

"Joses," Cettie choked out.

The two officers looked at each other, and one nodded. "What do we do, Lieutenant Staunton?" he said. "The magistrate left for the City."

"I know," said the mustached officer gruffly. He cast his eyes around the squalid place. "We need someone to act here. The children are starving. The woman has drunk away all her money." He pursed his lips. "I'll go up to Fog Willow. Fitzroy will come oversee this mess. He'll know what to do."

"You won't be back before dark," said the other nervously.

"Just barricade the door after I go. We'll come through the skylight anyway. I'll leave four men with you here and take Benson and Ricks with me." He craned his neck, as if just then noticing the wailing of the children. He turned to Cettie. "Go comfort them if you can, lass. What was your name again?"

"Cettie," she answered.

He looked at her long and slow and jerked his head for her to leave. Cettie hastened up the rickety stairs. There were two rooms in the attic. One had the skylight the officer would use upon his return, and the other was where the children slept, as far away from their guardian as possible.

If Miss Charlotte heard any whimpering, she'd march up the flights of stairs and thrash every one of the children, even if only one of them had been suffering. Cettie reached the room, and the children mobbed her immediately, frightened out of their wits. Officers had come in through the skylight. They were yelling at Miss Charlotte. Where was Joses? Did she have any food?

She felt as if the flood of concerns would knock her down. There was no food to give them. Some hadn't eaten in several days, including herself. Her bony arms and ribs were a testament to the famine. One of the little girls stroked Cettie's dark hair. The lights did not work upstairs, and the sun was failing. It was getting darker and darker.

"Come kneel down on the floor," Cettie offered in a whisper. She knelt first and drew them around her, hugging each one. She tried to explain that Joses had been caught stealing. There wasn't any food, but she hoped the officers would bring some. Looking into their desperate faces, she tried to smile. She felt like sobbing.

She hummed a popular dancing song for them. The shadows got thicker. The whimpering began to subside.

Joses was gone. He'd be locked behind an iron grate in a cell and left to die. No one other than her would remember him. No one would feed him. The thoughts pounded against her mind over and over as she hummed, trying to keep the young ones calm. Some sniffled. A little boy fell asleep on the floor at her feet.

How long would the officers be gone? The man with the mustache had said they were going to Fog Willow, one of the sky estates. What she would have given to just see a glimpse of it . . .

You'll never see one. You'll die in the Fells like the rest. Maybe Joses is the lucky one. Starving to death is quick. Painless. Like falling asleep. Fall asleep, Cettie. Fall asleep.

She heard a buzzing sound in her ears. The darkness of the room suddenly felt oppressive. The little girl she was hugging began to shudder and whimper.

"Shhhh," Cettie soothed, feeling a malevolence stir in the dark. It was the tall one, the tenement ghost who had haunted her for years. The one without eyes. Of course it would come to her on a night like this, when the suffering at Miss Charlotte's house was the most acute. Its whispering voice loved to taunt her, to choose the words that would torment her most. None of the other children could see the ghost. Or hear it.

But Cettie could.

CHAPTER TWO

BRANT FITZROY

Cettie couldn't remember a time when she hadn't seen ghosts in the Fells. One of her earliest memories was of one of them. Her guardian at the time—the one who had died—had fallen down drunk one evening, snoring loudly and obnoxiously. Cettie had curled up in the corner, unable to sleep because of the noise. The first sign of something amiss was a telltale prickle on the base of her neck, followed by a buzzing sound, almost like the drone of flies over spoiled meat, except deeper and more resonant. She sat up and stared at her guardian, only to see something hovering over him, leaning close as if smelling his breath. This thing was an outline of a person more than anything—a collection of sinewy shapes made of dust motes. And then it began to choke her guardian. The man's snores had cut off, and he'd fought for breath.

The ghosts hadn't started bothering Cettie until she was seven or eight years old. Some of them moved from shadow to shadow, slinking and crafty. But the tall one always strode into a room confidently, and the others seemed to give it deference. Whenever Cettie moved to a new dwelling, the tall one found her. As if it came *looking* for her. This had been going on for four or five years.

The other children started to whimper again. She went about her work, trying to shake off the feeling of threat and fear that came whenever her ghost did. She gathered the littlest ones around her, trying to help them lie down on the wooden floor in a circle around her. She smoothed their hair and whispered promises that food was coming.

"I can't sleep, Cettie," mumbled little Alice. "I'm cold."

"I'll hold you," Cettie promised, hugging the child close. All along, she kept an eye on the tall one, the one with no eyes. One time it had reached out a hand and touched her chest, its invisible claws passing through her skin and bones. Oh, the coldness, the numbness, the terror she'd felt . . . the sensation had lasted for days. The ghosts didn't attack little children. So Cettie surrounded herself and Joses with the young ones each night. It was the only thing that seemed to keep them at bay.

They will all starve. And when they are dead, who will save you from me? You cannot save them. You cannot save yourself.

Alice snuggled against her. Darkness was all around them, but somehow she saw the tall one even better in the dark. Cettie began to hum again, trying to comfort herself and the children. Although the dancing music had no words, she sometimes added them as she went along.

"I'm afraid, Cettie," whispered James in the darkness. "Is Joses coming back with food?"

Still humming, she reached over to caress his head. It was all she could do. Joses wouldn't come back with food . . . he wouldn't come back at all. She squeezed her eyes shut. Should she have encouraged him to stay home instead of wandering the streets looking for a way to steal food?

It is your fault. There were no ghosts here until you came. You are one of the night. And when you die, you will be like one of us. You are one of us already.

Go away! Cettie stopped humming and repeated the thought over and over in her mind, trying to drown out the ghost's twisted mind.

She didn't want to die. To be trapped in the Fells forever as a ghost that could only be seen by some.

She wasn't sure how long she wrestled against the being in her mind. She knew the sun would rise eventually—it always did. And when the light came, the tall ghost without eyes would sink into the floorboards. It lived in the cesspit, she believed. A place where it was always dark and fetid. She hated emptying the chamber pots down there. It was the only job she begged Joses to do for her.

When light finally filtered into the room, it wasn't the slow rise of dawn—it was a bright flare that stabbed at her eyes from the other attic room. Still, it made the ghost hiss and retreat into the shadows. *The skylight.* The thought was accompanied by the sound of boots landing on the roof. The officers had returned.

Some of the children had fallen asleep and no doubt dreamed of honeyed cakes drizzled in syrup. Others were still too hungry to sleep, and they scrambled to the wall to peer through the ripped chunks in the plaster. Cettie set Alice aside and rose; her knees pained her from the way she'd been sitting. Half crouching, she walked to the wall and peered through one of the gaps. She recognized the mustached officer. He was looking up, talking to another man, someone who wasn't wearing the uniform of the law.

The newcomer, an older man with lots of silver in his hair, looked like a banker—one of the upper crust. He had on a long coat and polished brown boots with gleaming buckles. He came down the ladder from the skylight, gripping the rungs with bare hands, which surprised Cettie. She'd thought everyone in the upper class wore gloves. The man blocked the light, which put him in shadow for a moment, and Cettie tried to adjust her position to see. The noise from the attic must have alerted Miss Charlotte, because the woman promptly let out a wailing cry that filled the entire house.

Footsteps in the stairwell announced another officer, one holding a frosted-glass lantern. He strode up to the lieutenant and the new arrival.

"She's come to and is begging us not to take the children away," the officer said. "Apparently there is no husband brave enough to return with all of us here. She has the deeds, smudged as they are, and earns her bread caring for these tramps. I had them checked with the ministry. It's legal. She has the right to care for them." He gestured toward the room where Cettie was watching from a hole in the wall. "Not much to live on, but she says she'll starve if we take them all away, Lieutenant Staunton."

"She does nothing but buy more drink," Staunton snorted angrily. "I don't believe her. The children are clearly neglected."

"Neither do I, but it's already causing a ruckus in the street. Many have stepped forward and offered to take the children, but they'll likely end up back here again if we allow it. This lot looks after their own."

Staunton grimaced. The bright light pouring from the skylight suddenly winked out. Cettie squinted, trying to see. Only a single lantern remained to light the dark. She felt the tall ghost moving toward her once again.

The lieutenant turned to the silver-haired gentleman. "We can't hand over the children to strangers, Vice Admiral," Staunton said. "What do you advise?"

"Let me see the children," the newcomer said. There was something about his voice. It wasn't gruff or impatient or scolding. There was hardly a word fit to describe it, but it was almost . . . gentle. Early on in life, Cettie had learned to quickly discern whether an adult could be trusted. Most of them couldn't be. But something deep inside her whispered that maybe this one was different.

"Back to bed," Cettie whispered to the other children gathered at the wall. "Be still. Be quiet." She felt the ringing in her ears again, louder this time. But the ghost with no eyes was no longer focused on her. A hissing noise was coming from it. She felt a whorl of hatred inside the being, directed at the newcomer.

But there was no time to process the information or make sense of it. She didn't want the officers to know the children had been eavesdropping—surely such an act would be punished—so she hurried to get the little ones settled around her again.

Through the walls she heard Staunton say, "This way, Vice Admiral."

None of the children had blankets, but there were a few dirty sheets, and Cettie covered as many of them as she could before the officers arrived. The door creaked open, and the dim light from the lantern shoved away the shadows. It was not bright enough to make Cettie wince. Nor was it bright enough to send the ghost away. The feeling of animosity pulsing from the being made her shudder.

Cettie had witnessed enough in her short years to know ghosts could affect humans, sometimes even hurt them, as had happened with her guardian. Only the younger children were safe. But until now, she hadn't realized *ghosts* could be affected by the living in return. The newcomer, who was clearly a military man because of the rank she'd heard mentioned, looked outraged by what he saw. Then he met Cettie's eyes. He spoke to her, singling her out from the rest.

"Have they had anything to eat all day?"

It made a spark light up in her heart. It was a tiny spark, but it was enough to embolden her.

"Indeed not, my lord," she answered, bowing her head, trying to please him. He looked startled by her words. She was trying to think of something else to say, a way to be useful to him, when he suddenly whirled around and began marching downstairs, no doubt to confront Miss Charlotte.

The officers followed the one called Fitzroy. The children continued to murmur, and Cettie told them that if they were good, the nice man would bring them food. That little spark of hope in her heart had built into a blaze. Something told her the man *would* help them. She left the circle of children and quietly stepped into the hall. She could hear the voices down below as Fitzroy tried to get Miss Charlotte to answer simple questions. The woman was still hysterical.

Moving quietly, Cettie stepped into the other room. She gazed at the ladder and then up at the open skylight. Without any forethought, she padded up the rungs and poked her head out the window, feeling her tattered skirt sway around her legs. It was a cold night. The breeze made her dark hair blow into her face, and she brushed the strands away. There was a rope ladder leading up to the floating zephyr.

Cettie bit her lip and squeezed the top rung of the skylight ladder. She didn't see anyone aboard the airship, but that didn't mean it was empty. Wouldn't the pilot of the vessel have remained behind? It hung just above the sloping rooftop—so close she imagined she could touch the bottom if she jumped high enough. Was this the chance she'd been waiting for? She'd dreamed of stowing away aboard a zephyr and going to a cloud manor. Clearly that was where the vice admiral was from . . .

She hesitated. If she snuck aboard, she'd surely be caught. Maybe Lord Fitzroy would take her with him if she asked? What harm could come of asking?

She felt the presence of the tall one in the room and hurried back down the ladder. It didn't need to use doors or hallways. It could pass through the cracked walls.

"Go away," she said in her most threatening voice. She didn't feel fear at the moment, just a blinding determination to escape the Fells.

Cettie left the room and rushed to the head of the stairs. She could hear angry words from below. Miss Charlotte wasn't pleased. Then Cettie realized that Lord Fitzroy was asking about *her*.

"I'll ask you again, ma'am. Who is the waif that puts the other children to bed?" he said.

"Her? I know who ye means, milord. Nothing fears her. Not her, milord. Saucy she is. Not even a thrashing will break her."

"What is her *name*?"

"Cettie," said Miss Charlotte with a hint of savageness in her voice. It made Cettie frown with anger. Should she hurry down the steps and try to defend herself? *No . . . be patient. He'll come back up. That's where the sky ship is.* "She taint like us, milord. She taint. She's not from this world. Not that un."

Cettie had never tried to be part of the Fells. Although she wore a ragged dress and her shoes had gaping holes in them, she'd always attempted to speak with dignity in the hopes of attaining something better.

Fitzroy was quiet for a while. The quiet seemed to unnerve Miss Charlotte, who started to gibber for forgiveness, for another chance to tend the children.

No! Cettie wanted to scream. *Don't believe her!*

"I will come back here in three days," Fitzroy said solemnly. "If there are not beds and blankets for those children, if there isn't food to spare in your larder, then I promise you, woman, by the Mysteries, your deeds will be revoked, and I will put you in prison myself. Do not test my patience in this. You've treated these children with shameful neglect. Beware when I return if I do not find all well here. Do you understand me?"

Miss Charlotte was gibbering again, but this time in relief. She was praising his name, invoking blessings on him, and weeping openly.

"Staunton, those children need to eat tonight and again in the morning. I will cover the expense. See it is done. I will not allow them to go hungry another moment." Fitzroy sounded disgusted.

"Yes, sir."

Then Cettie heard the march of approaching footsteps and retreated into the room, once again surrounding herself with the children. She knelt on the hard floor, pressing her mouth with her fingers, wondering what she could say. If she could get herself into a better situation, perhaps she could help Joses and ensure the little ones were well fed. And the tall ghost would undoubtedly leave, too. It would come looking for her, but surely it would not find her in one of the cloud manors. Her mind whirled frantically. Could she convince Fitzroy to take her away? Would he consider it? Hope blazed so brightly inside her that she leaned into it, even though her life experiences had taught her not to trust in miracles.

As the sound of the steps reached the top floor, the light from the zephyr came flooding back on, bathing the next room in radiance.

Please come back, she thought with desperation. *Don't leave me here. Please come back.*

Fitzroy didn't leave. He went straight to the cramped room where Cettie sat huddled with the children. He stood in the doorway, illuminated by the light from the next room. Cettie stared at him, trying to think of what to say. Could she ask to be his servant, to polish his boots? Surely he already had five servants who did that . . .

The ghost without eyes was there in the corner, seething at him. It was afraid of him. It *hated* him.

That only made her more eager to go with him.

Cettie hugged Alice and smoothed her hair, still searching for the right words to make her plea. *Please take me with you,* she thought. *Don't leave me here.*

Slowly, Fitzroy squatted down, bringing himself closer to their level, watching them all shivering. He lowered his head, and Cettie felt something stir in the room. It was deeper and warmer than the buzzing sound that accompanied the ghost; it felt almost like music. A warmth filled her heart, and she felt a pulse of . . . something fill the room. The tall one hissed and fell through the floorboards, as if a trapdoor had opened beneath it.

The warm feeling spread across the floor, over the walls, and even around the window frame. The whimpering of the children ceased at once. Those who were awake stared at Fitzroy in wonder. Even the sleeping children looked more at peace.

Fitzroy stood slowly, almost weakly—as if what he had done had exhausted him. His hands began to fidget, and he clasped them behind his back to still them. He gave the children a sad look and turned to go.

Cettie still couldn't believe what she had witnessed. The man had driven the ghost away. "It's gone now," she said.

Fitzroy stopped, lingering at the doorway. "What, my dear?" he asked in his gentle way.

"You *made* it go. It's gone now."

The bright light coming from the other room shadowed his face, hiding his expression from her, but his voice sounded worried. "Did you . . . did you see it?"

She slowly nodded.

"I'm coming back in three days," he promised. "I'll look in on you." His voice sounded raspy, as if he were struggling with his emotions. "I promise. I'll not abandon you."

Then he started walking down the hall toward the window and the rope ladder.

No! Cettie felt the blazing hope in her chest start to dim. No, he couldn't leave her behind. This man could keep her safe from the ghosts. She would do anything to go with him. She'd do the lowliest of jobs in his manor.

Cettie rose from the ring of children and went after him. She had no idea what to say or what to do, but the need to leave this place was overpowering. This was her chance.

A boldness seized her. Without thinking, she caught hold of his hand and stopped him. He turned, not angry, just surprised. There was a strange look on his face—at once pained and wistful.

The words came gushing out of her mouth. She hadn't planned what to say.

"Will you please adopt me?" she begged, clinging to his hand.

In their touch was unseen energy, binding them together. He seemed so familiar to her in that moment, as if she'd known him all her life. As if she'd held his hand a hundred times before. What a queer feeling, like the entire future had spilled out before them, shocking in its intensity, its reality. They both felt it. She could see it in his eyes. For a moment, they just stared at each other, caught in a singular moment that defied explanation.

"If I can," he whispered hoarsely.

CHAPTER THREE

FOG WILLOWS

Cettie of the Fells was flying in a zephyr.

She wasn't afraid—it was something she had always imagined doing, and rather than alarm her, the lift and sway of the vessel excited her. But she was still reeling from the scene at Miss Charlotte's house. She wasn't sure what had possessed her to ask that man to adopt her—or what had possessed him to answer as he had. The wonder of it had pulsed through her as she climbed the very rope ladder she'd eyed from the attic room.

Although she didn't know why she'd asked such a brazen thing, perhaps she'd done right to speak up. If she hadn't, she likely wouldn't be riding a zephyr into the sky in the middle of the night with a *vice* admiral. She would finally have the opportunity to set foot in one of the mansions floating in the sky.

The wind was bitingly cold, but she was too intent on soaking in every detail of the journey to pay it any heed. The interior of the zephyr consisted of a single aisle split by small weather-beaten benches on either side. There were rope handholds fastened to brass rings throughout. At the back of the zephyr was a narrow door that led to a compartment. The pilot was situated above that section, in a railed-off area. He stood in front of a big, anvil-shaped helm, and while the wheel didn't turn, he clung to the spars protruding from it. The pilot had some ropes hooked to his belt with loops, connected to the railing behind him. On the opposite end, at the front of the ship, a small ladder led up to the prow. A man crouched there, watching the path ahead. Cettie looked off the side of the ship and saw two more spars sticking out, angled like fish fins. Her fingers, gripping the rope handhold at the edge of the railing, were so cold they were numb. Her teeth were chattering, but she didn't care.

Fitzroy joined her at the edge of the ship and, without saying anything, took off his long gray coat and wrapped it around her shoulders. The bottom of the coat dropped all the way to the floor of the sky ship. She gazed up at him, looking for any hint of cruelty or anger in his face. She was a good judge of people. One had to be in the Fells. But there was nothing in his expression that caused her to worry.

"It's rather cold up here, Cettie," he said, squatting down to be eye level with her. Adults *never* did that.

"Are you really a vice admiral?" Cettie asked him.

A small smile quirked on his clean-shaven face. Light from the shining lantern hanging from a nearby ring revealed that his graying hair must have originally been black, or a very dark brown. He was much older than her, as old as a mountain probably. As he had given Cettie his overcoat, she could see he wore the coat, striped vest, and collar of an upper-class noble. His boots were an appropriate height, but they did not look overly fancy. He was still not wearing the customary gloves, and he kept worrying at his hands. There was a black tie at his throat, fastened tight with only a little slip of white appearing above and beneath it. The buttons on his dark coat were enormous, the size of coins. She fancied touching them but didn't dare.

"Yes," he answered, meeting her curious gaze with one of his own. "I once served in the Ministry of War, but no longer. I've been put out to pasture, as they say about the sheep."

"And do you live in the sky?" she asked him, biting her lip and hoping.

He nodded simply. "I do. My estate is called Fog Willows. We are going there presently."

Was this real and not a dream? No dream had ever felt so thrilling. No dream had ever made the wind run through her hair like this. But what if she awoke back in the tenements?

"Are you really going to adopt me? How many children do you have?" she asked, unsure if this was, in fact, an actual dream that she'd awaken from. He had children of his own. She had sensed that immediately in the way he interacted with her and the other children.

"I said I would try," he answered sincerely. "My dear wife must agree, of course. And we have three children. You seem close in age to our youngest. How old are you, Cettie?"

"I'm not sure," she answered, wrinkling her nose in confusion. "None of us have any birthdays. I think I am twelve."

"You speak very well for one so . . . young," he observed, and she felt a flush of pride.

"My papa taught me," she lied, giving him a smile. "He was the captain of a hurricane."

His eyebrow lifted. "Indeed? That is very impressive. Are you still hungry?"

"Very," she answered truthfully. She felt a twinge of guilt for misrepresenting herself.

"Lieutenant Staunton?" he asked. That's all he needed to say. The man obeyed him smartly, rummaging through the gear stowed on the sky ship for something to eat. That was real power, Cettie thought. To say a word and the thing was done.

"How do sky ships fly?" she asked, rubbing her hand on the railing. "Do they harness the wind?" Though she'd always wondered, it seemed even more curious now that she was riding in one. Up in the sky, there was no noise except the wind. No groaning of gears or rattle of belts like the sounds emanating from the grimy factories down below. Entire buildings would thrum with the motion. No, the sky ship moved smoothly, as if carried by two cupped hands from one shelf to another. The fact that she was actually *inside* a zephyr made her giddy. She couldn't stop grinning.

The man, her new benefactor, held up his hands and shrugged regretfully. "I can't tell you. It's one of the Mysteries."

If ever there was a word she simultaneously detested and pined after, that was the one. The Mysteries. It was the explanation adults used for nearly everything that seemed inexplicable, and it made her want to swear, which she never did.

"And it's the same that makes your manor float?" she pressed.

He nodded eagerly, not troubled by her sudden outpouring of questions.

"Do your children know the Mysteries?"

He shook his head no. "Only my eldest has begun to learn them, although the next will be starting school shortly. Would you like to learn them, Cettie?"

"May I?" she said as meekly as she could.

"I can't make any promises now," he said in his gentle way. "But if it is possible, I will try to arrange it."

"Why shouldn't it be possible?" she asked with confusion. "If you were to sign the deed away from Miss Charlotte, you would become my master."

"I know that, child, and I intend to do it," he said. "But a deed is different than an adoption, which is also encompassed by the Mysteries. The Mysteries of Law, to be precise. I'm not very good with that one. I will talk to my advocate soon, and he will direct me on the proper procedures. Adoption is a serious matter, Cettie. It is not undertaken lightly or granted quickly. Can I ask you a question now?"

She bobbed her head up and down. Part of her still wanted to stare off the side of the open-air craft and feel the wind blow her hair back. How far up were they from the ground? It felt like they had been ascending for a long time.

"Back at Miss Charlotte's," he said, giving her a penetrating look, "I used some of the Mysteries to protect the room where the children were sleeping. You said something to me. Do you remember?"

Her heart began to shrivel. "You sent away my ghost. The tall one."

"Your ghost?" he asked in confusion.

She nodded, the thrill beginning to lessen. But she felt safer up in the sky, safer with Fitzroy near. If anyone could protect her, he could. "Most places in the tenements have them. The spirits of the dead who cannot move on."

His eyes were deep and intense. "And you could . . . see it?"

She blinked quickly, not sure how she should answer. But she had already confessed the truth, so lying now would be pointless. "I can. Is that wrong, sir?"

"No, not wrong. Just very, very rare. Have you always been able to see them?"

She glanced down and nodded, feeling embarrassed. That it was a rare ability didn't make it a good one. When she glanced up at his face, she thought he looked disturbed by what she had acknowledged. "The tall one keeps following me. Every time my deed was sold, it would find me again."

"Here's something for the lass," said the lieutenant, returning with a crust of bread stuffed with some cheese and some sort of meat. She accepted it with relish and started to eat quickly, responding to the instant pangs of hunger in her weakened stomach. She hadn't eaten for several days and felt a little dizzy from it.

"What is going to happen to Joses?" she asked between mouthfuls, looking up at her guardian.

"Is he the boy who was caught stealing?" Fitzroy asked.

She nodded.

"Well, he would normally be punished for the theft regardless of the circumstances," he said, though his tone was by no means mean-spirited. "But since I am the magistrate at the moment, I can perhaps see to it that he is released . . . with a scolding?"

She grinned at him, feeling her worry for her friend start to diminish. The vice admiral insisted she concentrate on eating, not talking, so she leaned up against the sidewall of the sky ship to enjoy her food. She looked down at the view, but there was nothing left to see other than darkness and a few pinpricks of light, and she pulled back when her fear of heights began to make her dizzy. Looking up was much better. Her hair whipped around her face until she smoothed it behind her and let it fan out. The sky was so swollen with stars that it felt like she could spoon them up with a ladle. All her life, she had only seen the night sky from a window, not daring to go out into the streets after dark. She rested her hand on her arm and stared up at the stars. She was very sleepy but didn't want to miss the first sight of the floating manor.

"We're nearing Fog Willows, sir," said Staunton.

The words startled Cettie awake, and she realized she'd drowsed off while leaning on the rail. She was warm and comfortable in Fitzroy's jacket, and she lifted her head sleepily. Her potential guardian was chafing his hands and breathing warmth into them since he wore no special coat for the heights.

Seeing her blinking eyes, he motioned for her to join him near the front of the vessel. She walked down the narrow walkway in the middle, passing the small benches. Judging by the number of seats, a zephyr could hold up to ten people. She maneuvered past Lieutenant Staunton and reached the front of the vessel, staring up at the higher deck, where the officer was still holding the rigging ropes and viewing the way.

"Can she join you, Benson?" Staunton asked.

The man shrugged and patted the planks beside him. Cettie scurried up the ladder, feeling the wind cut around her as she sat at the prow of the zephyr. Surprisingly, it wasn't as cold as she had feared. It was still too dark for her to see much, but she could make out the shapes of trees and the sporadic beacons of light from lanterns down below.

"Are those lights coming from villages?" she asked Benson.

"No, they are markers set down to help us pilot in the dark."

"Are they lanterns?"

"Hush," he said with a partly amused smile. "It's the Mysteries, lass. I can't explain it."

Ah, there it was again.

"But they point the way toward Fog Willows," he said. "Fitzroy's estate here in the north. Gone and back quickly. We made good time. And there's no fog this morning, which helped us find it."

"Could we have found it in the fog?"

"Of course, lass! It sits *above* the fog. See it yonder?" he asked, directing his arm. "It's difficult to miss."

Her breath caught on a gasp. He was right. She'd been looking up in the sky, but now that he'd directed her gaze downward, she realized that they were going to descend into Fog Willows. Even though it was still nighttime, the estate was aglow. She could barely make out the tops of trees far below. They were still high up if the trees looked so small, yet she had a perfect view of the enormous manor.

Fog Willows was the most beautiful place she'd ever seen—so beautiful it brought tears to her eyes. She'd always wondered what the floating manors looked like. But this . . . this exceeded anything she could have imagined in her inexperience. She'd always thought they'd be boxlike houses, similar in construction—if not condition—to the ones on the crowded streets of the tenements. But this manor was the home of a king. The huge high windows of the estate shimmered up at her—an invitation to explore. It looked as if the home had been built into a mountaintop thick with huge pines and poplars, a mountaintop that had then been wrenched free by some titanic being and hoisted into the sky. She wondered what it would look like standing directly beneath it and looking up. Would it be like staring at an upside-down mountain? Surely the lights would be seen in the haze of mist . . .

As they made their swift descent, the details became clearer. Her eyes took in the glowing wonders beneath her—sheltered gazebos and outer kitchens, all with slanted roofs and cupolas, and trails carved into the rocks crisscrossing the estate. The buildings were connected by various bridges, and a waterfall straddled two of them, the water tumbling down from the heights and turning into mist before it could hit the ground. Willow trees surrounded by a pool of water in a ravine that seemed as ancient as the mountain itself.

Her heart cried out in wonder.

The zephyr angled toward the main house, and Cettie noticed a paved circular veranda off the main doors. Benson adjusted his position and rose, then began bellowing commands to the pilot.

"To port, hard as we go. Slow the descent by three stripes. Yes, three. More to the leeward. Aye, you're coming into position. Let's not broadside the vice admiral's house, eh, Klem? I don't think his lordship would appreciate that."

"Indeed," said the gentleman good-naturedly. He, too, had climbed the ladder, and he now stood behind Cettie, nodding approvingly. He clearly relished being on the ship, part of the command.

"Descend by three more stripes. Better make it four."

The sky ship lurched, and Cettie's stomach did a delicious little squeeze that made her gasp and cling to the rigging.

"My wife's youngest sister pilots a tempest," the vice admiral told her with an arch to his eyebrows, trying to impress her. He succeeded.

"A tempest? Really? And she's a girl?"

"A *woman*, of course," he corrected. "But, yes, she is female. Raj Sarin taught her how to fight as well."

"Who is Raj Sarin?" Cettie asked with interest.

"You'll be meeting him soon, I daresay. He's, well, he's my *bodyguard* officially. But truly, more of a friend. He is a Bhikhu. Do you know what that is?"

She shook her head no, but she was hoping to learn everything she could. This new world opening to her was the stuff of her wildest dreams. A floating estate, built onto a mountaintop. A ship that rose through the air. How did it all happen? Of course, it was all explained by the Mysteries, which meant it wasn't to be explained at all.

"The Bhikhu are a people that can fly just by bringing in their breath. It's quite amazing, actually. And a very handy skill to have when working from such heights. I must warn you, Cettie, to always stay on the paths. Some of the rocks below have loosened over the years. The power holds the stone up, not people. If you were to fall, you could fall clear off the estate." He scrunched up his nose. "There are certain protections, but it is possible to fall, so it's best to be careful. It's quite a ways down, as you can imagine."

"Slow down, lad!" Benson shouted down. "Four more stripes. Slower, slower."

"Would you like to do it?" the pilot snapped.

"I could, and I'd do it just as well as you!" said Benson, puffing his chest.

"Let's get the vice admiral home, lads; enough chatter!" Lieutenant Staunton said, his tone lacking patience. "It's been a long night, and I'd like to be back in bed before sunrise."

The zephyr came to roost at last just above the semicircular landing area by the doors. Cettie could see that a few servants were lining up below to greet their master. Staunton went to the railing and then looked over before dropping the rope ladder.

"I'll come to the offices in three days' time as promised," Fitzroy told the lieutenant, climbing down to the main level. He signaled for Cettie to follow him, and she did. "Make sure the woman obeys. I'd rather not put her in irons, but I will."

Cettie felt a flush of gratitude. She wasn't sure Miss Charlotte could stay sober that long. She secretly hoped she *would* end up in irons, so long as the children were kept safe. If Joses were released, he would undoubtedly take care of them and ensure they were fed.

Fitzroy climbed over the railing—the lieutenant gripping his arm out of courtesy.

"You come after me, Cettie," Fitzroy called back as he started down the ladder. She clambered after him eagerly, and soon they had descended to the landing platform. The glow from the lights made it seem like early morning. She gazed up at the monstrous house, which was even more elaborate and finely decorated up close. The very shingles on the roofs appeared to be made from quarried stone.

A woman stood at the head of the servants awaiting them. She was tall and very austere, with a perpetual scowl and cavernous wrinkles across her forehead, eyes, and cheeks. Her hair was combed back and secured with a silver pin. Her dress was plain, a dark forest green, and there was a brooch at her throat. She stood in a stately way, one gloved hand interlocked with the other, her elbows jutting out. Her stern blue eyes were fixed on Cettie. Was this the vice admiral's wife? She looked so cold, so dignified, not at all like the type of woman who'd gladly accept an orphan into her home.

"Mrs. Pullman," Fitzroy said, reaching for Cettie's hand and escorting her forward.

Ah, so Mrs. Pullman clearly wasn't the master's wife. Somehow, the revelation did nothing to settle Cettie. Judging by the set of key rings the older woman held, she was the keeper of the house—the most trusted position that anyone who wasn't part of the family could hold. Cettie had heard that all the sky estates had someone in that position.

The older woman sized up Cettie quickly, taking in every smudge, every ripped seam. The wrinkles in her craggy face stretched and smoothed in a way that clearly conveyed she did not like the look of Cettie. And Cettie instantly felt on her guard. She had trained herself to be wary and knew when people didn't like her.

If Mrs. Pullman had her way, Cettie wouldn't be staying long at Fog Willows.

CHAPTER FOUR

MRS. PULLMAN

"What have we here, Master Brant?" Mrs. Pullman asked as they drew closer to the keeper. Her strong accent indicated she'd been born in a neighboring country, a land that pulled their words and put meaning into the tone.

"Mrs. Pullman, this is Cettie. I just fetched her from the Fells, and she will be staying with us." He put his bare hand on Cettie's shoulder. Touching was a forbidden form of social intimacy in the upper classes, which was why the people who lived in the sky always wore gloves. That was what she had heard in her eavesdropping, anyway, but so far Fitzroy had proven to be an outlier. Glancing around, she saw that the man's staff all wore gloves.

The keeper's eyebrows startled upward at the familiar gesture, the crags in her face deepening. "For how long, Master?" she asked brusquely.

"Quite a while, it seems," Fitzroy said. "She will be living with us. I'd like to take her to see Lady Maren, but neither of us has really slept, and I think a new frock and some breakfast would also do before an introduction. Will you arrange it?"

"Of course," Mrs. Pullman said, never taking her eyes from Cettie. "I'll put her up in the servants' quarters, if it suits you. She's a bit young for a servant's frock, but we'll try to find something that *fits*."

Cettie thought it more likely that Mrs. Pullman would pitch her over the side of the estate as soon as they were alone together.

"No, not the servants' quarters, Mrs. Pullman," Fitzroy said, gesturing with his other hand to the building in front of them. "Here, in the main estate."

Mrs. Pullman almost tottered over at that. "The main estate?"

"Indeed." He turned and dropped to one knee in front of Cettie. The smile he gave her was cheery, but she could see the weariness in his eyes, the haggard look of a man with burdens. "I will see you again at breakfast, Cettie. Mrs. Pullman is the keeper of Fog Willows. She will take care of you while I rest and then attend to some business." His smile broadened. "You are safe here. There are no ghosts."

Cettie bit her lip, seeing the look of aggrieved ire in Mrs. Pullman's eyes. No, the keeper of Fog Willows didn't like this arrangement one bit.

"Thank you," Cettie stammered.

Fitzroy straightened, tousled her hair in a gentle way, and then turned to leave.

"What should I call you?" Cettie blurted out, feeling embarrassed.

He hesitated, his back to her, his hands clasped behind him. She could tell he was discomfited by the question from the way his fingers clenched into fists, nearly shaking. But he turned and gave her a wizened smile. "You can call me Fitzroy," he said. "That is the name I am most used to hearing."

Cettie tried a curtsy, but Mrs. Pullman's haughty smile assured her she'd failed. The other servants smirked at her, too, and her ears burned hot at the humiliation. There was much she needed to learn. But Cettie was an observer of people. She would figure out the customs of this new world. She was determined to succeed, to stay. It was her only chance.

Mrs. Pullman led her all the way to the end of a lengthy hall, turned left, and continued walking down an even longer one. At the end of that one was another turn, a series of steps, and then another deeper passageway bringing them back the way they had come. It led them past the dining room, into the kitchen, and finally to a winding stair-case at what seemed to be the farthest corner of the family mansion. Mrs. Pullman climbed the steps ahead of Cettie, having asked her to mind what she touched and not say a word. The stairs wrapped around the interior of a circular tower, and the climb wasn't too difficult. Even in the interior of the tower, there wasn't a smudge of soot. That struck Cettie as especially baffling. There was so much light, yet no candles, no puddles of wax on the floor. And no smoke. The air was so clear. They arrived at a room with a locked door, and Mrs. Pullman withdrew a set of black keys from her waist, searching among them for the right fit. She then fit the key into the lock and proceeded to stand there, solemnly, presumably waiting for something to happen.

Cettie felt a little nudge of pressure in her mind, as if she'd been poked. Then she heard the lock click. Mrs. Pullman swung the door open, revealing a smaller stairwell, wide enough for only one person, which led up around the turret again. As Cettie passed the door, she felt something about it tug at her, almost as if it were alive. She paused, trying to determine the source of the feeling.

"*Tsk*, come along, child," Mrs. Pullman scolded.

Cettie obeyed and followed her up the stairs. They led to an open room that was completely circular, the walls full of windows veiled by gauzy curtains. Cettie whirled around as she walked, finding about a dozen arched windows that faced every direction. The room was gently lit and contained a sturdy and comfortable four-post bed made of dark mahogany and loaded with mattresses and pillows and blankets. There were chests made of stamped leather, a cloak rack, and a small writing desk full of paper and styluses.

"This is my room?" Cettie gasped in wonderment, in love with it immediately. Rooms had four walls—this had none, only windows.

Mrs. Pullman chuckled coldly. "This is *my* room," she said deliberately, turning around to face her, commanding her attention. Cettie shrank from her physical size. She looked like the kind of woman who would beat a child. "This is my trust. I've worked here since I was a child. My mother was keeper of the house before me. I *earned* my position here. You are unfit to blacken the master's boots. Any urchin within a dozen leagues of this home would feel the privilege of standing where you stand. What makes you think such a foul creature as you deserves such finery? The rest of your kind will never see curtains so soft or blankets so warm as these in their short, miserable lives. I don't know what you did or what lies you told to convince Master Brant to bring you here. He is much too kindhearted. Unfortunately, that has always led him to be deceived by those who would take advantage of his . . . his generosity." Her jaw clenched with suppressed fury. "Like you."

Cettie felt herself shrinking inside. But deep down, the spark of rebelliousness began to sizzle. She didn't know what Cettie had suffered. She didn't know her at all.

Mrs. Pullman walked grandly to one of the curtained windows and pushed the veil apart. "Come, child."

The view was dizzying. It would look so different in the daylight, but it was already enough to steal her breath. Just below the window was the spine of a roof that ran parallel to the tower. It didn't just slope down—the roof was dangerously steep, carved with two crescent-moon shapes. Up close, she noticed the stone tiles of the roof were arranged in a colorful diamond-shaped pattern that spanned the length of the vast roof. As her eyes followed the pattern, she found herself studying the main manor house, with its turrets and spires and steeper roofline.

Partway across it was a series of bulwarks and an enormous cathedral-like spire. The landing pad was yonder, but the zephyr was gone. The enormity of the grounds, visible by moonlight, made it difficult to take everything in. There were a thousand places to explore, and her heart craved to do so immediately.

"*Those* are the master's rooms," Mrs. Pullman said, pointing toward the cathedral-like spire. "You saw where we met you and how far we walked to get here. These belong to me. They overlook all the grounds except for the servants' quarters, which are on the far side over there. They cannot be seen from here. I don't *care* to see them. The butler, Kinross, rules that wing. The rest is *mine.*"

Mrs. Pullman sniffed and released the curtain, blocking Cettie's view. She folded her arms, striking an imperious pose. "Now, young lady, let me be very clear with you. You will probably only be here for a few days. Master is very distracted. There are changes afoot in the government, and his ministry is pulling for more power. There may come a time, in the very near future, when our beloved master becomes the prime minister." Her wrinkles and crags smoothed out as she contemplated the idea with relish. "I cannot imagine someone better equipped to fill that role." Then the wrinkles crisscrossed again. "I cannot allow anything to distract him from this opportunity. Especially a poor, unwanted waif such as yourself."

Cettie began to grow restless with indignation and the threat of dashed hopes. Her blood was heating fast in her veins. She glared at Mrs. Pullman, feeling the woman poised to snatch something away, a treasure she had only just found.

"I see the anger in your eyes," Mrs. Pullman said knowingly. "If you desire to stay here in Fog Willows, then I suggest you watch your temper and mind your tongue! One word from me, and you will be taken back to the Fells where you truly belong. Cross me, child, and you will die in one of those abominable tenements, coughing on your own blood. I've seen it happen to the strongest of children. Even the wealthy who live below aren't spared. Do we understand each other?"

Cettie licked her lips, trembling. It felt like her new existence was already tottering, ready to crash down and shatter. A sick feeling spread in her stomach. She had no idea what Fitzroy's family was like. Maybe they all would wish her gone, too.

No, she couldn't let that happen. She would find a way to make them like her.

"Yes, Mrs. Pullman," she said.

A wrinkled smile. "See that ladder yonder, leading to the trapdoor? You'll sleep up there. In the attic. I'm sure you'll be grateful for a floor to sleep on at night. There are worse places for an urchin." Her eyes flashed with accusation.

"I know," Cettie whispered, working hard to keep her sense of panic down.

Mrs. Pullman glided over to a little table and picked up a small brass bell. The wrinkles on her hands showed bulging purple veins. "When you hear this, you will come down straightaway." She rang the tiny bell, and it gave off an interesting, birdlike sound. "When you go through the door at the bottom of the stairs, there is no coming back unless I open the door for you. Only I hold the keys to the locks. If you find a locked door, you let it alone. It is part of the Mysteries. You will wait for me, at the door, until I come to bed each night. Is that clear?"

"Yes, Mrs. Pullman."

"And if you speak a word against me, girl, I will know it. And you will regret it."

⌒

Cettie couldn't remember the last time she had worn a new frock. She'd been dunked in a bath in the servants' quarters and scrubbed like the laundry until she was pink and clean and then wrapped up in towels and changed. Her hair was then brushed out, and she wondered if Mrs. Pullman had ordered the servants to make her cry, given how vigorously they applied themselves to the task.

"You're a scabby one, you are," said the maid assigned to the indignity. "All skin and bones. You came from the Fells with Lord Fitzroy? Well, how does that rank? I was in a lottery for five years 'fore I got a chance." She continued to brush out Cettie's hair. "Your hair's too dark, miss. You look like a black goose, you do. And those are freckles, are they? I can try to take them off for you." She grinned in a mean-spirited way, turning Cettie's face this way and that as she scrubbed it. "Have to work extra hard now, because of you. Still have my regular chores to do now that it's daylight. Not that I'm complainin'. It's good to have work." She pursed her lips. "Your eyes are pretty at least. Not much to the rest of you There now, let's get that frock on."

After the ordeal was done, Cettie was hurried back to the main wing of the estate to the master's rooms. Her eyes could not get enough of the marvels and riches around her. Tall portrait paintings hung from gilded frames on the wall. Little vases of flowers and lovely mementos were perched on stands and tables. Cettie wasn't used to such splendor, and the value of what she saw baffled her. Just a few of these treasures could have fed dozens of urchins for months. There were no chunks missing from the plaster, and very little dust.

After climbing a wide swath of steps—so tall Cettie had to crane her neck to see them all—they reached a curious chamber. It was not a sitting room. In fact, there were only two small stools in the whole room. It was full of benches and tables, and on the tables were contraptions she had never seen, let alone dreamed about. Glass vials and metal stands, iron devices that looked like a bug's pincers, and a beaten-leather apron that lay discarded to one side. The device that caught her imagination most was a strange apparatus of glass vials nestled in an iron frame. It looked like a jewelry case, but instead of holding gems, the vials were half full of a silver substance.

Fitzroy stood at one of the tables, his back to her, writing something with the stub of a pencil on a set of bound ledger sheets. A huge curtained window loomed in front of him, and he gazed outside, prodding his bottom lip with the pencil.

The maidservant coughed to get his attention, and he turned around.

"Ah, Cettie. Here you are. I was growing anxious to see you. It's morning, but I should have known not to worry. Mrs. Pullman is always quite punctual. I'd like to introduce you to the rest of the family."

"What is that, sir?" she asked, unable to hold back her curiosity. She squirmed closer to the glass-and-iron contraption, trying to see it better.

"Oh, this? The container was a gift from my wife. The substance inside comes from the mines my family runs. She thought I might like it displayed in my office. It's become a little pet project, actually. Even though I focused on the Mysteries of War at school, I was always more interested in the Mysteries of Wind." He must have noticed the confused look on her face, for he added, "Are you familiar with the four branches of the Mysteries, Cettie?"

"I thought there were four branches of our government called the Ministries. Are they the same?"

"Yes, each ministry corresponds with one of the Mysteries. I took for granted that you'd understand my meaning. I am part of the Ministry of Wind presently. You see, when I left to fetch you last night, I noticed some quicksilver missing from the tube. Just a little. But my eyes must be getting old because it's there again today. I checked it over and over. I added these little marks to the glass a while back because I've noticed this phenomenon before. They help me to measure the changes in the quicksilver." He coaxed her forward and showed her the marks. To her astonishment, she noticed a small stone bowl next to the display. It was full of the silver, except it looked wet.

"Is that truly silver?" she asked, gazing at it.

"It's a type of silver. Look, watch closely." He took a little tool from the bench, like a spoon, and dipped it into the bowl. The quicksilver quivered and danced, which made Cettie startle. He then scooped some of it up and dumped it into his palm. Unlike water, it held together, but it moved and wriggled as he tilted his hand.

"Does it hurt?" she asked innocently, intrigued by the demonstration.

"Not one bit," he replied. "Hold out your hand."

She did so willingly, eyes widening. He tipped his palm over, letting the substance drop into her palm. Though she'd expected it to be cold or hot, it was neither. She giggled softly. It felt like the substance was alive and wanted to escape her hand and leap back onto the table. But she steadied herself and watched it with fascination.

"Put it back in the bowl, please," he said. "My wife is anxious to meet you. So are my children. Are you ready, Cettie? Do you think you could be happy at Fog Willows?"

Immediately, she thought of Mrs. Pullman and her warnings. Her confidence started to shrivel. But she was determined. She would do whatever was needed to ensure she could stay there. Nothing was worth going back to the Fells.

"I hope so," Cettie answered, dumping the quicksilver back into the bowl. It was quickly subsumed with the rest, and she wasn't able to see any further evidence of it having been a unique blob.

If only she could settle in as easily.

A certain type of woman will always have an impersonal contempt for other women. This woman deems all others as competition. Competition for affection. Competition for attention. Competition for reputation. Competition for power.

—*Lady Corinne of Pavenham Sky*

CHAPTER FIVE

LADY FITZROY'S CHILDREN

Cettie was prepared to like each member of Fitzroy's family, but after her encounter with Mrs. Pullman, she worried about their reaction to her. Her nerves prickled as she walked the grand corridor to the family sitting room with the master himself. Music was coming from the room, all trills and swelling sounds, and her tread slowed as she made her approach, her heart aching in wonder. She was used to street musicians playing fiddles and pipes, but this was so much grander. It sounded like dozens of musicians were playing at once, creating a rich fullness of sound.

A servant stationed at the door bowed to Fitzroy before turning the handle for them. As the door opened, the sound of the music gushed into the corridor, and the smell of breakfast drifted after it. She looked up and saw a smile on Fitzroy's mouth.

These must be his children—the boy looked to be at least sixteen, and there were two girls, the younger of which appeared to be around Cettie's age and height. Lady Maren was seated on the couch with a blanket covering her lap. There were smudges and shadows under her eyes, and a general weakness radiated from her. Cettie had encountered enough ill people in the Fells to recognize that the woman had some sort of lasting sickness.

As soon as Fitzroy entered, Cettie felt a subtle push against her mind, and the music ceased immediately. How curious! It was an unfamiliar feeling, one that made her slightly dizzy. Though there were some instruments in the room, no musicians were playing them. The two eldest children had been dancing together in the middle of the room by the couch where their mother sat, but they stopped whirling around the second the music cut off. Where had the music come from?

"Papa!" squealed the elder girl, rushing toward the door with a bright smile. She had long dark hair that was braided only on one side and the brightest blue eyes Cettie had seen. A dimple flashed on her left cheek as she hugged her father. "Is this her?" she asked, giving Cettie a quick and thoughtful look.

The young man came up next. He was lanky and nearly as tall as his father, but while he had a handsome smile, there was a look of distrust in his eyes. The youngest child held back, waiting with her mother on the couch.

"Cettie, these are my children," Fitzroy said. "This is Stephen, nearly a man himself, who decided to sprout this last year."

"Father," Stephen said, flushing in embarrassment.

"My second oldest," Fitzroy said, putting his arm around the daughter who had first approached him and hugging her close. The girl tilted her head against his chest and gazed at Cettie without any apparent hostility. "Seraphinia. We all call her Phinia."

The girl lifted her head proudly. "One of the Fitzempress heirs was named after me. She's a princess."

"That is true," Fitzroy said. "But everyone calls her Sera. My second eldest likes to take on airs as if *she* were the princess."

"I could have been one," the girl answered smartly.

"Long ago, perhaps," Fitzroy said. "There are too many royal cousins for our line to ever have preference. And the little one—who is about your own age, Cettie—is Felicianna. She's quiet and a little shy. We call her little Anna."

"How do you do?" Stephen said, bowing to Cettie. The guarded, distrustful look was still there. She didn't know how to respond to such a pleasantry.

Fitzroy released Phinia and then led Cettie over to the couch.

"Maren, here she is," he said in a gentle voice.

Despite her illness, Lady Maren appeared quite a bit younger than her husband. She looked scarcely older than Stephen, although she had wrinkles around her eyes. She wore gloves, as was the custom, and clenched a silk kerchief, which she brought to her mouth every time she coughed. Her very curly hair was held back by a headband.

Lady Maren's eyes had a feverish cast to them, but she smiled at Cettie in a pleasant, kindly way. "So you're the little girl he helped last night," she said in a whisper-like voice. "I'm so sorry, dearest, for the life you lived in the Fells." She reached out with her other hand, holding her palm up and inviting Cettie to put her hand there. She did, hesitantly, but genuine warmth seemed to exude from the woman. Lady Maren squeezed her hand, but it was a limp, weak squeeze. "You are welcome here at Fog Willows. You'll be safe here from those who hurt you."

"Thank you, ma'am," Cettie said gratefully. Her hope was rekindled.

Fitzroy looked pleased and sidled over to his youngest, who was trying to burrow into the couch cushions. He tousled her hair. "Come and say hello to our guest, Anna."

The youngest shook her head no, but she gave Cettie a shy smile.

Behind them, Cettie could hear the others talking.

"You've got to get that last turn right," Stephen said, scolding his sister. "It's left, then right, then back."

"That's exactly what I did!" Phinia returned defensively.

"No, you went right, then left, then right. You have to get it perfect, Phinia. You should ask Father to send someone up for lessons, or perhaps he can send you to one of the better dancing schools in the City before you go off to study. I don't want you to embarrass me."

"Always worried about yourself," Phinia quipped. "I just turned fourteen. No one is expecting perfection."

"Yes, they are," Stephen shot back. "There was a girl who was shunned because she stumbled during a dance. Neither she nor any member of her family was ever invited back to a ball again. I'm not trying to frighten you, Phinia, but I've seen it happen."

"Who was it?" Phinia challenged.

"Ardis Wimpole."

"Ardis Wimpole is a goose."

"And she's a goose who doesn't get invited to any more balls. You may act like you're sixteen, but you're not." He pitched his voice lower. "We'll practice again when Father is gone."

The family then assembled for a generous breakfast in a connected dining room. The sumptuous spread made Cettie tremble. Pangs of hunger made her want to cram as much food into her mouth as she could, but the almost bored way the Fitzroy children ate revealed that such fare was typical. Cettie savored a buttered roll, enjoying the airy dough and the warmth that spread all the way down to her belly. There was some talk and chatter during breakfast, but none directed at her.

Before too long, the meal ended, and Fitzroy *did* leave the room, mumbling about needing to get back to his duties, and Cettie found herself abandoned in the sitting room, not knowing what to say or what to do. Lady Maren, seeming to recognize her uncertainty, asked Cettie to sit down on the couch with her and watch Phinia and Stephen dance together. She said the governess would be coming soon to begin lessons. Once again, the music sprang to life out of nowhere. Cettie felt a tingling shoot down her spine.

"Ugh, why won't they play 'Genny's Market'?" Phinia complained.

"They play what they play," Stephen said in exasperation. "You can hear the counts, can't you? Five, six, seven, eight . . ." The two held hands and began a series of intricate steps and sways that was completely baffling to Cettie. The dancing was much more complicated than the boisterous peasant dances of the Fells.

"You'll get used to it after a while," Lady Maren said. "I used to love attending balls. Back when they were not so formal."

"I've never been to one," Cettie said in a small voice. She knew they were popular in the wealthier quarters of the Fells, and even more so in the City, but she'd only heard stories about them.

"Of course not. But you will, dearest." She stroked Cettie's hair. "This must all feel very strange to you. Do you have any questions?"

"Where does the music come from?" she asked, looking around. If she had to guess, the sound seemed to be emanating from the wainscoting on the wall by the fireplace, but she had yet to locate any apparent source.

"It's one of the Mysteries," Lady Maren said.

Cettie sighed.

"Why the frown?"

Cettie hadn't realized she'd made one. She quickly smoothed her features—wanting to be agreeable to the family. It was the only way they'd keep her.

"That's what everyone says. I just don't understand what it means. In the Fells, everyone thinks it is magic."

Lady Maren nodded sympathetically. "Yes, there is a bit of superstition where you come from. It's not magic, Cettie. It's an understanding of certain laws and powers. And since it is quite difficult to explain how the Mysteries work, we use that word with the uninitiated. Some knowledge, important knowledge, requires a price to be paid before it is learned. The secrets must be guarded. But they *can* be learned. Have you ever been to the City?"

"No, ma'am. I've never left the Fells. Not that I can remember."

"Here in the north, sky manors don't float directly above the Fells the way they do in the City. No, the manors are spread out and much smaller. There is less worry about them falling here if one of them fails."

"Does that truly happen?" Cettie had heard people speak of it, but it had always seemed more like a myth than a genuine possibility.

Lady Maren nodded her head. "It can, but the risk is small. People who live below the City do dread it. They must trust that those who live above them know how to keep that giant rock floating. It's been there for generations. The floating part is called Lockhaven, but some of us just call the whole thing the City because it's all connected, and zephyrs are constantly going up and down. In the City, there are many wonderful musicians. They have trained and practiced long and hard to master their various instruments. When all the instruments are brought together, it is called an orchestra. Do you know that word?"

"No, ma'am," Cettie answered.

"That's all right, Cettie. Do you see that instrument?" She pointed to a big box with gold trim and white and black keys. "That is called a clavicembalo, or just a cembalo for short. It's basically just a harp that was laid flat. When you strike the keys hard or soft, it plays music. It's an ingenious invention. When I went to school, I studied music." She smiled brightly, the shadows under her eyes fading a little as the memory swept her away. "Now, here is what I want you to imagine, Cettie. There are many orchestras in the City. They each have maestros, and they practice and play all day long and then perform at night. What you are hearing—right now—is one of those orchestras. Even though it is far away, we can still enjoy their music up here. Stephen and Phinia love to dance. I used to join them, but I'm so tired now." Her voice began to soften, and Anna crept closer, looking at her worriedly.

"How does the music get here?" Cettie asked.

Lady Maren smiled. "That is the part I cannot tell you. It is one of the Mysteries. But if you are good and obedient, when you reach Phinia's age, you will be sent to learn them, just as she will be sent.

Stephen knows some of them already." A dark look clouded her face. It immediately roused Cettie's curiosity, but she knew better than to press. Mrs. Pullman was correct about one thing; she was lucky to be here. Then Lady Maren's look changed, softening. "Ah, here is Mrs. Pullman with the governess, Miss Farnworth. Punctual as ever."

Miss Farnworth, who looked to be in her early twenties, had long blond hair and a gentle smile. Phinia begged for just one more dance before the instruction started. The governess's gaze shifted to the lady of the house, indicating the decision was hers.

Before Lady Maren could answer, Mrs. Pullman approached her and took her hand. "How are you feeling, my lady?"

"Tired still," came the reply. "Is Cettie all settled, then? Which room did you put her in?"

"She's staying with me, ma'am," said Mrs. Pullman in a sweet way. "I didn't want any of the servants to mistreat her." She gave Cettie a burning look, as if daring her to disagree. "Was she quiet as a lamb, ma'am? Or does she ask too many questions?"

"I don't mind. Thank you, Mrs. Pullman. Do let them finish one more dance. And, Miss Farnworth, please be sure to spend some time with Cettie as well. After Phinia leaves for school, you'll have two pupils to teach instead of one."

"Yes, Mrs. Pullman," Miss Farnworth said, and smiled at Cettie.

Mrs. Pullman then nodded at them all, sparing a final glance for Cettie, and left the room to see to her other responsibilities.

Cettie sat quietly on the couch and watched the brother and sister dance the final round. She liked to observe people, and she was quick to pick up on nuances and patterns. The dances they were performing were not random at all. Each song seemed to have a unique series of movements associated with it. Sometimes there was clapping to the rhythm. Sometimes the clapping came after a twirl. There was a method for each, but it would take time and study for Cettie to memorize them.

After the dance finished, they moved to the part of the room equipped with desks, tables, and chairs, and Miss Farnworth started on Phinia's lessons first. Stephen was quick to criticize his younger sister and constantly tried to show off the knowledge he had already received at school. But Phinia would not be bullied by his airs and liked to tease him back and challenge what he knew. They seemed to relish arguing. Anna did not say anything at all unless directly addressed. Eventually, Lady Maren fell asleep on the couch while the tutoring went on.

The afternoon stretched on, and Cettie found herself struggling to stay awake on another couch, reading a primer that Miss Farnworth had given her. Her days had always been so busy and full of chores that she'd had very little rest. She must have dozed off, because suddenly Stephen and Phinia were standing before her. Lady Maren had apparently left earlier, for her couch was vacant.

"Look, she's fallen asleep! How adorable!" Phinia said, laughing at her.

Stephen smirked. "She must be tired of sitting still for so long."

Miss Farnworth was trying to teach Anna something at a nearby table. Her tilted head indicated she could hear the exchange, but she did nothing to intervene. Rather, she pointed to the page again and whispered for Anna to keep reading.

Cettie flushed and blinked herself awake. Anna ignored her lesson and shot daggers at her older brother with her eyes.

"I'm only teasing," Stephen said, although his look denied it. "So you come from the Fells?"

Phinia elbowed him. "Papa said he's trying to get your deed. We have a very good advocate. The very best. His name is Master Sloan. He'll get your deed signed away."

"Father doesn't want her deed," Stephen said, his eyes narrowing. "I heard him tell Mother he's going to try and *adopt* her."

"Won't that be nice?" Phinia said with a gleam in her eye. "How lucky you are, Cettie. I adore your name. Is it short for something? Is it a nickname?"

"I don't know," Cettie answered, feeling badgered by the two of them. She wished Lady Maren were still there.

"It must be short for Celestina. Or Celestine perhaps. You will need to learn how to talk like us, if you want to be part of this family."

"Do you think she *can?*" Stephen asked in a snide tone. Then he smirked again. "I'm only joking, of course."

It was unfair of them to belittle her this way, to make her feel the awkwardness of her position even more keenly, but she was worried enough about her precarious state that she didn't want to retaliate.

"I know how to talk," Cettie said, a little defensively. She'd always had a reputation for speaking well. "My papa taught me."

"Oh, and who was your papa?" Stephen asked. "A brick maker?"

"He was the captain of a hurricane," Cettie answered, feeling more self-conscious by the moment.

Stephen and Phinia stared at her for a moment and then both burst into giggles. The sound made her ears burn. She clenched her fists in the fabric of the new dress.

"That's a *lie*," Phinia taunted after she recovered herself. Then she gave Cettie a disdainful look. "Only an admiral or a *vice* admiral can pilot a hurricane. We should know."

The sting of being wrong brought a wave of humiliation.

"Come on, Phinia," Stephen said, giving Cettie another ugly smirk. "We don't want to interrupt the little girl's lessons. As if she'll get them long. Mrs. Pullman thinks she won't last a week."

Cettie saw in Stephen's eyes the same disdain she'd noticed from the keeper. Now there were two of them determined to persecute her.

CHAPTER SIX

IN THE DARK

The immense Fitzroy estate was full of household servants, men and women who wore gray-and-blue livery and spent the day cleaning and tidying and serving the family. After the lessons, Miss Farnworth and Anna gave Cettie a tour of the mansion. Despite being shy, Anna held Cettie's hand in a gesture of friendship as she led her around. From one of the spires they climbed, Cettie could see the land all the way beneath the estate, and the perspective gave her the queer sensation that they were really atop a mountain and not hovering over the valley below. It was beautiful, but it almost made her stomach revolt. Not even the tallest building could have reached the underside of Fog Willows.

When evening came, the entire place started to glow again, though there were no candles. The light just appeared all at once, shining from behind frosted glass in the ceilings and walls. Cettie again felt that shivering sensation go down her spine, a prickle of awareness that made her giddy inside. Without asking Anna, she knew this to be another of the Mysteries.

The family spent the evening together reading books in the sitting room. There were shelves and shelves of books. Cettie couldn't read very well—what little she knew, she'd taught herself from the news journals the fish came wrapped in—but Anna had offered her encouragement. If she studied the primers from Miss Farnworth, Anna had said, she would soon be able to read every book in the sitting room. They were, after all, Anna's old primers, and she'd developed her skills the same way. Cettie studied the primer, trying to ignore Stephen and Phinia, who were neglecting their books in favor of making gestures and rude faces at each other, trying for a laugh or giggle. Fitzroy and Lady Maren sat together on the sofa.

At some moment in the evening, the lights began to dim of their own accord—as suddenly as they'd turned on—and Fitzroy folded his book closed and asked that his children go off to bed. As they bid one another good night, Cettie heard Phinia murmur that her papa looked very tired because he'd spent the previous night in the Fells. She shot Cettie an accusing look, and her brother offered a wry smile.

"Good night, Cettie," he said, but his tone was still not very welcoming.

Although Cettie was exhausted, she remembered her orders from Mrs. Pullman. She would not be able to retire until the keeper did. Earlier, Mrs. Pullman had made it sound as if she were taking care of Cettie herself, though she knew the older woman did not care to make her comfortable. As she walked down the now-abandoned corridor, the lights grew a shade dimmer, giving way to shadows. A little prick of worry stabbed her heart.

It was such a tall corridor, with its beams and struts and fanciful designs wrought by master craftsmen. She knew very little about the upper class, but she did know that estates like Fog Willows were inherited and had been passed down for generations. Fitzroy himself had once walked these corridors as a lad her age.

Cettie reached the kitchen and found the cook—she couldn't remember her name—still at work in the dimming light, trying to arrange some bread to rise in bowls. She offered to help, but the cook shooed her away with a disgruntled air, so she continued toward the steps at the back of the kitchen. It was dark in the turret, and she touched the wall with one hand to keep her way as she slowly ascended the steps, dreading the coming meeting with Mrs. Pullman.

The door at the top of the steps barred the way. Mrs. Pullman had told Cettie to wait at the stoop for her to finish her duties, saying the door would not open for anyone save the keeper. Not daring to test the handle, Cettie sat there, growing more and more sleepy with each moment. There was no way of knowing how long she waited, but she eventually fell asleep and was startled awake by the sound of shoes slapping up the steps. She rubbed her bleary eyes and saw light chasing away the shadows in the tower.

Mrs. Pullman appeared around the bend of the turret, holding a chain in one hand. A small square lantern was attached to it, the frosted glass like that of the walls of the mansion. Her eyes were deep and wary, and the wrinkles in her face bunched together when she saw Cettie waiting for her.

The tall, prim woman frowned. "So you did as you were told," she said in her drawn-out way of speaking. "I'm surprised. I expected little tricks. Well, these walls have ears, child. They tell me what I wish to know. You behaved today. You made no fuss, even when the master's children snubbed you. As they should."

The words came as a shock. Had Mrs. Pullman spied on her personally, or had she simply interrogated the servants, like Miss Farnworth? If she could spy on her, then Cettie would have to be very, very careful in what she said and did.

The older woman continued up the steps, the lantern swaying on the chain. Cettie couldn't take her eyes off it. She scrabbled backward and rose, pressing her spine against the edge of the doorway.

Mrs. Pullman withdrew her keys and opened the door, then gestured for Cettie to go in first and mount the steps. The room glowed with soft light. It was a beautiful, inviting place—warm despite being in a tower. Still, Cettie felt like shivering. She sensed something—a presence—and a horrible shudder went through her. She heard a faint ringing sound in her ears. Memories of past horrors began to churn inside her. She'd felt this before.

"You'll be sleeping up there," Mrs. Pullman reminded her. She handed the lantern to Cettie. "You'll need this. It'll be *dark*." The wrinkles stretched into a smile that sent a wave of foreboding through her.

Cettie grasped the chain and, steeling herself once more, walked to the ladder leading to the trapdoor.

As she started to climb, she heard Mrs. Pullman say, "Remember. Do not come down until you hear the brass bell."

Worriedly, Cettie climbed to the top rung and shoved open the trapdoor. The smell of wood and must struck her so strongly she nearly choked. She held up the light and saw the dusty boards. There were small boxes and chests littered throughout. It was no larger than a garret in the Fells, a small attic. The only windows were too high to see from, and she could hear the wind whipping against the walls. She climbed the rest of the way up, disturbing the dust, which scattered and spun in the light. There was a pillow and a blanket folded near the trapdoor. There was no bed.

"Go on," Mrs. Pullman said from below. "It's more fit for your station."

How many empty rooms existed in the sprawling mansion? How many beds lay empty? Surely the servants' quarters were more inviting than this empty, abandoned space. And yet, Cettie knew Mrs. Pullman was purposefully pushing her. She was trying to get her to complain to the Fitzroys.

Cettie climbed into the attic and closed the hatch behind her. She was exhausted, so she grabbed the blanket and pillow and settled onto the floor in an unused corner, her back against the wall so she could see the entire room. She thought about the children who had suffered with her at Miss Charlotte's and felt a pang of longing for their companionship.

She didn't know how to turn the lantern off, so she left it there, shining against her face. Perhaps it would be a help. Ghosts didn't like the light. The sounds of Mrs. Pullman getting ready for bed filtered up to her, but soon the room below grew quiet. Cettie wriggled under the blanket, trying to find a comfortable position.

The lantern went out.

Cettie lifted her head and turned, wondering how it had happened.

She settled herself on the floor, trying to get comfortable enough to sleep. Fitzroy had said there were no ghosts in Fog Willows. No, surely this was just Mrs. Pullman trying to frighten her. Her eyes slowly adjusted to the gloom and the dim light streaming in from the upper windows. There were no scratching noises declaring the presence of rats. Still, she sensed something in the gathering blackness—a . . . presence emerging from the dark. The ringing in her ears grew louder. Her heart began to beat a frantic, wild pace, for she instantly recognized it as a ghost. It wasn't the tall one. This one was different.

The fear that struck her was immediate and overpowering. There were no children nearby. There was no defense. Cettie pulled the blanket up over her head and shivered with dread. It was happening again, just as it had in the Fells. Were dark beings simply drawn to her? No matter where she went? She'd felt so certain that no ghosts would be able to rise to the manors in the clouds, and yet there was no denying what she sensed.

The ghost was in front of her, looming over her. Tears began to seep through her clenched eyes. She pressed her fists against her face, her heart beating a mad rhythm in her chest. "Go away," she whispered frantically, shuddering beneath the thin blanket.

The unseen entity lingered, brooding in the blackness of the attic.

"Go away, go away, go away," Cettie repeated, mouthing the words.

I just want to touch you. Just to touch. You are so warm. So warm.

She could sense things about it, little insights that sputtered to life and jabbed inside her thoughts. Her mind black with terror, she rolled over to face the wall, shivering violently.

"Please go away," Cettie begged.

You are so warm. So warm. So warm.

She waited, trembling, and then—with a spasm of dread—she felt a clawlike hand reach through her back and come out her front. Everything went cold.

SERA

CHAPTER SEVEN
THE BLOOD ROYAL

Every scullery maid kneeling in grime dreamed of becoming a princess. Every schoolgirl with pigtails, every hungry urchin, every milliner's daughter arranging feathers on customers' hats, every seamstress sewing beads into corsets, every baker's wife gripping a tray of warm buns from the oven, every coughing drudge forced to labor in the accursed cotton mills in the Fells. Every girl alive from one end of the boundless empire to the other, above and below.

Except for Sera.

"Seraphin Fitzempress, get down from the window. You know your mother doesn't like you daydreaming. Back to your lessons, please."

"I don't like it when you call me by my full name," Sera said, elbows on the sill, chin resting on her hands. The view from her window wasn't high enough for her to see over the garden wall. To see the rest of Lockhaven and the patch of the City that lay beneath them, she'd need to climb one of the trees again.

"I called you by your pet name three times, and you didn't answer me even once," said her exasperated governess Baroness Hugilde.

"You did?"

"I most certainly did. What were you daydreaming about this time? I shouldn't even ask. You were probably fancying yourself an underservant."

"You can never predict my fancies. I don't see why you even try. I was thinking that every girl living below Lockhaven wishes she were me . . . and how terribly wrong they all are. The most desperate one of them has more freedom than I do."

Sera could hear the indignant clearing of her governess's throat. "Freedom from hunger? Freedom from ignorance? Freedom from pride?"

"You're in a saucy mood this morning," Sera countered, giving her governess a nasty look. "Didn't you get breakfast?" Hugilde's forehead wrinkled with displeasure. There were many things Hugilde was *not* saying, she knew—as usual, Hugilde was trying to stay calm. Sera loved it when she provoked her governess to the breaking point and the older woman started scolding her in her native tongue. That was when the *real* Hugilde came out. All the other times, it was pretense.

The governess smoothed her skirts and adopted a look of tranquility. "And why does Your Royal Highness want to be a commoner anyway? Do you not stand to inherit the greatest treasure in all the world?"

Sera gave her a wry smile. "Who is to say that my grandfather would choose me as his successor? He has three sons in line for the throne, madame, and my father is the second eldest. I never see him calling on our manor." She turned back to the window. "I never see *anyone*." She sounded a little sorry for herself, and she wrinkled her nose, determined not to lapse into self-pity again.

"Ah, so my little Sera is lonely for companionship. I am not enough. But you must know the emperor does not make social calls. It's whispered that he prefers your father to his other sons. The emperor can pick whomever he chooses. It's not about being the eldest."

"That means he can also choose me. But how long must we all wait? I think Father despairs that he'll die of old age before he's given the chance to do anything important. Which is why I'm trapped here.

60

Waiting, waiting, waiting. I'm a slave really. And you, Hugilde, are forty years old, and I am twelve. Can you not imagine it might be pleasant for me to spend an afternoon with someone my own age? Or at least nearer to it? Sometimes the only way to escape is through my mind." *Or up a tree,* she thought eagerly.

Sera tilted her head sideways, wishing she could penetrate the fog of the city streets with her eyes and actually *see* the people down below. All her life, she'd lived in the sprawling, mazelike collection of palaces and manors called Lockhaven, but not once had she been allowed to walk its streets. Walking in the City below was doubly forbidden. Of course, she could see plenty of evidence of the world beyond hers. From her favorite tree, she had a perfect view of the chimneys and slanted roofs of Lockhaven. Occasionally, when the clouds were absent, she could see towers rising from below and the distant specks of wagons maneuvering in the crowded streets of the City. The people were too small to see, but she could imagine them.

The view from the window was decidedly less exciting, but at least she could still see the zephyrs and tempests and even hurricanes roaming the skies. Once, she had even seen a Bhikhu alight from one of the crafts and fly into another. She tapped the glass window with her fingers, closing one eye so she could touch the spots and specks of the distant sky ships.

"If we could get back to your lesson," Hugilde insisted, trying to master her patience once again.

"Why are zephyrs faster than hurricanes?" Sera asked dreamily. "Is it because of the size? Does that really matter?"

"I have no idea, Sera; that's a question better posed to the Minister of Wind."

"I would be happy to ask him if he could be brought to my high dungeon."

"Or do you mean high dudgeon?" Hugilde let slip a little jab.

Sera turned her head, a smile on her mouth. "You're getting impatient with me." She bounded off the couch, away from the window, and bent down to kiss Hugilde on the cheek. "I have so many questions, and you never know the answers. Let's walk in the garden."

"That is because you ask questions that don't *have* any answers, Sera. You always want to know things that no one knows. That aren't even part of the Mysteries. It's rather windy outside today. I would prefer we stay inside."

"Please, Hugilde. I'll listen better if we walk while we talk."

Hugilde sighed and relented—just as she usually did. Then she gathered up a book, and the two left Sera's study room and walked down the turret stairs to the back gardens. Their yard was impossibly small compared to those of other mansions. Only the sturdiest of trees thrived at such heights.

"Do you think Mother will let me go away to school to learn the Mysteries?" Sera asked, chewing on the end of her finger as they walked.

Hugilde gave her a scolding look. "Stop that. Princesses don't bite their nails."

"This one does," Sera answered sweetly.

"If your mother saw you doing that, she would . . ." Hugilde let out a harrumph and rolled her eyes.

The flagstones were set in sand, which was comfortable enough, but they did not go the direction Sera wanted to, so she left the path to wander in the grass, which was softer. It was still a little wet from a cloudburst that had struck the day before.

"I think she would be displeased," Sera said, still teasing loose the fragment from her nail, intent on goading Hugilde further. The grass felt delicious. "And then you would get in trouble because you are my governess. That's all you really care about, Hugilde. The possibility of getting in trouble and losing your position. You are so selfish, Baroness."

It almost worked. Hugilde's eyes bugged out, and she seemed on the verge of standing up and defending herself . . . except she realized just in time that Sera was once again only trying to provoke her.

Hugilde deliberately smoothed her skirts as she walked, something she often did to give herself a moment of thought. "Shall we proceed with your lessons again, Sera?" she asked with feigned sweetness. "Now that we are outside?"

"I want to go to school," Sera pleaded. "With children my own age."

"You are one of the heirs of the empire, Sera. You are not like other children."

"No, the problem is that I am *too* much like them." She wrung her hands and then started to run ahead, going straight for the tallest redwood in the garden. There was a row of them along the outer wall, waiting for her to explore.

"Your Highness!" Hugilde pleaded, starting after her. "Not today! We've not made much progress. If your parents saw you climbing that tree, please . . . Sera!"

Sera reached the sculpted tree. When she was little, it had been a struggle to reach the lower branches. She was short for twelve, but she was able to catch the lowest one and pull herself up before Hugilde caught up to her. Sera wriggled her way up the first branch, put her feet on it, and then started up the next. Hugilde reached the tree and lunged, trying to grab her foot, but Sera had moved higher in expectation of her governess's maneuver. The interior of the tree was perfect for climbing. The sagging branches offered a great shield from prying eyes. She continued to go higher.

"Please come down, Sera."

"Tell me something useful, then," Sera said over her shoulder. "Tell me something I *want* to know."

An exaggerated sigh came from her governess. "You are stubborn, child. This is not fitting behavior for a princess."

"It's fitting for an empress, though," she replied. "They can do whatever they want."

"The Mysteries of Law should be your specialty! You love nothing more than to argue."

"But I'm more interested in the Mysteries of War." Sera sighed, smiling with the thrill of the climb. She was almost to the highest spot, where she could see over the wall.

"War? Surely you are jesting with me again. Now, if you'll come down out of that tree and act at least a little like a princess, then I will tell you some gossip I heard from the north."

"Start off by telling me the gossip," Sera countered, "and if it is good, then I will obey you." She was almost there . . .

"You should obey me because I am your governess! In other households they can be quite severe with their students, you should know."

Sera reached the height of the wall and eagerly looked over. Fluffy clouds spread out beneath her, but her gaze was immediately attracted to an especially fat hurricane approaching Lockhaven from the west. She gripped the tree's narrow trunk and leaned toward the wall to get a better view of it. What cargo was it carrying from the City below? Or was this one full of soldiers? It looked like it was skimming the tops of the clouds as if they were the sea. Sometimes, she fancied if she could step off the walls, the clouds would catch her like giant pillows. "You wouldn't do that, Hugilde, because you're afraid that if I *did* become empress, I would have you tortured."

"Well, if you insist on being so headstrong, my only recourse is to tell you the gossip and then plead with you to come down. If your mother caught you standing in a tree again—but you know that she would not be pleased. Neither would your father. The news. Vice Admiral Fitzroy was called on to be a magistrate for a case up near his estate."

"Fog Willows," Sera said dreamily, gazing down at the clouds. She wished a strong wind would scatter them so she could have a better view. A few of the palaces in the wealthy neighborhoods of the City had turrets high enough to pierce the clouds. Those people could see Lockhaven clearly. Many of the royal families owned manors both above and below, but most preferred to remain above the soot, smoke, and smog. She leaned forward even more, grabbing the edge of the wall and resting her elbows on it. "What's interesting about that news, Hugilde? He's part of the ministry. Isn't the northern judge *here* at the moment?"

"Indeed, he is, discussing a labor dispute. Apparently Fitzroy was called in because the case involved children. Ones even younger than yourself."

Sera turned around, growing more interested. The branch she was on sagged under her weight. She felt like bouncing on it.

"Fitzroy said he intends to adopt one of them. A child from the Fells," Hugilde continued with a scandalized tone.

"That *is* news," Sera said, a queer feeling blooming in her heart. "When did this happen?"

"Not long . . . a fortnight ago, I think," Hugilde said. "He took the poor thing, a common urchin, I tell you, back to Fog Willows with him, and has asked his advocate to seek out evidence of the girl's parentage."

Sera didn't know many of the ministers. It was difficult to judge someone when you were rarely permitted to leave your room to wander the garden. Looking away from the view, she glanced at the hedge maze on the far end of the garden and the small benches in the midst of it. She loved the maze and would sometimes hide from Hugilde inside it.

"Lord Fitzroy is rather eccentric," Hugilde said.

Sera had heard that Fitzroy was different from the others. He never wore the latest fashions. He never gossiped. He refused to wear gloves—a decision that scandalized some people so much they refused to shake his hand in consequence. He was a distant relation of hers, but she'd only met him once.

"So Fitzroy's not satisfied to just take her deed?" Sera asked, feeling strange and conflicted about the news. A desire to meet the girl began to bloom inside her. Someone from the Fells would have stories. She would be interesting.

"Exactly," the baroness said, sensing that she had Sera's interest at last. "Getting a deed is no matter. Fitzroy has several already, including that young man from Holyrud."

Sera squinted. "I don't remember that one. Where is that again?"

"It's in another kingdom," Hugilde said, "but still part of the empire. You remember—the family went bankrupt, like so many do these days. All these schemes and risks. It's a marvel none of the mansions have crashed to earth recently. The last one happened ten years ago. How dreadful. The cottage beneath it was obliterated. It's all ruins now." The mere thought made Sera shudder. As much as she wanted to visit the world below, she didn't think she could live beneath Lockhaven permanently, always beneath the giant mountain's shadow. "But I think that young man's estate is still floating. It's being held by a bank. Fitzroy took the deed for the eldest son and is sponsoring him at school. The boy wants to become a doctor in the Fells."

Sera smiled and turned back to her view of the clouds and turrets. "I like him already."

"Goodness, Sera, the Fells in the north! Do you think living there would be romantic? I assure you, the waif that Vice Admiral Fitzroy rescued doesn't want to go back there. The average child there dies before reaching fifteen."

"Is that true?" Sera gasped in shock.

Hugilde nodded emphatically. "Of course it's true. I would not lie to you, Sera."

"But if so many die, why doesn't the emperor *do* something about it? That is awful!"

"What can be done?" the baroness asked helplessly. "The world is this way. Has been for some time. Someone must raise cattle and slaughter them. Someone must grow the wheat. The dress you are no doubt ripping was made down there."

"But if someone is hungry, you feed them, Baroness," Sera said, feeling her passions flare.

"In the tenements, they die of cold and sickness as well as hunger. They die because they have no hope and fling themselves off bridges. What would you have the ministry do, Your Highness? Erect nets to catch them? Many of them are too proud to ask for help. They see death as an escape from misery. But not everyone who lives down there is desperate. Many of them live very comfortably."

"Do you hear yourself, Hugilde?" Sera said, her voice beginning to quaver. "It is wrong." She felt tears prick her eyes. "At least Fitzroy did *something* about it. He took in one of them. I should like to meet her."

"But he left a dozen and took only one," the governess said, shaking her head. "What good can that do?"

"But does it stand to reason, Hugilde, that because you cannot serve *all* you shouldn't serve *any*? At least Fitzroy did something. That's more than Mother or Father do, and they've the means to help." She began to nip at her fingernail again.

It was precisely at that moment her parents entered the garden. She saw them coming together.

Sera had meant to climb down the tree earlier. And here she was, still in it, leaning against the wall *and* chewing her fingernail. The misery of the people—their people—had always afflicted her, and she felt tears welling up in her eyes. A blaze of defiance sizzled up her spine. Part of her wanted to climb up onto the wall, run to the far end, and jump into the neighbor's garden and escape. Maybe their gates were unlocked, and she could finally wander the streets of Lockhaven alone. Maybe she could meet someone who was not part of the household staff.

Her parents approached rapidly.

"Get down, young lady," Father said in a warning voice.

Baroness Hugilde turned, stammering an apology, her cheeks flaming with mortification.

Sera's mother was still quite young, for they had had their first and only child early. Their marriage had been arranged by their parents and was a sham. When they were out in society, they feigned happiness and ease and gave compliments to each other. But at the manor, there was needling and badgering and no attempt to conceal their dislike for one another.

Still, they could show a surprising unity when it came to trying to govern their daughter's interests. One of the only things they'd agreed upon was that neither of them could see their daughter alone, so as not to influence her against the wishes of the other. Hugilde had been carefully chosen because she represented neither side.

"You heard your father. Get down at once. This is *disgraceful* behavior from a princess."

Sera wanted to defy them. Up in this redwood tree, she could fancy herself free. She smelled the wonderful scent of the foliage, felt the wind in her hair, and saw the top side of the clouds better than at any place in her manor. Would her father compel her to obey? Would he climb up after her?

She put her full weight on the branch, stood—gripping the trunk with one hand—and looked down at her parents coolly.

"How far are we on today's lesson?" her father asked, clasping his hands behind his back. "I went by your room and found it empty and saw the baroness in the garden by herself."

His doublet and vest were the epitome of fashion. He was only a few years older than her mother, though his deep sideburns were stippled with gray. Sera's mother had a trim figure, perhaps too much so, and sometimes Sera would witness her parents arguing about food. She'd even overheard her mother vomiting in the privy closet. There was always tension when her parents entered the room. Tension about food, about her education, about something unsaid that never would be. Her austere father made her afraid, and she hated that feeling and was determined to conquer it. Her mother, in her fancy hats and ringlets, invoked her disdain.

"We were . . . about to . . . start," Hugilde said in a panicked voice.

"It's not her fault," Sera interjected. "It's mine. I wanted to see down below again."

"Another of your fancies?" Father said with a sigh. "When are you ever going to learn, Sera?"

The branch she was standing on cracked.

CHAPTER EIGHT

PRINCE REGENT

Sera's heart stopped as the branch gave way. She was falling, scraping down the length of the trunk, and if not for her father's quick reflexes, she would have broken her bones. At least. He was near enough that he caught her, but the impact had knocked them down. Sera heard screaming, both from her mother and Hugilde. The impact had only taken her breath away . . . and yet . . .

If falling from a tree felt like *this*, what would falling off one of the floating manors do to someone? There were stories that some of the wealthy, those who had lost everything, opted to jump rather than face their creditors.

Sera's father sat up, and she hugged him, filled with gratitude and remorse. He held her back, whispering soothing words, his anger replaced—for the moment—by intense relief.

"She's all right, she's all right," he said to her mother and governess.

"I'm not hurt," Sera said, squeezing him harder. "I've climbed that tree so many times. It's never done that."

"How many times must I tell you, Seraphin?" he said, pulling her face back and looking into her eyes worriedly. "Just because something doesn't happen constantly doesn't mean it won't happen at all. Many of the consequences we face are delayed. This principle governs so much in this world."

Yes, she had heard him preach this many times. A person can be dishonest once and get away with it. Twice even. Maybe a dozen times. But then the law finds out, and the punishment comes swift and fierce, paying in interest from the past. He had always taught her, from earliest childhood, that she could choose her actions, not the consequences of those actions.

The family retreated to the safety of the manor, a bit bruised and scraped, but otherwise unhurt. She knew that the relief her parents felt would be followed by stricter rules. And she knew that Hugilde wouldn't be easily convinced to let her go outside next time.

While Sera's lessons with the baroness were a particular form of torture because they were completely theoretical and had no application to anything in Sera's life, having meals with her parents was a level beyond it. Since there were only three in the family, Baroness Hugilde ate with them, too. As a matter of ritual, her parents often displayed their enmity for each other by sitting on opposite ends of the table with her in between—a ritual Sera detested.

Even worse, she was not encouraged to speak.

Sera wiped her lips discreetly on her napkin, spitting out the overboiled cabbage that had disgusted her, and folded it on her lap. Beneath the table, she shook it onto the floor. Hugilde noticed this surreptitious action from across the table and gave her a pointed stare, subtly reminding her that it was quite unladylike to spit out her food. Sera smiled at her primly as if nothing at all were amiss. Her elbow still throbbed from bashing it against a branch on the way down.

The conversation in the room was terribly dull. Father, who'd been schooled in the Mysteries of Wind, liked to prove his superiority by discussing the latest scientific discoveries and matters of the day. Mother, on the other hand, had been tutored in the Mysteries relating to religion, art, and writing—the Mysteries of Thought. Both had pressured her to follow in their footsteps, which only made her inclined to study something else entirely. The mayhem of the morning had already been discussed and a verdict rendered. She would be confined to her room for a week as a punishment. For once, she didn't argue for less time, because an injury such as a broken leg would have been much, much worse.

With a silver chalice in his hand, her father leaned back in his chair and swirled the contents, his tone rather demeaning as he addressed his wife. "And what do you think, my *dear*,"—he always said it in the most patronizing tone possible when addressing his spouse—"of Fitzroy bringing in an urchin to Fog Willows? I thought the man had more sense than that."

Sera perked up slightly, interested in the new direction of their conversation. She'd been thinking about the urchin ever since the baroness mentioned her.

Mother's blue eyes narrowed suspiciously, as if she anticipated a trap. "It is rather vulgar. Maybe it was just for a season?"

Father snorted. "Do you not remember what I told you yesterday? His advocate is seeking to do adoption proceedings. Adoption! It's unheard of!"

"Fitzroy has always been immune to the opinions of others," Mother countered.

Father took a deep swallow from the cup. "And what good has that done to his reputation? Very little, I tell you. He's a laughingstock among the gentry. I think it's all an act. He seeks to ingratiate himself with the populace. To curry enough favor to become prime minister. What do you think of that?"

"I don't really know," Mother replied, looking more uncomfortable. "His motives are entirely his own."

Father leaned back, cradling the cup between his hands, stewing in frustration. "If he didn't inherit that blasted silver mine," he growled, "he'd have to preserve his fortune like the rest of us. The cost of maintaining estates has dramatically increased. It's grinding us down." He stared off into space, his brow furrowed.

"Will we need to secure a loan?" Mother asked with a hint of worry.

He sneered at her. "I will not do that," he jabbed back angrily. "Our debts were all paid off when Seraphin was eight. We will live within our means. Do you remember when the manor jolted and began to drop? Some mistake at the bank, no doubt. It still gives me nightmares. I won't risk depending on others for credit ever again."

Sera remembered that day. The manor had trembled, and she'd felt that sinking feeling of going down. But it had steadied itself and returned to its moorings.

"Speaking of money, I would like to increase my allowance to help my sister in Chelton."

"Impossible." The answer was curt, venomous. Father's temper always flared when they talked of finances.

Mother leaned forward. "Surely, if we have no debts, then we can afford—"

"You know nothing whatever of the matter," Father said, cutting her off. He slammed his goblet on the table as he leaned forward. "Lockhaven is built on nothing but wind and promises. I grow more nervous by the day that the lord high chancellor and his underlings will lose all control or accountability. That one flawed phrase in a contract will send this entire place plummeting down to crush the populace of the City living below us. No, I would sooner take us to a small country manor, away from the corruption in this government. We get an allowance from my father and will live within it, unlike my brothers who borrow against a future that may not happen."

Sera could see that her father was about to explode into one of his rages again. So she took the opportunity to speak up, even though she knew she'd likely be scolded for it.

"I should like to live away from the City. Maybe we could visit Lord Fitzroy. I would like to see the girl from the Fells," she said, daintily picking up her spoon and sipping the broth.

Sometimes her interruptions provoked her father; sometimes he was amused by them. But, really, was it fair that a thinking person should be kept quiet throughout her entire childhood? It was a tradition, nothing more. It wasn't one of the Mysteries, surely.

Her father's head torqued to one side, his eyes flashing with mirth. "How many times have I told you not to speak during meals, Seraphin Fitzempress? If this were a dinner party, a child would never be allowed to speak."

She looked up at the ceiling. "This isn't a dinner party. I am young, but I still have thoughts. I still have ideas. I want to talk about things."

"And what kind of ideas can be tumbling about in that precocious head of yours that would be worth listening to?" her father asked, still giving her that bemused look. It looked perilously close to dipping into anger.

"But I don't understand why children cannot speak during dinner," Sera said.

"That's enough, Seraphin," Mother said. "You're provoking your father."

"But I want to know," Sera complained.

Her father's cheek started to twitch with anger. "When you disobey my instructions, it is an act of defiance. There is nothing, *nothing*, that I abhor more than defiance. If you will not be civil, then you will go to your rooms."

"My dear, she's just curious," Mother interceded. She didn't want to be left alone with him.

"And you think curiosity is grounds for indulgence? If she cannot be taught respect and manners at home, how will she do in society, where every lapse results in the sharpest displeasure and the most serious consequences? What happened in the tree this morning did not cause permanent damage to her. It did scar the tree. She must be corrected and brought to task for her own good. How else is she supposed to impress my father?"

Sera pushed away from the table and threw her napkin into the middle of the dishes.

"Seraphin!" Father seethed at her deliberate disrespect.

Sera stood up, feeling her cheeks flush with anger at being treated as though she were nine or ten. "I think Lord Fitzroy is a kind man. I've heard that his children *argue* during dinner. It's a good thing that he brought in that poor creature from the Fells. We should follow his example and do something like that."

The rims of his nostrils were white. She hoped she hadn't pushed him too far. He was normally very logical and composed, but the fists he was squeezing his hands into certainly did not look composed. "I think you've said quite enough, young lady." He gave Hugilde a sharp look and jerked his head for her to leave as well.

Sera took a roll with her and, holding her head high, marched toward the door, while Hugilde murmured apologies to her parents and excused herself from the table.

"You were too harsh with her, Husband," Sera could hear Mother scold.

"And you are too lenient. The child is positively reckless. She could have broken her neck this morning."

"She's your daughter."

"I wonder at that sometimes," muttered Father, causing Sera a jolt of pain. She was about to turn around and really provoke him, but Hugilde caught her look and grabbed her arm to lead her away—

Except she came to a sudden stop. The butler had opened the door with a florid face and rushed inside.

The verbal combat at the table abruptly ended, too, and the butler hastened to her father and whispered in his ear.

There was an immediate transformation, a look of shock in his countenance. Father rose to his feet, smoothing his jacket and vest and snugging his eating gloves more tightly around his wrists.

"What is it? What has happened?" Mother demanded, her eyes red from repressed tears.

"The prime minister is here," Father said curtly.

Sera turned and found the older gentleman standing before her in the doorway. He had wavy gray hair that swirled around a wizened, blocky face, but he was still a handsome man. And the many medals pinned to his coat showing his rank as lord high admiral as well as prime minister made him more so. The immediate hush over the room was like a spell. He smiled at Sera in a grandfatherly way and took her silk-sheathed hand in his leather-gloved one. The material was cold, and so was his entire person, which meant he had just arrived on a sky ship. Oh, to have the freedom of traveling in such a way . . .

"And good evening to you, Miss Fitzempress," he said, squeezing her hand. "I'm afraid I have interrupted dinner. Or was it just ending? I have not eaten myself this evening and may intrude on your hospitality."

He was commenting on the fact that she wasn't in her seat.

"Of-f course, Prime Minister," Father said, his anger gone but not the pasty look. "This is an unexpected arrival, surely. There was n-no word sent of your coming."

"None indeed," said the man. His name was Richard Welles, and next to the emperor, he was the most powerful person alive. Sera had never shaken his hand before. Even she, with her outspokenness, was humbled by his presence. "My private secretary is consulting with your steward at the moment. What is said here must remain confidential."

He squeezed Sera's hand again, giving her another smile, and then released it and approached the table, his hands clasped behind his back. He was broad chested and tall, the kind of man people were inclined to follow.

Father gestured urgently for Hugilde to take Sera away. The butler was already striding out of the room.

"No, she can stay. This impacts her as well," Welles said.

"W-who can stay?" Father stammered. "The governess?"

Welles looked annoyed. "No. Your daughter."

Hugilde blanched and hastily exited the room. Sera's heart beat fast. This was exciting. This was better than a fancy. Something was happening in *real* life. She pinched her wrist hard and felt the pain. Yes. It was not a dream. The butler carefully closed the door, sealing the four of them inside together. Sera bit her lip in anticipation.

"Your father has fallen ill," Welles said formally. "He had seemed in robust health for a man of sixty and two. There were no indications. Then his speech began to slur earlier today, his walking became awkward. He collapsed suddenly and has been totally unable to communicate since then."

Mother's eyes, already wet, began to gush anew. She pressed a napkin to her mouth.

Father's eyes widened with surprise. "An apoplexy, do you think?"

The prime minister sighed. "It appears so, Lord Willard. An astute observation, I should say, but not surprising coming from a man trained in the Mysteries of Wind. One does not have to be a *harbinger* to foresee that changes are coming to the empire. The emperor may recover quickly, rendering the need for this conversation moot. However, it has been my long experience serving in the admiralty that when a man has apoplexy, he is liable to have more, and the next will be even more debilitating."

Mother sniffled and waved her napkin. "But surely he can be healed?" she said through her tears.

The prime minister gave her a respectful, if condescending look. He cleared his throat. "It has also been my experience, ma'am, that while it is always good to *hope* for miracles, it is not wise to count on them. Laws are immutable, my lady. Consequences come to kings just as they do to the poor souls who live below. Both can die of a cough. And have."

Mother shook her head in misery and continued to wipe tears from her eyes.

Father was grasping the implications already. "You came here . . . first?"

The prime minister bowed his gray head. "I'm not a harbinger . . . *I* cannot see the future. But I can see clouds in the distance and know the winds will soon be fierce. Foremost, I am a servant of the people and naturally anticipate what may be best for all. What may be the most acceptable. If the emperor is incapacitated, then we will need a prince regent chosen by the privy council. While I might personally prefer that this individual come from my own ministry"—here he offered a curt bow to Sera's father—"I am pragmatic enough to recognize that the people would see a more natural answer from the Ministry of Wind. The emperor's condition being a medical one, there would be more trust if the regent came from that branch. He also made no will to specify his choice of heir. And, to put it bluntly, your two brothers are both spendthrifts and have racked up considerable debts. I think the privy council will look to this house."

Father staggered back into the table, his hand groping for something to steady himself. The feeling of dread in Sera's stomach yawned wide as the implication struck her like a fist. No, this could not happen. If this action put her even closer to the throne, how might her little freedoms be stripped from her?

"You think . . . you think that *I* could be prince regent?" her father whispered hoarsely.

"Yes. That is precisely what I think may happen. Prepare yourself, sir. If it does come to pass, you will need to form a new government based on your ministry. Beware the Ministry of Law doesn't outflank you. They are rather subtle. You might have papers thrust in front of you to sign and seal. Do not sign anything until this is resolved. You have no debt, which is rare for our class, and so their ministry cannot bar you from stepping into the role. The Ministry of War, of course, will stand ready to aid you should conflict arise, but we are in a season of peace, save for some minor trade disputes.

"I think it long overdue that the Ministry of Wind be given a turn at the helm of government. You might consider Fitzroy as your prime minister. The *ghosts* know the man wouldn't want it, poor chap, but he'd do an excellent job. But it's not my place to advise you. The Minister of Wind will hear of this shortly, if he hasn't already. I'm glad I reached you first."

"T-thank you, Prime Minster," her father said. A queer brightness lit his eyes.

"Would you like to stay and join our meal?" Mother asked, dabbing her eyes.

"Don't mind if I do," Lord Welles said cheerfully. "I never walk away from a meal," he said with a wry smile, looking down at the half-eaten plate that Sera had been forced to abandon.

He gave her a secret look and winked at her.

Just as thoughts are powerful, so are spoken words. There are words that are so powerful they can make cities float in the sky. To obfuscate such power from the masses—from the populace seething in the mills, the mines, and the manure— we employ other words. The rites of power are complex and must be studied. So we cloak them in language called the Mysteries. While there are infinite applications, there are four major schools: the Mysteries of War, the Mysteries of Wind, the Mysteries of Law, and the Mysteries of Thought. No one can master all we have learned of them. Even one branch of Law can take a lifetime to master.

—Lady Corinne of Pavenham Sky

CHAPTER NINE

TUTORS

It was not often that Sera was summoned to a meeting with her father and his private secretary. In fact, Hugilde's complexion turned a shade of green when she received the summons. Much had changed since the prime minister's visit; Sera's willfulness remained the same. The day was still young, and Sera had hardly had time to daydream, which she preferred to Hugilde's incessant repetition of boring lessons. How could she focus on a geography lesson when she'd barely traveled beyond her front door? What did investments mean when she had no way to spend the money she already had a right to?

The servant introduced her at the door to her parents' chamber, and she walked in, surprised that her mother was not present. This broke her parents' unspoken rule of never meeting with her alone.

Her father was seated at the study desk, an elegantly crafted piece of furniture that could have withstood a battering ram. Papers were strewn around, and his secretary, a man named Case, stood beside him, one hand planted on the polished wood. Sera didn't care much for the man. He was always sweating and seemed half choked in his tie and constricting vest, his golden spectacles crimping his nostrils.

"She's here, sir," Case said gently in her father's ear.

Father looked up from his papers.

"Where's Mother?" Sera asked brightly, gazing around the study. Father had a huge collection of tubes, racks, tongs, and weighing stones—the implements needed to study the wind, though he had never explained any of them to her. His study smelled crisp, like burned metal, a smell that had always been strangely pleasant.

"She's writing letters to members of the family," he answered tonelessly, glancing at the papers on his desk. "She does that often, you know."

"I was just curious," Sera said. "We normally don't have private interviews."

Case took out a silk kerchief and mopped his upper lip. He should have mopped his forehead. It was nearly dripping with sweat, and his greasy, thinning, dark hair was flopping around in it.

"I wanted to go over your new education schedule," Father went on, his mood curious.

Sera's brow wrinkled. "Isn't the baroness in charge of my education?"

"Not anymore," Father said. "She is your governess, true. But your education is about to take a dramatic turn."

"Am I going away to study?" Sera asked, feeling an eagerness kindle inside her. She would do anything to leave the cold, silent manor—it didn't matter where. The majority of her daydreams involved traveling through the clouds in a sky ship. The look on her father's face squashed that hope instantly.

"Don't be absurd," he laughed, seemingly delighted with himself. "We've finished our arrangements for your study. Your new tutors will be coming *here*, starting this afternoon. Tell her, Case."

A sour feeling entered her heart as the private secretary cleared his throat. "We have, ahem, Doctor Choate to teach her the Mysteries of Wind. Commander Falking will oversee her study of War. Ahem, for Law . . . you chose the firm of Eakett and Baggles, and the responsibility will be shared between the two advocates. And for the Mysteries of Thought, we settled on your private chaplain, I believe."

"Indeed," Father said smugly. "That will save a formidable sum while not sparing in the quality of her education. Your first lessons will begin this afternoon under Doctor Choate. He's an excellent man and very knowledgeable."

"Is he *boring*?" Sera asked. She wanted to learn more about the Mysteries—the prospect fascinated her—but she feared these new masters would teach her in the same way Hugilde did.

Father's brows beetled. "What difference should that make, Seraphin *Fitzempress*? Word of the emperor's apoplexy is spreading through the empire. That our humble family was chosen to help lead shows that all of our efforts have not been in vain. You are our only child. Someday, in the distant future, *you* may become empress. Your education *now* is therefore paramount."

"I don't understand," Sera said, the blood rushing in her ears. "Why cannot I be sent away for my education like others have been? Why limit my training to just four teachers?"

"Ahem, five," Case butted in with a finger. "Eakett *and* Baggles."

Sera wanted to throw something at him. "I had thought, Father, that when I turned fourteen, I would go away to study at a proper school." In truth, that prospect was the one thing that got her through the long, tedious days. There was a part of her that was excited to learn these things. The Mysteries, at last! But the crushing disappointment of not going away to study, of not meeting other children her age, tore at her heart. When would she be able to learn dancing? Would she be trapped permanently with Hugilde as a partner? All her life she had been surrounded by adults.

"It's an unnecessary expense," he answered gravely, steepling his fingers. "It will cost much less to have tutors brought here. And they are all capable, qualified *men* who will instruct you in the Mysteries. I will not tolerate any sluggishness or laziness on your part. You daydream too much, Seraphin. That must end. If this responsibility is thrust on us, then we must rise to it."

She bit her lip, squeezing her hands into fists. She hated crying. "What does Mother have to say about this?"

Father's cheek twitched. "I did not invite you here to negotiate with you. This change in circumstances will require me to travel frequently, and I wish to be assured that your education will accelerate in my absence. Think of this as an opportunity, Daughter. Most young women who go away to school are only given the opportunity to focus on the Mysteries of Thought or the Mysteries of Wind—and then only because of the musical component. The Law may be tedious, but as a member of the royal family, it's crucial for you to understand trade agreements and commerce. Even military strategy. Do you understand me, Seraphin? You have no siblings. You are closer to the throne now than you've *ever* been!" His eyes were alight with ambition. She wasn't sure if he was directing his words at her or himself.

"You've been chosen as prince regent, but that—"

"Ahem, *may* be chosen," Case corrected.

She turned to him, eyes blazing. "I don't think the prime minister would have come to tell us in person if it weren't already a foregone conclusion!" Sera said to Case, her voice rising as her temper flared. The secretary wilted beneath her tone of command.

"Enough," Father said in rebuke.

"I'm sorry. This is just so sudden. I want to learn, I do. I never thought that there was much of a chance that I'd become empress. At least not until I was much older."

"Of course not until then. Do you think you are remotely capable of such a heavy responsibility presently? Were my indebted brothers and I all to perish, you would still need a regent to rule for you until you came of age, and perhaps for some time afterward." He began to rise from the stuffed chair and planted his knuckles on the table. "But you are a Fitzempress. A blood royal. I think Baroness Hugilde has been far too lenient with you thus far. I've instructed Case to warn her, sternly, that should you fail to progress in your new duty of education, she will be sent away permanently, and I will find another governess who *will* manage your temper."

A shard of fear stabbed through Sera's soul. Though she did love to tease the governess, she was the only person in Sera's life who seemed to genuinely care about her. To know her. Hugilde was the only stable part of her world. "It's not her fault that I get lost in my fancies," she stammered.

"I know that," Father said pointedly. "You are responsible. Not anyone else. And you've failed to live up to our expectations. You've dawdled and overslept and wasted too much time on nonsense."

"I'm only twelve, Papa," she said, her voice choking.

His stern eyes softened with just a touch of compassion. "You're too easily distracted. Too impertinent and willful. I am your father, and you owe me your filial duty. Now that I am to be the prince regent." His voice became even firmer. "How can I rule others if I cannot rule my own household?"

Much of what he said was true, but that he was saying it in front of Case only added to her humiliation. The spark of defiance was beginning to boil now.

She lifted her chin and tried to calm her quavering voice. "Now that you'll be prince regent, you can do something to help the poor."

Father turned to look at Case, his expression changing to one of disappointment. He hung his head and shook it slowly. "The poorer classes have thousands of advocates speaking on their behalf, Seraphin. Much of the business of the lower courts is mired down in their complaints. Their savage conduct to one another. Their murders and robberies. No, if I am chosen as prince regent, my efforts will be poured into achieving what comes next. Being prince regent is just a precursor to becoming emperor. It takes great mental strength, a determined purpose to lead. I cannot be distracted by the pangs and pains of those thrashing about in the mire. They have made their world what it is down there. We have made ours. We rule them because it is our right, and they cannot make a city move. It's time you remembered whose blood flows in your veins."

"I do," Sera answered, steeling herself. "But if I were ever to become empress, I would help them."

He snorted. "You think it's that easy? For every urchin a man like Fitzroy saves, there are a thousand who die coughing or frozen. You cannot possibly imagine what it is like down there. If you walked the filthy gutters, dressed as you are now in your fine frock and custom shoes, if you walked there *alone* . . . you'd be torn apart like a piece of meat thrown to the dogs." He jutted his chin out at her, purposefully harsh. "They'd sell your hair. They'd sell scraps from your clothes. They'd even sell *you*. Cease this endless fascination with the lower world, Seraphin. You were born to rule the clouds. Let the Ministries run the commons as they have for ages. If you are to ever take your place here, it's time you started to *earn* it."

Sera didn't see it that way. The same government ruled both worlds. And that was where the problem lay.

~

Sera did her best that afternoon. During the lesson on Law, she thought her mind would explode from the boredom. There was nothing in the lecture that helped her understand how it applied to her or to the people below. Nothing that related to the things she did know and understand. Try as she might to focus, she began to fancy again. She even imagined what would happen if her mind did indeed explode—and repressed giggles at the thought of the shocked look that would pass over Baggles's face as her headless trunk slumped to the floor.

Doctor Choate's lesson was not an improvement. She gave it her best effort, for Hugilde's sake, even when her head began to throb and it became more and more difficult to conceal her yawns. There was nothing practical done, no demonstration of the Mysteries. Everything she was told flitted around in her head, like so many butterflies, only to go out her ears again. She fancied this, too, and it made her break into a giggle, much to the annoyance of the doctor.

"Do you find blood leeches so amusing?" he asked her with a wounded air.

She apologized and tried to be respectful. But the humor of leeches and butterflies was too much, and it started a terrible giggling fit that soon spread to Hugilde, who lost her composure as well, much to the doctor's severe annoyance.

By the end of the afternoon, Sera's stomach was absolutely gnawing itself to pieces, she felt faint from lack of food and the shortage of exercise due to her punishment, her head ached, and there was still one more lesson to endure. While she had always pretended to Hugilde that the Mysteries of War were the most interesting to her, in reality she felt more drawn to the Mysteries of Thought, something she wouldn't dare admit because it was the one expected from most young ladies. It was also her mother's specialty, and her father openly scorned it.

"Sera, they're here!" Hugilde whispered in a scolding tone, breaking her from the brief reverie. It was time for her lesson on the Mysteries of War. Rubbing her bleary eyes, she lifted her head and saw the middle-aged Commander Falking in his dark uniform jacket lined with enormous buttons on the front and the cuff, a sword belted at his waist. But her eyes immediately went to the person in his wake, a young man of fourteen or fifteen with dark hair that looked windblown from a sky ship. He was the most handsome young man she had ever seen. Her neighbors' children, whom she'd spied from climbing trees, were all uncommonly ugly, and she'd only been to a few gatherings with other young people. This young man put them all to shame. His eyes were fixed on her, his expression firm and serious, bound by duty. But there was something else in his eyes. It looked like *interest*.

"Pardon, ma'am," Commander Falking said to Hugilde in a voice that was nearly hoarse from yelling against the wind. "But I've had to bring this young man, William Russell, with me because of a previous obligation. Will's a lad I've been tutoring. Already a midshipman, as you can see by his uniform. I hold the deed to him, and he's spent the last two years under my command. We're a bit sunburned, Will and I, but we know our duty; you can be assured of that."

Sera could see it. His tanned face looked striking with his uniform. Her cheeks were suddenly very warm.

"He'll be joining us in the tutoring sessions until he goes off to study. Have high hopes for him. High hopes indeed. I thought it might help the young lady to study alongside someone more her own age. At least until he goes off to school in the autumn."

Definitely fourteen.

Somehow, Sera's headache had managed to vanish.

CETTIE

CHAPTER TEN

Sir Jordan Harding

Cettie stared closely at the glass tube, silently counting the little black tick marks in her mind. The well of quicksilver within it was placid, but to her it felt alive. Since coming to Fog Willows months before, Cettie had become hungry for knowledge. She had devoured the primers and children's books that Miss Farnworth and Anna encouraged her to read. The newfound skill of reading and the writings themselves had created a spark of some kind, and now a fire raged inside her.

One of her favorite places in the sprawling mansion was Fitzroy's study, with all its bizarre equipment and tools. She didn't understand the treasures of the room, but they fascinated her all the same. She loved wandering around and examining the glass vials full of quicksilver, the assortment of measuring spoons and stirring rods, the small pincers and crooked weights and measures.

Light rain dashed against the window, causing little specks of water to trickle down the panes. The bigger droplets, too heavy to stick, began to meander down the glass, gaining momentum as they picked up other drops. She couldn't predict which path they would take. Water drops were full of trickery.

The marks in the glass showed the level of the quicksilver had dropped again. Pressing her lips together, she stared into the vial and tried to understand why the glob was one tick, maybe a tick and a half, lower than the day before. She took the pencil with its wrapped paper end and carefully wrote down the number of ticks it had fallen. Pencils were another of her favorite things—rare in the Fells but extremely common at Fog Willows. They came in different shapes and sizes, and the points could be trimmed with little knives to make fine or broad impressions. Anna liked to draw with them. The one she had given Cettie was a treasure. Cettie took very good care of it.

"Cettie?"

The girl's heart began to hammer wildly. She'd been caught in Fitzroy's personal study, and by the master himself. Mrs. Pullman thought it a great impertinence that Cettie liked to visit this room and never failed to ridicule her about it on the days she came there. Somehow the old woman tracked her movements constantly, even though they were rarely in the same room for very long. At night, before sending her up to the loft, Mrs. Pullman would offer a withering critique about what Cettie had done that day. But she was unfailingly polite in front of Lady Maren and Fitzroy.

Cettie was afraid of Mrs. Pullman, but the boundless curiosity that had been unleashed in her mind could not so easily be reined in. She found herself coming back to the study again and again despite the old woman's censure. Despite her punishments. Still, the last thing she wanted was to be a nuisance to Fitzroy. She knew he enjoyed his study the best of any room in the house.

"I'm sorry," she apologized, trying to gather up her paper, but Fitzroy was already beside her, his brow wrinkled with concern, and he put his bare hand down on the paper, fixing it in place with his long, slender fingers. He was a trim man, never one to overindulge in food or drink. "Fastidious" was a word she had recently learned. She loved the power of words and how they could describe things.

"I'm not upset, child," he said in a coaxing manner. He squinted and bent his head lower, trying to read the paper. Her insides shriveled with mortification, and she grew hot and sweaty.

His lips pursed, and he bent lower. "My eyes aren't what they used to be. What have you written, Cettie?"

"I d-didn't know you were going to be back," she stammered, wanting to rush away, but that would only make her look guilty in his eyes. She hadn't done anything wrong . . . well, except for being in his study uninvited. Though she hadn't yet encountered him here, she was used to seeing him in the family rooms. Sometimes he would ask her to read aloud from her primer, and he gave her the same kind, interested, and indulgent attention he showed his own children.

He touched her shoulder with his other hand. "I'm not angry. I'm growing blind in my old age, and you've written so small. Are these numbers? Rows of numbers?"

She nodded mutely.

"You're measuring something?"

She noticed the water stains on his cloak and the drops still clinging to his graying hair. He had only just arrived.

"The quicksilver," she answered, squeezing her pencil hard, trying to keep its little stub hidden in her hand. She didn't want him to take it away from her.

"Have you . . . taken any of it from the tube?" he asked her softly.

She shook her head no emphatically. "No! But some is missing. It's lower than yesterday."

"Show me what you've tallied here," he said, dropping to one knee next to her. His eyes were brightening with interest.

She didn't want to disrupt his schedule, but his demeanor encouraged her to speak openly. If Mrs. Pullman happened by, she would be punished for this familiarity. And yet . . .

"I've seen you count the black marks on the tube." Cettie pointed with her finger. "So I started to count them, too. I count them four times a day and write the number here. Some days it doesn't change at all. Some days it does."

The corner of his mouth twitched. "Four times a day?"

She flushed with embarrassment. "I wanted to understand why it keeps changing."

"Do you measure it at the same times every day? Or just four different times?"

She shrugged. "Different times. Mrs. Pullman doesn't like it when I come here. I'm sorry for intruding in your study, Fitzroy."

He laughed to himself. "Don't apologize, Cettie. You've shown more interest in my work than any of my children ever have. I'm flattered, to be honest. So Mrs. Pullman scowls when she catches you here?"

Cettie kept her expression very calm. "Sometimes." When Cettie was silent about Mrs. Pullman's harassment, when she behaved meekly and in keeping with her station, the ghost didn't visit her loft. If she said or did anything against Mrs. Pullman, however, she would get a visitor in the dark. Somehow the old woman could control the ghost. Cettie lived in fear of displeasing her enough for her to unleash it.

He pursed his lips. "Well, you have my permission to be in here. I just ask you not to touch anything you haven't been taught how to handle. Do you know why?"

"Because it's your study. I try to put everything back just the way I found it."

"Good, good." He beamed at her. "That's very clever of you. I haven't noticed anything out of place. I say this not because I mind you rummaging around in here. I don't. But some of the things in here are rather dangerous. Do you see that vial over there? With the wax seal?"

She nodded with interest.

"That contains arsenic. It's a deadly poison, but it has other properties that are helpful in doing experiments. I'm always very careful when handling it. I wouldn't want anyone getting hurt. So, let me look over your numbers a moment." He carefully lifted the paper and held it close to his eyes, poring over the markings. "You have a steady hand, Cettie. Some of your numbers need a little work, but considering how recently you came here . . . well done!"

She flushed with pride at his compliment, suddenly gratified that he'd found her here.

"Why does the quicksilver move?" she asked him. She pointed to a set of numbers—the change had been quite dramatic about two days ago.

"This is very detailed. You drew a line between each day, yes? Very smart. And, yes, it changed rather dramatically that day, didn't it?" Pursing his lips, he shrugged. "It's a mystery."

Her shoulders slumped, and a twinge of disappointment followed. Another Mystery.

He caught her change in expression. "It's not like *that*, Cettie. It's not one of the capital *M* Mysteries." He wagged his eyebrows at her. "A mystery is something that's difficult to understand or explain. Sometimes it's impossible to explain. That is why we have these special schools—to educate people on what we do know, and all that we have yet to learn. I learned about quicksilver in school because it appears abundantly in my silver mine. But I didn't know, and I still *don't*, why the amount in this tube goes up and down. I don't think I ever would have noticed it if my wife hadn't given me this little contraption to store it in."

The butler, Kinross, appeared in the doorway. He smoothed his vest and inclined his head. Cettie liked Kinross. Sometimes when he passed her in the hall, he would secretly hand her a little wrapped treat.

"Sir Jordan is just arriving," Kinross said in his deep voice. "I think he saw you arrive home."

"He's out in weather like this?" Fitzroy said in surprise. "It must be important. Make ready to welcome him."

"Of course," Kinross said with a smile. Surely he had already given the order. He turned and left, and Fitzroy rose. He slid the paper over to Cettie with an approving nod.

"Is Sir Jordan our neighbor?" Cettie asked. She had heard Stephen and Phinia chatter about how outspoken and ridiculous he was.

"That's right; you haven't met him yet," Fitzroy said. "He was the captain of a tempest. We served together for many years. He's a dear friend."

"I should like to meet him, then," Cettie said.

Fitzroy was about to follow Kinross out of the room to greet their guest, but he paused and looked at her again. "When I got back from visiting the Fells, Anna asked me if you could stay in her room from now on." He lifted his eyebrows. "Would that be agreeable to you? I know you're staying with Mrs. Pullman, bless her heart, but I think you could do some good for Anna. The two of you seem to be forming a friendship. To be honest, I think she's always been more than a little afraid of the dark."

A cold, icy feeling slithered to life in Cettie's heart. Cettie had learned since coming to Fog Willows that she was not Mrs. Pullman's only victim. The keeper had firm control over life within the manor. To those who paid her respect and heeded her, she was generous and kind. But the servants who crossed her quickly came to regret it. If any of the servants were nice to Cettie, the next day they would shun her and give her fearful looks that told her Mrs. Pullman had interfered. Others were promptly dismissed for crimes the keeper deemed more serious. Cettie had already learned of one young scullion who had been sent back to the Fells. Stephen and Phinia were Mrs. Pullman's favorites, but Anna had always seemed afraid of her. And if Anna was also afraid of the dark, it was probably for a reason. She wouldn't see the ghost. She wouldn't know what was tormenting her . . .

Cettie adored Anna and would have infinitely preferred sharing a room with her to sleeping in the cold, drafty loft above Mrs. Pullman. But not if doing so would make her friend even more afraid. Not if it would put her in Mrs. Pullman's sights.

Fitzroy's eyes narrowed. "You've always had to share a room, haven't you?" he said in a soft voice. Then he lifted his hand reassuringly. "I'll tell Anna that I'm still thinking about it. You don't need to say another word. If you change your mind, just let me know."

She wanted to tell him. Her breath started to quicken, the words nearly tumbling out of her mouth. But if she spoke openly, the keeper would know. While she trusted Fitzroy to do the right thing, to protect them, he wasn't always home. Mrs. Pullman might wait to retaliate until the next time he left.

"Come, let's join Sir Jordan for dinner," he said, offering his hand. He'd been chafing it behind his back again.

Phinia sighed with impatience at her end of the dining table. Her voice was pitched low for Stephen, but Cettie sat close enough to hear it. "He thinks he's so funny."

"I just wish he weren't so *loud*," Stephen murmured back. "He and Father are such opposites." There was no denying that. Cettie could hear the man's booming voice before it reached the dining hall.

"I like Lady Shanron, though," said Phinia. "She's very fashionable. She's invited at Pavenham Sky once a month."

"I wish Father were invited there more often," Stephen whispered.

As the Hardings entered the room, the sniping comments between the siblings ended. Sir Jordan was broad shouldered and completely bald. Though he was the same height as Fitzroy, he dwarfed him in size. Lady Shanron was a regal dark-haired beauty, and her dress was as elegant as Phinia might have hoped—an expensive red damask gown the color of wine. Her outfit nearly matched the coiffed tresses that could be seen beneath her elegant feathered hat. In their wake came their four children, the eldest a brooding young man about Stephen's age, followed by two daughters, and then a fourth child, quite a bit younger—a son who looked so much like his father it was delightful.

It was as if a windstorm had blown into the room, and soon there were glasses chinking and bursts of laughter. Sir Jordan's manners were indeed very expressive, and he was not only quick to laugh, he could hardly offer up a sentence without doing so. Fitzroy's attitude was rather demure in comparison, but he had a pleased smile on his face, and Cettie could see that he genuinely enjoyed the boisterous company.

When they introduced Cettie to the Hardings, Lady Shanron was quick to compliment her on her pretty gown and dark hair. But she was more lavish in her praise of Phinia, and the two soon started to gossip together. Sir Jordan was pleased to meet Cettie as well and treated her not a whit differently than he did anyone else in the room.

They were well into their meal when the big man turned to her and said, "I would have offered to shake hands with you earlier." He winced as he tugged on his big leather gloves. "But my hands are aching at the moment. You'd crush my fingers, I'm afraid, little woman!" Fitzroy smiled at the comment. "Truth be told, my hands always ache when it rains. I can always tell when there will be a storm, because my knuckles will start to throb. I have the hands of a hundred-year-old man, and I am only fifty."

"Tell her why," Fitzroy said meaningfully.

Sir Jordan boomed out laughter again. "He always insists on me retelling this story, to my shame. I don't know why we continue as friends. Well, if you must know, when I was younger, I was quite a naughty child." He chuckled, his eyes twinkling. "I got into more than my share of mischief."

"You *still* get into mischief," Lady Shanron said from across the table with a flashing smile.

"This is true," Sir Jordan said. "It is a daily goal of mine to cause trouble in one form or another." He laughed heartily again. Cettie liked him very much and found her worries about the ghost and whether it had followed her were banished by his jovial manner. "I have several brothers, you see. Brothers make mischief. That is the rule. We were running about the manor, causing havoc as normal. I was trying to chase my younger brother, and he was about to slam the door. I thought it would be prudent to stop it by sticking my fingers into the gap." He winced and laughed at Cettie's shocked expression. "We all learn, little woman, that before we can be old and wise, we must at first be very young and foolish. The slamming door broke my fingers. On both hands."

Cettie gaped at him. "Did he get into trouble?"

Sir Jordan shook his head no slowly. "I have an absolute fear of doctors, my dear. I do not trust them. I hid my hands from my parents until the pain became too great. They insisted that the doctor be summoned, but I refused to see the man. I could be quite belligerent in my youth. And so my hands healed on their own. I can barely clench them, and not without great pain. But they did heal, and I didn't see a doctor. Nor will I!" He laughed loudly again.

"Sir Jordan and I were never midshipmen together," Fitzroy said. "But we did serve as lieutenants under the same captain. And when I was given my own sky ship, he began to serve under me. We have sailed through stormy skies together on many dark and frightening nights. And his hands could always tell when a storm was coming." He clapped Sir Jordan on the back. "Which is why it surprises me that you'd come to Fog Willows on such a night."

"This isn't a storm, Fitzroy," Sir Jordan said with a snort. "We've flown in much worse. No, I had to see you. I need your advice."

Fitzroy looked concerned. He glanced over at the man's eldest son, who was talking, limply, with Stephen.

Sir Jordan shook his head. "No, it's not about my eldest, although you can see the damage he's done by my lack of hair! No, it's about a speculation I'm considering. The glass business is faring badly at the moment. Profits have shriveled. I need to do something, Fitzroy, or I won't be able to afford Gimmerton Sough much longer."

Fitzroy pitched his voice lower. "Is it truly so dire?" he asked with concern.

All laughter drained from Sir Jordan's face. "It is," he said grimly. "I may lose the manor."

CHAPTER ELEVEN
DOLCOATH MINES

Mrs. Pullman entered the sitting room with Fitzroy after escorting the guests back to their sky ship so they could return to their own manor. Although it was only her first time meeting the Hardings, Cettie had found them to be pleasant and had especially enjoyed Sir Jordan's sense of humor in the face of his troubles. He had shared with her, in his light-hearted manner, about a time he had visited Fog Willows to find that Mrs. Pullman had set out a tray of cinnamon treats for the entire family to enjoy. After enjoying one of the tasty morsels, he had proceeded to eat the entire tray himself before the rest of the family arrived. And so Mrs. Pullman never let him leave Fog Willows without handing him a small parcel filled with the round treats. Cettie wondered how a woman who could be so nice and thoughtful in public could also be so cruel in secret. Fitzroy didn't see her darker side. He was completely blind to it. But, then again, Mrs. Pullman was quite efficient at her duplicity.

All too early, the light in the sitting room dimmed, signaling it was time for bed, and Cettie felt a flicker of dread once again. She had tried to be good that day, especially with the company. But she was still worried that she'd slipped in some way to earn Mrs. Pullman's displeasure.

Anna squeezed Cettie's hand. "I don't want you to go," she said softly. "I wish you would sleep in my room. I don't care what Master Sloan says about deeds; I already consider you as my own sister. Stephen and Phinia have each other, and they'll both leave for school before long. I've never had anyone, except Raj Sarin, and he's too old to be a true friend. I do wish you'd stay with me."

Cettie bit her lip, feeling the conflict war inside her. "I don't think I should. Maybe when we *are* real sisters."

"Papa!" Phinia said in an overly loud voice as she bounded up to him. "Some of the Hardings are going to have a dance tomorrow. Well, just to *practice* before their ball. Can you take us in the tempest? They said we could stay for several days. Oh please, Papa?"

Fitzroy glanced at his wife. Mrs. Pullman was sitting by her on the couch, holding her hand and stroking it. Lady Maren looked doubtful.

"I'm sorry," Fitzroy said. "But I'm going to Dolcoath on the morrow in the tempest. And then to Lockhaven. The prince regent has asked to meet with me."

"The prince regent?" Stephen asked in surprise, suddenly interested. "What for?"

"I don't know," Fitzroy said offhandedly. "Since the emperor's apoplexy, everything is chaotic there. That's why I need to inspect the mines."

"Can we take a zephyr, then?" Phinia pleaded. "Stephen could pilot it."

Cettie could see by the look on their father's face that he wasn't pleased by the idea. "I'll discuss it with your mother. The lights have dimmed. It's time for bed."

"That means no," Phinia said sulkily. "Come on, Stephen. We might have to learn how to fly like Raj Sarin."

A smirk appeared on the lad's face as he rose from the couch.

"Son," Fitzroy said, stopping him. "Would you like to go to Dolcoath with me?"

There was a look of conflict on the young man's face, which settled into a general attitude of resentment. "No, Father. I've been there often enough."

Fitzroy looked a bit disappointed, just a little wrinkle in his brow, as Stephen and Phinia left the room together, their heads bowed in conversation.

Anna rose from the couch, pulling Cettie with her. She approached Fitzroy, tugging Cettie after her. "Papa, Cettie hasn't been to Dolcoath yet. Can we go with you?"

Cettie knew the family owned a silver mine and harvested other rare metals also. She felt her stomach start to fill with butterflies of eagerness.

"Don't you want to go to Gimmerton Sough with your brother and sister?" Fitzroy asked Anna. Then he gave Cettie an appraising look. "Would you like to come?"

"I would," Cettie answered. "Very much."

Mrs. Pullman's wrinkles twisted into scowling knots. She shot Anna an angry look for having suggested the idea.

"Then you shall."

"Thank you, Papa!" Anna said, giving him an exuberant hug and kisses.

"Off to bed, both of you," Mrs. Pullman remonstrated the girls. She rose from the couch and addressed Fitzroy. "Isn't the weather too inclement for a visit to the gorge, Master?"

Fitzroy shrugged. "We're reaching the end of it, I think. The skies should be calmer on the morrow."

"If you say so," Mrs. Pullman said. "Go along, children. Mind the time."

Anna squeezed Cettie's hands in excitement, and the two started walking off. But they were still close enough to hear Lady Maren speak.

"Sir Jordan looked very troubled tonight. The two of you spoke a long while. Is it as bad as I fear?"

Fitzroy sighed. "I didn't know things had deteriorated so much. The business is floundering, and he has too many debts. He can't meet his obligations, and it seems unlikely to change soon. Many of his creditors are encouraging him to invest in a speculation."

"You warned him against it, though," Lady Maren said.

Cettie glanced back, but Mrs. Pullman was standing near the couple, and she gave her a disapproving frown. Cettie turned around and continued down the corridor, slowing her steps in the hope that she'd hear more.

"Of course," Fitzroy answered. "But I'm afraid he won't listen to my advice."

Lady Maren sighed. "I wish you didn't have to go to the City. You know I couldn't live there, Brant. Not after what happened."

"Shhhh," Fitzroy said soothingly. "Who knows what the prince regent wants? It could be any number of things. It doesn't mean he'll ask me. And what happened . . . that was a long time ago. Many people have forgotten it."

"I haven't," Lady Maren said. "I doubt I ever will."

~~~

Cettie was relieved that her sleep had been undisturbed that night. Mrs. Pullman had decided not to take revenge on her for whatever reason. But maybe it meant that Anna would be punished instead. The thought of that happening made Cettie worry.

Fitzroy had accurately predicted the weather. The dawn sky over Fog Willows was devoid of clouds the next morning, while coils of thick mist lay beneath it. Everything had a damp, pleasant smell. The scent of a fresh rainstorm was so different in the cloud manor than it had been in the Fells. Down there, rain turned the streets into mire. It brought forth the unpleasant odors of overflowing cesspits—the basement chambers where refuse was put. Living in the sky, the air smelled like wet stone and damp trees.

As Cettie shivered on the landing platform, Mrs. Pullman standing at her back, she watched the vice admiral's tempest rise over the steep shingles of the manor. It dwarfed the zephyr she had ridden to Fog Willows months before. There were three masts, one jutting from the top, and one jutting from either side. The sails were not unfurled yet, and she saw the master's servants scrabbling around on deck to make the craft ready for the voyage. She had seen tempests flying over the Fells before, but none so close that she could see the rigging and hear the shouts of command.

"Now, you do as you are told," Mrs. Pullman said from behind, her voice full of warning and a hint of disgust. "I will know if you've misbehaved at all. Why the master should condescend to bring *you* to the family mines, I'll never know. He's taken leave of his senses. But don't get underfoot, whatever you do."

"I won't, Mrs. Pullman," Cettie said deferentially.

"The master has concerns weighing on him now," she continued, tugging her shawl tighter against the cool breeze. "He may get called to serve as prime minister." Her voice throbbed with pride. "If that happens, things will change. He will be gone from Fog Willows much of the time. You and Felicianna have been too friendly with each other. That will not be good. For either of you. Don't encourage her. Or she may get a visitor to *her* room instead."

Her words began to sour Cettie's expectations about visiting Dolcoath. Rather than respond, she kept her expression stoic, her eyes on the airship.

"Didn't you hear me?" Mrs. Pullman said in a threatening voice.

"Yes, Mrs. Pullman," Cettie said weakly.

The tempest lowered down to the landing platform. Anna waved to her from the gangway, but she looked subdued, not as excited about the travel as Cettie had anticipated. The sky ship came parallel with the circular yard, and two uniformed officers stood ready with a ramp, which they fixed into place.

"Don't forget what I told you," Mrs. Pullman muttered.

Cettie, anxious to be away from her, walked up the plank and entered the massive sky ship. Anna's eyes looked wan from lack of sleep, and she touched her stomach as if it ached.

"Are you all right?" Cettie asked her.

Anna shrugged and took her hand. "I am now."

Soon they were airborne, and Cettie's stomach thrilled at the sensation. Fitzroy wore his usual jacket, vest, and knee-high leather boots. His hands were clasped behind his back, and a small private smile brightened his face as he stood near the helm, the wind ruffling his graying hair. Once, long ago, he had been a sky-ship captain in the Ministry of War. The longer Cettie looked at him, the more she wondered why he had left that life behind.

At the bottom of the sky ship, there were thick sections of glass wedged into metal girders. Anna had explained that it was another way to exit the sky ship from beneath, and the crew needed to be able to see what was under the vessel before it landed. The two girls lay on the glass on their stomachs, watching the treetops below as they crossed the land. It had terrified Cettie at first because it felt as if they would plummet down to the earth, but the glass was thick and sturdy.

The bowels of the sky ship were intriguing. There were no machines or cranks or wheels, no obvious mechanics. The sky ship was very quiet as it glided across the countryside, passing over vibrant farms and narrow ridges. Cettie had passed over it in the darkness and now realized how wide the world was outside the Fells. She'd once imagined the entire world nothing but a continuous series of dirty, ill-kept, narrow streets that went at odd angles to one another. The only escape, she'd thought, was up in the sky. But the city where she'd spent her whole life was only a tiny part of a much bigger whole. Why did so many people stay in the dirty, stinking cities when *this* lay beyond?

Anna rested her chin on her forearms and pointed out different sights as they cut their way through the air.

"Is this the ship your father was captain of?" Cettie asked dreamily, gazing down at the view.

"Oh no," Anna said. "The Ministry of War doesn't let the captains keep their own ships. This is a merchant-class tempest. Father uses it to transport the silver after enough has been harvested."

"Has he ever been attacked?" Cettie asked. "A ship full of silver would be worth something."

"Yes," Anna said. "The crew all used to work for Father in the ministry. And Raj Sarin is a Bhikhu. Not many captains have someone like him in their employ. I'm so glad we could go with Papa. You'll love Dolcoath."

"What's it like?" Cettie asked, intrigued. She scratched an itch on her cheek.

"Well, it's very dirty," Anna explained. "Most mines are. But where we are going is the birthplace of Fog Willows. When the mine was discovered, you see, they built the manor house on the rocks and peaks of the mountain atop it. There were tunnels crisscrossing beneath it. Eventually, when it was done, it was lifted up."

Cettie turned her head to look at her friend.

"Lifted up," Anna went on, seeing the confused look in Cettie's eyes. "You know, through the Mysteries. Papa said there are a lot of underground springs in Dolcoath. Much of the silver that's been found there was underwater. So the waterfalls of Fog Willows are what pull the water from the mines. That's why the waterfalls we've walked past at home are always running. They're fed by the springs within the mines."

That didn't help at all. "But how does the water in the mines get all the way up to the manor?"

Anna shrugged. "It's one of the Mysteries. There are so many, Cettie. Which Mystery would you like to study when we go to school?"

"Do you think I will be able to go?" Cettie asked in a hopeful voice.

"Of course! Papa doesn't break his promises. I think you should choose the Mysteries of Wind. He says you like his study best out of all the rooms in the manor."

"I do like it. What is that down there? Oooh, there's the gorge! You can see it!"

Both girls lifted their heads and rested their chins on their hands while their elbows pressed against the glass. The sky ship began to descend, and a thrilling sensation went through Cettie's stomach again.

"The only way to get in or out of the gorge is by sky ship or wagon," Anna said, pointing down. "It takes a long time for wagons to come up and down that road, and it's dangerous, too. The families of the workers live in cabins along the road. It's so green, isn't it? I love Dolcoath."

The view was indeed majestic. The gorge was a series of intersecting hills and mountains that went as far as the eye could see. She could see the road cut into the mountainside, and small plumes of smoke spiraled up from where cookfires burned below. The sky ship suddenly plunged down into the neck of the gorge, and Anna and Cettie started giggling involuntarily. Jagged rocks and rugged trees rose from the nearly vertical cliff walls, and Cettie found herself thinking of Fog Willows.

"Where did the manor come from?" Cettie asked, scanning the treetops as they made their descent. She was trying to find the place where the stone had been gouged away.

"You can't see it," Anna replied. "It was over a hundred years ago. More trees have grown up since then. The land has healed, but there's still somewhere we can go to see where the manor was yanked away. There's a river that runs along the base of the gorge. The water is so clear it's like glass, and if we go there, we'll be able to see the spot.

Father will have to go down into the mines with the governor of the mines, Mr. Savage, but one of the workers will take us on the river walk. They don't mind. It's better than carrying rocks."

One of the ship's lieutenants came down to tell them it was nearly time to disembark. They'd be climbing down a rope ladder from the bottom of the ship, which Cettie was excited about. There were workers gathering at the landing pad beneath them, many with shovels and pickaxes. They were coated with gray dust and brown dirt. Shacks and dwellings, carts and wagons sprang up haphazardly around the gorge.

Cettie and Anna awaited their turn before climbing down the rope ladder. Fitzroy was already on the ground, talking to a strikingly tall young gentleman with a hawk nose and a shock of black hair riddled with stone dust, which made him look older. He had an angry look, and his eyes narrowed as the two girls approached.

"And who have we here?" he asked Fitzroy.

"That's Mrs. Pullman's son," Anna whispered nervously to Cettie. "His name is Serge Pullman, but everyone calls him Mr. Savage. He yells a lot."

Now that Cettie was closer, she could see the familial resemblance, and his brogue was similar to his mother's. He was in his early thirties and looked as if he'd been around the mines all his life. He wore a waistcoat and high leather boots, like Fitzroy, and his collar was trussed up in a silk tie around his neck, which he tugged at with a hooked finger.

"You recognize my youngest, of course."

"Ah. It has been some time since she's come to Dolcoath. And is her companion the foundling? I see that it is. Mother has told me of her." He gave Cettie a meaningful look, then turned back to Fitzroy. "The mine has run dry again, Master. I sent a man on a horse to bring you word since I wasn't expecting you so soon. We've reached another dead end. That's why so many workers are idle."

Cettie heard her friend gasp with surprise, and her own heart flailed inside her chest. This could not be good news for Fitzroy. What if his finances took a tumble like the Hardings' had? Why, then, would he adopt another child into the home?

Fitzroy was imperturbable. "I'll go down with you, Mr. Savage. Let's see how things stand. I'm glad I came." He turned toward the girls, trying to smile kindly at them, but the look didn't quite reach his eyes. "Anna, take Cettie on the river walk. I'm sure she'd like to see it. Is there someone who could go with them, Mr. Savage?"

"I'll send the doctor's lad," Mr. Savage said. "They've not been as busy lately. Creigh!" He shouted the last word, and a young man of about fifteen stepped through the crowd and approached them.

He had thick brown hair and a prominent dimple on his chin. His jacket had been shed, but he still wore a tie—an ugly brown-striped affair—and the black cuff identifying him as a doctor's assistant circled his white shirtsleeve. He was a handsome young man with a pleasant smile and kind eyes.

"Yes, Mr. Savage?" he said, striding up. His leather boots were in tatters, and one had a gaping hole. Cettie could see a dirty sock protruding from it.

"Ah, young Adam," Fitzroy said with an approving smile.

Cettie felt Anna's hand squeeze her own so tightly it hurt.

Fitzroy had been clenching his hands behind his back, his palms red and irritated, but he opened his palm to gesture toward the girls.

"Would you escort these two on the river walk this afternoon? If you can spare the time?"

"Spare the time." Mr. Savage chuffed. He gave Adam Creigh a curt nod, making it an order.

"Of course," the young man said. He brushed his hands together, and puffs of dust came from them. Like Fitzroy, he wasn't wearing gloves. "It would be my privilege."

Fitzroy turned to Mr. Savage. "There haven't been any incidents at the grotto?"

"None at all," he replied. "And, besides, it's still daylight."

CHAPTER TWELVE

ADAM CREIGH

If Anna's tightened grip on Cettie's hand hadn't been enough to suggest it, her complete lapse into silence the moment they started the river walk confirmed Cettie's suspicions. Anna harbored feelings for Adam Creigh, and her natural shyness made it absolutely impossible for her to speak. That required Cettie to shoulder the burden.

She heard the river before she saw it, but as they walked along a dusty footpath where all hints of vegetation had been ground away by the constant passage of wheelbarrows, Adam stopped them at a warped wooden table on which sat several rocks gleaming with flecks of silver. He lifted one of them and handed it to Cettie.

"The mines of Dolcoath," he said simply, angling the rock so that it caught the midafternoon sunlight. It sparkled with tiny flecks.

Cettie took it and examined it keenly. She'd never held raw silver before, or at least not the stone from which it came. "The pieces are so tiny," she observed.

Adam nodded in agreement. "It takes a great deal of work to mine it. It's backbreaking work, and most of the laborers here in Dolcoath have been at it for generations."

"Have you tried?" Cettie asked, handing him back the sample.

He nodded vigorously. "I wanted to experience it. Pushing the carts and steering the barrows all day has made me more grateful I'm training to be a doctor. Some of the old men in the camp are so withered and broken they can never work again. But Fitzroy won't dismiss any of them. He's a good man."

"He is indeed," Cettie agreed.

"This way, please," he directed. The pathway ahead plunged into a lush green landscape with towering trees and plants of all sorts growing out of the rocky walls of the gorge. The river was placid as Cettie gazed up at the overhanging trees. She could barely see the tempest hovering above where they had landed. They continued on the path, which cut through the gorge, and Adam kept an easy pace for them. Anna bit her lip and kept glancing at him, her cheeks flushed a pretty pink.

It would have been impossible, even for a zephyr, to descend into this part of the gorge. The stone banks on either side were irregular, and many areas were so thick with leaves and vegetation that the sun was impossible to see.

"That's my favorite tree," Adam said, pointing to a thin-barked tree that Cettie couldn't name. It had thick boughs that stretched out over the river, perfect for climbing. "See how that branch comes back and joins the trunk again? It looks like an elbow, doesn't it?"

Cettie held up her hand to shield her eyes and saw what he meant.

"What's it like, training to be a doctor?" Cettie asked farther down the trail.

"Mines are dangerous places to work. We see a lot of injuries."

"It must be very dark in the mines."

He turned back and shook his head. "There are strings of lamps down there, but it's peculiar the way everything echoes."

The first river crossing was a small bridge made of two slim tree trunks connected by nailed-down boards. There were no rails to hold on to, but Adam did not even pause before starting across it. The makeshift bridge bounced with his every step.

"It's fun," Anna said, seeing Cettie's worried expression. "You won't fall in."

Even if she *did* fall in, it would only get her wet. The bridge wasn't high above the water, and the clear flow passed just underneath it. Cettie stifled her doubts and proceeded across the planks. The bridge did sway a little, but she crossed it easily enough, and Anna followed.

Adam waited at the other end to help each of them down the final step.

"The trail gets narrow up ahead," he warned. "Just stay near the rocks, and you'll do well. How old were you when you first did the river walk?" he asked Anna.

She lowered her eyes, her cheeks flaming. "Six . . . I think."

"Why did Fitzroy ask about the grotto?" Cettie inquired.

He shrugged. "Some think it's haunted. No one is allowed to go there at night."

"Do you think it is?" Cettie asked, feeling a twinge of worry.

He shook his head. "The people here are superstitious," he said, hands on hips, gazing up at the dense foliage around them. "It's hard to imagine that Fog Willows was born from these rocks." He slapped the nearest boulder with his hand, as if he were stroking a horse. "Come along, then," he said cheerily, and continued on the way.

They crossed two more bridges, and each time, Cettie gazed down at the water beneath her. There were no fish that she could see, no muck or murk. There was no stagnation, only a fresh, endless supply of crystalline water. The walls of the gorge were rugged and uneven, and it looked as if huge segments had been twisted and broken loose, creating the jagged edges. It was difficult to comprehend that her new home had been lifted from this very place. Never had she realized there could be so many shades of gray, but they only made the stone more beautiful. In several places, tree roots had expanded in cracks and seams. Life clutched at the rock, gripping it with tenacity.

Farther on, they encountered a massive series of boulders blocking the way forward, but Cettie spied a makeshift ladder leaning up against the barrier, and a path had been constructed out of wooden planks ahead. Iron poles had been wedged into the rock walls at short intervals to hold the path up. To her eyes, it looked very precarious.

Adam, without a moment's hesitation, mounted the ladder and climbed to the rickety path. Her heart quailed a bit, but she was determined to be brave. If the path was sturdy enough to hold the robust young man, surely it would support her, too. He stood at the top and waved them on encouragingly.

"You first," Cettie said to Anna, but the girl shook her head covertly.

"I couldn't talk to him. You're doing a better job of it. You go first."

Cettie sighed and gripped the ladder. It shook a bit, and she closed her eyes. Adam knelt by the top of the ladder and gripped it in both hands.

"You can do it," he coaxed.

Cettie planted one foot and then the other, climbing to the top slowly and meticulously. It felt like the ladder might suddenly pitch over at any moment, sending her plummeting into the river. She gazed up into Adam's eyes. Was he the kind of young man who would tease her for such a fancy? Maybe even shake the ladder? But his eyes were full of encouragement, and he continued to grip the ladder tightly to minimize the shaking. When she arrived at the top, he once again held out his hand and helped her climb onto somewhat firmer ground.

She thanked him profusely, grateful that challenge was done.

"Just stay close to the wall," he said. Then he gripped the ladder again. "Come on, Felicianna Fitzroy. You've done this plenty of times."

But he waited until both girls were up on the ledge before continuing down the planks. Again, there were no handrails to hold on to, and Cettie kept as close to the wall as she could, but the footing was uneven, and it required her constant focus. The river was farther down now—probably the distance of a second story of a street-level shop. The waters were deep and tranquil.

"Some of the miners like to come here and jump in the water," Adam said over his shoulder. "It's very deep at this part."

That was something Cettie of the Fells would never have considered. She had a slight fear of heights and didn't like steep staircases or coming too near the edge of a drop. It felt different to look over the edge of a perfectly safe sky ship than to crest a path on which a stumble could be fatal. Besides, it was completely against the rules of decorum. Young ladies did not jump into rivers. Most of the rules of society were not passed down, she had discovered—they were taught in nuances, looks, glances, and subtle smirks. Cettie often felt she were a blind girl, trying to cross a room and continuing to stumble into furniture she couldn't see. But despite—or perhaps because of—the titters from Phinia and Stephen and the glares from Mrs. Pullman, she was determined to learn the proper order of things, and to walk without fear of colliding into some tradition no one bothered to teach her.

The planks hugged against the rock wall and bent around a sharp angle. On the other side, the path led down over some smaller rocks before joining the level of the river again. In the distance, she could hear the gentle rushing of a waterfall. When they reached the rocks, Adam bounded up to the first one and waited, extending his hand again to help them clamber up and over the impediments. His bare hand.

One of the questions of etiquette that had puzzled her for months was why Fitzroy did not wear the gloves favored by the upper classes. Adam did not wear them either. Could she broach the subject with him without embarrassing herself—or him? She didn't feel brave enough to ask her benefactor.

After he assisted them back onto the trail, Cettie steeled her courage and asked her question.

"I've noticed something," she said, almost blurting out the words.

Adam turned back and looked at her quizzically, inviting her to speak.

"Since I came to Fog Willows, everyone I've met wears fancy gloves. There are dinner gloves, dancing gloves, writing gloves. Even the sky-ship officers wear thick gloves to protect from the cold. Yet Master Fitzroy doesn't wear them. At least, I've never seen him wear them. I could not help but notice that you don't wear gloves either . . ."

Adam stooped down and picked up a rounded stone from the riverbank. He examined it for a moment in his bare hand, then rose and threw it into the river, angling it so that the rock skipped a few times before plunking in. Anna's eyes were fixed on his face, and Cettie could tell she was just as eager for his answer.

Silence settled on them, making things uncomfortable. Cettie felt like she had blundered again.

When Adam finally turned to look at her, his expression was difficult to interpret. He didn't seem upset, necessarily, more melancholy. His answer was delivered in a low, measured voice. "Let me try to explain it. When I was ten, I used to live in a manor like Fog Willows. My father risked everything in a speculation. He trusted his men of business, whom he thought were his friends. I think he asked Fitzroy for advice, though maybe he was too embarrassed to.

"I still remember when the creditors came and took everything away. Every sofa. Every writing desk. Everything." His face was very grim. "It still wasn't enough to settle the size of the debt. The *mountain* of debt." His eyes flashed. "So my father sold a deed for me to Fitzroy. I didn't know it at the time, but my father had been sick all along. His speculation was a last gamble to try and right his financial situation. I was only ten, not old enough to have learned the Mysteries. But I'm grateful that my father chose Fitzroy. He holds my deed until I am eighteen, and then I must make my own way in the world. What I study, when I go away to school soon, will be my only means of supporting myself." He brushed his hands together and glanced at her. "I owe Fitzroy everything. But the more I have gotten to know him and understand him, the more I wish to *emulate* him."

Cettie's eyebrows shot up. It was a word she'd never heard before.

He saw her look and explained, "Has he told you the story of the man and his son who needed to sell their mule?"

Cettie could see in Anna's delighted look that she knew the story well. "No, he hasn't."

"Then ask him to tell it to you. In that one story, you'll learn just about everything you need to know about what makes him the man he is." He looked down the trail. "Shall we?"

The river walk ended at the edge of a huge cave. Living water gushed down the rock walls, filling an enormous pool that drained into the river they had journeyed along. Sunlight streamed in on the far side of the cave, indicating there were gaps in the rock to allow it in. Boulders were strewn around the opening, wet and slippery. The ground was unstable, but there were some flat portions to stand on.

"It's so beautiful," Cettie said, staring in wonder.

"This is the grotto," Adam replied, arms folded as he gazed at the pool. "The pool isn't very deep. Up to your knees, perhaps, and it goes around that bend. There are smaller caves back there. But we will not go that far."

"Do people go in there? I thought you said it was haunted."

"I don't let others' fear stop me when I know something is safe. Just like with the sky manors, there are boundaries. I always stay within them."

"Does the grotto connect to the silver mine? Is it part of Dolcoath?" she asked him.

He shook his head. "No, these are the headwaters of the river. There's an underground spring here, and the water comes out through the rocks *above* us. Remember the leaf we passed along the trail that we all took a drink from? All the water here comes from the same source."

"I see," Cettie said. She glanced at Anna, who was looking surreptitiously at Adam.

He showed no awareness that he was being observed, and continued to gaze at the grotto. "I never grow tired of the view. I'm not the only one who ventures here. Sometimes the village daughters come here during the heat of the summer," he said, hands on his hips. "Their mothers act as chaperones. The young men aren't allowed to come at the same time, of course. Propriety."

Cettie crouched by the edge of the pool and dipped her fingers into the cold water. It was completely transparent, just like the large glass windows at the bottom of the tempest. Broken chunks of stone loomed above her head, reminding her of the floating manor she lived in. There was no doubt a matching edge at the bottom of Fog Willows. She sensed an affinity between the two places, a shared soul. She wished she could have been alive back when the manor had first been made. In her mind, she could almost hear hammers and the grunt of workmen, the creak of ropes and squeal of pulley wheels. The coldness of the water made her fingers numb, but she enjoyed the small discomfort as her imagination wandered free.

She felt a sudden throb of fear in her heart. It was as if something had awoken inside her mind, some preternatural awareness of danger. The cold, numbing sensation told her there was something in the caves behind the veil of the falls. Something alive. Something blocked off from the common world. She knew it as surely as she could sense the presence of a ghost. A mind prodded at hers, urging her to come into the pool. To wander deep into the grotto—behind the bend where she wouldn't be seen.

This was no ghost.

Fear knifed through her heart. She started to tremble, and not from the chill of the water. The compulsion to step into the water was powerful. Darkness wreathed her vision, causing ripples of panic. It was like the entity was fixing her wrists and ankles with strings, eager to use her like the street puppets she'd occasionally seen in the Fells.

"I think we should go," Adam said, his voice suddenly firm and serious.

His words loosened the strange presence's grip on her mind.

She looked up at him, saw him staring into the grotto, his eyebrows knitting in worry.

The thing's grip tightened again in an instant. Loose strands became strong cords. Cettie couldn't move. Her muscles were locked, seized into place. She wanted to rise out of her crouch, but the thing's pull on her was fierce.

Adam turned and looked at her, saw the fear in her eyes. His lips pressed into a tight line. She knew without asking that he felt it, too. "We're going. Now."

"If you think we should," Anna said quietly. She sounded a little baffled by his sudden haste.

"Come on, Cettie. Get up." He offered his hand to help her rise. She wanted to reach for it, but her muscles were still gripped by that terrible power. She couldn't speak. Couldn't do anything. It felt like someone was choking her.

The compulsion to wade into the pool crashed over her in waves.

Adam's hand gripped her arm firmly. "Easy now, up we go." He pulled, and she felt the bands once again begin to loosen . . . but they did not break. Her eyes pleaded with him to take her away. She still couldn't speak.

"Anna, you may need to run ahead for help," he directed. "I'll bring Cettie. Come along, it's going to be dusk all too soon."

An angry sensation flooded her mind. It made her want to jerk her arm free, to strike Adam across the face, to grab a rock and bash his head with it. She had never had such violent inclinations in her life, and she was ashamed of her surging feelings despite knowing they didn't come from her.

Think the word, and you will undo the barrier. Don't be frightened.

She didn't know the word, but it felt as if she had only forgotten it. If she could concentrate, she would remember it. Then she could say it. Then whatever was caged within the grotto would be freed. Part of her mind rebelled against the idea, and she tried to squeeze the strange feelings out. If only she could get away . . .

One step over a rock. Then another. As Adam led her away from the pool, a frantic, thwarted sense of fury continued to pump into her mind from behind. She glanced back, convinced that she saw a hulking shape within the shade of the grotto. It made her mind go black with panic.

Open the barrier. Open it.

She came to herself a few moments later, the grip of the grotto broken. She could hear the birds again. Had they been silent, or had all her senses been focused elsewhere? She noticed that Adam's arm was around her back, his hand pressing against her side. His other hand clutched hers, as if he'd been dragging her away from that dark place. She felt the urge to look back.

"No, don't look," he said warningly, coaxingly. "We'll be all right if we stay on the path."

Anna clambered over the rocks ahead, walking with firm purpose and agitation. Taking a deep breath, Cettie let the fresh scent of the trees soothe her. Her heart was finally ceasing its reckless charge.

"Are you feeling better?" he asked her softly, discreetly.

"Much so, thank you," she whispered. She could speak again!

The rushing noise from the grotto was fading now. The trail led up to the wood planks held up by the iron poles. The water was placid and smooth, flowing effortlessly away.

She looked up into Adam's worried face. "What . . . what was that?" she asked in a mouselike voice.

He shook his head. "I don't know. I've never felt like that before today."

In her heart, Cettie felt the dreadful conviction that it had come because of her. Because of some darkness inside her.

That certainty horrified her.

CHAPTER THIRTEEN
THE POOR MAN'S MULE

When they returned from the river walk, they learned that Fitzroy had gone down into the mine and would not return until later. They stayed at Mr. Savage's home, which was the largest dwelling at the bottom of the ravine, fenced in with a small stone wall mounted with iron spikes. The servants were more humble than the ones who worked at Fog Willows, but they fed and entertained the young women as best they could.

Cettie sat by the window seat in the library, feeling the cool breeze from the gorge waft in. The noise of the day's work had come to an end. She imagined it was nearly the hour that the lights began to dim at Fog Willows, and yet word had not arrived from her guardian. The lack of news unsettled her, even more so after the strange ending to their afternoon excursion. She had chosen a book of fables from Mr. Savage's sparse library, but she found herself distracted by every noise she heard from outside—the occasional bark of laughter from passersby, the crunch of gravel, the sound of crickets.

And then, in the distance, she heard a roar that sent a prickle of fear all the way down to her toes. Had she done something to unintentionally release the creature trapped in the grotto? Had she, unwittingly, thought the word that would release it? Her uneasiness enlarged to worry. Something was wrong, and she feared it was all her fault.

"What was that?" Anna asked, setting down her book.

It felt as if a ghost's hand had reached in and clutched Cettie's heart. She began to shiver, but it was not because of the chill breeze.

Anna joined her at the window seat, and together they gazed out at the night. The only view was the stone wall and a little scrub of a garden. Reaching out, Cettie slid the window closed and bolted the latch. Although a pane of glass offered scant protection, it made her feel a little safer.

Anna reached out and put her hand on Cettie's shoulder, giving her a comforting look. "We're safe here, Cettie. You needn't worry."

Safety. It was a feeling that Cettie had never truly experienced. Safety was for the privileged. Safety was a secret garden that no one else could access. She doubted she would ever truly feel safe. Wrapping her arms around her knees, she rested her cheek on them and stared at the reflections of herself and Anna in the glass. She squelched a pang of jealousy at the sight of Anna's beautiful golden hair and reassuring smile.

Finally, after what felt like an eternity of silence, voices from the corridor announced the arrival of Mr. Savage and Fitzroy. Mr. Savage spoke loud enough to shake the halls. "I imagine the whole valley heard the roar. Send Mr. Tanner, Mr. Cooper, and Mr. Flint with an arquebus each to patrol the street. I want men on watch all night long!"

The door of the sitting room opened, and Cettie drew her legs down as the men entered. Adam Creigh accompanied them, speaking in a low voice to Fitzroy. The serious look on the young man's face only made her worry more. Fitzroy thanked him and whispered something in reply, and Adam strode away.

Mr. Savage put one hand in his vest pocket and stood, angling his head and staring at the young women in the corner. His gaze seemed accusatory when it settled on Cettie, but he quickly shifted his attention to Fitzroy. "Are you sure you won't spend the night? It would settle the people who live here, surely, knowing you are among them."

Fitzroy sighed and shook his head. "I will stay as long as I can, but I have an appointment with the prince regent on the morrow. We should have left hours ago, but I wanted to inspect the mines myself."

"The prince regent?" Mr. Savage said, inclining his head. "Well, the young ladies will rest better, I think, up in the air." His expression became stern as his gaze met Cettie's. There was a sour look, one of disapproval.

"Might I trouble you for some tea?" Fitzroy asked Mr. Savage. He nodded and departed to make the arrangement, leaving the two girls alone with their guardian. Anna hugged her father affectionately, but her eyes were worried. She was not immune to the strange mood that had settled upon the night. He bent down and kissed her hair, and Cettie saw little bits of stone rubble in his graying mane. She felt a sudden pang of jealousy, wishing she felt closer to Fitzroy so that she could hug him as Anna did . . . or that he would at least give her a little pat on the head. Loneliness threatened to choke her with tears.

Fitzroy kissed Anna again and then came to Cettie and gazed down at the book she had discarded. She held it up so he could read the spine.

"Ah, I had such a book myself when I was younger," he said. Then, pitching his voice lower, he said, "Adam told me about the adventure of the river walk today. Can you tell me what happened?" He sat down at the edge of the window seat next to her, looking concerned.

She did her best to explain it, to describe her feelings and how she'd felt paralyzed by fear. Even now, it felt like some terrible creature was hunting her. As she told him the story, the feeling of shame returned—the worry that she'd drawn the being—making her miserable. Tears threatened to spill out of her eyes, and she wiped them preemptively, trying to stop them.

"It's not your fault," Fitzroy said, shaking his head. "There is no way you could have known how to release it."

Cettie and Anna both looked at him in confusion.

He sighed. "The rumors are wrong. The being held within the grotto is not a ghost. It's something far more dangerous."

"What is it, Papa?" Anna asked softly, her tone betraying her fear. "I thought the river walk was safe."

He looked at his daughter and then at Cettie. "It *is* safe. The creature's name isn't important, but it feeds on fear. The protections of the grotto have always kept it safely contained in the past. They should be infallible. The creature's influence is usually never felt during the day. No one goes on the river walk at night, however. That is forbidden, and for good reason. But the safeguards in the grotto are not the only ones. We will not be harmed if we stay within the boundaries of protection set for us, and Mr. Savage is sending men with arquebuses to patrol the borders of the mining village."

He paused, then added, "I suspect that the reason it revealed itself to Cettie is because it sensed that she still carries a great deal of fear. If a creature like that ever got loose in the Fells . . . I shudder to think on it. No, if this is anyone's fault, it is mine for not considering how special Cettie is . . . how delicate she is to impressions. Adam knew just what to do, and he got you both safely back." He smiled with fondness. "He's a good young man. I see a lot of promise in him. Just as I do in *you*." He gave Cettie a warm smile.

Anna hugged her father again and kissed his cheek.

Another distant howl sounded in the darkness outside, sending gooseflesh down Cettie's arms. The way he spoke of the creature told her it was another one of the Mysteries, which somehow made it more frightening. How many unknown evils lurked in the world, waiting for her to discover them? Could Fitzroy be right? Had the creature only reacted to her fear, or was it something else, something more that had drawn it to her?

Fitzroy's mouth turned into a low frown, and he patted Anna's hand and asked if she'd go fetch his tea. She did, leaving them alone together. Cettie felt like she should tell him about the ghost at Fog Willows. The one controlled by Mrs. Pullman. It was only right, even if it ended with the keeper sending her away when he was gone. He needed to know the truth about the ghost . . . and about the woman he trusted with his household. If any harm happened to him or his children, she would never forgive herself.

"Adam will be coming with us to the City," Fitzroy said, folding his arms. "I'll be taking him and Stephen to school soon. It's time for Adam to learn the Mysteries. I'm glad he was there to look after you."

"So am I," Cettie answered. She swallowed, growing more nervous. Her stomach began to clench and twist with dread. She didn't want to lose her place at Fog Willows.

"Is something troubling you?" he asked.

She nodded, looking down. Words jumbled around in her mind. How could she express her feelings? "I don't belong . . ." she started, but those were the only words she managed to get out before anguish overwhelmed her and she began to cry. Hot tears burned her cheeks. Her throat seized up, and no more words could come. She tried to blurt everything out to him, but she couldn't give voice to her feelings at the moment. They were all tangled and ugly, and she wished she could shrink to the size of a dust mote.

His gentle hand touched her shoulder. There was a look of pure compassion in his eyes. His lips trembled, but he did manage to speak, even though she could not.

"It will take time, Cettie," he said, "for you to feel truly comfortable where you are. Change is never easy. Were it not for happenstance, I could have been born in the Fells and not Fog Willows. Adam Creigh deserves more than what he has, but he doesn't let the vagaries of fate stop him from taking action. And neither should you. You are a bright, intelligent young woman. You are a true friend to my daughter, unrelentingly compassionate, and fiercely loyal. And you have a determination I find very rare in someone so young. My own children lack it, because of their ease in life." He sighed and shook his head. "No one truly belongs anywhere, Cettie. We each are given a life to live. And we live it as best we can."

She bit her lip. "When you first found me," she said huskily, trying to dry her eyes with a sleeve, "I said my father was the captain of a hurricane. That's a lie. I'd told it so many times I'd come to believe it."

His lips pursed, as if he was trying not to smile. "It's all right, Cettie. I am grateful you trusted me enough to tell me the truth."

"Even if you already knew it?" she asked.

He turned his head slightly. "Trust is as fragile as an egg. But I have gentle hands. I won't break yours."

The comfort and relief that washed over her made her feel infinitely better. She was about to tell him about Mrs. Pullman when the roaring sound burst out again, this time even closer. He took his hand away and started to rub it. She noticed scrape marks and even dried blood on one of his fingers. His hands had taken a battering that day.

Noticing her worried expression, he set his hands on his lap. "It's getting closer," he said simply.

"What can we do?" she asked.

He looked perplexed. "I don't think it can get past the defenses." Fitzroy clapped his hands on his knees. "One day at a time. One worry at a time. As my grandfather used to say—it is folly to cross a bridge before you come to it, or to bid a ghost good evening before you meet him." He smiled, and Cettie could tell he relished the quote. He found the discarded book and picked it up, turning it over in his hands. "It's still a ways off. And Adam said I've neglected your education. That I haven't told you the parable of the man, the boy, and the mule."

Cettie nodded eagerly.

He stared down at the book, thumbing through its pages. "I heard this one when I first went away to study the Mysteries. It was shared with all of us, but I don't think all of us heard it the same way. That's the thing about stories. They can touch on truths that some people just are not ready to hear. The tale goes like this. Long before the first flying castles and sky ships and cauldrons of molten steel—before the Fells—life was simpler. A man and his son needed to sell their mule to buy food to last the winter. So they started walking to get to the market, which was very far. They met a fellow traveler along the way who criticized them for not riding the mule. So the man, realizing that his beast of burden wasn't being used for its purpose, put his son on it to ride. But when they arrived at the first village on their path, some men in the square scoffed and said how inconsiderate the son was for making his father walk. They stopped and watered the beast, and so the father ordered the boy to walk while he rode. Again, they reached the next village, and what did they hear? Some washerwomen complained that the father must be evil to force his son to walk while he rode. Ashamed by their words, the father decided to change yet again. Do you know what he did?"

Cettie shook her head no, eager for him to continue.

Fitzroy wagged his finger at her. "So they *both* rode the mule into the next town. By this time, the mule was getting very tired, and when they reached the next village, they were ridiculed for being lazy and working the poor beast half to death! The market was in the very next town, and they feared they'd not be able to sell the poor creature, now it was so spent. And so the father and son cut down a sapling, lashed the mule to the pole, and carried *it* to the next town. You can imagine what the townsfolk thought as they saw the father and son laboring and exhausted as they approached the town. Who were these country bumpkins who carried a mule on their own shoulders? As they crossed the bridge into town, suffering the jeers and taunts of passersby, one of the ropes broke loose, and the mule kicked free. The boy dropped his end of the pole, and the beast fell into the river and drowned."

"No!" Cettie said, mouth wide open.

Fitzroy nodded sagely. "A man with a crooked staff had been following them into town. As he passed the grief-stricken man and his son, he said, 'Please all, and you will please none.'"

He leaned back against the edge of the window seat, folding his arms. "The longer I have lived, Cettie, the more those words have rung like a bell in my heart." He paused, staring at her with farseeing eyes. "What do you learn from the story?"

She was still reeling from the horrifying ending. "Don't listen to other people. That poor mule!"

Fitzroy smiled at her. "The mule died rather quickly, I should think. The man and his boy had nothing to sell. They may well have starved to death that winter. You see, they lacked a plan from the start that went beyond the need to sell the mule. One of the things I have noticed in life is how others use the bludgeon of ridicule and shame to beat us off our intended track. It wasn't that the villagers gave poor advice. They just lacked the ability to see the travelers' circumstances for how they really were. The first group of villagers didn't know how far their journey would be. The second didn't know the sacrifice already made. By changing to suit the crowd, they heaped trouble on themselves. And because they listened, they failed to provide for their own needs."

Cettie was beginning to understand. It felt like Fitzroy had opened a window of sorts and let in a breeze of ideas.

"Is that why you do not wear gloves?" she asked him, remembering Adam Creigh's comment from earlier that day.

Fitzroy's eyes twinkled. "I'm not old by any stretch, only fifty, but I have seen fashions come and go. When I was younger, some matriarch in the City complained that the bodices of young women were too low. It was a scandal." He fanned himself theatrically. "And now almost everything is covered. There are no soft bodices; they are all made of bone to shield the eyes. Scarves and hats disguise ladies' necks and hair, which they once wore in elaborate styles. And everyone wears gloves to protect against the temptation of physical touch." He shook his head, frowning. "I'm probably getting too old, because I see evil in either extreme." He chuckled to himself. "You fall off a bridge by going off either edge. Try to steer in the middle."

She looked him in the eye, feeling so *full*. Not with food—it wasn't *that* sensation—but with peace and gratitude and respect. Even a feeling of safety, despite knowing that there was a beast loose in the forest—one that she still worried she might have unintentionally set off. Unintentionally freed. She reached out and laid her hand on his.

"I will never lie to you again, Fitzroy," she promised. She meant it. And as she spoke the words, she *felt* it, like a jolt going through her heart.

His other hand capped hers. "I believe you, Cettie."

And she knew he would hold her to that promise.

It was after midnight when the creature approached the village. Tension hung in the air like the strange fog that had settled over the hamlet during the night. Fitzroy had insisted that Cettie and Anna wait in the sky ship, ready to float upward at a moment's notice, but he was down with Mr. Savage's guards, holding an arquebus himself. The village gate was barred shut, and the men stood on the rampart above it, ready for a possible bombardment. Adam stood beside Fitzroy, gripping a lantern to provide light to the men.

"Let them be safe," Anna prayed, shivering. The temperature had fallen considerably. The pilot of the tempest remained at his post, but his eyes were fixed on the scene unfolding beneath them.

Cettie could feel the thing venture closer yet. She looked over the railing, the puffs of mist coming from her breaths joining the fog to obscure the scene even more. The hair on the back of her neck tingled.

Do not fear me, little one. All these I will hurt. But not you. Open the gate.

Cettie shuddered, feeling her mind darken as she heard the creature's thought whispers.

"Do you see it? Can anyone see it?" Mr. Savage yelled.

One of the guards shot off his arquebus. Another man let out an oath.

"Steady," Fitzroy said firmly. He raised his weapon to his shoulder and aimed into the darkness.

"How did it get loose?" Mr. Savage demanded. "Is this that girl's doing? Seems mighty convenient it got out right after she left the grotto. The beast's never escaped the protections before."

Cettie's heart quailed at the accusation.

"Steady, Mr. Savage," Fitzroy said, ignoring his comment. "Mind the moment. It cannot get past."

"It got out of the grotto," he said angrily. "How could that happen?"

"I see it!" Adam shouted, pointing.

"Easy, Mr. Creigh," Fitzroy said calmly.

"It's coming," Mr. Savage warned.

Open the gate. Do not fear me.

Cettie squeezed her eyes shut. Anna started to whimper with worry. "Come back, Father. Come to the ship."

The sharp crack of the arquebus sounded, making Cettie gasp and peer into the mist. A bellow of rage sounded. Of rage and pain. It was wounded. Cettie saw its hulking shadow retreat.

"Good shot, Fitzroy!" Mr. Savage said.

Cettie saw her guardian lower the arquebus. The beast slunk away into the night. But it was only wounded. She sensed its wicked, brooding thoughts, its growing hatred for the man who had struck it.

And then it was gone.

SERA

Some think that politics should be the fifth Mystery. But of all the phenomena observable to society and students, the relationships between people are not unknowable. Just as a plum will drop to the ground after falling off a table, so our fellow creatures respond in predictable, even self-injurious ways. Women, above all, want to be perceived as desirable above other women. They will go to great lengths to ensure this. True, our society has prescribed this, but this tension has always existed. That is why there is fashion and why the milliners and dressmakers and hairdressers will never lack employment. And it is why fashion will never stand still. It must change. It always changes. Men, above all, desire power. Either for public office or simply, as in the case of my husband, to be known as the wealthiest of them all. Power is a heady thing, and men will put themselves in desperate circumstances in order to achieve it. For who can resist the whispered urge of feeling important?

—Lady Corinne of Pavenham Sky

CHAPTER FOURTEEN
FITZROY'S REPUTATION

Sera found herself secretly looking forward to Commander Falking's lessons each afternoon. She'd try to feign indifference, but she would keep watch for his sky ship from her window. It was hard to feel indifferent to a set of warm brown eyes that would surreptitiously glance at her from a warm brown face that was always pensive—to look away from warm brown hands, always scribbling so studiously with a pencil. She adored William Russell, whom she called Will in her mind. He addressed her as Miss Fitzempress.

One afternoon, however, a different airship set down at the manor at the time Commander Falking and Will normally arrived. It was a tempest class that she'd never seen before. She watched from the window as a tall man disembarked, followed by a young man and two young women. There had been more visitors now that Father was prince regent, but most of them arrived in zephyrs.

Due to the size of the tempest blocking the landing porch, she didn't notice the arrival of the zephyr bearing Commander Falking and Will, so she was caught kneeling on the seat, her eyes fixed on the sky.

"Sera!" Hugilde whispered harshly to get her attention. When Sera turned, she saw Commander Falking suppressing a cough on his fist at catching her in such an unladylike state. Will's brazen smile caught her off guard, and she felt her cheeks flush.

"Excuse me," Sera said, practically jumping off the seat. She felt a little dizzy at having been discovered in such a pose.

"It's quite all right, ma'am," Falking said in his crusty voice. "I used to gaze at sky ships when I was a lad. Stop smirking, Russell. It doesn't do you credit."

The rebuke startled the young man, and he straightened up and took his usual seat, looking discomfited. Sera quickly went to her desk and began to arrange her papers for the class, still feeling quite self-conscious. She caught Will glancing her way, offering an apologetic smile, which she eagerly returned.

"You have an august visitor today, ma'am," Falking said as he paced in front of their makeshift classroom. "It does this house honor."

Sera turned to Hugilde in confusion before shifting her attention back to Commander Falking. "The tempest, you mean? I don't know who the visitor is yet. No one has told me."

Falking frowned at the comment and shrugged. "It's all the gossip in Lockhaven, ma'am. The tempest belongs to Vice Admiral Brant Fitzroy. He used to be with the Ministry of War, but now, as you know, he's with the Ministry of Wind. Not that we wouldn't accept him back, eh, Russell?"

"Yes, sir," Will said dutifully.

"Lord Fitzroy," Sera said in wonder. She had always wanted to meet him. She knew that he had two young daughters, one her own age and one older who—distastefully—shared a derivative of Sera's name. Thankfully, she went by Phinia instead. But Sera was most intrigued by what she'd heard of Cettie of the Fells. Could one of the young women have been her? The lesson that stretched out before her suddenly felt like a form of torture.

"Yes, he's to be the new prime minister, if I'm not mistaken," Commander Falking said with a hint of smugness. "Your father could choose worse, and he's taken long enough to replace Welles. The man has a good reputation despite some previous scandal. I rather doubt the younger generation even knows about it."

"Scandal?" Sera asked curiously, her interest bubbling over. "What do you mean, Commander Falking?"

"It's not really my place . . ." he hedged. He cast a pleading look to Hugilde to assist him.

"It is your place," Sera corrected him. "You are my teacher. You are supposed to educate me in what makes a proper example. I've only heard the good about Vice Admiral Fitzroy, none of the bad. I must learn to judge a person impartially. Would this not be a good opportunity? Especially since the man is about to be declared our prime minister?" She blinked at him, showing firmness of voice and expectation.

"If it please you, ma'am," Falking said, coughing into his hand. "Do you know the story of how Fitzroy saved six sky ships from being destroyed by a ferocious storm?"

Sera shook her head no. Will leaned forward, his eyes widening with interest. This felt more real than most of their lessons, which focused on long-ago conflicts, historic wars that were as dry as dust. *This* interested her.

"Well, the event earned him the reputation of being a harbinger of sorts. That's one who can presage the future. Their squadron was on a dangerous assignment, going across the sea. It was a routine voyage, of course, but storms can be unpredictable in that quadrant. You must always keep a weather eye open, as the saying goes, eh, Russell?"

"Yes, sir."

Sera frowned. "Can't a sky ship go through a storm?"

"Minor squalls, of course," Will said. "But no captain would willingly sail a vessel into a storm."

"Quite right, young man," Falking said, clearing his throat. "Disastrous consequences. Simply disastrous. A hurricane-class sky ship is called such in the expectation that it *could* survive one. But no admiral worth his salt ration would willingly fly into one. We cannot speak of the Mystery that keeps vessels aloft. But let's just say that a sky ship is still made of wood and iron and struts that can be blasted apart by lightning. So, as the story goes, Captain Fitzroy was part of a squadron heading west. The evidence of a coming storm was not conclusive. Fitzroy signaled the commodore to warn him of danger. He didn't have any proof, mind you, but he felt something was wrong. The commodore, anxious not to lose time, ignored the warning." He frowned and shook his head. "It's a common saying, ma'am, that men are promoted to the point of their greatest incompetence. I've been offered my own command and have turned it down. It's a grave responsibility being the leader of a squadron of sky ships. Not everyone is suited for its rigors. *Ahem*, and so a squall turned into a storm. The commodore's ship was blasted to fragments, sending every man aboard plummeting into the sea."

Will's knuckles turned white at the thought, his gaze deadly serious. Sera could only imagine the horror of such a thing.

"The commodore of the squadron died in the blast. The second in command, another captain within the squadron, panicked and relieved himself of command." He chuckled softly. "Everyone turned to Fitzroy, who had predicted the storm. He ordered the sky ships to beach in the waters, even though waves can turn quickly into mountains. And they started rescuing survivors, those lucky souls who managed to survive the fall. There were six ships in all. Two were lost. It was a miracle they all weren't brought down. The men worked all night long, fighting against the storm as they tried to save as many men as possible. When it was over, the ships were waterlogged. It took days to pump out the water, but it was done, and they went aloft again. Made it to port. News had already traveled to the City that they'd been destroyed. Fitzroy was treated as a hero, and he was made commodore and, shortly after that, rear admiral. He was young, but a promising officer, a good leader of men. He's calm under pressure. Not many are."

Sera scrunched up her nose. "Nothing you have said is very scandalous, Commander Falking."

He smiled. "No, I'm not at that part yet. You see, admirals are part of high society, ma'am. Fitzroy struggled in that role. He did not ingratiate himself to the society folk. He was a bachelor still, as many in the fleet are, because the duty weighs so heavily. It's not easy being the spouse of such a person, always being left behind. But they say a young woman caught his eye. She was vivacious and beautiful, with an excellent singing voice and a disposition toward poetry. He was entranced by her, but she had given her heart to a known scoundrel. Fitzroy waited patiently for her to see the truth about the one she'd given her heart."

"This is Lady Maren?" Sera interrupted, wrinkling her brow.

Falking nodded. "Yes, ma'am. It so happened that Lady Maren was invited to a ball here in Lockhaven, even though she wasn't normally included in such circles. To have merited an invitation to this particular ball was an honor of consequence, because it was held at the home of Lady Corinne at Pavenham Sky. And, as you already well know, she dictates the code of fashion among the upper crust. Well, Lady Maren made a spectacle of herself at the ball by seeking the young man's attention. You see, he'd become engaged to another young woman—one of far more consequence than herself! She was shunned by society for her behavior." His face was stern with disapproval. "She ruined herself and her hopes. Some said she even tried to *do herself harm*." He shook his head meaningfully. "But Fitzroy looked past her disgrace. He salvaged her reputation by asking her to be his wife. No one else would have. She'd slighted him for a lesser man, yet he forgave her. They were married shortly thereafter and have three fine children.

"Even so, Lady Maren's health has been poor ever since. He resigned his commission to tend to her, but he was given the rank of vice admiral—a promotion that was underway at the time of his resignation—as a mark of honor . . . and also to provide him with an additional pension of sorts. Mines can be temperamental things." He paused, brooding a little. Then he brightened. "It's nothing in comparison to the pension he'll receive as prime minister, of course! He's a good man. It's been nearly twenty years since his wife's disgrace. I think even Lady Corinne can finally overlook the indiscretion now."

Sera thought the story was terribly romantic, and it raised Fitzroy even higher in her esteem.

"Now, if we can start the lesson," Commander Falking said. "Let us apply the principles of the impact of storms on sky ships to the impact of war on them. The Battle of Triffinger is an excellent study of both of these points."

—

Sera was outraged. Her blood was scalding, and she stamped her foot when she found Mother at her needlework in the drawing room.

"Case won't open the door to let me see her," she said accusingly to her mother.

"Really, Seraphin. You must learn to control your anger. This is not the proper way to address your mother."

She stamped her foot again. "Tell Mr. Case to open the door! I want to see her!"

Her mother rubbed the bridge of her nose and set down the needlework. "I set Mr. Case there for a reason, Daughter. In all honesty, I'm amazed Lord Fitzroy would bring someone like . . . like *that* into our home. It's disgraceful."

"It's compassionate," Sera said in a huff. "This may be my only chance to meet someone from the Fells, Mother." Not to mention another girl her own age.

"You are Seraphin *Fitzempress*," her mother said in a haughty tone, her voice struggling for patience. "You shouldn't even be thinking such thoughts, let alone desiring to act upon them. They are different from us. The blood of the noblest families runs in your veins. What you stand to gain as a princess of the realm is beyond imagination."

Sera took a step closer to her mother. "But shouldn't we try to help them? If I could help one of them, like Lord Fitzroy did, I would—"

"Stop! I beg you, child, stop! You are not going to see that . . . that *urchin*. Next you'll be asking for her to be brought over as a playmate, and then you'll want to visit the noxious place that birthed her. You are special. You are different. It is time you began to act like it." Her mother's eyes were wide with turbulent emotion. "If you only knew . . . if you only knew . . ." Her voice trailed off as tears began to gush from her eyes.

Sera was used to her mother's emotional spigots. The side room door opened, and Father stalked in, his face enraged. His clothes had grown fancier with his promotion to prince regent, and she'd noticed that he was putting on weight. His smiles had become fewer and further between.

"He has rejected it!" Father said with a biting tone. He looked offended. "The presumption of that man! I can scarce believe my own ears."

Mother turned on the couch, trying to wipe her eyes. The gesture was not lost on Sera's father, who regarded her with disgust. "Control yourself, woman."

"I am trying," Mother said angrily. "But Seraphin wanted to go *meet* that child. I've forbidden it, of course."

"For once you do something to her credit," Father snapped. His eyes seemed to shoot flames at her. "His attitude is disgraceful. Go to your room while your mother and I discuss this between ourselves."

Curiosity compelled Sera to speak. "Lord Fitzroy refused to become prime minister? Why?"

Father's lips trembled. "Because of that child of the Fells. He won't send her away. Not to a boarding school. Not to an orphanage. I don't know how much he's spending on researching her parentage, but it's robbing his legitimate heirs of future wealth. What nonsense! And he *dared* to bring her into our home without asking first. I told him to take her back to Fog Willows and never impugn the dignity of Lockhaven again. If word of this gets out, we'll be stained by it. How reckless."

Sera was in a state of shock. Her ears were ringing as she tried to absorb the information. "Are you saying, Father, that you made it a requirement of becoming prime minister that Lord Fitzroy give up that little girl?"

He looked at her as if she'd grown another nose. "It is well within my right as prince regent to call whom I *will* to form a government. Do you think I want a prime minister who is distracted by a protracted legal case? He already has an ailing wife, as if that weren't disadvantage enough. But he flatly refused to send her away to a place better suited to her station. He wants the position, mind you. He has ambition enough—I could see it in his eyes. The wealth, the power, the esteem. Oh, he wants it. He must be doing this to spite me. To make me *beg* to have him. And suffer insults and derision from the other ministries? I think not! No, this is completely unacceptable."

"But who will you call to be prime minister now?" Mother asked worriedly. "I thought surely Fitzroy would do it."

"So did I," Father spat out. "I thought he was a reasonable man, but he's too emotional to make a logical decision. We should have seen it with his decision to marry someone so beneath his station. Now he's trying to adopt someone even lower." His expression was black with rage.

Sera felt completely different. Fitzroy was a man of principles . . . a man of his word, and her father wished to punish him for it.

"This makes him lesser in your eyes? In both of your eyes? I should think it would speak to his leadership. He is a strength to the empire. A man with vision. You . . . you both disgust me!" Sera said angrily, and then whirled and ran out of the room, hearing her parents splutter and shout behind her. It would cost her later in some consequence she didn't deserve, but she could not regret it. Tears stung Sera's eyes, and she clenched her fists to try to quell them. She dashed down the corridor and saw that Mr. Case was no longer guarding the door. But as Sera ducked her head inside, she saw the chamber was empty. So she ran down the corridor, hoping to reach the landing platform before it was too late.

As she raced up the stairs, out of breath, the two doormen blocked her. Left with no other alternative, she pressed her face against the window. Through the beveled glass, she saw a blond-haired girl bound over the railing from the plank and disappear on board. Fitzroy followed her across the plank to the tempest, holding another young woman's hand. The girl had dark hair, almost as dark as Sera's. The girl was looking up at her protector, so Sera only saw her profile. Her heart raged inside her, and she wanted to pound the glass with her fists until it broke. She wanted to ask them if she could stow away on board.

The unfairness of the situation made her so furious. Fitzroy would have been a wonderful person for that position. He would have improved the lives of the less fortunate.

Which is why, she realized, her father had ultimately refused him.

CHAPTER FIFTEEN
EAKETT AND BAGGLES

Of all Sera's tutors, the ones she enjoyed the least were the advocates—Masters Eakett and Baggles. They were both a study of contrasts. Eakett was tall and charismatic. Baggles was short and dumpy. Eakett liked to roam the room, hardly standing still, full of energy. Baggles would sit in a chair, often complaining of a sore back, and his speaking voice was dreadfully dull. The man refused to respond to her goading, and if she asked a question he deemed irrelevant, he'd completely ignore it by continuing with his lecture. It was infuriating.

Master Eakett, she realized, was losing patience with her inability to grasp the aspects of the Mysteries of Law that he was trying to teach her. He had a sturdy head of hair—thick, dark, wavy curls—above his face. He wore a smug look, one that had no doubt developed over years of reciting and regurgitating senseless facts.

"Now, let us try this concept again," Master Eakett said, sighing with frustration and kneading his forehead. "Delegation of authority. Can you give me an example, my dear, of when it might be used? Perhaps an example involving your father, the prince regent?"

Sera's mind had been wandering, and only at the end of his sentence had she realized he was addressing her again. "Can we talk about deeds, Master Eakett?" she asked.

His lip quivered with suppressed impatience. "We were discussing delegation of authority, ma'am."

"Well, *you* were discussing it. But I wasn't paying close attention."

"Obviously," he snorted under his breath.

"It would help me understand the Mysteries of Law better," Sera went on, "if I could connect them to something that *does* interest me, and I'd like to learn more about deeds. How do they work? How long have they been in practice?"

He started pacing, his brow furrowing as he debated the prudence of which authority to please—the father or the daughter. He gave her a measured look, puffing out his cheeks and submitting to what he clearly felt was an indignity.

"Very well, if it please you. But we must quickly return to the topic at hand. You are already well behind where most of my students are—"

"Thank you, Master Eakett," Sera interrupted. "I appreciate your indulgence."

". . . and I really don't see how studying deeds is going to expand your knowledge. In your lifetime, it is unlikely that you will ever have to personally engage in the practice. It is not a recent custom by any standard. It began at least a century ago when the Ministry of Law was in power." He was always determined to make his points.

"But it interests me, Master Eakett. I thought the practice dated back much further. Proceed."

"A hundred years isn't recent. They were a solution to a problem regarding rights and ownership. A deed is the right to control the destiny of someone or something. Take a sky ship, for example. One can acquire the right to use it to travel from one city to the next. It can be kept in a hove for months at a time or used daily to soar over the treetops. The one who holds the deed controls the use."

"I don't care about sky ships," Sera said with unconcern. "I never get to ride them. But people are connected in such a way, too. The right to control *them*."

"Precisely. Say, for example, a man owes a debt. It might be from gambling or from a failed business endeavor. It might take him, under normal circumstances, twenty years to repay the debt. Let's say he is forty-five years old—"

"That's very old," Sera said.

Master Eakett's brow furrowed more. "That's *my* age, ma'am."

"I'm very sorry," she apologized. Hugilde gave Sera a disapproving look and quickly turned away, covering her mouth.

"Let's say he is fifty-five years old, then. As his age increases, he is more susceptible to sickness and disease. The crushing weight of a financial obligation has been known to send even younger men to an early grave. But this man has a son who is twelve years old. That's very young." He gave her a pointed look, showing that he was trying to get his revenge on her. "The younger man's capacity to pay off the debt is higher because he has more years left to him. Yet," he added, wagging his finger, "because he is young, he is also unskilled. A deed is arranged, and the boy is committed to service the debt holder for twenty-four years. Four to cover his training and twenty to resolve the issue. The debt is now transferred to the boy of twelve, and the father avoids going to prison."

"But that's not fair," Sera said with anger. "It wasn't the boy's fault that the father incurred the debt."

"Alas, that is true," Master Eakett said. "But while that is an extreme example, youngsters are traded every day in the world below. Many of them have deeds assigned to them. If the lad tries to escape, he can be pressed back into service, and time might be added to the deed for his misbehavior."

"How awful," Sera said, her heart twisting with anguish.

"It is the way of life," Master Eakett said with a shrug. "Nearly every servant in your own household, ma'am, has a deed of service. But most consider it a luxurious privilege to be serving someone of your station rather than cleaning gutters down below. You won't find anyone complaining about working in Lockhaven."

Sera found herself thinking of Will Russell, who would be leaving shortly to attend to his schooling. What kind of service would he be compelled to do afterward? How many years of his life would be spent meeting the obligation? It struck her forcibly that she knew so, so little about the lives of other people . . . about the very empire that she was in line to serve.

"And any parent can make a deed for their child?" she asked, her cheeks flushing with heat. "The child has no choice?"

"None whatsoever, ma'am," he replied with a shrug. "You cannot trust a child to act in its own best interests. Look at your own case, ma'am. If you were left to yourself, would you be studying the Mysteries of Law at all? Probably not, given your limited powers of concentration. But your father could, legally, assign a deed for you. And you would have no say in it, even after reaching the age of majority."

The thought filled her with dread. Not that Father *would* do it to her—he was too conscious of his reputation for that, and, besides, he loved her—but because he *could*.

"What's the difference between a deed and an adoption?" she asked next.

"I think I have answered your question, and we should get back to the principle of delegation of authority, which is much more relevant to your life."

"Yes, but I want to know."

He looked up to the ceiling, as if supplicating a higher power. "Is this about that little girl from the Fells? The one Fitzroy is trying to adopt?"

"Of course not," Sera lied, shaking her head.

"Because I've been given express instructions from the prince regent not to discuss that case with you."

"I would never ask you to disobey Father," Sera said. "I was just curious because my tutor of the Mysteries of War has a young man with a deed. I was wondering if adoption breaks the terms of it."

Sera didn't know if he believed her ruse, but he answered her nonetheless. "Ah, I see. Well, as I explained, a deed is signed for a specific term to cover a specific obligation. That young man, the one you speak of, may have an obligation to serve in the military. It would be for a fixed period of time. Were someone to adopt him, the terms of the original agreement would still need to be met in some way. It usually involves a lump-sum payment."

"What does that mean?" Sera asked.

"It means the payment of the entire debt plus interest. The deed may have been written to exonerate a debt of ten thousand, for example. With interest, it becomes twenty thousand. So it would cost someone a minimum of twenty thousand to clear the deed and adopt the young man. It is much more practical to transfer the deed from one person to the other. For example, and I'm just using this as an example, that little girl from the Fells had a deed. Lord Fitzroy has assumed it, and so she lives at his estate now and must do whatever he tells her to do. In order for him to adopt her, they must find the original document that set the terms of her service. Given that she's an orphan and lived in the Fells all her life, it is not likely the terms of the deed are very long—she wouldn't have been expected to survive the fulfilling of them. Still, Fitzroy's advocate must hunt down the original document. What if it was burned in a fire? What if it was destroyed by water?"

Sera leaned forward, very interested.

Master Eakett flushed, realizing he'd done exactly what he'd initially refused to do. "Ahem, it's time we returned to the topic at hand. Delegation of authority."

Sera was not pleased. But she knew it would be a mistake to push Master Eakett to learn more. He would likely balk from discussing the subject altogether.

"Just to be clear, Master Eakett," Sera said, "in your estimation, how many children born in the empire are signed away into deeds at a young age?"

"The majority, I should think," he replied. "Even the wealthy are always at risk of losing their rank. Of course, a young man or woman who is educated would naturally have a shorter term of service. Maybe only ten years. Or five, depending on the training. A young man with the aptitude to become a surgeon, for example, may incur a deed to pay for schooling and then owe a period of service healing others before practicing his trade with a richer clientele in a higher estate. The young man you spoke of, in the Ministry of War, might have an obligation to serve as part of the crew of a hurricane. Now, if we can get back to the matter at hand . . ."

Sera had persuaded Hugilde to talk to Commander Falking before their afternoon lesson. She'd feigned an interest in a certain battle, and her governess had promised to ask him to come prepared the following afternoon. It provided Sera with exactly the opportunity she had hoped for—a chance for her to whisper with Will.

"I learned about deeds today," she said, leaning toward him so that he'd hear her better. She kept her eyes focused on Falking to ensure he wouldn't notice her indiscretion. "How long must you serve the Ministry of War?"

Will didn't answer right away. A quick glance revealed his discomfort.

"Would you tell me?" she pleaded. "I want to help you if I can."

He picked up his pencil and began fidgeting with it. "I'll get in trouble if I talk to you too much," he whispered, one hand shielding his mouth. His eyes were fixed on Falking.

Sera was undeterred. "I have an idea," she said. "Write it down while you are taking notes. And then leave the letter with me before you go. I'll read it later. Will you do that for me?"

"You want me to write you notes?" he asked, his voice sounding very doubtful.

"Yes. Yes, I do. And since I'm a Fitzempress, you won't get in trouble. I'm ordering you to do it."

She watched as his lips pressed into a firm line. He started tapping the desk softly with the pencil, and, for a moment, she was certain he would say no.

"What do you want to know?" he finally whispered.

A thrill of victory. She'd give Hugilde a big kiss for innocently helping her. "Everything. Tell me about your deed. How many brothers and sisters you have. Where you're from."

He looked even more uncomfortable. He was taking a serious risk if he heeded her. If Falking found out, he'd be rebuked. Or not invited back. Sera could only hope he'd be willing to take a chance. He'd be gone soon, and she wanted to know more about his background and his deed—and not just because Will intrigued her. She had been denied the chance to meet Cettie of the Fells; this was the only way she could learn anything real about her people. Her teachers didn't want to give her the knowledge she wanted to hear, only the crusty knowledge they thought someone of her class should have.

"Yes, Miss Fitzempress," he said.

"Thank you, Mr. Russell."

Commander Falking strode over to them, and Sera felt a twinge of guilt for her small act of rebellion. But as she tasted the guilt, she found it sweet. Being naughty was always a little thrilling. She looked forward to reading his note and asking him questions in return.

Falking cleared his throat. "I'm pleased to hear, ma'am, that you've taken such an interest in the Battle of Skyfell. Many a good man died that day. I hope you will not become queasy about the carnage. It may be your privilege, in the future, to order such conflicts. War is a terrible thing. It is great but terrible."

"Have the people ever revolted against the emperor?" Sera asked, noticing that Will had started to write some notes surreptitiously. She wished to keep Falking's attention on her.

"Oh yes," Falking replied with confidence. "Once the populace even tried building a tower to reach our lofty heights. That ended with much confusion. I shall tell you the story."

Sera smiled in pleasure. That sounded like a story that would actually interest her. She was anxious to hear it, but even more anxious to read Will's note.

CHAPTER SIXTEEN

BELOW

Miss Fitzempress,

As it may become my future duty to obey your commands, I have undertaken to fulfill your request. My father, Blain Russell, was a successful merchant in the City. His father had been a carpenter by trade and was called upon to build cabinets for those living in Lockhaven. My father inherited his business and prospered. As a child, I would often join him on his journeys up to various manors aboard sky ships, which must have started my fascination with the military. My father's success in designing and building cabinetry led to many associations beneficial to my family and my future education. When I reached the age of ten, my father had already put aside sufficient funds to pay for my schooling and a commission to the rank of lieutenant, assuming that I earned my merits.

Unfortunately, my father was called on to do business with a man I will not name for fear of future retali-

ation. He engaged my father on false pretenses, and after my father completed the work, which was extensive, he utterly refused to pay his debt. I can only guess as to his motivations, but there are rumors that a speculation had gone bad. Perhaps he could no longer afford to pay the agreed-upon amount. When my father tried acquiring an advocate to plead his case, he was shunned from Lockhaven, and his business plummeted. As did my prospects.

I accepted the rank of midshipman, and my father took out a deed on me to prevent further disaster and possible homelessness. The deed against me is for thirty years, the life of a soldier. I do not condemn him for his choice. As for my own choices, I have none. The Ministry of War may ship me to the farthest reaches of the empire. I have no say in my destiny, except to declare that I would prefer this fate to constructing cabinets. I hope that if I serve the empire, and you, to my utmost ability, I may earn a sufficient reward to liberate myself from the deed. It will not be easy.

It could also be much worse. An officer who has studied the Mysteries of War cannot, I am told, be shot down by an enemy. I do not know by what powers this is realized, but I will eagerly await learning this Mystery, even if it results in a departure from you and your considerable kindness to me. I am grateful for my patron and for the opportunity it has given me to make your acquaintance.

Yours devotedly,
William Russell

Sera read the letter at least six times, and each time it made her burn with more indignation on William's behalf. Had it been within her power, she would have forgiven the debt herself and made him a free man once again. She would have forgiven the debts of all the children who'd been essentially sold. This explained why he was so reserved, why he brooded while he studied with her. It was certainly a pity that—

"What is that?" Hugilde said in a worried voice, snatching the letter from her hands.

"Give it back to me," Sera demanded, her cheeks turning hot. Normally she was more careful, but she'd been so immersed in thought she'd forgotten the letter was still in her hand.

"I came here to brush your hair before bed, Sera, and I find you in your nightdress, the buttons still undone, and here you are staring out the window, completely insensible. What is this?"

Hugilde began to open it, and Sera rushed off the window seat and tried to grab it back. "That is mine, Hugilde! You may not read it."

"I most certainly will, young lady," said her governess archly. She was taller than Sera. Much taller. That drove Sera to a frenzy.

"I order you to give it back!" Sera said, tears of rage beginning to stream down her cheeks. Another grab for it proved futile.

"Sit down," Hugilde snapped back. "You are behaving like an animal, Princess. Where did you get this? Who gave it to you?"

"Please, Hugilde!" Sera begged. "You are the only person who truly loves me. You will break my heart if you read it. Please, give it back to me."

Hugilde was wavering. The letter was half-open, and she was warring with herself. "I am your governess. I am responsible for your moral character, and I will be held accountable for your misdeeds. You are still very young. Before I choose whether to read the letter, you must answer my questions. If you refuse, I will take this note to your father immediately."

Hugilde may well have dunked Sera's head in a frozen bath. It sobered her quickly, and she began wringing her hands. She cursed herself for her constant daydreaming.

"It's from William Russell," Sera said in a subdued voice. She watched closely for Hugilde's reaction.

The governess closed her eyes as if a death sentence had been passed on her. "By the Mysteries, that boy is too bold!"

"It's not his fault, Hugilde! It's mine. I . . . I made him write it."

Hugilde's eyes flew open with incredulity.

"It's true, it's true. Dearest Hugilde. Sweet governess." She began to pace, trying to think of what to say to stave off disaster. "It's not what you think. It's not a love note. He would never do that. After Master Eakett explained about deeds, I asked Will about his—"

"*Will?*" Hugilde said in dismay.

Sera winced at her indiscretion. "I m-meant William. Please, Hugilde, don't be angry with me. I have lived my entire life surrounded by adults. I'm not allowed to see my cousins except on rare occasions, and even then, I'm chaperoned. I adore you, Hugilde, but this is the first opportunity I've had to know someone my own age and someone who has lived in the world below us. I just wanted to know about his deed, that's all. He's not from the tenements. No, not that low. But his life has been very different from mine. I need to learn about life outside of this manor, Hugilde. How else am I to do it?"

Hugilde puffed out her cheeks and sighed. "So this is not a love note? The boy is handsome enough. I wouldn't put it past him."

Sera bit her lip. "You think he's handsome, too?"

"I have eyes, don't I? I may be thrice his age, but there's no doubt he'll make a striking officer. And you are Seraphin Fitzempress and could do him a bit of good someday, as I'm sure he is very well aware." She fanned her face with the letter.

"Are you going to tell Father?" Sera asked meekly.

"I *should* tell him," Hugilde said with a snort. "But if I did, Mr. Russell would be punished for your sin."

Sera stamped her bare foot. "It's not a sin to write a letter, Hugilde. Don't be ridiculous."

"You're only twelve, Sera. It starts like this, innocent flirting. But there's a certain intimacy involved in correspondence." She pursed her lips. "While I trust you would not lie to me, Sera, if I am to keep this secret for you, then I need to know what is in this letter. May I have your permission to read it and judge for myself whether I should tell your parents?"

Sera stared at her governess, wishing again that she had been more guarded.

"I wish you wouldn't read it," she begged.

Hugilde arched her eyebrows, gazing down at her young charge and waiting for permission to be granted.

"Why cannot I have at least one secret?" Sera pressed.

Hugilde's look softened. But she didn't relent. "Princess, I know you will find it difficult to believe, but I was once a young woman, too. I know what it feels like to pine and sigh and daydream. But I am also older and wiser than you, and this is the reason that I am the governess and you are my pupil. Trust is as fragile as porcelain. It is beautiful and shining when it is whole, but it is worth nothing when it is broken. And how easily it breaks . . ."

The words struck Sera in the heart. She sighed and turned her back. "You may read it."

While Hugilde perused Will's letter, Sera finished buttoning her nightdress and then returned to the window seat, folding her arms around her knees, hugging herself. She felt like the loneliest girl in all the world. Someday, when she was eighteen, she would be granted a yearly income that would hopefully enable her to choose her own servants, her own household. And yet she feared it was just a fantasy. That her parents would choose a husband for her before she reached her majority. That she would be controlled for the rest of her life and live in misery as her parents did. Would she be as subject to their authority as Will was to his deed? As she waited for Hugilde to finish the letter, she let more tears creep out of her eyes again, seeping into the thin fabric at her knees. She liked feeling sorry for herself every once in a while.

"Thank you, Sera," Hugilde said. She dropped the letter on the window seat in front of her and then fetched the brush and began brushing out Sera's long dark hair. Sera kept her face tilted toward the window, too embarrassed to speak.

"It was a fine letter," Hugilde went on after a while. "He expressed himself well. I assume that he wrote it during Commander Falking's lesson?"

"Yes," Sera whispered, surprised at Hugilde's mild response. She didn't seem so shocked anymore.

The teeth of the brush went through her hair, and Sera winced, scrunching her nose. She didn't like the way it felt when her hair was tugged. It made her nose itch and caused little stabs of pain to radiate across her scalp. Hugilde knew she was sensitive and tried her best, but sometimes Sera wanted to shriek at her to be gentler.

"Well, I would prefer it if you'd write your response this evening so you can focus on your lesson tomorrow afternoon. Your father is paying for you to learn, Sera, and no one appreciates it when their money is wasted. Especially him."

That was true. Father was certainly a miser. His good fortune in becoming the prince regent had done little to change that.

"That makes sense," Sera said, still feeling disconsolate.

"After you've written it, I want you to give it to me to read. And then I will speak to Commander Falking. If he agrees, and I think that he will because he's a worldly man and recognizes that you will be a powerful woman someday, he will give the note to Mr. Russell."

Sera lifted her head and turned, her entire outlook brightening. "You will help me, Hugilde?"

The matronly woman smiled and leaned down to kiss her damp cheek. "As I told you, Sera. I do remember what it feels like to be young."

A burst of happiness went through her, and she turned and hugged Hugilde close, burying her face in her governess's waist. "Thank you, Hugilde. Thank you so much!"

Hugilde stroked her hair, and Sera felt a shimmer of peace. She pulled back and looked up at her governess. "Why did you never marry?" she asked. It was an impertinent question, but she longed to know the answer.

Hugilde's countenance fell, but she did not stop stroking Sera's hair. "When I was younger, eighteen, I was in love with a dragoon."

Sera blinked in surprise. "I know what that means now," she said, grinning. "Commander Falking would be so proud. They are the men who train with arquebuses and shoot from the sky ships. They are skilled at hitting their marks. I think that is what Will would like to become."

Hugilde smiled and nodded. "They have great skill, and it is difficult training. Well, I had gone to school with this boy, and he was learning the Mysteries of War while I was studying my subjects. We were from the same rank, so there would not have been an impediment there. I think Father liked him well enough." Her smile faded. "When I was twenty, there was a brief war. A rebellion in one of the kingdoms of the empire. Those seem to occur repeatedly, no matter how hard we strive for peace. Many young men lost their lives. Including my beloved. He fell to his death after his sky ship broke apart."

Sera's eyes bulged. "How awful!"

Hugilde nodded in agreement, her eyes distant. It was an old pain. But Sera could see it still throbbed. "There were so many deaths that year. And not enough young men for all the young ladies. In my generation there are many like me." She smoothed Sera's hair again and planted a kiss on her forehead. "It's not Mr. Russell's fault that he's indebted. I have seen it happen often enough."

Sera's brow furrowed. "What do you mean? Are you saying it was deliberate?"

Hugilde frowned and resumed brushing her hair. "You are still very young and have enough outrage to last a lifetime. I've lived in this world long enough to see corruption for what it is. I've heard enough conversations among our kind. It was different when the Ministry of Thought was in power. I was little then, but I remember it as a gentler time. The people below are kept there for a reason. When one of them shows enough ambition or skill to rise, they are rewarded and encouraged and praised. They are fattened, like a hog to be butchered. And then they are brought to their knees. Men prey on other men. They gain some inherent satisfaction from devouring each other financially. That is the Mysteries of Law, despite Master Eakett's protestations and talk of *delegation of authority*." She sniffed with cynicism. "Those are just words they've invented to soothe their guilty consciences. Everyone who's mired down below has a deed in some form. And like the masters pulling a puppet's strings, the wealthiest make them dance to the tunes that they play through the walls. We are corrupt, Sera. But we pretend to be virtuous." As she finished the final strokes with the brush, she set it down and quickly tied Sera's hair into a night braid.

"Write your letter," Hugilde said. "Give it to me in the morning."

Sera wanted to weep for her governess. She wanted to weep for Will Russell. In all the lectures she had listened to, with their outlandish vocabularies and nuances and dry-as-dust details, she had never heard her society summarized in such an eloquent and shattering way. The size and weight of the injustice felt like a mountain crushing the earth.

There was a reason her parents wanted to keep her ignorant, she realized, and it sickened her. They wanted to preserve the natural order of things—or what they felt was the natural order. The suffering down below was *calculated*. It was overseen.

It was *administered*. It was no accident that someone from Lockhaven had let Will's father take the fall for *his* bad dealings. Who cared if an honest cabinetmaker suffered so long as a sky manor kept floating? And her father, who'd made his attitude toward the working classes quite clear, meant to ensure that it stayed that way. She clenched her small fists.

Poor Will, she thought disconsolately. His father had tried to escape the game, only to end up yoking his son to the same fate. It wasn't fair. It wasn't right.

Sera's heart burned with anger. And that anger filled her with resolve on one thing. She would be a free woman. No matter what her father said or did, she would not marry before she was eighteen. She would make her own decisions.

And she would find a way to help those living in misery down below.

Hugilde stroked Sera's hair and looked into her tear-swollen eyes. "It has been like this for a very long time," she said.

Sera struggled to maintain her composure. "I know. But that doesn't make it right. It doesn't mean that it cannot change." She paused, then added, "And I do mean to change it."

CETTIE

They say that fortune favors the bold. To gain greatness, one must risk disaster. Some, like Brant Fitzroy, refuse the game entirely and so are left without the greatest prizes. Others step forward willingly and grasp the reins of opportunity. Some will stand. Some will fall. But the thrill is in the risk. When one defies the odds and emerges triumphant, there is no greater reward. It was not always this way. Back when the Ministry of Thought ruled, debts were forgiven. The idle were indulged. But those old practices have changed. The possibility of gaining riches stimulates the mind of rich and poor alike. Both strive for it.

Some people gamble with coin. Some gamble with reputation. From the lowliest of footmen dicing in the street to the most austere advocates betting on the outcome of a trial. Those who rise in the ranks of society can rise quickly. If they only dare enough.

—Lady Corinne of Pavenham Sky

CHAPTER SEVENTEEN
OUTCAST

Something had changed because of the visit to Lockhaven. Cettie had sensed it while walking away from the prince regent's manor back to the sky ship. Fitzroy's mood had altered noticeably, and while he was as courteous and polite as ever, he was also brooding. His eyes were wrinkled with disappointment. And she didn't know why.

She and Anna stood at the edge of the tempest, watching as the floating city shrank behind them, constantly swiping hair out of their faces as the fierce winds battered them. Anna pointed out the various manors and named who ruled them. But it was too confusing to remember any of them. The tempest shuddered at the sudden gusts, and there were creaks and groans that Cettie hadn't noticed before.

"There's a storm coming," the captain told Fitzroy in a warning voice. "I can smell it."

"Oh, there's already been one," Fitzroy answered dryly, but it was obvious he wasn't referring to the weather.

"That one is Angelica," Anna said, pointing to a large brick manor. "Named after the old master's wife."

Cettie leaned over the rail, trying to study Lockhaven, knowing she may never get a chance to go there again. It was the seat of the empire, the repository of all the wealth of its dominions. The opulent manors she had seen while flying south were dwarfed by the sheer size of the place. The City cowered beneath it, wreathed in fog, but a few towers protruded up through the clouds. Though she had heard City folk complain about the shadow cast by Lockhaven, it felt different to actually see it—it was as if a massive mountain had been turned upside down and lifted into the air. She could only imagine the size of the shadow it cast over those who lived below. The floating part of the City was crammed with towers and manors, though there were small swatches of green for the tiny parks. Some of the manors were built into the side of the rock, and there were a dozen or so waterfalls that cascaded off the sides of the massive edifice, the water flowing down below. Fitzroy had told her that most of them emptied into the river that ran beneath in the City.

A sudden break in the cloud cover gave Cettie a look at the wide stretch of tenements lining the river, so smothered with fog and smoke as to be nearly invisible except for chimney stacks. It was not the Fells, which were up in the north, but her stomach twisted into a knot all the same. She feared she would end up back there despite all her efforts to be honest and obedient.

Lockhaven was encircled with hurricane and tempest sky ships, some moored and tethered by long, thick chains. Several ships were either docking or leaving.

"There are so many people living down there," Anna said, gazing down at the spectacle. "I don't think it's possible to number them all."

"I can never get used to the view either," Adam Creigh said, startling Cettie. She hadn't heard him approach and sidle up next to her. Nor had Anna. There was a certain wariness in his tone of voice. Anna's cheeks began to flush.

"It's beautiful," Cettie said, still struck with amazement.

"Lockhaven? Yes," he answered gravely. "But I was commenting on those living below. The mass of human suffering down there. We're too far away to hear it, but I'm sure if we were closer, it would be nothing but coughing and sickness." He gripped the edge of the railing, his mouth turning down into a frown. "What can be done about it? When there are so many in need?" He sighed and straightened. "And this is just one city in the empire." He vaguely gestured at the scene with his hand. "It's like this everywhere, in every court overseen by every arch-duke. Grand balls, beautiful music, talks of politics and the weather. Yet at what cost?" He looked at her with sympathy. "What do you see when you look at it?"

She didn't know why Adam was addressing her and not Anna. Maybe the incident in the grotto had changed something between them. Maybe it had earned her his compassion. Whatever the reason, she was grateful for his company; in a way, he was an outcast, too.

"I see so much," she answered, shaking her head. "The waterfalls, for example. Some of them land in the river, but the ones on that side"—she demonstrated by pointing—"fall on the city itself. The people who live down there must think it rains every day. What must it be like to live under a shadow so vast, knowing that the floating part of the City could fall at any time and crush everything you've ever known?"

His mouth broke into a knowing smile that pleased her. "I'd never thought of that, but I'm sure it must be troubling. The river down there is so polluted with human filth that few are willing to drink from it. They see the water falling from Lockhaven as a Mystery."

"It *is* a Mystery," Cettie said, gazing back at the scene. "It is getting so small now. I feel like I could pinch it with my fingers." She squeezed one eye shut and used her thumb and forefinger as if she could catch the entire floating rock between them.

⌒

Cettie awoke to the realization that she wasn't moving anymore. A small squall had hit the tempest, and she and Anna had gone down below to rest while the winds raged around them. The lack of movement wasn't the only change—the mattress she was on was much thicker than the pallet she'd lain on in the tempest. She lifted her head from a soft pillow and felt heat radiating nearby. Anna lay beside her, her face peaceful, her lips slightly parted in sleep. Cettie blinked and sat up. She was wearing the same dress as the previous day, but she was in Anna's room, and a beautiful morning light streamed in through the gauzy curtains.

Instantly, she felt a spasm of worry that Mrs. Pullman was going to be angry with her. But Cettie hadn't gone to Anna's room willingly—she'd fallen asleep and been carried there. At least the keeper had not retaliated yet. She hadn't been awakened by the bone-chilling cold of a ghost. Relief swelled in her heart.

She left the bed carefully so as not to wake Anna. Borrowing one of her friend's brushes, she brushed her dark hair, using the vanity mirror, something she ordinarily didn't have at her disposal. Then she set the brush down and went outside into the hall. Her stomach was grumbling.

She didn't want to go to the kitchen and risk encountering Mrs. Pullman, so she walked down the corridor toward the sitting room, hoping there would be a tray of something to eat. Her footsteps slowed as she passed a closed door—one she'd never seen open. In an earlier tour, she had asked Anna where it led, but Anna had never been inside either. It was a room only Mrs. Pullman entered, and it was always locked. Cettie wondered what was inside it, because each time she passed the door, a strange feeling emanated from within. Something that made a part of her mind shrink. Something poisonous. She shrank from it without understanding why.

The elder Fitzroy siblings were already in the sitting room, talking in low voices, but Phinia cut herself off the moment Cettie walked in.

"There she is," she said darkly to her brother.

Stephen, who was seated on the couch, turned, and his face instantly went from serious to angry. It was immediately clear that something had angered the two siblings. More to the point, something to do with *her*.

"What are you doing here?" he asked in a challenging tone.

"Looking for something to eat," Cettie answered in a quiet way, feeling the immediacy of trouble yet not understanding what was causing it.

"She's hungry," Phinia snorted.

What custom had she upset this time? Had they seen her wearing this gown last night?

Stephen rose from the couch and walked toward her. Phinia continued to glare.

"Don't you understand what you've done by coming to Fog Willows?" Stephen said hotly.

"I don't think she knows." Phinia sounded surprised.

Stephen frowned, though his gaze looked no less angry than it had before. "It's just like Father to not tell her."

"Know what?" Cettie pleaded. "Please tell me."

Stephen was close to her now. He wasn't very big, but his nearness was intimidating. He looked down at her with bald accusation. "Mrs. Pullman told us that the prince regent offered Father the chance to become prime minister. And he refused . . . because of you."

Cettie was no longer hungry. She felt an instant thrum of disappointment for Fitzroy. Who better deserved such a post than he? And then she remembered her first meeting with Mrs. Pullman months ago. This was the honor the older woman had long coveted for her master, and her dream had been shattered. Fear struck her in the heart—if Stephen and Phinia were this angry, Mrs. Pullman would be absolutely vindictive. Servants had been unceremoniously returned to the Fells for much lesser sins. And if she controlled the ghost, perhaps she also controlled the severity of its attacks . . .

"I don't understand," Cettie said, shaking her head. "Why because of me?"

"She really is stupid," said Phinia.

Stephen's look was condescending. "I wish I didn't have to go back to school so soon. I'm going to get ridiculed over this mess. Cettie, it's quite simple. Try to understand. The prince regent is not the only person who thinks it is entirely inappropriate that someone of Father's station is trying to adopt someone of *yours*. The prince regent asked Father to send you away. There are places you could be sent that would be preferable to the Fells. Special schools for the poor. Father already paid off your deed, he—"

"He did?" Cettie gasped, interrupting him. "He never told me that."

"It wasn't very much," Phinia said with sarcasm. "But finding even one of your parents is proving difficult. Still, Father insists he is going to adopt you. The prince regent—"

"Let me explain it, Phinia," Stephen shot in. "If Father were named prime minister, his willingness to help an urchin like you would be seen as an agenda for reform. And it's true. That's just the sort of thing Father would try to do if he *did* get the role. The prince regent would have none of it. He gave Father an ultimatum, according to Mrs. Pullman. And Father walked out." His jaw clenched. "And what makes it worse is that the silver mines have stopped producing anything but quicksilver, which is pretty useless. You can't mint coins out of liquid metal, you see. So not only does Father have to pay for our schooling now, which is indeed a burden, but he also has to pay our Mr. Sloan to hunt the Fells for a man or a woman who didn't even want you to begin with. The salary of being prime minister was more than what Father was earning per annum before. It would have solved all of our problems. And now, we run the risk that we'll go *bankrupt* because of you, and Fog Willows will come crashing down to the ground and break into rubble because it costs *money* to keep it afloat."

Whether or not Phinia agreed with her brother didn't matter. It felt unfair of them to heap all the blame on her shoulders. Fitzroy was acting in character—and his nontraditional behavior had begun before Cettie was even born. But that didn't lessen the pang. It made it worse. Cettie stared at the two siblings mutely, feeling despised and utterly responsible for the family's current predicament. She was going to cry, and she didn't want them to see her.

Unable to speak, she turned and rushed out of the study. Escaping the room wasn't enough, though, and she fled the confinement of the manor altogether. It was drizzling outside, and the sky was leaden with gray clouds. Over the last months, she'd learned the various walkways that wound through the grounds. On a day such as this, she knew she wouldn't find anyone else wandering outside. The light rain felt cold against her cheeks, and soon her hair was thick with it, her dress damp.

There was a gazebo with a cupola on the far side of the manor grounds, which she knew would provide some cover from the rain and a place to be alone and out of sight. She especially didn't want to see Mrs. Pullman. Something told her the woman would be fiercer than a dragon. As Cettie ran along the slick trails, part of her was tempted to just slip and stumble and fall off the edge. Fitzroy had mentioned some protections but not how they worked. Would some strange providential barrier stop her from falling? Or would she plummet down to the ground far beneath the estate—back to the place where the eldest Fitzroy siblings thought she belonged? How would Stephen and Phinia react to that? The thought of self-destruction terrified her, as did the image of falling from that great height, and she shoved it from her mind.

As she turned the corner of the trail, the gazebo came into view. To her bitter disappointment, someone was already there. It was Raj Sarin, the Bhikhu, the master's bodyguard, whom she had scarcely spoken three words to in all her months at Fog Willows. He was standing, feet apart, dropped low in some sort of pose. His hands and arms were doing a mirrored set of motions, and his breath came in and out in short spurts. The sequence changed as he straightened, and Cettie found herself watching him. Catching herself, she was about to run back the way she'd come when Raj Sarin turned his head and noticed her.

"Good morning, Cettie!" he called to her. There was a twinkle in his eyes as he gestured for her to come to the gazebo.

Her dress was nearly soaked through, and she was cold and miserable and self-conscious. She had been crying and hoped that her eyes weren't too red and puffy. Raj Sarin continued with some of his movements—his arms circled each other slowly before jabbing out quickly and raking downward. He repeated it again and again. It was a bizarre ritual, but it captivated her.

He didn't stop his practice when she reached the gazebo. It was wide enough in the center for him to perform his routine, so she slunk onto the bench and watched in fascination.

Finally, after several minutes, he stopped the ritual and then turned and bowed to her, pushing a fist against an open palm in a form of salute. Raj Sarin was short and pudgy, which seemed unusual for one of his training. His hair was scraped clean with a razor, but he had a salt-and-pepper beard that nearly covered his neck. His dark eyes met her own, and she felt an immediate kinship with him. He had a slightly haunted look, as if he, too, had seen many sorrows in his days.

"What were you doing, Raj Sarin?" she asked him. Though they'd spoken infrequently, he had always treated her with respect and kindness. *He* would not mock her for not knowing what she should.

"Practicing," he answered with a smile. "I come here every morning. You never know when brigantes may attack Fog Willows." He raised his eyebrows at her and smiled. "It is best to be prepared." He clasped his hands behind his back and started pacing. "So, Cettie of the Fells. You were running just now. You look upset. Let me hazard a guess. You put a cockroach in Mrs. Pullman's breakfast and were caught?"

Cettie started with surprise because he had said it so seriously. "No, Raj Sarin."

He frowned and nodded. "Let me try again. You were carrying sixteen porcelain dishes for Kinross—because of his gout—and dropped all but three."

Cettie bit her lip and shook her head no again. She felt the tiny beginnings of a laugh.

He pursed his lips as he continued to pace, running a hand over his cone-shaped beard. "This is truly a mystery, but I will solve it. You were blamed, unfairly, by the master's eldest children for being the cause of hunger in the world, for heat on sunny days, and for rashes on the sick and afflicted?"

Cettie stifled a giggle. In just a few moments, he had made her feel enormously better. "You were a little closer to the truth that time," she said.

"Ah, I see, I see," he said, his eyes twinkling again. "I heard something to that effect from Mrs. Pullman first thing this morning. Would you like some advice, Cettie of the Fells?" He dropped down into a stance again and started moving his arms slowly, one following the other.

"I would appreciate your counsel," she answered. "You must be very wise."

"In my country, they call hurricanes *typhoons*. If you are at peace with yourself in your center"—he tapped his heart with his spread fingers—"then you can stand on a beach during a typhoon and it will only rustle your hair. If you have any." He winked at her. "If you are not at peace, then the typhoon will blow you away." He continued with his motions, turning in a full circle as he did them. "When Fitzroy met me, I was a slave to the poppy dust. I was fat, and I'd forsaken both my training and my wits. He gave me another chance at a new life. And every morning, I come to the gazebo and do these drills. They have helped me conquer my mind. They have helped me realize that I sought fulfillment in something that could never *fill* me.

I would never forsake a practice. Not even if a hurricane were blowing. And so I control my mind. And so I control my peace."

He paused midmotion. "Would you like to learn, Cettie of the Fells, how to control your mind?"

She rose from the bench, her eyes widening with hope, her heart feeling swells of relief. "I would, Raj Sarin."

"Then I will teach you," he answered with a smile.

CHAPTER EIGHTEEN

BELONGING

Raj Sarin told Cettie that the art he practiced had an ancient name called the Way of Ice and Shadows. Most practitioners simply called it the Way. He offered to teach it to her, and Cettie eagerly accepted.

The mind, Raj Sarin told her, was affected by everything the body did. This series of exercises he practiced was taught not only to improve strength and quickness, but also to allow the mind to focus, to rid it of distracting thoughts and worries. Each part of the routine that he taught her, and he said there were thousands of others, had a name. *Heron swooping on water. Rooster claws at seed. Black dragon spreads its wings.* It was a whole new world, with a whole new language to accompany it, and her mind immediately craved learning more.

She was in the middle of *crane gliding on waters* when she saw Fitzroy and Anna approaching them from the manor. That particular movement had her standing on one leg, her back arched, one fist pointing outward, her other arm jutting the other way to counterbalance. Her whole body felt alive and invigorated, but standing like that made her feel incredibly foolish in front of Fitzroy and her friend. She was about to drop back down, but Raj Sarin clucked his tongue in warning, reminding her that she had not finished holding it to the proper count.

As the others approached, her self-consciousness increased, and the strain of the pose made her limbs begin to tremble. It had not been difficult before, but she was suddenly desperately aware of her damp dress and rain-soaked hair and the wind and the cold.

"Now you are finished," Raj Sarin said, releasing her from the pose.

Cettie lowered her leg and rubbed her arms, feeling the tingling sensation all the way to her fingertips. She couldn't help but glance back at Fitzroy and Anna.

Raj Sarin interposed himself in front of Cettie, blocking her view of them. "One of the reasons I practice *here*," he told her gently, "is to avoid what just happened to you. Your mind was calm, your breathing was guided, until you felt yourself being *observed*." He held up his finger, his eyes narrowing with seriousness. "To fully master your mind, you must learn not to react to being observed by others. We naturally seek to please. To be acceptable. And in so doing, we give others—even our loved ones—power over our minds." He shook his bald head and gave her a fierce look. "Never let another person have control over your thinking. It is yours by right and by destiny. My greatest shame occurred when I relinquished control of my mind to a powder. When we practice next, you will hold your poses until the last count, no matter who sees you." He gave her a small bow of his head, his fist salute, and then he backed away just as the noise of Fitzroy's boots reached the edge of the gazebo.

Anna rushed up to Cettie and embraced her, hugging her tightly. "I was so worried."

"I told you she was here at the gazebo," Fitzroy said in a calming way. "I'm pleased to see Raj Sarin has started teaching you."

"This morning was her first lesson," Raj Sarin said with a bow.

Anna kissed Cettie's cheek, catching her by surprise. She looked at the other girl with confusion. "What's wrong?"

"When I woke up and you weren't in my room, I was afraid something had happened to you," Anna said. "I found Stephen and Phinia, and they told me about what they'd said to you. That they hoped you would leave Fog Willows. Phinia even teased that you might have . . . might have jumped off!"

The quip hurt, especially since she'd considered the possibility for the briefest of moments, but there was no denying Anna's concern was deeply felt.

"So I went to Papa, who always knows what to do," Anna said, turning to her father and smiling with relief.

Fitzroy still looked concerned, although he was trying not to show it. He shrugged, but she noticed his hands were behind his back—probably itching.

"I will have a word with Stephen and Phinia," he said somberly. "I do always try to hear both sides before rendering consequences, and they need to be given a chance." He looked Cettie in the eye earnestly. "What did they tell you, Cettie?"

She swallowed, unsure of what to say, but then she remembered that she'd promised never to lie to him again. She didn't want to get Stephen and Phinia in trouble. That wouldn't earn their love or respect. But the promise she'd made to Fitzroy needed to be kept.

"They told me that you were not going to become prime minister. Because of me."

His lips pursed, and a brooding expression came over his face. "They shouldn't have said anything of the sort. How did they learn of it?" he said to himself, half muttering.

Cettie took another breath. "Mrs. Pullman."

Fitzroy gave her a solemn look and nodded in understanding. "That makes more sense." He sighed and shook his head.

"But it's true!" Cettie said forcefully. The patter of rain against the shingles of the gazebo grew more pronounced. It would be a wet walk back to the family manor, and Cettie was dreading it. If Mrs. Pullman could see beyond the walls of the manor, then she'd just given the woman yet another reason to destroy her.

Fitzroy met Cettie's gaze. His bitter smile said it plainly enough. "It *is* true, Cettie. And I would be dishonest to say that I'm not struggling to come to grips with it. It would have solved . . . multiple problems." He chafed his hands and pressed his palms firmly together and tapped his chin with the edge of his forefingers.

Cettie's heart flinched, but she stepped forward and looked at him pleadingly. "Then you must send me back to the other children."

"Shhhh," Fitzroy said, shaking his head, stopping her from saying more. "No more of that," he said kindly, his voice tightening. "But what gives a man, even if he is a prince and a regent, the right to compel a man to act against his conscience? To toss down values he has held long before you . . . before *you* were even born?" He struggled to compose himself. The rain continued to patter even louder, and the gutters of the gazebo were soon churning with the flood. There was something unsaid in his words. Some long-ago hurt. Some resolve made of stronger stuff than dreams. "He may as well have asked me," he said with thick emotion, "to carve out my honor and cast it aside. I will not do it, no matter who asks it of me. That he would ask tells me much about the kind of leader he will be . . . and the kind of prime minister he desires."

"And you might as well carve out a part of my heart, too," Anna said, grabbing Cettie and hugging her. "You are my sister. As if we had the same blood. Please don't go. Stephen and Phinia were just being selfish. They are, you know."

The looks on their faces humbled Cettie. She had never felt wanted before. She had never belonged to a family before. It was a dizzying, heavy feeling, one that made her joints weak. The looks of utter sincerity on their faces, and the small grin and nod of approval from Raj Sarin, made fresh tears spring into Cettie's eyes.

"No more talk of such nonsense," Fitzroy said. "I will have a discussion with Stephen and Phinia. And Mrs. Pullman."

Cettie winced.

Fitzroy reached out and touched her shoulder. "*Trust* me, Cettie. I will do it in a way that doesn't implicate you. When I was captain of a sky ship, I would get reports of misbehavior from the men. Gambling belowdecks, for example, could lead to enormous problems. Lost wages, fistfights, even duels. I made it my practice not to respond immediately to reports, especially those told to me in confidence. I made it seem more like happenstance that I had found out." His thumb came up and grazed her cheek, interrupting the fall of a tear. "I don't want them to dislike you. In fact . . ." He looked deep into her eyes. "I want them to be as fond of you as Lady Maren and I are." He gave a wink to his daughter. "And Anna, too. Why don't you two run back to the manor? Raj Sarin and I have a matter to discuss about your training."

"Yes, Father," Anna said, beaming. "Can Cettie stay in my room from now on?"

Fitzroy arched an eyebrow at Cettie, clearly leaving the decision to her.

It would be a risk. This would make things worse with Mrs. Pullman. But if she stayed with Anna, it would be more difficult for the keeper to seek out a private audience with her, wouldn't it? It might also make it harder for her to seek vengeance on Cettie without revealing her true nature to all. Maybe it would even be better for Cettie to sleep in the same room. If the old woman *did* send a ghost to torment them, Cettie would see what Anna could not. She'd know to call for Fitzroy.

He had the power to banish them. And she knew that he would.

Maybe she finally had a solution to her problem.

Cettie nodded gratefully, and Anna squealed and gripped her arm. Hand in hand, they ran back into the rain. Cettie glanced back once to watch Fitzroy speaking to Raj Sarin.

There was a feeling in her heart. No, it wasn't a feeling. It was a whole jumble of them all crowding in on her at once. Gratitude, respect, admiration, loyalty, concern, compassion, and the desire to please.

For the first time in her life, she realized what that special mixture was called.

Love.

No sky ships approached Fog Willows that day. It would have been too dangerous to fly. The storm continued to rake the windows of the manor all day long, but Cettie felt safe from the cold. As Cettie gazed down at the willow trees, the long limbs being thrashed by the storm, she pitied them. Her morning had been blissful—a warm bath, a change of clothes, a delicious meal, and a dear friend—and she knew her life had changed for the better.

It had been a few days since she'd checked the glass tubes in Fitzroy's study, so she made her way there before dinner and withdrew the book she had been using to record the tick marks on the glass. She checked her previous entries and started counting the ticks, surprised by how much the level had changed. So much of the quicksilver was gone. She counted it again—just to be sure—and got the same number and wrote it down. Why had it changed so much in a few days? Had someone come into the room and stolen the curious metal? She tapped her bottom lip with the pencil, staring out at the rainstorm and thinking about her day—the horrible confrontation with Phinia and Stephen, the gazebo, and her wonderful talk with Fitzroy and Anna. To remember the day, she drew a little square covered in small parallel lines to represent the rain. She had not done that before, but it was a special day for her—the day that Fitzroy had made her feel truly wanted.

"What are you doing in here, Cettie?"

She turned in startled surprise. It was Adam Creigh. It seemed he had been passing along in the corridor and had stopped upon noticing her at the desk. The servants were used to Cettie being there. Her heart was still racing from surprise, but Adam didn't look accusing, only curious.

"I'm counting the tick marks," she explained. Holding the pencil, she pointed it toward the glass tube without touching it.

He approached the desk and looked over her shoulder at her ledger. "May I?" he asked.

Cettie nodded, only a little embarrassed, and he slid the book over and started glancing down the columns of numbers she had written there. He flipped through some of the pages, his head bent over the scrawl.

"So you are counting the tick marks on the glass," he said. "And the numbers change every few days, is it?"

"Yes," she answered. "We don't understand why. Fitzroy has been studying it a long time. I thought I would help keep track."

He nodded, impressed. "What does this mark mean?" He pointed to the square she had just drawn.

"It's raining today," she said.

"Ah. Do you know where quicksilver comes from?" he asked.

She wrinkled her nose. "The silver mines at Dolcoath."

He nodded. "I've seen it when it comes out. It sticks to the rocks in little globs. You have to harvest it. There isn't much we can do with it, of course. It's a curious metal, though, the only one that is liquid. Don't ever taste it, Cettie. It's poisonous. I treated a man who had swallowed some after losing a bet with other miners." He shook his head at the memory. "The man died. What a bad bet. People gamble over the strangest things."

Cettie's eyes went wide. "That's awful."

"It was awful. I can't wait to go to school to learn everything I can about the Mysteries. When you are fourteen, you will as well."

Cettie smiled. "I hope so. It makes me so curious when I see the evidence of them. Like the music coming through the walls."

"Exactly!" Adam said, his eyes gleaming. "Down below, most people are very superstitious. They don't *want* to know. Even if they were given a chance to study at the schools, they'd be too afraid. Why aren't you?"

"I don't know," Cettie answered. "I've always enjoyed learning. I love to read, love to observe things. I didn't know how to before I came here, but now . . . it feels like I'll never stop asking questions. Maybe I have too many."

Adam chuckled. "It's not possible to have too many. You have a mind for the Mysteries of Wind, I should think. Is that your preference?"

"I think so," she answered truthfully. Then she bit her lip. "That is, if Fitzroy can afford to send me to school. I've heard he's already paid off my deed. He's spent so much money on me already."

Adam cocked his head to the side. "Well, if it came down to it, he should probably send you to school before me. My father had the opportunity of saving his wealth to pay for my education. He gambled it away on a speculation instead. You never had the opportunity. I would hate to see you deprived of it."

She was touched by his concern. "But I feel the same way," she said. "It wasn't your fault that your father . . . lost his money."

Adam shrugged. "In a way, I'm glad that he did. Who is to say what kind of man I would have become if I'd kept my father's wealth?" He gave her a knowing look. "But I shouldn't speak ill of the family. I owe them everything, and I'm not complaining." He slid the book back to her. "Have you ever been to the far side of the grounds, down past the willows? There is a rookery of sorts there. Some of the most interesting species of crow make their nests in these heights. Have you seen it?"

"I haven't," Cettie said with interest.

"If you and Anna would like to see it, we can go there tomorrow perhaps? I think she would like it, too. I'm not certain she knows about it."

Cettie wondered at his words, at his desire to show the nests to Anna as well. But perhaps this was a good sign for her friend. She felt indebted to Anna and wanted her to be happy.

"I think we'd both like that," Cettie said.

"Tomorrow, then," he said, bowing his head to her. He started to leave, then paused and turned back. "It wouldn't be proper, you know, for the two of us to be alone together like that. I hope she's willing to come. I think you'd especially like it."

She felt her cheeks burning a little. "Thank you."

"We'll see each other at dinner, then," he said with a smile, nodding once again, and then departed.

CHAPTER NINETEEN
BEHIND LOCKED DOORS

The lights in the sitting room dimmed, signaling the end of dancing practice, which always wrapped up the day after the children's studies ended with Miss Farnworth. The strains of another song had just begun, but the sound had faded into silence before the notes could be heard. Phinia let out a groan of displeasure and quickly turned to her father, who was sitting in his favorite stuffed chair reading a book.

"Father, just one more dance, please. It's 'Genny's Market'!"

In the time Cettie had spent at Fog Willows, she had become familiar with the tunes of the family favorites. Each one had an interesting and peculiar name and a rhythm and a series of steps all its own, which had slowly begun to form in her mind. One of the brother-and-sister pair's favorites was "Genny's Market."

Fitzroy glanced up over his book. He looked weary and tired, and Cettie could see that he would rather send everyone off to bed. Lady Maren was already asleep on the couch.

"Just one more," he said. "And only because it's 'Genny's Market.'"

Phinia threw her arms around Fitzroy's neck and kissed him. There was the familiar pulse in the air, the quiver of some hidden magic, and the music filled the room again. It had already started, but they hadn't missed much.

With the arrival of Adam Creigh to the manor, Anna finally had a dance partner who wasn't Cettie. Her cheeks were flushed from the exercise and the closeness to the young man she admired. Cettie knew the moves and wished that she could have joined them, but she lacked a partner. She watched Anna and Adam with a little thrill of excitement. The dancing looked so enjoyable. Her favorite part was when the dancers circled each other, the gentleman's hand on the lady's back, gazing into each other's eyes—which was the custom, of course. Many a young woman had undoubtedly swooned to be held in such a way with an admiring gaze fixed on her. Social dancing was how individuals from any class fell in love with each other. But it was also a calculated thing, a test of sorts. Missing a step, turning in the wrong direction at the wrong time could cause a fall from grace and prevent an invitation into more elevated social circles. As Cettie watched, it made her think of the Way of Ice and Shadows and how each movement was sculpted to a purpose. She had a precise mind, and such things appealed to her. She wanted to get it right.

All too soon, the song ended, and the two couples clapped.

"I hope they play it at the Hardings' ball next week," Phinia said.

"Are they still having the ball?" Fitzroy asked with concern.

"Indeed," Stephen replied, reverting to the formal tone he usually took when addressing his father. "Mother says the invitation already arrived."

"I should think they could ill afford it," Fitzroy answered, shaking his head.

"But they always host one before everyone leaves for school," Phinia said. "It's tradition."

"Not all decisions are a matter of cost and calculation, Father, surely," Stephen said. There was a tone of judgment and superiority in his voice that grated on Cettie's nerves.

Fitzroy did not respond to the subtle rebuke. Surely if Stephen took as much interest in learning about the household and its costs and the struggles happening at the Dolcoath mines as he did in high society, he would be more discreet. Fitzroy's forbearance was admirable, and Cettie wished her own heart didn't flare up with resentment whenever Stephen and Phinia showed their ingratitude to their parents.

"Thank you for being my partner tonight," Anna told Adam, blushing furiously.

"I enjoyed it," he replied, offering a short bow. Then he looked at Cettie. "The rooks, then? Tomorrow?"

Cettie smiled and nodded cheerfully.

Now that the music was ended and the lights were dimming throughout the manor, it was time for bed. Though Mrs. Pullman hadn't acted last night, Cettie could not help but fear she would send the ghost to them tonight. Part of her wished to warn Anna, and yet . . .

Mrs. Pullman would surely find out, but that wasn't the only thing that stopped Cettie. She could not forget the look on Mr. Savage's face the night of the river walk. He'd blamed her for releasing that fearsome beast. What if Anna decided Cettie—and not Mrs. Pullman—was the problem? What if Fitzroy and Lady Maren agreed? She hadn't belonged to this household for nearly as long as the old woman.

Wouldn't it be best to wait until the ghost arrived? Until it could be seen—and stopped—by Fitzroy?

Anna grasped Cettie's hand and pulled her away. Stephen and Phinia began to talk excitedly about the Hardings' ball and whom they expected would be there. Once they were in the hall, Anna was fit to burst.

"I had such a good time this evening," Anna said, squeezing her hands. "He's so gentle and thoughtful. And so tall—he's nearly as tall as Stephen. Adam did the dances very well, don't you think?"

"He did indeed," Cettie said with an encouraging smile. "The two of you looked very charming together."

"Do you think so? It makes me so eager to attend school. They teach all of the dances there. There are so many, and the dancing masters can be quite strict. I'm grateful Stephen has been teaching us."

As they turned the corner, they nearly collided with Mrs. Pullman, who gave them each a stern frown. She was holding her lamp, as she always did at night. Cettie felt a chill from her presence, something that choked her good spirits. Anna looked frightened and shrank slightly back.

"Why aren't you two already abed?" she asked in a scolding tone. "The lights dimmed a quarter hour ago. The master will be displeased."

Anna's countenance shrank even more from the rebuke, and Cettie felt Mrs. Pullman's eyes turn to her next. It was the first time they had been so alone since her return from the City. The gaze of the older woman could have turned someone into stone. Cettie could feel the animosity seething from her. It was a look that tried to do harm.

"We were with Father," Anna said in a subdued voice.

Mrs. Pullman's frown deepened. "You coaxed him for another dance, I take it? How insensitive. Your father's troubles weigh on him like stones. And you think only of your own needs. Well, you are children, after all." She jerked her head. "Off to bed."

Even though her voice was a dismissal, she glared at Cettie with a look of warning—a look that guaranteed her revenge would indeed come in its own due time.

Anna pulled on Cettie's hand, and the two of them walked hastily away. Cettie glanced back and saw Mrs. Pullman staring at them still, her face wrinkled with her deep frown. A chill ran through her, and she quickened her steps.

As they walked down the corridor, they passed the locked door that had hooked Cettie's attention. The same strange feeling emanated from it, compelling her attention. She slowed her steps to gaze at it. A hunger of curiosity swept through Cettie's being, even though the feeling made her slightly ill.

It was as if a song were beckoning to her, only it was not music she heard. But it had the *feeling* of music. A song that was being played wrong.

When they reached Anna's room, they started getting ready for bed. On Fitzroy's order, Cettie's few belongings had already been moved to a chest at the foot of the bed.

"I'm so grateful you decided to stay with me," Anna said after shutting the door. "Sometimes, when I get scared at night, I'll go to Phinia's room, and she's not very pleasant about it. And she'll be leaving for school herself, which would have made me the only child left in the manor. I was afraid I'd be so lonely." She gave Cettie such a dear look.

Cettie knew what that felt like. The two girls helped each other unbutton their dresses. "I'm grateful, Anna. Mrs. Pullman isn't very happy with either of us."

"Mrs. Pullman is angry that I went to Father. She knows that I did. She's the keeper, how could she not know it? It takes a little while for her anger to cool, but it will."

"How did she come to work at Fog Willows? She doesn't seem the kind of person . . . well, she isn't exactly the kind of person I thought your father would hire." It was as much as she felt she could openly say.

Anna turned and looked at her in confusion. "She isn't."

Cettie was taken aback.

"I keep forgetting that you don't know these things already. Our grandfather brought on Mrs. Pullman and her son. Her husband died of illness long ago. I don't remember how it happened, but he died young. Mrs. Pullman was hired because she was like Grandfather. She thought like him and acted as he would. But Grandfather and Father were very different."

"So he's no longer alive?" She immediately chuffed at herself. "That was a foolish question. He must not be if your father inherited Fog Willows."

The girls slipped on their nightclothes and crawled under the thick blankets. "Grandfather was very strict," Anna said with a small smile. "Father has told us stories about him. When he was young, they took in the daughter of a family whose fortunes had been blighted. It happened a lot more back then, I think. Out of duty, Grandfather brought the girl home to Fog Willows. She was fourteen, and Father was sixteen and away at school. When he got back, the two of them became friends. Well, more than friends! They fell in love. Grandfather was so upset when he found out. He was angry that he had taken in the girl. He charged Mrs. Pullman with keeping them apart."

Cettie listened with fascination. It was difficult imagining Fitzroy as a young man Stephen's age. And it was especially difficult imagining him acting spoiled like Stephen. But the story was already helping her see Mrs. Pullman in a new light.

"What happened then?" Cettie asked eagerly.

"Well, the two of them were determined to marry, despite Grandfather's wishes. Father did not have any siblings, so if Grandfather didn't choose him to inherit Fog Willows, the family would lose control of the manor. So he took steps to separate the two. Father was sent to the Ministry of War with a commission. The girl—he's never told us her name—was sent to the Fells." Her voice grew quieter. "Father doesn't speak of this very often. I've heard most of the story from Mother and Phinia. Mother came from a wealthy family, all sisters and one brother, but when her father died, her brother became greedy and refused to give his sisters anything. They were forced to live down below even though they'd spent their lives in a manor in the clouds. Sometimes they were invited to society gatherings in Lockhaven out of pity. Or for something to gossip about."

"How could their brother do that to them?" Cettie gasped in outrage.

"It's one of the Mysteries of Law," Anna answered. "Once my uncle had full control of the estate, he overrode the things that his father had set in place to care for his daughters. Having a good advocate is so important. Everyone says his wife made him do it."

"So what did your mother and her family do? How did they live?"

"My grandmother, on my mother's side, is a relation to Sir Jordan Harding. That's how my parents met, through him, at one of the balls the Hardings like to throw."

It made much more sense now. And she could imagine someone like Stephen doing a similar thing to Anna, but not to Phinia. "Could your father send Mrs. Pullman away if he wanted to?"

"It's not that easy," Anna said. "And Father isn't like that. He's very patient. Mrs. Pullman is absolutely devoted to him and Fog Willows. She cares more about his future than he does. But she certainly takes more after Grandfather's style. She's very capable, though. Running a manor this large isn't easy. Not many have the strength of will to master all the responsibilities, I should think."

Cettie noticed the light in the room had dimmed just a little more. "Mrs. Pullman hates me."

Anna frowned. "That's a strong word, Cettie. I'm sure she doesn't. I think she saw the pain it caused my father to be separated from the girl he loved. Maybe she's afraid that Stephen will start liking you!" She giggled softly.

Cettie shuddered. "I don't think that's possible!"

"Well, if you become adopted, then it cannot happen. You'd be like my true sister. Which you already are." She leaned over to kiss Cettie's cheek.

Weariness stole through Cettie, and she rested her head on the soft pillow, such a stark difference from sleeping on the bare wooden floor. Although her body was tired, her mind was still awake. The room became darker still. Soon, she could hear Anna's breathing change as she fell asleep.

Cettie waited for that prickle of awareness to go down her back. The anticipation of it tortured her. She silently begged the ghost to stay away, to leave her alone.

The slow tread of footsteps came down the hall. It was a familiar sound. It was the sound of Mrs. Pullman's shoes. Cettie cringed at it as terror began to wriggle up her throat. The sound of the footfalls stopped at the door of the room. Cettie could feel Mrs. Pullman standing there; she could sense the emotions of anger and determination.

Please don't come in. Please don't come in.

The feeling of safety she had had earlier dissipated in an instant. She felt alone, even with Anna sleeping beside her, and she felt vulnerable. All her life, the adults she had known had failed her. Her own parents, whoever they were, had neglected her. Each household she had lived in since, each person who had taken her deed, had failed her. In the end, Fitzroy would fail her, too. No one was *that* good.

Mrs. Pullman was biding her time, training the next generation. Stephen would become like the grandfather, not like his own father. In time, Mrs. Pullman's will would rule once again at Fog Willows, and it would be for the good of the family. The grandfather had become prime minister for a season, after all. The family's fortunes had changed because of his shrewd decisions. He had been a true Fitzroy. But the waif had to go. She had to be persuaded to leave.

Cettie didn't understand why all these thoughts were jumbling inside her head. Why it felt that she could *hear* what Mrs. Pullman was thinking as she stood outside the door. The thoughts were dark and terrible. They made her feel sick inside.

And then she heard a key slip into the lock and twist. The lock clicked fast into place.

This is the room. But not tonight. Not while the master is here.

Yes, madame.

Cettie recognized the voice of the thought. She had heard its taunts before. Cettie shrank beneath the bedsheets. It was the tall ghost. The one with no eyes.

It had finally found her.

CHAPTER TWENTY

ROOKS

It was a long, anxious night. No matter how Cettie tried to control her thoughts, she could still hear it over and over again, the clicking noise of the key in the lock and the silent exchange between Mrs. Pullman and the ghost. How had Mrs. Pullman summoned the tall ghost to Fog Willows? How had she known that it was the one Cettie feared most?

She knew it wouldn't come for her that night, but it *would* happen. Mrs. Pullman would get her way, no matter what. And she wouldn't just punish Cettie—she would punish Anna, too. Anna, who wouldn't even see the thing that tormented her. The thought of her friend suffering made her screw up her courage. She would explain the situation to Fitzroy before he left them again. She had to, even if Mrs. Pullman witnessed her doing it.

Cettie awoke the next morning to the sound of the lock being turned. It was dawn, and Mrs. Pullman was already up and around. Anna still slept, and for a moment Cettie was tempted to lie abed. But she rose, dressed quietly, and then made her way out to the gazebo trail to practice with Raj Sarin. The cold made her shiver, but the storm had passed, and the clouds had all been tamed, though they lingered in the western sky. It was a beautiful morning, and although she was tired from lying awake half the night, she felt a throb of hope that things would get better after she finally shared the truth with Fitzroy.

"Good morning, Cettie *Saeed*," Raj Sarin said with a smile of greeting, not interrupting his stance, which she recognized as *crane searches the water for fish*.

She quickly joined his posture, mimicking his actions. "What does Saeed mean? Is it from your mother tongue?"

"It is," he answered. "It means . . . Cettie of the Clouds."

It was Raj Sarin's way of saying that she *belonged* at Fog Willows. Her heart warmed at the sentiment. By the time she had finished the exercises, she was no longer cold, and she had learned several new stances and forms.

Anna was up and getting ready by the time Cettie returned. She normally slept in later, but she could be counted on to rise early if the reason was good, and apparently spending time with Adam Creigh was an ample enticement.

The family ate the morning meal together punctually, except the schedule was a little laxer on the days when Fitzroy wasn't home. When one of the children showed up later than usual, he would sometimes say, in his understated way, "Early is on time." Cettie didn't know what it meant, but she always strove to be early to breakfast.

The meals were never eaten in silence. Phinia was very exuberant and always had something to say, and Stephen could be counted on for his share of witty remarks. Anna was usually quiet around the others. Adam's presence at the family meals shifted the normal routine. He received much of the attention as the family asked him about his experiences working with the doctor at Dolcoath.

"Mama," Phinia asked breathlessly, "is Adam invited to the Hardings' ball as well? They know he is staying with us, surely." Without even waiting for an answer, she turned her eyes on his eagerly. "You're a very good dancer now, Adam. I shouldn't be ashamed to stand up with you at the ball. Just try not to squash my toes!"

"I will do my best not to," Adam replied, trying not to smile. He seemed discomfited by all the attention.

Lady Maren and Fitzroy sat next to each other, not on opposite ends of the table as some couples did. They usually held hands during breakfast, which Cettie found very charming. Lady Maren gave her husband a covert look and then answered, "Yes, Phinia. The invitation specifically included Mr. Creigh." She paused a moment and, before Phinia could interject another comment, added, "And Cettie is also coming."

A look of disappointment clouded Phinia's face. "Oh? But she's not of age, Mother."

"Neither is Anna and she is coming, too," Lady Maren said pointedly. "And I do recall a certain young lady who begged and received permission to attend her first Harding ball at twelve. We will all be there to help chaperone. It's not my youngest two that I'm worried about."

A strangled silence fell across the table. Phinia's cheeks were flushed, but she wisely said nothing.

"My sister may be paying a visit soon," Lady Maren went on in a more cheerful tone.

"Which one?" Stephen asked, always in control. Always a little aloof.

"Aunt Juliana."

Phinia's enthusiasm was restored. "I adore Aunt Juliana! Has she finished the trading deal with Atovincia? She's so clever. Will she be coming to the ball?"

"If the weather holds," Lady Maren said. "I wish everyone could come, but my mother is getting very old, and Ariah has her hands full caring for her." Cettie watched as Fitzroy gently stroked his wife's knuckles with his thumb. He gave her a tender look, one that promised a visit in the near future. Cettie wondered whether Lady Maren's sisters lived above or below. No one had ever told her, and it seemed wrong to ask.

The morning meal ended shortly thereafter, and Adam fulfilled his promise by taking Cettie and Anna on a walk of the grounds. They passed over the stone bridge that connected two separately floating sections of the grounds. Even though the sky was clear, there were clouds beneath the bridge, which made the crossing less frightening. Cettie and Anna held hands as they went over it.

"When we were younger," Anna told Cettie, "we used to have to dance across the bridge. Stephen said it was the only way we could keep from falling off. He was only teasing, but he said it so seriously that we all did it for years."

"I remember that," Adam said with a chuckle. They walked at a languid pace, never rushing. Adam pointed out some of the rock formations and their similarities to Dolcoath.

"The tree roots have burrowed into the seams and cracks of the stone and cling with a tenacious grip. The trunks are even firmer up here than their sister trees in Dolcoath. I asked Fitzroy about it, and he said that it's because of the wind. Trees become hardier when exposed to rougher environments. The trees of Fog Willows, even the willows themselves, are tougher because they live in the clouds than they would be if they grew in a calm, quiet valley down below. He wouldn't explain *why*, but he said I'd learn it in school."

"I can't wait to go to school," Anna said with a sigh.

"At the schools, you study all of the Mysteries, do you not?" Cettie wondered.

Adam nodded encouragingly. "Yes. But you must pick one to master. They are far too intricate for one person to learn them at that level. Now, do you see that outcropping of rock over there?" He gestured with a finger. "We're going down that little ridge off the path. That's where the rooks are roosting."

Cettie felt a pulse of alarm. It was such a long way down. "Fitzroy warned me never to leave the path."

"He showed me the rooks himself," Adam said. "And I already obtained his permission to bring you here this morning." He gave her a reassuring smile. "Staying on the path is a wise course, especially when an area is new and the risk of danger is high. It will be all right."

She trusted his assurance, and, before she knew it, she was scrambling over the rocks with the others. Mrs. Pullman's tower loomed above them, and she couldn't help but wonder if the keeper of the house was watching them from one of the many windows. That was an unnerving thought, but she tried to focus on stepping gracefully from one broken rock to another. Anna clung to her hand as they both negotiated the path. Adam bounded easily ahead of them, and soon all three were flushed from the descent. They followed the gorge but had not yet begun to climb up the other side.

"Watch for the moss growing in the shadows," Adam warned. As they reached the bottom of the small gorge, their view of the manor was obscured.

When they reached a spot with a long gap between the rocks, Adam waited on the other side and held out his hand, helping each of them step across.

"We're almost there," he said. They continued along the bottom of the gorge, and the way became tangled with rocks and scrub. When they rounded an outcrop of rock, they started up the other side, which was steeper. It was an enjoyable climb, not too difficult but strenuous enough that it made breathing a struggle. But the noise of the rooks banished any thought of discomfort.

At last, they reached their destination, and Cettie could see the proud black birds perched in the trees on the edge of the mass of rock.

"We won't go any farther," Adam said, finding a large lopsided rock and gesturing for them both to sit down. He squatted at the edge of the boulder. A trickle of sweat raced down the side of his face, but he seemed oblivious to it.

"The crows up here are bigger than they are down below," he explained, directing their eyes toward the birds. "If you look at the upper third of the branches, you can see their massive nests. The trees are all full of them. They're easier to see in the autumn when the leaves have fallen. The trees are skeletal then, and the nests stand out."

Cettie squinted, watching one of the birds as it landed in a tree. "I see a nest!" she exclaimed. She pointed to Anna to help her.

"Excellent!" Adam said. "There are probably forty to fifty birds living in this rookery. A group of this size is called a parliament."

Anna looked at him in surprise. "Like the government? How curious."

"I thought so as well," Adam said. "Fitzroy explained that these birds have unusual customs. For example, they mate for life. If a bird loses its mate, it will not attach to another bird for the rest of its life. We don't see that behavior mimicked in our world, do we? The other curious thing about them, and what earned them the name parliament, is that they will gather around a single crow in a cluster. They'll grunt and caw as if they're debating a law. And then, as if the judge has found the crow to be guilty, they will all pounce on him and peck him to death!"

"How awful," Cettie said, shrinking inside. "Have you seen it happen?"

"I have," he answered. "It happened my first time here, when Fitzroy showed me this place."

"Why do the crows kill one another?" Cettie asked.

Adam rubbed his chin. "No one knows. But like all Mysteries, it's just waiting for someone with the right mind to come along and answer the question." He rapped his knuckles on the stone beneath him. "I mean, if you drop a stone, it will fall. Unless it doesn't. Once you understand the principle of something, it is no longer a Mystery."

"There are so many of them," Anna said, gazing in wonder at all the birds. It seemed as if the rooks had finally taken notice of them, because they were growing noisier and noisier.

"Noisy brutes, aren't they?" Adam said with a laugh.

Cettie was grateful he had suggested bringing them there. It was enjoyable seeing this new aspect of Fog Willows. How many more hidden places existed here?

The sun warmed Cettie's shoulders as the three of them sat on the rock, talking and observing the birds.

"Look, a zephyr!" Anna suddenly called out, pointing. It was coming from the west, so they had a full view of it as it approached the floating estate. There was no doubt that it was coming their way.

Seeing it brought back memories of her first ride up to Fog Willows. How long ago it seemed. Other memories started to surface as she watched the airship approach. Of the scoldings and beatings Miss Charlotte had given her. Of the desperate feelings of hunger that had ravaged her insides day and night. She thought about the children sometimes. Their whimpers and cries at night. The ghosts of the dead that haunted the tenements. Especially the tall one. A shudder ran through her.

"Are you all right, Cettie?"

Adam was gazing at her in concern. She tried to smile, but it felt forced. She simply nodded.

Cettie Saeed. That was the name Raj Sarin had given her.

Cettie of the Clouds.

Right now, she felt more like Cettie of the Fells.

She looked at Adam. "When the rooks pass judgment, do any of the other crows intervene to save the one condemned?"

He looked at her curiously, then shook his head no.

"A zephyr always brings news," Anna said, squeezing her arm. "Let's go back."

By the time they reached the path, the zephyr had already landed. They could see it suspended above the landing pad, the rope ladder dangling. It looked exactly like the zephyr that Lieutenant Staunton had come on. As they approached, a little breathless from the pace, Cettie realized the man standing there *was* Lieutenant Staunton. He looked just as she remembered him, and a pit opened in her stomach. Worries came wriggling out, like a loose brick overturned to reveal a nest of cowering insects.

"Hello again, ma'am," Lieutenant Staunton said, nodding to her.

Cettie's throat went dry. Was it coincidence that he'd returned?

Then she saw Fitzroy coming from the doors wearing his thick overcoat, the one he had given her to keep her warm. He was being called on again. No, he couldn't be leaving. Not so soon.

"What is it, Father?" Anna asked with true concern. Adam's brow furrowed.

Fitzroy saw Cettie and paused, his brows drawing together. He looked agitated and distressed. "I thought I'd have to find you at the rookery. I'm glad you are back." He turned to Adam and Anna. "If you'd give us a moment, please."

"Of course," Adam said in a hushed tone. He and Anna stepped away.

The ground was tilting. Cettie felt herself go dizzy.

"Cettie," Fitzroy said. "Do you remember Lieutenant Staunton?"

"I do," she answered thickly.

"He brought news from my advocate, Mr. Sloan." He was wringing his hands behind his back. That wasn't a good sign. His voice dropped even lower, and she struggled to hear it. "He thinks he's found your parents. I need to go with him to be sure. I'll return as soon as I can."

CHAPTER TWENTY-ONE

THE FELLS

Cettie feared she would vomit. The news didn't fill her with excitement; it filled her with blackness. She had no memory of her parents, other than the dim impressions of a man, possibly her father, in uniform. Whoever her parents were, she had been deeded as a small child. Some of the homes she'd been sent to had been very bad. If her parents were truly alive, they'd never looked for her. They clearly didn't care that *she* was alive—and yet they could ruin everything.

She didn't want to leave Fog Willows. She didn't want to abandon her new life. Tears stung her eyes, and she looked down, feeling miserable.

Fitzroy put his hand on her shoulder. "Mr. Sloan is very good at what he does. Things are not totally certain. That's why I want to go myself."

She looked up at him, her heart in her throat. "Can I come, too, please?" she begged. If she stayed, Mrs. Pullman would attack her and Anna tonight. She'd send the tall ghost in to torment them.

He frowned. She could tell he wanted to save her pain. That he was experiencing pain himself. The pain of dashed hopes. The pain of a wretched decision.

"I think it would be for the best if you did," he finally answered. "Fetch a cloak."

She did as he asked and quickly boarded the zephyr. The return went quickly compared to the journey to Lockhaven or Dolcoath. It was strange how close they were to the Fells, which felt a lifetime away. Her sense of distance and perspective had altered.

As the zephyr glided down, Cettie stared at the approaching ramshackle roofs, her heart full of pain and dread. As she began to smell the soot, her body trembled. In her mind, she thought about *snake resting in a pool* and *fierce tiger rakes its claws.*

Courage, Cettie Saeed, she told herself. *It is better to know than to not know.*

A gentle hand touched her shoulder, and when she looked up, she saw Fitzroy's concerned face. Surely part of him was tempted to let her go now that her parents had been found. It would free him to receive the office he had wanted, to rise to a position from which he could help other children like herself.

"How are you holding up, Cettie?" he asked her in his kind way.

"I'm not afraid," she answered. And, truly, fear wasn't the feeling that troubled her. It was the suspense of not knowing what would happen to her. It was the dread of possibly returning to the Fells permanently. Of fending off the ghosts each and every night.

"You're a brave little woman, then," he said wryly. "I'll be afraid for both of us."

"Are you afraid, Fitzroy?" she asked him in surprise. She remembered how boldly he had stood against the creature from the grotto—the menace that had threatened the village of Dolcoath.

"I don't want to lose you to this place," he said, eyes full of despair as he gazed at the scene unfolding below them.

It was true. Things got lost in the Fells. People were taken, abducted in the streets during the day and found murdered in alleys blocks away. Even worse things happened at night. There were gangs that preyed on anyone weaker than they. It was no wonder that so many people set their hopes on the lottery that might give them a chance to work in one of the cloud manors.

A pigeon rose from a rooftop and flew past the sky ship in a whir of feathers and cooing. For a moment, Cettie feared it would crash into them.

The streets below were thronged with people, and the sun shone high overhead. She saw the rubbish carters and could hear the muck scrapers as the zephyr glided over to a large central square where a few other sky ships were moored just above the roofline. There was a huge fountain down below spraying jets of water into the air, and washerwomen were gathered around the rim, tending to their chores. Little children played beside the women. Other children were working, wringing water from the garments.

Cettie had never been to this part of the Fells before. It looked a little cleaner than the areas she'd occupied, although there were easily a thousand pigeons roaming the cobbled square below, pecking at crumbs and gutter drippings. The air smelled of pungent, damp rags. Some older people were sitting on the steps, selling their handmade wares for a pittance, their faces lined with seams and crags. These were the people who were too old or injured to work in a factory any longer. Cettie's heart filled with pity as she saw their wrinkled faces.

"Down we go, sir," said Lieutenant Staunton. He glanced at Cettie, eyes hardened to the suffering below, the sort of misery he dealt with daily. Fitzroy climbed out first, and as Cettie followed, she witnessed a hive of urchins throng him, begging for coins.

"Get on, then!" Staunton shouted down at the crowd. "Hurry down, lass. I need to dispel that rabble."

"It's quite all right," Fitzroy said. "Good day, children. I have a meeting with my advocate at the present, but if you wait for me in the square, you'll each get a farthing when I come out." He was instantly surrounded by cheering children. As Cettie reached the cobblestones, someone bumped into her from the throng below.

"Watch it, boy!" Staunton growled. The rope ladder quivered as the lieutenant hurried down. Cettie felt a hand grip her elbow, and she turned and looked into the eyes of Joses, her companion and friend from Miss Charlotte's.

He had a feverish, hungry look in his eyes, the same wasted cheeks and smudges that she'd always tried to clean away. His dark hair was matted with dirt beneath his jaunty cap, but his blue eyes were still keen.

"Joses!" she gasped, giving in to the urge to hug him despite his filthy clothes.

He whispered in her ear. "It's a sham, Cettie. A trick. Don't fall for it."

She looked at him in concern—what was a trick?—but he released his grip and melted into the press of children crowding Fitzroy, though taller than most of them. Fitzroy turned to her as several young girls started tugging at her dress and begging her for a coin.

"If you please, miss . . ."

"Can you spare a farthing, miss . . ."

"You have pretty hair, miss . . ."

"Go on! Go on!" Staunton railed, and the little girls scattered in fear. His gruff manners and angry tone were enough to warrant obedience, but his uniform made it prompter than usual. "Clear away! Now!"

As the mob of children began to disperse, Fitzroy joined Cettie's side. She searched the crowd for Joses and finally caught sight of him turning a corner into an alley. He stopped once, looking back at her and nodding, and then slipped away.

"I wish I got down faster," Staunton grumbled. "That lanky one has been eluding us for months."

Cettie stared at him. "Joses?"

"That's the one," the officer said angrily. "He ran away from the shelter and has taken up with a street gang. Refuses to work for the deed that was signed. Ungrateful brat. Gave up a chance to learn to live in the streets night and day. Did he steal anything from you?"

Cettie shook her head. "I don't have anything to steal," she answered. Her feeling of disquiet returned. What had Joses meant? Did he know something?

Staunton pursed his lips and then guided her and Fitzroy to a two-story building wedged between other professional buildings. Sloan and Teitelbaum, the sign said.

"Go on!" Staunton glowered as the children slunk nearby, always keeping out of reach. Cettie saw the washerwomen at the fountain observing her with disdain. They probably thought she was some rich heiress . . . not one of them. The faces were all unfamiliar, but they had a universal look of hardship and weariness. The sun struggled to get past the haze.

Fitzroy took her elbow and guided her up the tall steps. Her heart churned with emotion—worry for her friend, concern about what she was facing, and curiosity about meeting the advocate who had been working on her adoption. The front entry was dark, and she felt something press against her mind, an awareness of sorts that felt stern and brooding. After she crossed the threshold, the strange feeling left. The inner corridor was cramped, and they had to walk single file, but it opened to an office with several wooden desks and walls that were crowded with shelves and cupboard doors. There were several young men there scratching with pencils. Most of them had their heads down at their work. One of them, a very young man probably her own age, had stopped writing when he saw her. A little flush came to his cheeks, and a timid smile surfaced on his mouth before he looked away.

There were filthy windows high up on the wall, letting in a slanting shaft of light. Motes of dust hung in the shaft like a flurry of tiny snow. She'd forgotten the way soot marred everything in the Fells. Cettie's shoes thumped noisily on the floor planks, and she gazed around at all the small brass knobs on the cupboard doors. She glanced back at the young man who had smiled at her and found him still staring at her. When she noticed him, another little flush came to his cheeks, and he hurriedly looked away and went back to his work.

They encountered two old men inside the inner sanctum. One was sitting in a stuffed chair and holding a silver cane. He had a warm smile, feathery white hair around the sides of his head, and just a little hair on top that was combed down the back of his head. He had spectacles on the bridge of his nose. Within the chamber, Cettie felt as if dozens of eyes were watching her. She sensed the presence of power. It seemed to thrum from the wooden panels on the walls. Throb from the floor. Vibrate in the ceiling. It felt as if the room were a living being that held deep secrets. And perhaps it did . . . the Mysteries of Law were at work here.

The other old man sat at the edge of his chair, arms folded and one hand tapping his lip with a sturdy finger. He had gray hair, not white, and it was thick and groomed and very full. He was short in stature, but had a powerful gaze and intense eyes. He did not look unkind, just more serious than the one sitting in the stuffed chair.

Fitzroy cleared his throat. "Mr. Sloan, Mr. Teitelbaum. Thank you for the summons."

"Thank you for coming so promptly, Lord Fitzroy," said the white-haired man. He lifted his spectacles higher so he could get a better look at Cettie. "This is the young woman at long last?"

Fitzroy bowed his head and introduced her. "This is Cettie. I'd like you to meet Mr. Sloan"—he gestured to the white-haired man who was smiling—"and Mr. Teitelbaum." The gray-haired man nodded solemnly.

"I asked Mr. Teitelbaum here to go over the facts with me," Mr. Sloan said. "We were discussing them before you arrived. This young lady is rather famous in this office," he said with a chuckle, taking off his spectacles and turning them over in his hands. "Many of our advocates have been working on her case for months. I'm glad you brought her, Fitzroy. She should be one of the first to hear the news."

"So you've found them? Found her parents?"

Mr. Sloan inclined his head. "One of them. Let me say what we have come to learn and how we learned it. I will be brief because the couple we interviewed is waiting in Mr. Teitelbaum's chambers."

Cettie felt a throb in her heart and started trembling.

"Indeed," Fitzroy said, clearing his throat. "I should like to meet them."

"Of course. Now to the facts. We have been unable to find the original deed to this young woman, but we did discover what we believe to be a copy of it. Her name, as we have come to learn, is Celestina Pratt. Cettie is a derivative. The father, Mr. George Pratt, was discharged from the Ministry of War for excessive gambling debts. He was a sharpshooter for the admiralty—a dragoon. He has had an ill turn of luck in parting ways from the ministry and continues to accumulate excessive debt. He's strong, soft hearted, and embarrassed by this whole affair. He trains young officers who cannot afford to attend regular school. His wife, whom he calls Lady Admiral, is clearly too young to be the mother of the child. The mother, as we understand it, is still unknown. Apparently, the child was conceived in a sort of dalliance and deposited, as a babe, on Mr. Pratt's property in the Fells. He cared for the babe the best he could, but his lifestyle made the situation life-threatening for the child, and he'd already fallen on hard times. So he signed her away in a deed to raise money to settle some of his debts. He'd intended to come for her after meeting his obligations, which, unfortunately, he has proven incapable of doing."

Cettie felt as if the world were spinning around. So they still had not found her mother . . . and from what they'd said, they likely wouldn't. Her heart hammered in her chest.

"What kind of debts, Mr. Sloan?" Fitzroy asked hoarsely.

"It's a considerable sum, Fitzroy."

"And I would like to know it."

Mr. Sloan looked to Mr. Teitelbaum and then back again. "By our best reckoning, Mr. Pratt is in debt to the order of forty thousand."

It was such an astonishing number that Cettie gasped aloud.

"Good heavens," Fitzroy blurted.

Mr. Sloan nodded. "As you can see, he is in no position to take back his daughter. I have interviewed Mr. Pratt several times. He had no knowledge of my intention or on whose behalf I was working. I found *him*, not the other way around. There is no intent to blackmail or wrong you. But he, of his own volition, offered up sufficient detail that corroborated what was written in the deed."

Cettie felt like an egg, so fragile she could crack if squeezed too hard. She hungered to meet the man. Mr. George Pratt.

"And there is no record of the mother, then?" Fitzroy asked. "She would have rights over the child as well if she is still living."

"That is true," Mr. Teitelbaum said, "but we have no way of locating her. Mr. Pratt's interests are substantial in this case. You clearly hold the deed and control the child's fate until she is of age. Most children in the Fells never come of age." He said the words so bluntly he made Cettie flinch. "You cannot proceed with an adoption without getting Mr. Pratt's consent. And should he learn who you are, he may very well seek substantial remuneration for that permission."

"In other words," Mr. Sloan said. "He could ruin you."

CHAPTER TWENTY–TWO
Truth Will Out

When Mr. Teitelbaum left to fetch the guests, Cettie felt a mounting sense of pressure. The man George Pratt had to duck to enter the door. He looked uncomfortable in his formal, soot-spotted coat. His boots were so thick and laden with buckles that they jangled as he walked. He had a bluff face, brass-colored hair, and a mustache that came down to the edges of his chin. His hair was slicked back, and he wiped the sweat from his brow with a soiled handkerchief clutched in his gloved hand. She felt a flicker of recognition, but her childhood memories were so distant and vague she couldn't be sure of anything.

Halfway through the door, he paused, then turned awkwardly sideways and tried to let Lady Admiral enter, only he blocked the way.

"Go on in, George," she said with a hint of annoyance. "You're already halfway through. Go on, you big brute."

He shuffled in sideways, exposing a small woman who was closer to Cettie's age than to his. Lady Admiral was no more than twenty, if that, and Mr. Pratt was easily in his thirties.

She had light brown hair and a trim waist and a perpetual look of annoyance. Even though she was young, she had a keen eye and quickly sized up the visitors in the room.

"Who is it?" she demanded quickly. Then her eyes found Cettie's and skewered her with mistrust. "Ah, is this the chit?" She folded her arms and arched an eyebrow.

Cettie's heart quickened, but the big man, Mr. Pratt, still didn't look at her. In fact, he seemed determined not to.

"If you please, Mrs. Pratt," Mr. Sloan said, gesturing for her to be patient.

"I've been waitin' long enough," said Lady Admiral. "Is this the girl? Is this the one you are trying to wheedle on Mr. Pratt and I?"

"Please, Mrs. Pratt," Mr. Sloan said. "Be silent."

Cettie felt something stir in the room, something that streaked past her mind, and suddenly Lady Admiral was gaping like a fish, shocked into silence. Mr. Sloan gave Fitzroy an apologetic look and then shrugged slightly.

"Sometimes we must do what we must do to further the conversation along," Mr. Sloan said. "Mr. George Pratt. Surely you are wondering why we have called you into this meeting with Vice Admiral Brant Fitzroy?"

Mr. Pratt, upon hearing the title, snapped to attention, his huge right arm coming into a salute.

"Be at ease, Mr. Pratt," Fitzroy said apologetically. "I'm no longer with the Ministry of War."

"Pardon my attire, milord," said Mr. Pratt with a husky, weary voice. "I should have worn my regimentals. My apologies!"

Fitzroy waved his hand. The matter was of no consequence. "Mr. Sloan tells me that you've fallen under difficult circumstances."

"Yes, sir. That would be the case, sir." He stood erect still, gazing at the ceiling beams and not down at them.

"How have you accumulated such an impressive load of debt?" Fitzroy asked.

"Mainly from borrowing it, milord. I have schemes, you see. But no head for numbers. I go to bed one night and the amount I owe is one number. And I wake up the next, having done nothing but sleep you see, and it's grown like a monster. I don't understand it, sir. The only thing I can do is borrow more to get out from under it. But I'm a hard worker. I'll work until my bones are gray. Ask Lady Admiral. She can tell you as much."

Cettie did look at Lady Admiral, who was straining against some invisible power that prevented her from speaking. Her complexion was turning a shade of purple. She stamped her foot, but still no words would exit her mouth.

Fitzroy frowned. "Mr. Sloan tells me you are aware that you fathered a child approximately twelve years ago."

"I did, sir," he huffed. "It was a mistake, surely, wild oats and all. I'm ashamed to admit it in the present company of my wife." She swatted him with the back of her hand. He cleared his throat. "I knew it was wrong at the time." He cleared his throat and tugged at his collar. "I've always been brash, milord. Haven't always thought to the end of the row, if you catch my meaning. She was lonely and unloved, poor thing."

Cettie felt more and more awkward for the man. He wiped another layer of sweat from his brow. Even though he was so large and powerful, his mind seemed almost childlike.

"And you have no idea of the lady's identity," Fitzroy pressed. "She was a stranger to you?"

"Indeed, sir," he said with a huff. "I never knew her name. I'm ashamed to admit it, even now. It was wrong of me, sir."

"And so the child was brought to you as a baby," Mr. Sloan said. "And you found yourself unfit to parent this child, so you signed a deed."

"Indeed, sir!" Mr. Pratt said hoarsely. "If you pardon the play on words."

Mr. Sloan rolled his eyes. He looked to Fitzroy for approval. Fitzroy's mouth was a firm, thin line. He nodded curtly.

"Mr. Pratt, it is our belief that the child we are speaking of is the young woman standing by Lord Fitzroy. Your wife's inelegant comments earlier may have given you that information too soon. I think she is shrewd enough to realize what this is about."

Mr. Pratt wiped his mustache with the sodden linen and then coughed into his fist. "If I am understanding you properly, Mr. Sloan, you are telling me—as Lady Admiral told me before we came—that the young woman standing by his lordship is, in fact, the child from the deed I signed. That is my understanding."

He still wouldn't look at her. Cettie's heart yearned for him to look upon her with some kindness, but he seemed so awkward, so uncomfortably embarrassed, and he would do nothing but fidget and stare blankly over their heads. Despite everything, she wanted him to hold her, to show any spark of emotion or tenderness.

"Why do you think you are here, Mr. Pratt?" Fitzroy asked calmly.

"Lady Admiral believes, ahem, that you are returning the . . . the child to us to care for and pay for. I'm in reduced circumstances, milord. It pains me, but it's true. If I hadn't married my landlord's daughter, I would have gone to debtors' prison already."

Fitzroy gave a sharp look to Mr. Sloan, who nodded to affirm the statement.

Mrs. Pratt stamped her foot and pointed to her mouth, giving Mr. Sloan an angry glare.

Fitzroy sighed. "And you have no further knowledge of the child's mother? Her approximate age? Her physical description? Some clue that would help us locate her?"

"She wore a veil, so I could not see her face," said Mr. Pratt. "She never spoke to me, so I do not know her voice, nor would I know it if I heard it now. The assignation was arranged by servants. I was blindfolded, if you please, and went by zephyr."

"Was it in the City?" Fitzroy asked.

"It may have been Lockhaven, but I don't think we flew that long. We went *up*. That's all I remember. I've already told you, milord, that Lady Admiral and I cannot afford to keep a child. I've already spent the deed money I got for her. I'm buried under a mountain of debt that, frankly, blots out the sun. I'm married to my landlord's daughter"—she hit him again—"and have only three young officers at my shooting school. In a word, I'm sinking, milord. I can't take the girl on. But if you make it an order, I will square my shoulders and do my duty. I owe the empire my allegiance after all."

Lady Admiral gawked at him as if he were the most foolish man in the world. She stamped her foot again and lividly gestured at Mr. Sloan to release her power of speech.

Cettie felt a throb, as she had many times when one of the Mysteries was enacted, and suddenly words were spluttering from Mrs. Pratt's mouth. "I've never been—you've got no right! If you think that I'm going to—!"

"Please, Mrs. Pratt," Fitzroy said. "We have no intention of forcing you to take this young woman home with you. Mr. Sloan, you may proceed with the negotiations. I'm taking Cettie out of here at once."

Anger burned in his eyes as he snatched her hand and escorted her firmly from the room. As they left, Lady Admiral continued to rail against the two advocates until the door closed, but not even a mumble could be heard on the other side of the wooden door. Cettie turned back and gazed at the door, surprised that such shouting had instantly been silenced. Many of the young men at the tables had glanced up from their work on hearing the commotion. The young man who'd smiled at her gave her a sympathetic look.

"We can't leave here soon enough," Fitzroy muttered.

They left the workroom and started down the narrow hall leading to the main square and the fountain. But Fitzroy paused in the corridor, hand clenched into a fist. She had never seen him so emotional or upset. He was furious and barely able to contain it. As if suddenly realizing he'd paused, Fitzroy turned and gave her a sheepish smile.

"I'm sorry you had to witness that, Cettie," he said. "I should have come alone." His mouth pressed into a firm line.

She blinked up at him, feeling pummeled by raw emotion. Her father had hardly looked at her. She was a reminder of a lapse of judgment from his younger days. His young wife was clearly in control of him and all that he did. Cettie pitied them and the harshness of their lives.

"What do you think will happen?" she asked Fitzroy.

He reached out and smoothed her hair. "Once they learn that I am seeking to adopt you, Mrs. Pratt will try to squeeze me in hopes of gaining a sizable sum. If her father is a landlord, then she is already used to this form of torture. It grieves me that the world has become this way. How quick everyone is to renounce responsibility and foist it on others. But if there is a farthing to be made, they will be as tenacious as wolves. This change in our society has happened so abruptly." He sighed and shook his head. "When I was younger, it wasn't this . . . mercenary. It is almost as if it has happened by design. When the Ministry of Law took power, many years ago, things began to change. The prime minister back then had a saying that I found quite chilling, but true."

Cettie was so grateful to him at that moment. His anger was directed at the system, not at her. He was preparing to go to battle to win her. He wouldn't cast off his promise.

"What was it?" she asked him, feeling her throat catch.

Fitzroy looked at her. "He said, almost smugly, that *interest* never sleeps, sickens, or dies. It neither visits nor travels, it takes no pleasure, and it is never discharged from its employment. Interest has no kinfolk to watch over and care for." He chuckled to himself. "He was almost gleeful when he said this next part. It is the soul of the Mysteries of Law. Once in debt"—he wagged his finger at her—"*interest* is your companion every moment of the day and night. You cannot shun it or slip away from it. You can never dismiss it. It yields neither to entreaties, demands, or orders, and whenever you get in its way or cross its course or fail to meet its demands, it *crushes* you."

He gave her a fierce look. "After I heard him say that, I determined to free Fog Willows from the debt my ancestors had accrued. Every day, I am given an offer to go into debt for something or other. It staggers the mind, the amount of debt that the empire controls. If an obligation fails, a sky manor can come crashing down."

Cettie's eyes widened with horror.

Fitzroy nodded. "It has happened, Cettie. The fear of it drives even sane men into taking on impossible quantities of debt. And then they lose their manors another way. It is all part of a game we willingly play. The game of risk and chance." He shook his head. "I refuse to play it. Shall we go? Is there any place you'd like to see while we are here? Your friends from Miss Charlotte's, perhaps?"

Cettie remembered the chance meeting with Joses. "I would like that, Fitzroy. When we arrived, I forgot to tell you that I saw Joses."

"You did?" He looked surprised. "I didn't see him amidst the throng. He shouldn't be wandering the streets during the day."

"The lieutenant said Joses left Miss Charlotte's house and joined a gang. Did you know that?"

"I did not. I knew you would be anxious about your friend. Let me inquire further. Did he speak to you? I was mobbed by those children when we arrived."

"He gave me a warning. He said it was a sham."

"What is a sham?" he asked her, confused.

"I don't know. That's all he said."

He looked at her and nodded. "I will have Staunton on the lookout for him. But the Fells are very deep. They can swallow someone who doesn't want to be found. And sometimes someone who does."

He offered his hand, and she took it willingly.

He was about to leave but then paused once again. "The truth always comes out in the end, Cettie. Mr. George Pratt has learned this lesson to his detriment. I learned it long ago. There truly are no secret acts. One day, all will be revealed." He smiled. "Even your past."

SERA

One of the most powerful tools in the influencing of human beings is praise. While we all disdain flattery, and its self-seeking motivation, the well-earned praise of someone we admire can lift the weight of a burdensome obligation and grant courage in dark hours. Withhold it, however, and you may drive a man nearly mad to attain the smallest morsel. This is the power that society wields. It shapes the destinies of empires. A little praise can end a war. Exposing a fault can start one.

—Lady Corinne of Pavenham Sky

CHAPTER TWENTY-THREE
RUMOR'S THOUSAND TONGUES

Will was leaving soon to start his schooling in the Mysteries. It pained Sera to think she might never see him again. She had never had a friend before, someone with whom she could share her thoughts and ideas without fear of judgment. Each time he and Commander Falking came for the tutoring sessions, Hugilde would give her another secret letter after they left, having read it first to ensure it was harmless banter between two young people. But Sera looked forward to reading them despite her governess's role in their correspondence, and she spent hours crafting her replies, sometimes going through six or seven sheets of paper to perfect her messages.

Each subject her tutors taught her was getting more and more difficult, and Sera found herself struggling to keep up with her studies. Her mind wandered terribly during classes, and she was beginning to sense the growing impatience of those her father had hired to tutor her in the Mysteries. She asked so many questions that occasionally she earned a scolding, along with a reminder to keep to the topic at hand. Why could she not force her mind to be more tranquil?

Hugilde was of no help, of course.

"Sera, you are too distractible," the governess scolded one afternoon. They were strolling through the garden together, hand in hand. Even though Sera was growing older, she was still affectionate by nature, and since she got so little of it from either parent, she enjoyed being close to her governess. Hugilde steered them away from the trees, however. Sera could still see the scar from the limb she'd broken on the day that had changed her life forever. Her fall had diminished the thrill of climbing.

"You must learn to *discipline* your mind."

"But how do I do that, Hugilde? So many things fascinate me. I can't help asking questions. I love to learn. But I don't want to learn all the dry facts my tutors want to teach me. None of it relates to anything."

"You are a spoiled child; that is your problem," Hugilde said.

"I am not spoiled!" Sera countered. "I don't get anything that I really want. Sometimes I feel like a prisoner."

Hugilde rolled her eyes at the dramatic statement. "Do you even hear yourself, Sera? Prisoners are forced to labor. You are being forced to sit still and *learn*. In order to master the Mysteries, one first needs to master herself. When I was younger, a student daydreaming would get rapped on the knuckles with a cane." She arched an eyebrow at Sera, trying to make her feel coddled, no doubt.

"Father once grabbed my arm and shook me," Sera said archly.

"You were six," Hugilde said. "That was many years ago."

"And he gets upset with me constantly now," Sera continued. "Becoming the prince regent has placed an enormous burden on him, I know that, but he has no patience anymore. I don't think yelling at someone makes them want to change. It only makes me more determined to be wicked."

"Hush, Princess. If you visited the Fells for one afternoon, you'd see that you are nothing more than a pampered princess chafing at her lessons. We've all been through it, dearest."

Sera ran her fingers through the hedge leaves as they walked. "I'm going to miss Will very much. Commander Falking can be so boring. I wish I could go away to school. I know I would learn better if I were away from here."

"You don't need to go to school. The masters will continue coming to you. It hasn't always been that way, though."

"I know. And it disappoints me every day." She saw the entrance to the hedge maze and tugged at Hugilde's hand to enter with her. When she was a child, she used to run ahead of Hugilde and try to lose her in the maze. She loved to hear her governess's frustrated complaints and threats as she hid amidst the hedges—almost as much as she enjoyed seeing the relief in Hugilde's eyes when she was finally found.

"Can I show Will the hedge maze?" Sera asked brightly. "I think he would love it."

"We don't have enough time for the lesson most of the time, much less for such nonsense."

"Please, Hugilde!"

"No, Sera."

The young princess stopped and tugged on Hugilde's hand. "But he's going away in a fortnight. Can't we spend our last lesson walking through the gardens? I'd love to show him this place. It's so small, yet so beautiful. It's part of my life that I *could* share. You and Commander Falking could walk with us. It wouldn't be improper."

"If your father found out," Hugilde said, shaking her head, but Sera could see she had already begun to win.

"Father is busy all the time," Sera said. "I only see him at dinner, and he's getting fatter every day. I think the chief requirement of being prince regent must be eating treats."

"That is a wicked thing to say." The words were delivered in a serious manner belied by Hugilde's smile.

"Is it wicked that I said it, or is it wicked that it's true?"

"Some days, you are simply impossible."

Sera smiled and bowed. "Thank you. Now please, Hugilde. Can't you arrange it? I see the way Commander Falking glances your way. He's a bachelor, you know, and I think he'd enjoy spending some time in your company. You're very striking."

Hugilde put her hand to her cheek. The little blush there was noticeable. Sera felt a little guilty for manipulating her.

"Do you really think so?" the governess asked.

Sera's plan worked like a miracle. Commander Falking thought it was a splendid idea to take a little walk in the gardens he had admired from his zephyr. He chuckled and said he wished that he could take Sera with them for a ride above the City, but he knew the prince regent would never consent to such an outing. Instead, they would spend the last lesson out of doors, discussing military tactics in the open air.

Thrilled by her success, Sera prepared for the outing by choosing one of her best gowns and even asked her maidservant to spend extra time doing her hair. She had written a final letter to Will that expressed her hope that they could continue their correspondence after he was away at school. She'd expressed her gratitude for his friendship and wished him the very best success in his chosen field of becoming a dragoon.

When the day finally arrived, the sky threatened to ruin all her plans. Thick thunderheads had appeared, and Sera found she could not pay any attention to her morning lessons for fear a downpour would crush her hopes. Why did a storm have to arrive on that day? The week previous had been the most beautiful weather in a month, ideal for taking a stroll. Occasionally a few taps of raindrops on the window would wilt her feelings, but they didn't last long. The sky was preparing for a massive storm, but it was not ready to be set free. Sera wished with all her energy and focus that the rains would be delayed an hour more.

When Commander Falking and Will arrived, the rain still hadn't started, but she was concerned that the portent would dissuade everyone else from the adventure. She was thrilled past words when Falking said, "I hope, Your Highness, that you won't let a little water frighten you away from the outdoors?"

"Not at all, Commander. I was afraid that *you* wouldn't want to go out."

"Tush," he said with a wry smile. "I've flown through worse storms than this. Even if it does start to rain, it will give you better appreciation for what the Ministry of War endures to defend the empire."

And so they started their little walk in the garden. None of the groundskeepers were out. Everyone in their right mind seemed to be hunkering down, waiting for the storm to hit.

The wind was gusting, so the four of them had to stay close to hear one another. Commander Falking offered his arm to Hugilde, and she took it, and then Will did the same to Sera. She felt as if a hive of bees had been unloosed inside her chest.

"The greatest risk a soldier takes is being aloft during a storm," said Falking. "Do you know why?"

"Would it be the lightning?" Sera asked over her shoulder.

"That is a good guess, but it is exceedingly rare. Though I've seen lightning strike from ground up to the hull of a ship. Did you know it went both ways?"

"I did not," Sera said with excitement.

"It's part of the Mysteries of Wind, naturally, but anyone who sails the skies learns them to some degree. No, it's the wind itself that causes the trouble. It is unpredictable and malicious. A man can be blown from the rails if he's not careful."

"How terrifying," Sera said. She glanced at Will with concern. He saw her look and shrugged. He didn't seem afraid at all.

"A sudden storm can catch a ship unawares," Falking continued. "Nothing is more powerful than the raw force of nature. No one knows when one will come, and they can shake a ship to pieces. The sky can be clear in the morning and then violent before dusk. The winds are a risk in every operation we undergo."

Just as he said the words, a sudden gust hit them and blew the hat clean off his head, sending it flying. He lumbered after it, and Sera and Will started laughing at the sight.

They were near the hedge maze. Hugilde was trying not to laugh as Falking attempted to chase down his errant hat. Sera had already learned that the size and shape of an officer's hat was important and that losing it would be a huge embarrassment to the commander.

The impulse to sneak into the maze with Will was overpowering. Maybe it was the sudden chaos of the wind. Maybe it was her disobedient spirit. Maybe it was too difficult to endure the utter boredom of her life.

"Come with me," she said. Their arms were already hooked together, and she tugged him toward the entrance of the hedge maze. There was a flash of indecision on his face. It lasted only a moment. He flashed a smile and joined her.

"Sera! Sera! Wait!" Hugilde chuffed.

Into the maze they dashed. Sera knew it very well. She was gasping and trying to quell her laughter all at once. There was a part of the maze that had a succession of quick turns, which she took to put distance between them and their pursuers. Hugilde would be furious at the trick, and no doubt the commander would be out of sorts, too. But this was the last time she would see Will. Maybe the last time forever, and she wanted to make the moment last. The sounds of pursuit could be heard from the hedge, but the rushing of the wind made it difficult to make out any words. Sera kept low, pulling Will after her, and then they stopped to rest and giggle in a little nook in the maze. Sera was trying to control herself, but the image of Falking chasing his hat made her double over with laughter. She couldn't stop. Tears were in her eyes.

Will leaned back against the hedge, looking back the way they had come. He was laughing, too, looking free and unguarded. She blinked up at him, enjoying this new, carefree side of him. He was capable of having fun. Despite his discipline as a soldier, he was still a young man at heart.

"Will we get in much trouble?" he whispered to her.

"Very much, I'm afraid," she answered, wiping hair away from her face. The tops of the hedges were shaking with the wind. It sounded like a great beast was rustling them. "But it's my fault. It's *always* my fault."

"I came willingly," Will said.

"No, you were my protector. You saw me run off ahead and didn't want anything to happen to me. That's what you must say. Trust me, Will. I know how to get *out* of trouble, too."

The corner of his mouth quirked up as he watched her give her little speech. He glanced back. Some heavy raindrops began to fall. "Do we stay here until they find us?"

She shook her head. "Let's go deeper. There are some benches we can sit on."

"What if the rain gets worse? Shouldn't we head back now?"

"You're not afraid of a little water are you, Midshipman Russell?"

He didn't *look* afraid. "My uniform will keep me warm and dry, Your Highness. You, on the other hand . . ." He gestured to the gown.

"Sera? Sera?"

It was Hugilde.

"There's a gazebo in the middle. Come!"

They both moved as quietly as they could. Her shoes trod more softly than his sturdy boots, but the noise was minimal compared to the raging wind. More heavy drops of rain struck her in the face— a feeling she *relished*. She'd rarely felt so much energy, so much zest for life. Being indoors each day had starved her for nature. They were nearing the gazebo when suddenly Will caught her arm. His fingers were firm and strong.

She turned, whirling around to look at him. He pressed a finger to his mouth. Then she heard it. The sound of a woman's voice. It was coming from just ahead of them.

Will leaned close and whispered in her ear. "Do you hear that? Someone's talking."

It was not Hugilde. Scrunching her brow, Sera ventured a little closer to the sound, walking carefully and quietly.

"Who is it?" Will whispered again, keeping close to her. He looked worried now.

They were near the gazebo. She still couldn't see it over the hedge tops, but she knew it was there. Sera didn't recognize the sound of the voice. They were close enough now that she could begin to make out some of the words.

"I wasn't sure what to do with this information," the woman said. "Naturally, I would like to avoid a scandal. I think you would as well."

A deeper voice muttered, "Yes," the response too quick for her to make out the man's voice. Sera's eyes widened with fear.

"I don't know what Fitzroy learned in his interview with the soldier, but he's a clever man. He may start putting the pieces together. The woman's identity was never revealed. The soldier didn't know her name. The fool got many details wrong, but if he learns that it was your . . . well, I'm sorry to be the one to tell you this. I can see that you're hurting."

"No, I'd rather know the truth. And you will keep it discreet? Can I trust you to?"

It was her father. He was alone in the gazebo with a woman who was not her mother. This woman was telling him something about Vice Admiral Fitzroy. Sera's mind raced with worry and concern. Her cheeks were heating up, and she had the urge to confront them.

Will tugged on her arm and nodded toward the exit, but she could not leave before she heard more.

"I cannot thank you enough, Lady Corinne," her father said in a low, angry voice. "There is much . . . damage you could have done with this information."

"I don't have all the facts, Prince Regent," she said. "I don't need to have them. Rumor has a thousand tongues. I'm just grateful that you heard it from me first. I am loyal to the empire. To you. The Ministry of War has been in power for too long. I had hoped that Fitzroy would have his turn."

"He would have if not for that abominable little girl," Father spat. "Now . . . in light of what you've told me . . . this makes things worse. For everyone."

"I'm sorry, Prince Regent. You can be assured of my discretion. If I hear anyone else speak of it, I will let you know. It may come to light regardless. The truth will out, as they say."

"Maybe it needs to," Father said with anger and resentment. "One good turn deserves another. I overheard it discussed that one of your neighbors in the north is practically bankrupt. The Hardings. Perhaps the news will be of use to your husband. Ah, it's raining harder now. Come, let's get back to the manor."

"Of course. One scandal is enough for a day."

The noise of their shoes gave them only a moment's warning. Will looked frantic as he gripped Sera's arm, and the two of them raced away from the gazebo. Sera no longer worried about finding Hugilde—she needed to escape before her father caught them. Suddenly, all the maze looked the same. She turned left, instead of right, and she and Will ended up in a dead end. Stamping her foot in frustration, she whirled and went back the way they had come.

"Do you hear something?" the woman's voice asked.

"Someone's here," Father said angrily.

Sera took the right way just before they turned the corner and then collided into Hugilde. She would have fallen on her backside if Will hadn't smashed into her from behind.

Hugilde's hair was damp, and she looked furious at having been eluded for so long. "Young lady!" she gasped with outrage.

"Father!" Sera squeaked.

Hugilde's eyes widened with shock.

"What's the meaning of this!" Father shouted from behind them.

CHAPTER TWENTY–FOUR

VENGEFUL PRINCE

Sera normally was ready with an excuse for any occasion, but in that moment, words failed her. Her foolishness had led to this—she'd been caught by her father, and caught with Will Russell no less. She looked at her father's angry, accusing face, and her courage wilted.

Hugilde, unfortunately, didn't seem to know what to say either.

"Forgive me, Prince Regent," the governess panted. "Seraphin slipped into the hedge maze, and I've been trying to catch her."

"But why isn't she having her lessons? Who is this young man?" The look of anger was growing steadily hotter.

"William Russell, my lord," the young man said, his voice tightening with humiliation and dread.

The prince regent said nothing more. He gave Hugilde a withering look and curtly jerked his head, dismissing them all. The rain was coming down in earnest now, and Sera felt everything crumbling around her. She knew she was in disgrace, and her stomach twisted into queasy knots as she marched, head bowed, out of the hedge maze. Will said nothing. His cheeks were flushed, his eyes sparking with anger, his mouth turned down with dread.

Commander Falking was waiting for them outside the maze, and he scowled with anger at her, adding to the horrible emotions seething in her breast. He'd found his hat, at least, but the memory of him chasing after it didn't seem funny anymore. She couldn't remember a time when she had felt so terrible.

Commander Falking and Will slunk away to their sky ship, and Hugilde took Sera back to her room to change her from her wet dress to a dry one. The governess toweled Sera's hair vigorously, her lips pressed into a thin line.

"The letter!" Sera gasped, remembering it all at once. "Did you give it to Commander Falking?"

"How can you think of that at such a moment?" Hugilde hissed.

"But it was the last letter I was going to give him," Sera said, her voice quavering.

Hugilde slammed the brush on the table and covered her face with her hands. Her shoulders were trembling.

"Hugilde—what's wrong?"

The governess's eyes were full of despair as she lowered her hands. "I know your father, Sera. He has changed for the worse since acquiring his new position. He's going to dismiss me. Commander Falking will be dismissed as your tutor as well. Your father can be a vengeful man."

"But it's not your fault," Sera said in confusion. "It's my fault. I'm the one who ran away."

"He won't see it like that," Hugilde moaned. "I have nothing else, nowhere to go. Without a good reference, I'll never get another post as governess."

Sera stared at her in growing horror. "No, Hugilde! I won't let him!"

Tears started streaming down the governess's cheeks. "You don't have the power to stop him," she whispered morosely.

Sera was fired up with indignation. With her hair half-tangled, she pushed away from the vanity desk and barreled out of her room. The servants knew that a storm was raging inside the manor, and no one would meet her eyes. As she marched down the hall, her new-found courage began to waver. But, no, she would not lose Hugilde. She would not be the cause of Commander Falking's failed career or any harm to Will.

She heard the shouting before she reached her mother's room. Instinctively, she had gone to her mother first in the hopes of plead-ing for her to intervene. Her father's valet was standing in front of the door, his face somber. A dark mood hung in the air. Tension was etched on the man's face. Clearly he could hear every word from inside. He gripped the door handles firmly behind his back.

"Let me in, Charles," Sera demanded.

He shook his head no. "Sorry, my lady."

Sera squeezed her hands into fists. "Open the door, or I will scream."

Charles's eyes widened with astonishment. She'd never threatened him before. He was clearly uncomfortable and in distress. Everyone in the manor seemed to fear for their jobs at the moment.

Before he could answer, the handles jerked, and Charles spun away in surprise. Her father's butler, Mr. Case, strode out of the bedroom, his face livid. He snapped his fingers, and Charles fell in tow next to him, leaving the door ajar.

A feeling of blackness emanated from the room. Sera could hear her mother sobbing. It stole Sera's courage and made her feel weak and scared. The mood had never been starker in their unhappy home, and the tension was unbearable. Sera's breath came in rapid gasps. She trembled from head to foot. Every instinct warned her to flee, to find a sofa to hide under until the storm had passed. But if she did that with-out first making a case for herself, she was afraid of what she might lose.

Sera pushed the door open and strode inside.

"I will show you once and for all, woman," Father said in a low, dangerous tone of voice, "that *I* am the master of my own house."

He turned to leave and saw Sera standing meekly in the doorway. The look in his eyes hardened at the sight of her. While he'd never been an overly affectionate father, something inside of him truly had changed. This was a different look. A *hateful* look. She had never seen him look at her this way before.

There were things she had wanted to say. Demands, really. But his expression silenced her. She stared at him as he strode out of the room, not giving her another glance.

Mother was sobbing on a sofa, unable to speak. Sera went to her and held her. And she wished she had never been born.

⌒

It took some time to coax answers from her mother, and they were mostly unintelligible. Father had demanded to know if she had been unfaithful to him. She had tried to defend herself, to deny the accusation, but he had clearly not believed her. Sera thought about the woman whom Father had spoken to in the hedge maze, the one who had given him the strange story. Not only did this affect Mother's emotional state, it affected Sera's future as well. If there was any shade of doubt that she was a true Fitzempress, it would affect every aspect of her life.

One of Mother's ladies-in-waiting hurried into the room in distress. "My lady, the prince regent has ordered the butler's staff to ransack your private rooms! They are spilling out every drawer. What are they looking for?"

Mother's tear-blotched face quivered with emotion. "What they will not find." She hung her head and began crying again. Sera stayed behind to comfort her, although it felt strange to be doing so. Normally it was her mother who tried to soothe her tempers, to coax her into being good. She had witnessed her parents fighting before. But something between them had changed. Something irrevocable.

Bursts of noise came through the manor. She heard a few shouted commands—her father's—and soon everything went chillingly quiet. Sera's mother had fallen into an uneasy sleep, and Sera rose from the couch and walked back to her room in a daze.

The door was open, and she saw her father standing inside alone. It felt like hours had passed since the fateful walk in the garden.

Father was pacing, holding up a couple of folded sheets of paper. Sera's heart plunged even lower. Father was reading Will's letters to her. The rest of them were heaped on the desk. Every one of them was precious to her.

Anger pulsed through her, awakening her. She strode forward. "Those are *mine*."

The look he gave her stopped her in her tracks. "Well, at least I see now how my expenditures on your education are being put to use. Encouraging the advances of a lowly midshipman." He chuffed. "As they say, the apple does not fall far from the tree."

"What does *that* mean?" Sera asked hotly. Her cheeks were burning.

"You are too young to understand," he replied. He tapped the current letter against his open palm and then gathered them all up. "Well, this ends Falking's career, too. I thought he was a man of better sense."

"It wasn't his fault," Sera protested.

Father raised an eyebrow. "There is plenty of fault to go around, young lady. I hired your tutors to discipline you. Not to become a slave to your whims. In what sort of world do you think it would be proper to encourage such advances?"

"I'm lonely, Father," she said, trying to muster more courage. "They weren't advances. Mr. Russell is my friend."

Her use of the parental title made him flinch. "Leadership is loneliness," he said after a pause. "You had no right to encourage this young man. And you've ruined his career as well. He was going to leave for school, I understand." His eyes flashed with vindictiveness. "Not anymore."

"No!" Sera said, shaking her head. "You cannot do this. It is unfair."

He arched his eyebrows. "I cannot? You forget my rank. Why is it that I am afforded more respect outside my own manor than I am within the walls of it? That I am treated with dignity and accommodation everywhere else? No, it is time that my household learned proper respect. If there is insufficient penalty for disobedience, then the situation will remain unchecked. I'm grateful that I discovered your little secret today, Seraphin. I assume, judging by the contents in these letters, that you have written to this stripling as well?"

She swallowed and nodded curtly.

"Well, you will write to him one last time and demand that he return all of your letters. Every single one. If he refuses, I will make his life so miserable he will wish to flee to the Fells. Hugilde said he was a promising young officer. Thanks to you, he will rise no higher."

Sera trembled with outrage. "Why are you punishing him for my misdeeds? It was all my fault!"

"Don't take that tone of voice with me, young lady. I cannot expect someone so young to exercise good judgment. Which is why I've dismissed your governess as well. I expected better from one of her maturity. She confessed to being a willing accomplice. So you see, little Seraphin, it is not all your fault."

He arranged the letters into a neat, little pile.

"As of now, I am also canceling your other tutors. Their reports have been highly disappointing anyway. You've made so little progress in the Mysteries, I've been told, that it's really quite hopeless. I'm suspending your education. I'll not waste another farthing on it while you daydream." His words cut her to the quick. Yes, something inside him had changed. Something terrible.

"Am I to have a governess at all?" Sera gasped.

He pursed his lips. "I don't see the purpose. You're ungovernable. No, I will assign you a maidservant. Someone of *my* choosing."

His words were beating her down. Everything familiar and comfortable was being stripped away from her. Her privacy—once her only solace—was forfeit, and though she had found the classes tedious and pointless, she was desperate to cling to them now that they were being ripped away.

"Please don't send Hugilde away," Sera begged, tears coming to her eyes. She wrung her hands. "I'll accept anything else that you do to me. Just don't send her away. She's the only one . . ." She could hardly speak through her emotions. "She's the only one who truly loves me."

Maybe something in her plea touched a chord deep inside him, for he frowned, and the heat of his temper dulled slightly. He still looked altered, but there was a gradual softening.

"You're in no position to make demands of me," he said firmly, but in a hesitant tone that gave her hope.

"I know," Sera said. He was hungering for something. Respect? Deference? "I've been a horrible daughter. I've disappointed you over and over. But please don't take Hugilde away from me. Don't make her suffer for my sins."

Father pursed his lips again. "I'll reconsider it. I don't think you can change, Seraphin. You haven't shown a willingness to work hard and stick to a task. Perhaps that's not your fault. Perhaps you were *born* this way." He grunted. "Show me that you can be obedient. And I may bring her back to my household."

There was nothing certain in his choice of words.

But it was all Sera had to cling to.

CHAPTER TWENTY-FIVE

LORD HIGH CHANCELLOR

Sera knew of the land-dwellers' superstitions about ghosts. There were not such stories in the sky above, of course, and Sera had never met anyone who claimed to have encountered one. But according to gossip she had heard from Hugilde, the spirits who were trapped down below often attempted to influence the living in malevolent ways. They had the power to turn someone's heart cold. To change someone's personality in short order. Even, in some cases, to drive the life out of the living. Hugilde had told her there were carnivals in the City where strange women attempted to make contact with the dead through glass orbs and other such nonsense. It was frowned upon by high society, of course.

Sera felt that her father had been touched by a ghost or that she herself was becoming one.

Even the servants avoided meeting her eyes as she wandered disconsolately down the corridors of the mansion. She was dreadfully lonely without Hugilde, and it only took thinking about her dismissed governess to make her burst into tears. There were no more tutoring lessons to attend, and she worried that she might retreat so deeply into her reveries that she would no longer be able to find her way out. One of her favorite daydreams was imagining Father getting shoved out of a hurricane and plummeting into the Fells.

It was during the afternoon of one such ghostly walk along the manor's balustrade that she saw a sky ship, a tempest, looming in the yard. She hoped it was Vice Admiral Fitzroy, although she doubted it would be. The cut and trim of the sky ship was different from the one she had seen him arrive in a month before. Father's butler arrived at the front door, and soon she heard the noise of her father's shoes clicking on the marble tiles. Sera paused, her hand still on the railing, and watched from above.

"Chancellor Erskine!" Father said eagerly, arriving at the doorway and pumping the man's gloved hand vigorously. Sera had never seen the lord high chancellor before. He was a middle-aged man with dark hair and a well-cut coat and vest. His hair was windblown, with a lot of gray in it, and he had a goatee.

"Prince Regent," Erskine replied with a bow. "I came as soon as I could." Because of the cavern-like hall, the sound of their conversation reached her quickly.

"You are the Minister of Law as well as the lord high chancellor. I knew I could depend on you. My *wife*"—he almost spat out the word—"has hired an advocate to defend Seraphin's rights. A man by the name of Mr. Durrant. I want him dismissed. Immediately."

Chancellor Erskine sighed audibly. "I cannot exactly *do* that, Prince Regent," he said with the hint of a whine in his voice.

"You are the lord high chancellor!"

"I am, Your Grace, and I serve at your pleasure. If it were up to me, I would snap my fingers and it would be done." He did snap his fingers. Sera squeezed the rounded rail and listened with growing excitement.

"But alas, I am also the Minister of Law. Our empire is bound by traditions and precedents. Unfortunately, and it is unfortunate given the current estrangement between yourself and . . . *ahem* . . . your wife, she felt the need to seek her own counsel. I don't know who recommended Durrant to her, but he's a canny, savage sort of man. He grew in fame defending murderers from below—"

"Impossible!" Father shouted, his voice swelling with rage and disgust. "I'll not allow such a man to enter my house and speak to my servants!"

The chancellor looked discomfited. He started to pace in the entryway. "Oh dear, oh dear," he mumbled. "This won't be pleasant. This won't be pleasant at all."

"What do you mean? Speak up, man!"

The chancellor looked plaintive. "Your Majesty, the Mysteries of Law must be upheld. Were you to attempt to overrule them, or even break them, it would put your position in jeopardy. You were selected to be prince regent because of your noble birth and because, quite frankly, you were deemed to be the sort of man who would uphold tradition. Why, if you were to forbid Durrant from speaking to anyone, including your daughter, the privy council might depose you."

"Can they do that?" Father gasped, stepping backward.

"I'm afraid they can, Prince Regent. The laws were designed to prevent one person from having too much power. You have the right to declare no confidence in the prime minister you selected to replace Minister Welles. You can dismiss any of the other positions that rule the empire, my own included. But your rank could be revoked by that same power. And after such a short period, it would cause a scandal. It grieves me that I must be the one to explain this to you, my lord. Of course, my only desire is to serve your interests."

Sera scrutinized the politician below and felt the man was more likely serving his own interests. Still, his words had awakened the flames of hope inside her. Her mother had begun to take action. Her life wasn't necessarily over.

"But it is my house," Father protested. "Surely I can bar entry to anyone I deem inappropriate!"

"Naturally!" said Erskine. "But you cannot prevent Durrant from speaking to those witnesses he must speak to in order to do his duty. You could, for example, send your servants to his offices below and hold the interviews there. At your expense, of course."

The last comment was a particularly effective line of reasoning against her father, Sera knew. He hoarded his wealth and rarely parsed out funds for any reason, even good ones. Young though she was, she saw that the chancellor was manipulating her father. By positioning himself as a friend, not an adversary, he had deftly begun to guide her father toward the path of thinking that Erskine himself preferred.

"This is outrageous," Father grumbled, scowling at the man.

"It is the law," replied the chancellor helplessly. "Do you have any questions I may answer for you before Durrant arrives? When will he be coming?"

"He *told* me he'd be arriving before dinner and that his interviews may last into the evening. The audacity!" Sera could hear the desire for revenge in his tone.

"Advocates aren't known for their sensitivity," Erskine said, wincing. "He has been hired, no doubt, to protect your wife's and daughter's interests. I've heard that you canceled some of Seraphin's tutors. Is that so?"

"Indeed. She was wasting her time and *my* money."

"Ah, I see. That is truly egregious. Only a wayward child would do such a thing." His censure lacked conviction, however, and Sera sensed the man was once again trying to placate her father. "You have the right to dismiss a tutor, a governess, whomever you wish. But you cannot *legally* deprive your daughter of an education. There are schools that will take in the lowest of the low from the worker class. No child who wants an education will be deprived of one."

"Surely that is not true!" Father gasped.

"Oh, I assure you that it is. We in the Ministry of Law do not educate the masses on their rights, for surely it would overwhelm the empire to provide an ample education to every person, male or female. Imagine the chaos that would ensue! The expense!"

"It would be wrong to teach a guttersnipe," Father said angrily.

"Indeed so. But Durrant knows of this law and will no doubt use it in your daughter's favor."

Father was pacing restlessly. Then he stopped and glared. "Who is going to pay for Durrant?"

"Ultimately, you will," said Erskine with a sigh. He put his arm around her father's shoulder. "No doubt he will educate your wife regarding her rights to her marriage portion as well. A portion that she has the ability to bequeath to her children."

Sera almost squealed at the news. She gripped the banister so hard her fingers were burning.

"But how can that be!" Father complained. "Our funds have been united for many years. There are no separate accounts."

"Oh, Durrant will separate them!" Erskine said with a chuckle, and, on earning a sharp look from her father, it turned into an adjusting cough. "As I said, it grieves me that I must be the one to educate you on the formalities of Law. You have always favored the Mysteries of Wind, which frankly I know very little about, so you did right to seek my advice. Be prudent, sir. You must hire your own advocate to defend *your* interests. If you would like recommendations now that you've dismissed Masters Eakett and Baggles, I would be happy to oblige."

"Yes," Father said, looking stunned and dazed. "Yes, I would. I thought, perhaps, that *you* would advise me."

"Oh no! It wouldn't be proper to do that, Prince Regent. I no longer have a private practice. It would be a sign of corruption. No, I had to sign a delegation of authority when I became the Minister of Law. Let me warn you, though. These proceedings will likely get very . . . messy. It's a shame really. When word of your scandal reaches the ears of the populace, it will tarnish your family's reputation."

"*My* scandal?" Father blustered hotly. "It wasn't my fault . . . this is madness!"

"I'm not sure what you mean, my lord," said Erskine tonelessly. But Sera could see that he did.

"Nothing," Father snapped. "Well, thank you for your time. I would appreciate a recommendation from you on another advocate."

"I will be happy to provide several," Erskine said. He patted Father's back and guided him toward the front door. Then Erskine looked backward, his gaze following the banister rail up to where Sera was crouching. A small, kind smile came to his mouth. He dipped his head to her.

꘡

Mr. Durrant was a wickedly funny man. It was as if he believed every person was corrupt and untrustworthy and felt duty bound to comment sarcastically on it. Although he was slight of build, he had a clenching grip that made Sera wince when they shook hands in greeting. Mother was in attendance for the first part of the meeting, but then Durrant asked to speak to Sera privately. He was balding on top, but the plenteous hair on the sides and back of his head had been combed in such a way as to form little curls. There was one little lock of hair that he had deliberately combed down to his forehead into a little curl—an open defiance of his balding forehead. He had a sad, somber mouth and was always folding his arms, as if his frail body could never get warm. The man looked older and more seasoned than her parents, an impression heightened by the saggy flaps of skin beneath his eyes.

The door shut, leaving Sera and Mr. Durrant alone together.

"So."

He was gazing at her, arching one eyebrow and then the other as he sized her up. His lips pursed, and he clucked his tongue and shook his head.

"I understand," he went on after a very long pause, "that you prefer to be addressed as *Sera* instead of your given name, Seraphin Fitzempress."

"That's true, Mr. Durrant. I know it's a peasant's—"

He winced and shut his eyes, holding up a finger as if her words had pained him. She immediately quieted.

After another lengthy pause, his heavily lidded eyes opened, and he stared at her. "Never, never, never explain yourself. Not to anyone, even to me. First, it will get you into trouble in the law." He gave her a cunning smile. "Second, you owe no one an explanation. It's none of their business. You are who you are, and that's that. End of story. Point. End. Finished." He gazed at her again.

Sera stared back at him with avid interest. His words hadn't offended her. In fact, they'd stirred inside her a little delicious feeling of warmth. A feeling of independence. Had *he* been her tutor in Law, she could tell she would have learned plenty.

"What I have come to learn about you so far today, Miss Sera, is that you have an indomitable will. I spoke at great length with your governess, Hugilde. A remarkable woman. Very helpful. She misses you terribly. I've advised her not to seek other employment at present. I believe, in due course, she will return as your governess."

"Do you indeed, Mr. Durrant?" Sera asked eagerly.

"I do, as much as I would also counsel you to put your trust in no man, myself included. But as your future estate is paying for my services, I render my advice freely. You choose what to do with it." He folded his arms even more tightly. "Yes, I've spoken to your governess, your chambermaids, your mother, your tutors. Through their eyes, I have painted a little picture of you in my mind." He scrunched his nose and cocked his head to one side. "You are twelve years old. But you ask questions that only the wise and aged would ask. You have, as I've heard it said, an old soul. You will make a fine empress someday."

Sera blinked in surprise.

"I've startled you. Why?" he asked.

"This is not how I thought our interview would go," she stammered.

"What? You were expecting me to waylay you with questions? Hardly. I already had the answers to my questions before I came here. This is about the succession. When your grandfather dies, a new emperor . . . or empress . . . will be chosen." He yawned. "The prince regent has already proven himself a disgusting tyrant." He shrugged. "No offense."

"How is he a tyrant?" Sera asked.

"He has wrangled a higher stipend than his predecessor's even though he only has one child to support and not many. He has deployed the military in several questionable ventures already. Mostly, I'm afraid, he is too apt to heed those who flatter the most. Tyrants do that, you see. Some on the council think that you might make a more promising ruler. You are too young to inherit the throne in your own right, and it's clear that your father seeks now to disqualify you as the heir to the empire. You are, after all, his biggest competition. His brothers are both buffoons and so corrupted by bad business decisions and crippling debts that neither stands much of a chance at being chosen." He reached up with one hand and twisted the little lock dangling across his forehead. "So let me be frank with you, Miss Sera. By defying your father's wishes, I run the risk of his excessive wrath. I mean to become a thorn in his side. A blister. A canker. A wart. And I do it in the hopes that *you* will achieve your rightful place as empress and will find it, in the goodness of your heart, to reward me for my troubles and travails. There, now I've said it out loud. You can pretend to be shocked!" He gave her a wily smile.

Sera liked him. She liked him very much.

"So if you already knew everything about me before you came here," she asked. "Why did you come?"

"Excellent question. I came to tweak your father's nose. To prove to him that he couldn't stop me without great trouble and even greater expense. And I came because you need someone who will answer your questions." He spread his hands apart and gestured to her. "So ask them."

Sera leaned forward. "Is it true that Father cannot prevent my education? That I would have the right to study at a school even if I had no money or connections?"

"It is absolutely true. There are laws dating back centuries allowing it, but we like to shroud things in mystery in order to keep control. Have you ever wandered down the hall and encountered a locked door and felt something behind it . . . something that beckoned to you? Why are there so many locked doors in the manor, Miss Sera?"

She bit her lip. "I don't know."

"Precisely!" he said, eyes blazing eagerly. "And that is the way they want to keep you. Locked out. If you are to become our empress, you need to know much more than you do now. Your tutors have tried to progress your knowledge from fact to fact, as they were taught." He shook his head. "That is not how the Mysteries were explained in the past. In the past, even the very young could master them. And so can you. Why haven't you mastered them yet, Miss Sera?"

She felt something bubbling up inside of her. "Because I've not been given—"

He winced again, wagging his finger at her. "Never, never, never explain yourself. Not to anyone, even to me."

She looked deeply into his eyes. Her education had finally begun in earnest.

CETTIE

It is not uncommon for young people to test the boundaries imposed by society. Fashions may alter as quickly as hairstyles, for people are driven by their natures to seem unique. The young chafe at the rules and prohibitions against the trim of a bodice, the brim of a hat, the requirement to wear gloves when interacting with others, or how low one must nod to avoid seeming flirtatious. I like to quote a previous Minister of Thought, Master Driggs, who said: "No one person, however brilliant or well-informed in the Mysteries, can come in one lifetime to such fullness of understanding as to safely judge and dismiss the customs or institutions of his society. These customs are the culminations of the wisdom of generations of experiment in the crucible of history. A youth boiling with emotions will wonder why he—or she—should not give full freedom to his or her desires. Alas, we have learned from sad experience that if the young are left unchecked by customs, morals, or traditions, they may well ruin their lives before they mature sufficiently to understand this essential truth; desire is a river of living fire that must be banked, cooled, and channeled by copious measures if it is not to consume in a flood of burning chaos both the individual and society."

—*Lady Corinne of Pavenham Sky*

CHAPTER TWENTY-SIX

THE HARDINGS' BALL

Cettie had never seen Fitzroy wear gloves until the night of the Hardings' ball. Anna had insisted that Cettie don a pair herself, but she had demurred because Fitzroy didn't wear them. Anna had laughed and said that he always did for a ball; everyone did.

Anna, Cettie, and Phinia all wore short-sleeved gowns, but their silk gloves went well past their elbows. It was an unfamiliar feeling to wear them, and when Cettie looked at herself in the mirror, her hair done up in curls and ringlets with pins to fasten it in place, it felt as if she were looking at a stranger. None of the little ones at Miss Charlotte's would have even recognized her. She was no longer so thin and wasted, her cheeks gaunt. She *looked* like one of the family, but everyone present would surely know about her background.

Anna had tried to reassure her that the Hardings were delighted to have her attend. It was not a high society ball, like those held at Pavenham Sky—the rules and strictures would not be enforced. Nonetheless, her stomach was fluttering as she waited with her 'sisters.' Fitzroy, Stephen, and Adam were getting the tempest from the docking yard, and Phinia boasted that it was Stephen's first time piloting it—with supervision.

Phinia looked overeager for the event. While Anna's and Cettie's gowns were modest and simple, Phinia was preparing to enter society, so hers was more elaborate, and she'd fastened a large white plume in her hair.

"I don't know why I'm so nervous," Phinia tittered. "I've been to the Hardings' balls so many times. Just think—in two more years, you both will be coming out."

Anna rarely responded to Phinia's light banter. She just smiled and nodded.

"Oh, doesn't Mother look lovely?" Phinia said with a sigh. Cettie turned and saw Lady Maren coming down the steps, holding the banister as she took each one gingerly. Mrs. Pullman held her other arm as if to brace her. Seeing Cettie gathered among the girls, some of the lines on Mrs. Pullman's face stretched, and although she smiled, there was a hint of a grimace to it.

Since Cettie and Fitzroy returned from their trip to the Fells, Mrs. Pullman had focused her energies on persecuting Anna instead. The youngest of Fitzroy's daughters was scolded more, and so was Miss Farnworth, who had been chastened for being too easy on Anna. Fitzroy had not left since his return, and Cettie had the feeling Mrs. Pullman was biding her time, waiting for an opportunity like spiders waited in their webs. Even so, Cettie still had not brought herself to share the truth about the keeper with Fitzroy. *Before he leaves,* she promised herself. *I'll tell him before he leaves.*

Upon reaching the landing, Lady Maren embraced Phinia, who kissed her mother's cheeks. Anna greeted her in kind, and Cettie followed, planting a small kiss on her cheek as she'd done before. Feeling the glare of Mrs. Pullman, she pulled back quickly and felt a twinge of self-consciousness.

"You all look so beautiful," Lady Maren said, smiling. "I'm grateful I'm well enough to attend the ball tonight. I haven't always made it to the Hardings' ball, but I have fond"—her expression slipped just slightly—"*memories* of them."

Mrs. Pullman stroked her lady's arm. "If you need to come home to Fog Willows early, you do that, my lady. The younger girls can come home with you." Her eyes narrowed just a little, and she cast a subtle glance Cettie's way.

"I wouldn't want to ruin their fun," Lady Maren replied, oblivious to the undercurrent in Mrs. Pullman's comment. "I used to be able to dance all night long at Gimmerton Sough."

"Will you dance with Papa tonight?" Phinia asked excitedly.

"I plan to," Lady Maren said, pleased, swishing her skirts. "Your father is an excellent dancer."

A shadow loomed from the great windows, and everyone turned excitedly as the tempest approached, except for Cettie, who dreaded the thought of coming home early. No, she would stay as long as Fitzroy did. The tempest lowered to the edge of the landing and then dipped too low and nearly disappeared. Phinia giggled at Stephen's botched arrival as the servants pulled open the doors and escorted them out. Cettie glanced at Mrs. Pullman over her shoulder. The imperious keeper of the house stood in the doorway with her arms folded.

A ramp was extended, and the family was escorted one by one across the plank. Cettie was the last to cross, and Fitzroy held out his black-gloved hand to her. She found she didn't like wearing gloves—it added a new and unwelcome separation between them—but the thought was quickly tossed out by the ascent of the tempest.

Cettie watched as Fog Willows dropped away, her stomach thrilling with the sensation. They had all worn wraps for the journey. Fitzroy took Lady Maren belowdecks, but the children all stayed to watch the view. Stephen stood at the helm, wearing a light blue jacket and black breeches and boots. He cut a fine figure and almost looked like a man grown. Adam stood behind him, wearing a brown-striped vest beneath his black coat. Both boys looked serious and thoughtful.

Fitzroy returned a little while later and kept casting nervous glances at his eldest at the helm. His hands were clasped behind his back, and Cettie could see him chafing with discomfort. She approached him, and he must have heard her step, for he turned and greeted her.

"Are you anxious about your first ball, Cettie Saeed?" he asked her, smiling wryly at his use of the nickname that Raj Sarin had given her.

"Why should I be?" she replied. "I'm too young to dance."

"That is true, although the Hardings have been known to forgo propriety on occasion. And I've seen you dance on occasion, Cettie. You do it very well."

"Thank you," she said. "May I ask you something?" she added quietly. The question was burning inside of her.

He turned his full attention from the helm to her. "Of course." Since they'd returned from seeing his advocate, he had been more restrained, as if the weight of his many burdens was crushing him.

"This is a small thing, really. I don't mean to pry."

"You can ask me anything, Cettie. What is it?"

"You're wearing gloves. You never do that."

He gave her a small smile. "Are you sensing an inconsistency in my character?" he asked.

She flushed. "I probably shouldn't have asked."

He shook his head. "Of course you should. I am grateful that you did. Much of what we do, we do without thinking. We do out of habit. I wear gloves at balls out of habit, but there is another reason, and I don't mind explaining it. At Fog Willows, I do as I please. You know I don't condone all the restrictive fashions of the day. They have gotten extravagant in recent years. Things were much simpler before Stephen was born. But some people are quite accustomed to them, and they've become uncomfortable touching hands. It shows too much intimacy, if you will. At a ball, there are forms that require multiple partners as you work your way through the line, like 'Mulberry Lane.' I can choose my partner or set for the most part, but I'd rather not make someone else uncomfortable needlessly because of my opinions on the dictates of fashion. Especially a lady." He gave her a little bow. In a teasing tone, he said, "Do you deem the reasoning for my inconsistency acceptable, Cettie?"

"I do," she replied, smiling.

The Hardings were some of their nearest neighbors, but it still took some time for them to arrive at the Hardings' estate, Gimmerton Sough. It was a much smaller manor. Each one, she had come to learn, had its own unique structure. Gimmerton Sough looked like an ancient castle that had been plucked out of a river or moat. In fact, the stone on the lower portion was a deeper mottled gray, perhaps the result of centuries of high and low tides. The castle was made up of two main sections connected by a double-arched stone bridge. One end was narrow, rounded, and featured a tower and a flag. The other was much larger and seemed to be the main part of the estate. There were crenellations on the walls around the castle, everything was set at an angle, and the stone was uniform in color. The fortress was only two stories high, but there were huge, towering windows interspersed symmetrically along the walls. What was most interesting about it was its location: the manor was nestled in a floating pond.

Other sky ships had already moored at the estate, and many hovered over the waters of the pond. A small green park stretched to the entrance, and Cettie saw a zephyr unloading a few passengers onto the lawn. It was still late afternoon, but the tradition was to have a large dinner in the ballroom before it was cleared away for the dance.

Cettie gripped the handrail, nervous about her first foray into society.

After landing and disembarking, Cettie and Anna held hands as they entered the estate. They were greeted boisterously by Sir Harding and his wife, and the ruckus in the ballroom quickly drowned out Cettie's concerns. Music filled the hall—light, airy notes from strings and horns. She was used to the sounds now and could even name the composers of the pieces she heard. Ten other families had joined in the gathering, each one coming from their own floating manor. She had heard their names before, but hadn't met many of them in person. Fog Willows did not receive many visitors.

During dinner, Cettie was amazed at the expensive porcelain dishes and the sumptuous courses served in them. In her mind's eye, she could imagine all the little children at Miss Charlotte's who had so little to eat. There would be leftover food from this feast—tons of it. Did any of it go down below? Was it thrown away?

After the meal was done, the servants began to clear away the dishes, and the tables were moved to open the hall for the dancing. Most of the older youth clustered together, and Cettie noticed that the Hardings' daughter, who wore a stunning gown that made her look older than sixteen, was very attentive to Stephen. Phinia and Adam joined the thicket of young people, too, but Anna and Cettie wandered the hall and listened to the different conversations as they passed.

Abruptly, the noise and chatter ended, and a hush fell over the room.

Cettie tried to see what had caused the sudden reaction and noticed an elegant couple was standing in the doorway to the ballroom. All eyes were fixed on them, and it was obvious their arrival was both unexpected and astonishing. Not even a whisper broke the silence.

The butler thumped his staff on the floor, a formality that had been overlooked for all the other guests.

"Admiral Robert Lawton and Lady Corinne Lawton of Pavenham Sky," the butler announced.

Even in the Fells, Cettie had heard about the grandeur of Pavenham Sky. The Lawtons were considered the wealthiest couple in the empire. His success in business following his military career had exceeded everyone's wildest expectations. Whenever a venture or risk was to be made, he was part of it—and while others lost, the admiral never did.

Sir Harding and his wife, Shanron, were the first to greet the couple. The Lawtons did not look impressed, but they thanked their hosts for the invitation, explaining that they'd decided to come on short notice.

The music began to play, and the young people came together on the dance floor. Sir Jordan tried to make his new guests comfortable, but they seemed disinterested in what he had to say. They gazed around at the tapestries, the floor, with looks of impassive judgment. Admiral Lawton was tall and slender with a serious face, thinning hair, and a large, thick mustache that entirely covered his upper lip and most of his bottom lip. His suit was gray with light silver trim, paired with a silver necktie. His wife, Lady Corinne, was a haughty-looking woman with dark curly hair pinned high on her head, just visible beneath the crown of a turquoise hat with ribbons and plumes of matching color. Her scarves and fancy jacket matched her hat, and even her gloves were turquoise. The only skin visible on her person was that of her smooth cheeks. She looked older than Lady Maren, and her husband was much older than her. She had a proud mouth and watchful eyes.

"They've never come before," Anna whispered to Cettie as she observed the newcomers. "The Hardings invite them every year because they are important, but I've never heard of them coming. Not once."

"Why do you think they did?" Cettie whispered in response.

"I've no idea," Anna said. "Look, Papa is talking to the admiral now. He made his fortune in the Ministry of War and then put it to use in the Ministry of Law. He's the one who gave Papa his rank, even though he had resigned his commission. He respects Papa, I think. But I'm surprised Lady Corinne came."

"Why?"

Anna pitched her voice lower, but Cettie could still hear her above the music. "They haven't been to a ball together for years and years. The last one was in Lockhaven, before my parents married. Mama broke a rule and was shunned from society after that."

"A grudge can last that long?"

Anna nodded, eyes wide. "It can last forever."

The ball continued, and servants rushed around serving drinks and platters of fruit and pastries. All the families came to pay homage to the Lawtons. The two were gracious, but Cettie noticed that they didn't seem to engage in any deep conversation.

"With all the dancing, it gets so warm in here," Anna said, lowering her wrap down to the crook in her arm where Cettie's arm had linked with hers. "We won't be invited to dance for certain. No one would deliberately risk offending Lady Corinne."

The young men and women were all enjoying themselves, but the air of boisterousness that had prevailed earlier had dimmed. Cettie watched the dancers with a pang of envy. She would have danced her heart out if given a chance, regardless of what Lady Corinne or Admiral Lawton thought of her.

At the next dance, Fitzroy escorted Lady Maren to the row to join in "Sky Ship's Cook," which was a particularly lively number. The clapping became more pronounced when he joined the dance, and the mood lightened.

Anna sighed wistfully. "I would so love to dance." Cettie squeezed her hand. They'd practiced this dance together at home, and they could both do a passable job of it.

The beautiful music came from the walls, just like it did at Fog Willows. They stopped a servant for porcelain cups filled with punch and stood by the wooden panels from which the music emanated. It provided the best view of the hall.

Cettie felt the sounds rising from her feet and filling her with an even stronger urge to join the dance. At least they could see the whole room from their vantage point, though the music masked what they were saying. Some of the matronly women were gathered together on lounge chairs, gossiping merrily while their husbands traded quips by the fireplace. The Lawtons stood to the side, aloof from everyone else, not participating yet seeming perfectly comfortable not doing so.

Cettie saw Sir Harding's mother, a normally jovial woman whose gray hair was arranged tidily beneath a feathered hat, lean toward another woman. Cettie thought if she just strained her hearing enough, she'd be able to hear what the old woman was saying. It was a whimsical thought, but for a moment, she believed it was possible. A drowsy, lulling feeling came over her. The room began to fade, the noise hushing as she fell inside herself. Something awoke inside of her, an awareness—a feeling—that tickled down her spine. She felt herself swaying slightly, as if a small breeze from the sky beyond the stone walls had penetrated and moved her.

And in that daze-like state, she *did* hear the old woman's voice, clear as a bell, as if she had been standing at her left shoulder.

"And you know what I think, Mrs. Simmons?"

"Tell me what you think, Mrs. Harding," asked another proper voice with much eagerness.

"I think, Mrs. Simmons, that Fitzroy hunts for the child's mother because he secretly believes she's the girl he loved and lost to the Fells."

"Do you really think so, Mrs. Harding?"

"I do indeed. He never recovered after losing her. Lady Maren has been a consolation, dear thing, and I adore her for finally seeing Fitzroy's true worth compared to that *scoundrel* she once humiliated herself for." Her words were delivered breathlessly, and Cettie felt the awareness that she was eavesdropping on a very private conversation. She thought she should pull herself loose, but she couldn't. She burned with curiosity.

Somehow she knew they were talking about her life.

And they didn't know that she could hear them.

CHAPTER TWENTY–SEVEN
The Hardings' Fall

Cettie felt a thrum of power deep within her skin, exuding from her pores. As she listened to Sir Harding's mother talk, she felt herself connecting with the estate. She was aware of the music coming from the walls. She felt the subtle jets of air that rose from the slats in the floor, trying to cool the ballroom full of energetic dancers. She felt the wood and the stone, the polished marble and the glass. Everything spoke to her, almost as if she'd come awake and could hear the very house speak. The feeling was almost impossible to describe. It was overwhelming, and it made her dizzy and excited and intrigued all at once. The Mysteries were speaking to her. She had typically only felt malevolent forces, like the tenement ghosts or the beast in the fog at Dolcoath, or slight twinges and nudges when the Mysteries were invoked by someone else. This feeling was different—brighter and more peaceful.

"Well, the man Maren loved *was* a scoundrel," said Mrs. Simmons. "He married that other girl for her wealth, and she wrung out his heart. If his aunt hadn't kept supporting him, he would have been lost to the Fells years ago."

"I know," Mrs. Harding said emphatically. "But she won't cut him off. I've heard my son say that the man still pines after Maren, that he considers his marriage a mistake. He would run off with her if given a chance, the devil! But Lady Maren wouldn't do that, even if she were tempted. Look at them dance. It cheers my heart to see it."

Cettie was so absorbed in their conversation she didn't hear Anna talking to her until the other girl tugged at her arm.

"What's wrong, Cettie? Are you unwell?"

She was jolted back to herself with such suddenness the room started to tilt and sway around her. If Anna hadn't been holding her arm, she might have stumbled. Her energy seemed to wilt, and a dreary fatigue made her feel like fainting.

"I think I'm all right," Cettie said, reaching for something to hold on to. Her knees buckled.

"You're not well," Anna said with concern and helped her to a nearby chair. "It is very warm in here. Are you feeling faint? Do you want to go home?"

"No!" Cettie said forcefully. Her stomach clenched with queasiness, and she was afraid she'd retch on the polished floor. But she was even more afraid of Mrs. Pullman.

"Let me fetch you something to drink," Anna said.

"Not the punch," Cettie said anxiously, clutching her stomach. The thought of the sickly sweet juice made her feel even worse. Anna hurried off to intercept a servant, while Cettie gripped the arms of the chair, trying to stay upright.

The song ended, the dancers bowed to each other, and the room began to bubble with conversation again. Stephen was talking to the Hardings' daughter, who eagerly listened to his every word. Phinia was searching for another dance partner before the music could start up again. As Cettie watched them, her vision began to narrow, as if black curtains were veiling her eyes, and she gripped the edges of the chair harder. She saw Admiral Lawton and Lady Lawton standing aloof, ignoring Lady Harding's attempts to engage them in conversation.

Lady Lawton wasn't listening to her host at all. Her eyes were fixed on *Cettie*. She said nothing, just gazed at Cettie with her impassive, unfriendly eyes.

Anna arrived. "It's water," she said, offering the glass goblet. Cettie gratefully drank from it and felt her dizziness start to fade.

Suddenly, the lights in the ballroom began to flicker. At first Cettie thought she was back at Fog Willows and it was the signal that it was time for bed. But the gasps of alarm from the dancers indicated the situation was not normal.

A strange, sinking feeling rippled through the hall.

"What was that?" Anna gasped in concern, gripping Cettie's chair.

The lights flickered again and began to dim. A sinking feeling, the kind she'd felt in the sky ships, jolted her stomach. Could the estate be falling?

The ballroom door opened, and a woman came rushing in, her face pale with panic. The sinking feeling stopped, and the lights instantly became brighter. The feeling of being connected to the manor swelled inside Cettie again, despite her weakness. The feeling was almost overpowering in its intensity. The music stopped, and the lights were dimmed, although this time it was done deliberately.

"I wonder what's happening," Anna said with dread.

Cettie saw Fitzroy striding toward Sir Jordan. His mouth was moving, and she desperately wished to hear what he was saying. Again, as if responding to her wishes, she heard his words as if she were standing right next to him.

"You must send the guests home immediately, Jordan," Fitzroy said. "It will take time to summon their ships. We need to get off the estate right now."

"I don't know what's happened, Fitzroy," Jordan said with a worried voice. "My keeper said the keys aren't working."

"It's clear they are not. If things fail, we could all die. Make an announcement. We need to get away at once."

Cettie heard another voice enter the conversation. It wasn't familiar to her, yet when Fitzroy turned to face the newcomer, she moved with him. It was the admiral.

"May I be of assistance?" he said calmly. Lady Corrine stood next to him, their arms interlocked.

Sir Jordan was flummoxed. "The estate is sinking," he said in a half whisper.

"That much is obvious," the admiral said.

"We must evacuate the guests," Fitzroy said sternly.

The admiral held up his hand, just slightly, urging caution. "Let's not cause a panic, Brant. I'll be concise. The reason Lady Corinne and I came tonight is because I learned the Skempworth investment failed. It will be announced in the morning to the public. I believe, Sir Jordan, that you had a sizable stake in the investment. Is that true?"

Sir Jordan produced a handkerchief and mopped the sweat from his balding head. "It failed?" he gasped in shock. His jaw must have trembled, because Cettie could hear a distinct quaver in his voice. She remembered that he had come to Fog Willows seeking Fitzroy's advice about the investment. Fitzroy had warned him against it, but it would appear he'd moved forward anyway.

"Utterly and completely," Admiral Lawton said dispassionately. "It was a risky venture from the start."

Sir Jordan looked at him in horror. "I've lost everything."

"Indeed, sir, you have," the admiral said. "I came here tonight to be of assistance, if you will let me. You've broken the covenant that holds Gimmerton Sough in the sky. *That* is why the keys have stopped responding. Without intervention, the estate will fall within the hour. You never should have held a ball when you were under such financial distress."

Lady Shanron had joined them. "I didn't think it could happen so fast," she said in a small, shaking voice. Cettie felt her body start to tremble. The weariness she'd experienced earlier was compounding, but she struggled to maintain her focus, to listen to the words being spoken across the hall.

"The law is merciless, Lady Harding. It brooks no excuses. You risked the lives of every person you invited here this evening. I sense and can tell that you did this unwittingly."

"Of course," Fitzroy said, putting his hand on Harding's shoulder. "What can be done, Admiral?"

"Unless someone assumes the debt burden of Gimmerton Sough, it will be lost. Are you prepared to do so, Brant?"

Cettie heard the brief intake of breath. "No, Admiral. Not at present."

The room felt like it was tilting, and a spasm of fear rocked her. Was the manor falling again?

"I thought not. You manage your own resources in a capable manner. I respect that. Sir Harding, I propose that the ball continue. I will cover the debt burden and will lease out the manor in the hopes of recouping my loss. It may take some time to cover this . . . embarrassment. You are not the only man ruined this evening, sir. If that is a consolation to you."

Sir Jordan looked grieved beyond words. "Where will we go?"

The admiral shrugged. "That is up to you to decide. If we have an understanding, then I will have my advocate speak with yours to work out the arrangement. Conclude the ball as planned."

"Admiral, I cannot say how grateful I am that you—"

Admiral Lawton cut him off. "My only condition, Sir Harding, is that you do not mention my involvement in your public disclosures. I seek no recognition and would prefer this were handled with discretion. Do I have your word, as a gentleman?"

"You do indeed, sir," replied Sir Harding.

"This was an unfortunate matter," Admiral Lawton said. He had displayed no emotion during his speech. Cettie wondered how he had kept his composure. Her vision had narrowed to a small, tight circle now. She was part of this moment, part of this manor. She could feel the emotions of the fortress as if it were a living thing. It grieved losing its master. Sorrow wrenched her heart, larger and vaster than anything she had experienced in her life. The emotions flooded her, overwhelming her—drowning her.

Anna cried out in concern as Cettie slumped from the chair, the chalice dropping from her hand and shattering on the floor.

Her body felt as if she had climbed a hundred thousand stairs. Every joint and muscle ached. When Cettie regained consciousness, she could not at first open her eyes. She wanted to see, but it was impossible. Her eyelids felt too heavy. She was lying on a soft bed with blankets pulled up to her chin. A damp rag bathed her face. Was she back at Fog Willows?

Her chin itched, but she couldn't lift her hand. Even though her eyes were closed, she sensed the light, and the pale peach skin of her eyelids glowed. She felt lips brush her forehead.

"Come, dearest. Wake up. Please wake up."

It was Lady Maren's voice, so pleading and gentle—and worried.

"I'm awake now," Cettie whispered.

She felt more kisses, kisses of gratitude. "I'm so grateful. I haven't left your side since we carried you here."

"Are we back home?" The sheets smelled different. So did the pillow. It was a strange place.

"We're at Gimmerton Sough," Lady Maren said, stroking her nose.

Memories from the ball came rushing in. "Is it safe?"

"Yes, you're safe. The castle is almost empty now. Everyone has gone." Lady Maren pulled some of the blankets away and took her hand. Cettie tried to squeeze it, but her fingers were too weak. "Dearest, something happened last night. Something very rare. It happened right as you fainted. The Hardings have fallen on hard times. They have lost their estate to a wealthy man here in the north. If the admiral had not come last night, we might have all perished."

Cettie had listened to the conversation. She wasn't sure if the admiral's arrival had been a mercy or a ploy for personal gain. She kept that thought to herself.

"Where are the others?" Cettie asked.

"They're on the tempest, waiting. It's barely dawn. I was so worried about you," she said, kissing Cettie's brow again. "A long time ago, I was very sick. I almost died." Her voice trembled. "My older sister waited up all night for me. Afraid for me."

"I remember that night," Fitzroy said softly, tenderly.

Cettie hadn't heard the door open, but she was relieved to hear his voice. A smile quivered on her mouth.

"How are you feeling, Cettie Saeed? I think we should go, if you feel you are able. Raj Sarin will be worried about you, too." The two of them were nearby, Lady Maren on a settee and Fitzroy beside her, his hand on her shoulder. Cettie liked seeing them together. Whatever Harding's mother believed, she thought them perfect together.

Cettie tried to sit up, and they helped her. She was still exhausted, but her strength was slowly returning, bit by bit. Her gown was wrinkled and her knees wobbly, but with each of them supporting one of her arms, she was able to walk.

As they left the room, the quiet of the manor astonished her. It was a feeling of utter desolation. The light she had experienced beamed in from the window in the room. None of the hall lights were shining, but all the doors had been opened so that the curtains could chase away the shadows. All the energy and vibrancy of the ball were gone. Cettie felt a shudder go down her spine as she sensed unseen ghosts lingering in the dark. The protections and wards had failed. Fear made her start to tremble. If there were similar wards at Fog Willows, then her theory was correct: Mrs. Pullman was indeed letting the ghosts in deliberately.

Even if Cettie *did* attract the tall one, she wasn't the one bringing all the ghosts into the manor.

"You're safe, Cettie," Fitzroy said to her. She looked up at him and saw his confident smile beaming down at her. She would be safe with him. But she could feel the ghosts pressing in around her, yearning to touch her. Unfortunately, she wasn't safe without him, not even at Fog Willows.

They walked slowly down the long hall, the cavernous space quiet beyond the noise of their shoes. Cettie bit her lip, looking at the huge sheets obscuring the artwork. Then they passed a closed door. Cettie stopped walking. It reminded her of the locked door at home—the one only Mrs. Pullman accessed. She could sense it just by staring at it. Beyond the door was the feeling of a mother weeping over a dead child. The heartsick suffering was so oppressive, so vast, that Cettie shrank and stepped away from it.

"Cettie?" Fitzroy asked with concern.

She wanted to go away. She wanted to run. It was almost as if she could hear wailing coming from the room, even though it was silent.

"Come, dearest," Lady Maren soothed, tugging at her arm. "Come away."

She heeded them, but the moment would forever be branded on Cettie's mind. She would always remember Gimmerton Sough as a place of keening, of suffering, of dashed dreams.

And the memories would haunt her.

CHAPTER TWENTY-EIGHT
HOUSE OF KEYS

The mood at Fog Willows was somber in the wake of the disgrace of the Harding family, even more so after Phinia and Stephen and Adam left for their schooling. Cettie was determined to tell Fitzroy about Mrs. Pullman before he left. The time for waiting had ended—the ghost would be unleashed as soon as he was gone. When she found him in his study, she tried to speak, but her throat constricted, and a terrible power overwhelmed her, rendering her speechless. The feeling did not leave her until she slunk away from his room, unseen. It was then that she realized that she was powerless to tell him. Mrs. Pullman's influence was stronger than she had dared to believe.

Fitzroy left soon afterward, having promised to set Sir Jordan up with temporary work at the Dolcoath mines. The miners were harvesting quicksilver, while Mr. Savage sent crews in to try to discover new veins.

Cettie tried to speak to Fitzroy again as he bid her good-bye in front of the tempest, but her lips were sealed. A feeling of doom descended upon her as she watched the ship pull away.

Later that day, Anna and Cettie roamed the manor's corridors disconsolately. Cettie tried to tell her friend about the choking feeling that came over her whenever she tried to speak of Mrs. Pullman's influence, but the same power made it impossible for her to communicate the problem to Anna. A storm threatened outside, so neither of them wished to risk an outdoor excursion.

Not all topics were forbidden her, though.

"What frightened me so about the other night," Cettie told Anna, "was how fast Gimmerton Sough fell. It wasn't very long ago that Sir Jordan asked for advice about the speculation."

"He should have heeded Papa's advice," Anna said somberly. "Now we've lost our best friends and neighbors. I will miss them so."

"As will I," Cettie said. "It must cost a great deal of money to afford an estate like theirs."

"And Gimmerton Sough is not even half the size of Fog Willows," Anna said. "It's lucky that the Lawtons came when they did."

Cettie frowned. "I'm not sure it was luck at all. I think they *knew* it would happen and came to take advantage of the situation."

"Do you really mean that, Cettie?"

Cettie hesitated, wondering if she was being too forward. But she trusted Anna enough to speak frankly. "I heard them speaking, Anna."

Anna gave her a surprised look. "What do you mean? You weren't near the Lawtons at all that night."

Cettie sighed. "I may not have been standing by them. But I could hear them talking. While I was there, I felt this strange . . . power come over me. I could hear people across the room. As if I were standing right next to them. That's why I fainted, Anna. It wasn't the heat from the ball. It was because I felt so drained by the experience."

"It's the Mysteries," Anna said with deep respect.

"What do you mean?" Cettie asked.

Anna stopped in the middle of the hall and squeezed her forearms. "I mean that you can sense the Mysteries, can't you?"

Cettie felt her insides wriggling. "I *think* so."

"Yes, it must be that," Anna said seriously. "Come with me." She grabbed Cettie by the hand and started to tug her down the hallway. She spoke in a low, cautious voice. "Mother used to be very strong in the Mysteries. You know how I told you about the ball she attended in the City? The one where she broke a rule? She had fallen in love with a young man who did not have very sterling morals, and she confronted him at a ball. Though there were people watching and listening, she used all her force of will to attempt to persuade him to give up the other girl and her fortune. She . . . she became very sick that night, and it took her a long time to recover her strength. That's another reason I was so worried about you. You fell sick, just like she did."

Cettie bit her lip. "Can the Mysteries make someone ill?"

"Yes! It requires great mental energy to harness them. Father says he's always exhausted after using them."

"Where are we going?" Cettie asked. She knew instinctively where Anna was taking her. Toward the bedrooms. Toward that one locked door. Her heart began to beat faster with worry.

But there was no need for Anna to answer. They soon arrived at *the* door. Though it shared the appearance of any of the numerous doors within the manor, the feeling it exuded set it apart. Just as before, Cettie sensed something beyond the door, something that beckoned to her. Not with words, but with a keen intelligence. She swallowed, suddenly fearful.

"I've only seen Papa and Mrs. Pullman go beyond this door," Anna whispered to her, squeezing her hand. "Father said he won't let any of us in until we are ready."

"What's in there?" Cettie whispered in response.

Anna shook her head no. But Cettie could sense the presence even more strongly now. Before she had been half-asleep to the feeling. Now, she was fully awake. The feelings she had experienced at Gimmerton Sough had been dreadful and scary and horribly sad. These were different. She sensed honor and integrity. She sensed a strong will and a gentle hand. It reached out to her mind as if welcoming her in. Without realizing it, she reached up her hand and rested her palm against the wooden door.

Her mind instantly exploded into a lightning storm of thoughts. She felt the thrumming power of the manor, the existence of every living thing within it, come rushing into her in a single vortex of blinding, rushing, thriving life. Every corridor at that moment was laid bare to her, every footfall, every muttered word. Her senses expanded beyond her normal reach, sinking deep into the awareness of something inexplicable. It was as if the light from a thousand suns had radiated through her mind all at once, leaving her too dazzled to think and unable to shield herself from their rays. Yet there was a shadow inside the light. A sickness—a taint. Maybe it was coming from Cettie herself.

But, no, in the middle of it all, she sensed Mrs. Pullman. Cettie saw her erect stance, her stern frown, her serious demeanor. She was the keeper of the house, the one entrusted with Fitzroy's keys. Cettie sensed the older woman was equally aware of her, and, for a brief moment, their minds merged into one. All that was Mrs. Pullman was stripped bare, and Cettie saw that beneath the sternness, beneath the caprice, beneath the brooding soul lay a woman who felt unworthy of her station. Fitzroy's father had led her to believe Fog Willows was too much for her, that being a good keeper lay beyond her abilities. Fitzroy's father's erratic criticism and general air of disdain had shaped her into the woman she'd become. Her greatest fear was being dismissed, so she had made herself indispensable. Every aspect of the manor ran according to her will and regimen. But beneath that strong, confident front, her deepest, darkest fear was that she might be let go anyway. To avoid that fate, she would do anything.

As that realization struck Cettie, she realized that Mrs. Pullman was physically inside the room at that very moment. Worse, she knew her defenses had been breached.

With unmasked fury, Mrs. Pullman wrenched hard on Cettie's thoughts and pulled her loose, prying the two of them apart. A ripping feeling, visceral and painful, stabbed through Cettie's mind.

The door swung open, and Mrs. Pullman was standing before her. Anna gasped in fear and dread.

Cettie could see the fury blazing in Mrs. Pullman's eyes as she stood there. "And what are *you* children doing here?" She asked it in her usual haughty way, but her voice was thick with emotion. "The master wouldn't be pleased to learn I caught you snooping about."

Anna wasn't bold enough to speak up to authority. She shrank from Mrs. Pullman's visible wrath. "I'm very sorry."

"You should be, child," Mrs. Pullman said waspishly. "You knew better than to bring her here. Go."

Anna tried to pull Cettie away, but Mrs. Pullman gripped her by the arm. "I said *go*, child," she warned Anna.

Anna shrank back, tears springing to her eyes, and fled down the corridor. Cettie stood there, her arm smarting with pain as Mrs. Pullman squeezed it, digging in with her fingers. An old fear snapped to life. She wondered if Mrs. Pullman was going to drag her away right at that moment and send her back down to the Fells. Or maybe she would simply throw her over the edge of the manor.

She didn't. She released Cettie's arm. The wrinkles on her face twisted into grotesque shapes. She was barely mastering herself.

"You do not belong here," Mrs. Pullman said in a choking voice. "You've never belonged here. And you'll bring disgrace on this house. The master should never have brought you home. Were it not for Miss Felicianna, you'd be back in the Fells this very night."

Cettie trembled inside as Mrs. Pullman's thoughts and corroding will pummeled her mind. A sense of blackness and despair struck her forcibly, making her want to cower. But she resisted the urge. She clung to the belief that no one controlled her destiny but herself. Mrs. Pullman was like the villagers from the tale of the father and son and the mule. She was afflicted with the same self-doubt that she spewed on Cettie. It was Mrs. Pullman who secretly felt she did not belong, who tried to prove herself day and night by her tireless work. But no amount of work had erased her feelings of unworthiness. Cettie walled herself off from the poisonous thoughts. Even though her arm was throbbing, she tightened her little muscles, squeezed her hands into fists, and stared at Mrs. Pullman with determination.

The two locked wills.

"Go," Mrs. Pullman whispered angrily.

Cettie walked away.

Later that night, after the lights of the manor had dimmed, Cettie and Anna huddled beneath the warm blankets in Anna's room.

"I don't see how your father can keep someone when she . . ." Cettie said with a throb of injustice, but her throat immediately seized up again. She frowned in frustration.

"Mrs. Pullman acts differently sometimes when he is away," Anna said, snuggling closer. "She's never been kind to me the way she is to Stephen and Phinia, but she's getting worse. There's something . . . wrong with her."

I'm going to find a way to tell him, Cettie thought darkly. She was determined to endure her mistreatment no longer.

Anna swallowed and shivered. "We should tell Mother what she did tonight. She shouldn't have done that."

Cettie thought a moment. She could not talk about the ghosts, but she would say as much as she could. "No. Mrs. Pullman is stronger than her." A horrible thought struck her. Mrs. Pullman didn't like any stain of disgrace on the Fitzroy household . . . She certainly wouldn't consider Lady Maren an appropriate wife for Fitzroy. Though everyone agreed that the lady's health had been foundering for years, no one knew the precise cause. "Maybe . . . maybe she's even the reason your mother is so sick. I don't know. I don't like the way she treats you, Anna, and she's doing it because of me. She's controlling everything in this house. She even . . . nngghh . . . I have to make it stop." But first she would have to get through the night. They both would.

As was usually the case, Anna fell asleep first. Cettie was having difficulty relaxing; her mind was reliving the confrontation with Mrs. Pullman. Just touching that door had triggered an awakening inside her again. She was drained, but not as drained as the night of the ball. New vigor had been granted to her.

Later, much later, she experienced the strange prickle down her back. The room was dark. The manor was still.

Cold. A pit of cold filled Cettie's stomach, and her teeth began to chatter. Anna groaned in her sleep, beginning to fidget. Fear twisted inside Cettie's stomach. It was a familiar sensation, like a remembered stench, but she had not experienced it in a long time. It was the tall one. It was coming down the hall.

Sickening panic. It was coming. The ghost was coming. She felt it drift noiselessly down the hall. Anna let out a whimper, still asleep. Cettie tried to move, tried to get out of bed, but her muscles were locked, just as they had been at the grotto.

Cettie started to gasp for breath as her mind went black with sickness. It was coming. It was coming. And she couldn't move.

She felt it enter the room, a clot of blackness in the shadows. Suddenly Cettie couldn't breathe. It felt as if an icy hand had clutched her throat.

Hello, little one. Do you remember me still? Did you think I wouldn't find you again?

And then Anna started to scream.

CHAPTER TWENTY-NINE

STORM

Anna couldn't stop shrieking. Cettie tried to wrench free of the sheets, but she was frozen. The ghost was in there with them, and she had no idea how to banish it. She tried to will it away with her thoughts, pouring all her energy and will into it, but she didn't know how to make it obey her as it had obeyed Fitzroy. There was knowledge he had that she lacked. Then Anna started to thrash and writhe in the covers, her screams piercing the air. Cettie watched in a helpless state as the ghost floated toward her friend.

"Go away, go away, go away," Cettie pleaded through tears, wishing she could hug Anna. Wishing she could take all her friend's fear on herself. The hysterics went on for what seemed like forever before Cettie saw the tall one reach its clawed hand through Anna's chest. Anna, finally awakening, sat up and started sobbing. She breathed in choking gasps, looking frightened but unable to see the eyeless ghost poised over her. Cettie thought it was *smiling*.

Anna started making a choking sound, and Cettie, in pure desperation, flung aside the wraith's power. She needed help right away for her friend, and, despite her earlier hesitation, Lady Maren was the only person she could think of to go to in the midst of the crisis. Rushing from the bed, she struck her shin against the footstool and fell in a heap from the pain. The pain helped her shift her focus away from the fear, and she managed to get up and limp to the door and hurry out the corridor. She felt the tall one coming after her. Although her shin throbbed, it was of no concern at all. At least she was leading the ghost away from Anna. At least her friend would be safe. She saw a light coming from down the hall. It was the same kind of swinging lantern that Mrs. Pullman carried.

And then the keeper rounded the corner, the light from the lantern in her bony hand making her face look frightening.

Stifling a scream of her own, Cettie raced in the other direction, determined to find Lady Maren. The corridor was lit by moonlight through the high windows. Cettie's bare feet padded down the hall and then up some stone steps. The distance from the ghost allowed some of her wits to return. She hurried to the door to Lady Maren's bedroom. She rapped on it quickly and hard, bouncing from one foot to another, covering her mouth and trembling uncontrollably. Summoning her strength of will, she gazed down the hall for any sign of movement in the shadows.

The door opened. It was Elizabeth, Lady Maren's lady's maid, looking confused. "Cettie? What are you doing here?"

"Anna!" Cettie said, not sure what to say.

Elizabeth rubbed sleep from her eyes. She turned, Cettie felt a slight pressure in her skull, and the light came on in the room.

"Did you send for Mrs. Pullman?" Elizabeth asked in concern.

Cettie slipped past her, earning a gasp of surprise, and hurried to Lady Maren's bed. She was already awake and coming out of the sheets. Elizabeth grabbed a shawl for her lady and hastily put it around her shoulders. Lady Maren was disheveled and weak, but her eyes were full of concern.

"It's Anna," Cettie whimpered. "You must come."

Lady Maren asked no questions. She put her arm around Cettie, and the three of them, Elizabeth included, rushed back to Anna's room. When they arrived, the light was shining dimly, and Anna was asleep, being held and soothed by Mrs. Pullman. In the half-light of the room, Anna looked peaceful and tranquil. Mrs. Pullman stroked her hair. The hypocrisy of it made Cettie want to brutalize the older woman.

"What happened, Mrs. Pullman?" Lady Maren asked wearily.

"Just the night terrors," Mrs. Pullman said. "Like she used to get. Something has brought them back on."

"I thought she was sick," Lady Maren said with relief.

"It wasn't the night terrors," Cettie said, staring hotly at Mrs. Pullman.

Mrs. Pullman's eyebrow arched innocently.

Lady Maren turned to her. "She used to get them all the time, Cettie. She hasn't had one since you started sleeping in her room. You're just not used to them."

Cettie grew more frustrated. "I've seen night terrors. I know what they are. This was different. It was a—" And then her throat blocked, and she found she could neither swallow nor speak.

"Was what?" Lady Maren asked in concern. She looked closely at Cettie, wanting to understand.

Cettie's throat was constricted once again. It felt like she was choking. The fear she had felt earlier began to writhe to life again.

"I'll get her some water," Elizabeth said, hurrying from the room.

But no amount of water could loosen her words. She wanted to say the word "ghost," and she simply couldn't. Mrs. Pullman continued to stare at her with a knowing smile. The keeper had left the door unlocked, she realized, just so Cettie would realize how very helpless she was.

The ghost returned the next night, and the night after that. Mrs. Pullman had started locking the door each night to prevent Cettie from waking Lady Maren. But that was another subject that Cettie was forbidden to speak up about. No matter how hard she tried, she couldn't use words that would have explained the situation. And Anna couldn't explain what was happening either. To her, it seemed a dark, horrid dream, and she grew to fear the night. To fear Cettie's company.

Finally, after several days of Anna's fear steadily escalating, Mrs. Pullman persuaded Lady Maren that things might improve if Cettie were no longer sharing the room. Lady Maren was dubious of the claim and said she would try it out for one night.

And, of course, that night Anna slept peacefully. The weather took a sudden turn for the worse, which Cettie feared would delay the return of Fitzroy, who would surely set everything to rights. Cettie sat by the windows, watching the droplets of water chase each other down the glass as a storm battered Fog Willows. She felt impotent against Mrs. Pullman's machinations. Anna had become extremely withdrawn around everyone, including Cettie. The two had been very close before Stephen and Phinia had left for school, but a shroud now seemed to hang over everything. Cettie took the change badly and feared that a fissure was splitting them apart.

Despite the situation, Cettie refused to abandon hope. Mrs. Pullman hadn't expelled her yet. Something was holding the old woman back from that final act of domination. Fitzroy would return and put things right; she had to believe that. She wanted to be useful to him, so she made sure to go to his study every day and update the log she was keeping on the level of the quicksilver. After updating the information, she added a little square and drew the rain in. She wondered how long ago it was that it had last rained, so she went back through her previous entries and saw the little mark she had made on that day. Something struck her instantly.

It was the same number of tick marks she had just written down.

Cettie frowned and began chewing on the end of the pencil. She compared the two entries again. Something snicked inside her mind. Maybe it was because of the rain lashing the windows outside. Maybe it was because she knew Fitzroy was prevented from returning to the manor because of the storm. Maybe it was some intuition deep inside her that had always known and was just now revealing itself.

She flipped between the pages, watching the numbers change. Some days they changed dramatically. Most days they stayed the same as the day before. But there were subtle, regular shifts. Sometimes the quicksilver went down. Other times it went up. She and Fitzroy had pored over the instrument for months, trying to make sense of it. But Cettie had an impression, a guess, that the quicksilver was reacting to something they couldn't see.

It was like opening a window and letting in sunshine. Cettie dropped the pencil and went back and studied her markings again. She had been tracking them for months, almost since she had first come to the Fitzroy manor. The changes all happened within a few ticks of each other.

What if, somehow, the quicksilver was responding to changes in the weather?

A pulse of pure giddiness washed through her. She picked up her pencil again, going back to each entry that shared a similar number. The excitement of the idea thrilled her. Staring out the window, it felt as if the sky were cheering her on instead of threatening her. The rain continued to dribble down.

With the pencil, she wrote a little note for herself next to the boxes indicating rain. *When the silver falls, a storm will come.*

She stared at the glass and the shiny liquid within it. Then she closed her notebook and determined to test her theory.

The opportunity came almost immediately. After three days of perpetual rain, during which the level had stayed the same, the amount of quicksilver in the glass tube changed again. It changed dramatically between morning and night. Cettie made an observation during dinner that she thought Fitzroy would come back in time for dinner the next night.

"It has to stop raining first, Cettie," Lady Maren said, looking more weary than usual. "He won't pilot a tempest in a storm unless it's an emergency. It's too dangerous."

"I think the storm will end tonight," Cettie said innocently, sipping broth from the spoon.

"I hope it does," Lady Maren said.

The evening went on in its somber manner, as it had for days now. Even though the attacks had ended once Cettie had gone back to the garret, Anna grew anxious each time the sunlight began to fail. Mrs. Pullman had become very solicitous to the girl, and crooned to her each night as she tucked her into bed, no doubt attempting to win over her affections and her loyalty. Cettie clenched her fists, wishing she were older and more capable. Wishing she knew how to best the older woman.

The next day, Cettie awoke in the garret and waited for Mrs. Pullman to let her come down. The rain had stopped beating on the shingles during the night, and the air smelled clean and fresh through the upper window of the garret. But no bell rang inviting her down. All was silent below.

The daylight increased and still no Mrs. Pullman. Cettie paced restlessly in the garret. She'd never been locked in for the morning. When the morning passed and there was still no sign of relief, Cettie's mood turned desperate.

It was late in the afternoon when she finally heard Mrs. Pullman's footsteps down below. The bell rang.

Cettie scrambled down the ladder, her stomach sick with worry and hunger.

Mrs. Pullman seemed worried. "The master has returned," she said, looking hard at Cettie.

Cettie felt a thrill of comfort. "I'll tell him what you did," she said, clenching her fists.

"Just as you told Lady Maren about the *ghost*?" Mrs. Pullman asked, her wrinkles dancing across her face. "You think you can best *me*, you ungrateful little guttersnipe?" Mrs. Pullman taunted. She towered over Cettie, looking down at her with proud disdain. "You think about this, young lady. If I can rob you of being able to speak, do you not think I could also take away your hearing? Your eyesight? Hmmm?" She gave Cettie a hateful look. "You imagine what that would be like, child. A deaf-mute. I'd put you back into the Fells like that. Consider what *that* would feel like. How helpless you would be. How long do you think you'd last, child? I'm warning you. Now, the master wants to see you. He's heard you've not been feeling well today. You'll let him know that you're feeling much better now, won't you? That I've been caring for you myself in my own rooms. Do we understand each other?"

Cettie faced her, feeling a mixture of dread and rage. "I hear you," she answered softly, not trusting herself to say more.

"I'm glad you hear me, child," Mrs. Pullman said. "My voice may well be the last sound you ever hear. You remember that. Now go downstairs. Say *nothing* about what we've talked about. I will know if you do. These walls have ears, child. I think you know that by now. There is nowhere you can escape me in Fog Willows. I'll know if you try to betray me again."

"Yes, Mrs. Pullman," Cettie said, squelching the fire inside her.

"You be back on the stairs after the lights go dim. Don't make me find you."

"I won't, Mrs. Pullman."

"Good." She gestured with her head. "On your way now."

Cettie went down the inner well of the tower, seething all the way. Before going to see Fitzroy, she went to the study and looked at the glass vial. The level of quicksilver was at exactly the same level as it had been the day before. She marked it in the log and wrote another note.

The storm passed.

Then she tried to write the word *ghost* on the page. But her wrist seized up, her fingers locked, and she couldn't use her arm. Closing her eyes, she began to clear her mind, to breathe in and out slowly, as Raj Sarin had taught her. After a few moments, she felt her arm muscles loosen. She tried to write the word again.

Again, her fingers seized up with paralysis.

Cettie stared hungrily at the page, wanting to give Fitzroy a clue. She tried to write *it is back*.

But she could not manage even that.

CHAPTER THIRTY
THE MYSTERIES OF WIND

Fitzroy was in the sitting room when Cettie arrived. Music wafted in from behind the wooden panels, and the servants looked brighter than they had in recent days. For a moment, Cettie stood just outside the doorway, watching the family tableau before her. Anna clung to her father's arm, sharing a chair with him. She had shadowy smudges beneath her eyes and a sickly air. Lady Maren sat on her couch, a blanket on her lap, and husband and wife were talking together with animated expressions.

Cettie wanted to know what they were saying. She felt awkward intruding, but she, too, was relieved to see Fitzroy. His presence brought a calming feeling, and, besides, it would curb Mrs. Pullman's worse behavior. She was anxious to tell him the news of her insight, but that could wait. Clearly he was talking about something of importance. She wished she could hear what he was saying.

With her thought, she felt a throb of power, and suddenly their voices reached her ears as if she were actually standing amongst them.

"I had no idea their marriage was in peril," Lady Maren said.

"It was not common knowledge at first," Fitzroy said in a low voice. "News of it struck Lockhaven like a storm. Now no one can talk of anything else. Those who knew the royal couple recognized that they've always had little love for one another. The prince regent's new advocate is encouraging him to divorce his wife now and seek a replacement. Others counsel him to wait until after the investigation."

"An investigation?" Lady Maren pressed.

"Yes, the Ministry of Law is investigating their relationship. There are rumors that Seraphin Fitzempress is illegitimate. I don't know what to think myself, but it seems highly unlikely. I must say, the way they've kept their daughter isolated is appalling. They scarcely ever allow her to leave the house."

"That's strong language, Vice Admiral," Lady Maren said with a tone of teasing.

"My apologies, Maren. I've long felt sympathy for the princess. Her lack of affinity for the Mysteries is likely a result of her parents' silent war. They have used her as a shuttlecock. It's deplorable."

"So what happens now? What is the latest you have heard?"

Fitzroy grunted. "Honestly? It's likely a ploy by the Ministry of Law to seize power. Durrant is an ambitious man. He's defending Seraphin's rights. The prince regent will not be able to cast his wife and heir aside without compelling evidence. This thing could rage on for years, which would shift the power back to the Law. There could be a new prime minister called before the winter snows."

Cettie felt a little light-headed from using her newfound power, but she was grateful for it. She knew hardly anything about the princess, but what she'd heard made her feel compassion for the Fitzempress girl. Though their backgrounds couldn't be more different, she knew what it was to feel isolated and cut off from the wider world. Her entire childhood had been spent that way.

"I'm grateful you made it home safely, my love," Lady Maren said, reaching for Fitzroy's hand and squeezing it. "Cettie said you'd be home today. I haven't seen her all morning."

"Mrs. Pullman said she wasn't feeling well," Fitzroy said. "That she's been attending to Cettie's needs personally. How considerate she always is. She knew I'd be worried about her. I hope she's not too unwell?"

"She's in the doorway, Papa," Anna said, pointing.

Their eyes turned to her, and Cettie felt as if she'd been caught eavesdropping. Fitzroy's face brightened immediately when he saw her, but she came in slowly, hands behind her back. She felt like crying and didn't know what she should say or do.

"She does look pale," Lady Maren said as Cettie approached them.

"She does indeed," Fitzroy said, coming down to sit on the couch next to his wife. "Mrs. Pullman said you started sleeping in her rooms again after Anna's night terrors returned."

It was true. Cettie bit her lip. She nodded, saying nothing.

"Are you feeling better this afternoon?" Lady Maren asked.

Cettie brightened a bit and nodded. "Much better, thank you."

"Well, it may storm again," Fitzroy said. "The Hardings are settling in Dolcoath. It is quite an adjustment for them. Sir Jordan has lived a soldier's life and a gentleman's, but now his work is more strenuous. He's working in the mines as an overseer under Mr. Savage. The position is temporary. I hope I do not have to close down the mines."

"Is it as bad as that?" Lady Maren whispered, her tone suddenly grave.

Fitzroy shrugged, looking anxious. "A silver mine that produces globs of quicksilver is not very profitable. I sent for an expert from the Ministry of Wind to advise me about the mine. He's very busy, though, and cannot come for several weeks. We'll know more then."

"But then the winter will be here," Lady Maren said with concern.

He patted her shoulder. "We have ample funds to last past the winter, my dear. Closing the mines will save in costs, but I'd rather not sell the lands quite yet. There may be something we just don't know yet. Serge is doing all that he can." He gave Anna a hug and a kiss on her cheek before standing. "I'll be in my study until dinner." Then he bent to kiss Lady Maren's hair.

She smiled up at him. "I'm glad you are back. We've needed you."

Fitzroy smiled with pleasure and started to leave. But he stopped and extended his elbow to Cettie. "Would you join me?"

Gratefully, she accepted it and followed him back to the study.

When they arrived, he bent over the glass tube and started counting the ticks under his breath. "Have you still been measuring them, Cettie Saeed?" he asked with a wry smile.

"I have," she answered shyly. Her log was sitting on the table, and she pushed it toward him. "I think I know what is making the quicksilver move."

"Oh really?" he asked with genuine curiosity. He opened to the last page, where she had written her note from the day before. Bending his head closer, he observed the page. His expression gradually changed as he stared at her words.

He chuckled under his breath, looking dismissive for a moment. Then he caught himself, and his lips pressed firmly together. He flipped back for several pages. His brows knit together, and she stared at him, hoping that he wouldn't make fun of her. Perhaps he had already tried her idea and knew it was wrong.

Fitzroy tapped his bottom lip with a long finger. He was silent for a long while. Then she felt it, the subtle pulse in the room. There was something happening inside Fitzroy. Some feeling that *she*, too, was sharing. He glanced at her serious face, her eyes boring into his. *Believe me*, she wanted to say.

His lips pursed. "It's so tempting," he said in a soft, clear voice. "To want to dismiss this. Every instinct screams that it's preposterous." He reached down and tapped the page. "Not what you've written. But that you *could* have written it. I've prided myself these many years for being more open-minded than others." He let out a deep sigh. "Why does part of me want to reject this? There is a little war happening inside my mind at this moment. This very moment." He turned and looked at her, giving her a curious stare.

"I don't know why," she answered. "But I think what I found is true. Only I didn't find it. I think the truth found *me*."

He cocked his head at her and slowly nodded. Then he glanced back down at the open book. She could see from his fidgeting that his hands were bothering him again.

"Cettie, do you know why one of the Mysteries is called the Mysteries of Wind?"

She shook her head no.

"Because it asks the age-old question—where does the wind come from? You cannot see the wind. It is invisible. But you can see its effect on the treetops, on water, on your hair." He smiled and tousled hers. "You cannot see it, but you can feel it. You know the wind is real because of the evidence of it. But no one has ever been able to explain where it comes from or what it is. There are stories, legends more likely, that there are celestial beings who control the winds of the earth. They unstopper their vials and unleash the winds for a time. Then they stopper the vials again, and the wind ceases. That isn't true, of course, but it is what our race came up with to try and explain the unexplainable."

He squinted at the tick marks on the glass orb. "When the quicksilver goes down, it means there will be a storm." He rubbed his chin and stared at the table. "What you are inferring, then, Cettie, is that there is a force that we cannot see that pushes down on the quicksilver. It is invisible. It is inside the glass tube, just as it is pressing down on us in this very room. How would we test this new truth?"

Excitement sprang up inside Cettie. Something she had done had been helpful. She blinked quickly. "I could keep counting the tick marks each day, and when the level of quicksilver changes, we could see if the weather changes too."

"Naturally," he answered. "We will be doing precisely that. But I'm trying to think of a way we could test it sooner—without waiting for the next storm to arrive."

"We could go to a storm?" Cettie suggested. "And bring the tube with us?"

Fitzroy grinned and snapped his fingers. "Precisely! Grab your cloak."

Fitzroy had chosen to use his zephyr because of the speed and quickness of the flight. He wore his heavy coat and his gloves as protection from the cold wind. The zephyr sped away from Fog Willows, and Cettie's stomach thrilled with the motion, her cloak whipping behind her. She gripped the railing with one hand and held up the glass vial with the quicksilver with the other. Fitzroy piloted the zephyr himself, and they lurched into the sky.

As soon as they were a good distance from Fog Willows, she opened her mouth to speak, eager to tell him about Mrs. Pullman's true nature. But her throat seized shut just as it had before. It frightened her that Mrs. Pullman's power over her extended far beyond the walls of Fog Willows. Somehow Mrs. Pullman had put something *inside* of Cettie herself that forbade her to speak of her mistreatment. Certainly this had happened to other servants as well, which was how Mrs. Pullman had managed to stay in power for so long.

She would have to find another way.

As the sky ship sped away from the manor, Cettie kept glancing back at the tube and then noticed that it had already changed. The slight bumpiness of the journey made it difficult to count, but she did so.

"It's already changing!" she called to him against the keening wind.

"Let's try lower, then!" Fitzroy shouted back. She felt a pulse of power come from his direction, and then the zephyr began to descend. The air was cold and clear, and the wind chilled her face and ears. Her hair streamed behind her.

She gripped the glass tube hard and watched as the quicksilver changed before her eyes. "It's going down farther still!"

The zephyr swooped down until it was parallel with the valley floor. A river churned beneath them. Cettie saw a small hamlet ahead and feared they would strike the houses' chimneys if they went much lower.

Fitzroy aimed for a farmer's meadow and brought the zephyr down so low they could jump out onto the grass. There he stopped.

"What is the reading?" he asked her.

She counted it and then told him.

"Even lower than at Fog Willows," he said. "Write it down. Clover Valley Hamlet. Then the number."

Cettie quickly scribbled down the note.

"Up from here!" Fitzroy said. As soon as they boarded, he went to the helm, and suddenly the zephyr shot straight into the air, lifting away from the meadow with a rush. The craft rattled and shook with the motion, and Cettie had to grip the railing again to steady herself.

Fitzroy laughed. "She's not used to going straight up! I'm glad we're doing this *before* dinner. Some people can't abide the sensation of rising and dropping."

When they reached a certain distance, he stopped the zephyr mid-air. "Mark the measurement, Cettie Saeed!" he called. The wind was much stronger now.

"It's the same as when we left!" she answered after making the count.

"Is it, now?" he said with jubilation, and started to laugh heartily. "Let's go higher up!"

Again the zephyr lurched vertically, pressing Cettie harder against the floor. It did feel as if a giant hand were pressing her down. Queasiness filled her stomach, but she kept her gaze riveted on the glass tube, watching as the quicksilver quivered and rose.

"It's rising!" she shouted with giddy excitement.

"Are you getting cold? I want to go higher."

"Go higher, then," she called back. Her cheeks and nose were feeling the effects of the drop in temperature. But the sky ship raced still higher. Breathing became more and more difficult. They were much higher than Fog Willows now, and her lungs were burning. The zephyr halted. The winds were so loud she couldn't hear Fitzroy calling to her, but his arms were gesturing for her to count again.

She did so and tried to write it down, but her fingers were so cold they were cramping. Breathing was painful.

After she finally managed to scribble down the number, she nodded to Fitzroy, and the zephyr started plunging like a stone. Her stomach rose into her throat as they plummeted, and she let out her air in a joyful scream. She began to float off the floor of the zephyr, almost like Raj Sarin could do merely by taking a breath. Her stomach flipped and flopped and squeezed, and her chest felt like it was full of flapping birds all caged at once. The descent slowed, and she felt the press of the floor again. Then the zephyr settled to a stop in the sky.

She gripped the railing, breathing much easier now.

"Sorry if I terrified you," Fitzroy said apologetically. "I haven't done these maneuvers since the Ministry of War. A sky ship can go any direction the pilot intends, but it's dangerous going too high. There is no air left to breathe."

"I felt that," Cettie gasped, trembling with the thrill. "How high have you flown?"

He smiled and shrugged. "Higher than that—to the point where the whole crew needs to hold their breath. It's easier to surprise an enemy coming from above than from below."

"I would imagine so," she replied. "The higher we went, the more the quicksilver rose. There are many ticks in between the low point and the high point."

Fitzroy folded his arms. "So the level of the quicksilver changes depending on altitude. That makes sense. Fog Willows is moored at a consistent height. It takes much more effort to move her than it does a zephyr, which is why this is the best way for us to test your theory. We will measure it at different times of day at different elevations. It may be a combination of factors. I think, Cettie, that you may have uncovered a truth about the wind that has been hidden for thousands of years. The change in the quicksilver must reveal when the wind is shifting. And when it shifts, it brings storms."

She felt her cheeks tingling with blood again. "I didn't discover it myself. Without your equipment, without your teaching, I would never have even tried."

"I appreciate your modesty, Cettie. I've heard that all the great strokes of genius came as an idea out of nothing. An observation suddenly catching afire in the imagination. There is a source of truth greater than ourselves. I think it chose to teach you because you were open and willing to listen. I may have been too proud."

She doubted that was true.

"What does it mean, Fitzroy? What would happen if we could know of a storm before it comes?" she asked with excitement.

The wind raked through his graying hair. "It means, my dear, that it may well be possible to predict when storms will come and go. Do you know how useful the Ministry of War would find this knowledge? How it would benefit the Ministry of Law in terms of trade? Do you imagine how many lives it could save?"

CHAPTER THIRTY-ONE
Storm Glass

The following weeks were some of the happiest Cettie had ever known. Her breakthrough had enlivened Fitzroy. It was the kind of discovery that happened once in a century, if that. She knew she couldn't have done it on her own. But it felt as though fate or some strange happenstance had brought the two of them together.

The implications of the discovery needed to be tested before Fitzroy would risk sharing it with the prime minister. And he would need to share it with him carefully so that the prime minister could not steal the findings and claim them as his own. So, with Cettie as his assistant, Fitzroy began to set up glass tubes in various locations—in his brother-in-law's house in the City, in Dolcoath, in each of his vessels, and in the homes of colleagues whom he knew and trusted. At several times during the day, he arranged for servants to count the number of ticks at each of these stations and send them to him at Fog Willows to record and study. This was done through a means of communication that was apparently one of the Mysteries.

They needed to come up with a name for the contraption they were inventing as it went through several iterations in order to make it more portable and easier to read and count. In the end, it was Cettie who named the device. *Storm glass.* Fitzroy thought it a splendid suggestion.

The first test of its accuracy happened at the Dolcoath mines. The readings on the quicksilver at the various stations would change every few days, but not always at the same time. Distance, both vertical and horizontal, played a factor. But one day the level dropped sharply at Dolcoath, even though the skies were clear at Fog Willows. Fitzroy sent a warning to Mr. Savage and Sir Jordan that a storm was coming. Then, one by one, all the storm-glass stations began to signal the approach. Cettie watched the windows anxiously for signs of clouds. The wind picked up and blew the weathercock around. The clouds appeared in the horizon by late afternoon the next day. Cettie reported the change to Fitzroy at once, and he grinned at her as the distant storm approached Fog Willows with jagged bursts of lightning.

It was a magnificent storm, with booming thunder that shook the walls of the floating manor. All the servants had been ordered inside to hunker down in preparation for it. All the sky ships were grounded because of it, and Cettie felt safe and secure inside the manor, even though she still slept in the garret above Mrs. Pullman's room. She was willing to stay there so long as Anna wouldn't be tormented. The storm glass in the City never registered the presence of the storm, and it died out before reaching the populous location.

Then all the stations returned to normal, and the skies cleared up again.

Fitzroy reviewed the records afterward, and together they used a chart to map out the approach and duration of the storm. At every station, the advent of the storm had been predicted by the falling of the quicksilver in the glass tubes.

"It's unmistakable," Fitzroy said in awe as Cettie leaned forward, her chin on her wrists. He used a strange pincerlike device to measure the distances between the locations on the map he pored over. He folded his arms, shaking his head slowly. "There is a warning every time.

And did you notice how deeply it fell? I think the faster and more pronounced the drop, the more violent or long-lasting the storm may be."

"What did Mr. Savage say about the storm after it was through?" Cettie asked.

Fitzroy chuckled. "He thought my warning was odd, but when the storm happened, his next response was to call me a *harbinger*—one who can see the future. Imagine this, Cettie. Imagine a world in which every sky ship is equipped with one of your devices. Every major city throughout the empire will have them, too. Just think—we can know the weather in the farthest reaches of the empire, even sitting here at Fog Willows. And this season is the perfect opportunity to test it, for storms will come regularly from now until winter."

Cettie beamed at him. "When are you going to tell the prime minister?"

"Soon," Fitzroy said. "This was our first major test. I'd like to do a few more before spreading the news to our leaders. We have uncovered a Mystery, Cettie. It will likely be a state secret, one that only a privileged few will ever know." He looked at her approvingly and lightly touched her nose. "And you will be one of them."

His praise made her flush with warmth. "I can't wait until I can go to school," she said, staring at the cylinder of glass capped with a pointy end. "I want to learn more of the Mysteries."

"You will go to one of the finest schools in the empire," Fitzroy said. "You already have a strong affinity for the Mysteries, Cettie. It usually begins at a young age. I'm surprised you haven't already felt the stirrings."

She looked up at him. "I have."

He paused, giving her a secret smile. "I thought perhaps you had. Do you remember the night of the Hardings' ball? The night you fainted? I've been meaning to talk to you about that."

"Of course I do," she answered. "Something strange happened to me that night."

"Tell me," he said, but she could see in his eyes that he already knew.

"While I was watching the ball, I felt something calling to me. It was as if the manor were alive, and I could hear what it was hearing and feel what it was feeling." She looked down at her hands.

"Go on," he coaxed.

She felt a little twinge of guilt—she knew spying wasn't a thing ladies did, or at least not one they admitted to—but pressed forward. "I saw Sir Jordan's mother talking to Mrs. Simmons. I w-wanted to know what they were saying. And then I could overhear their conversation, as if I were standing there next to them."

"Extraordinary," Fitzroy whispered.

"I felt as if maybe I *shouldn't* be listening in, but I couldn't help it. I didn't *try* to do it. It just happened."

"While I normally don't condone eavesdropping, that you can do it at all is nothing short of astonishing. It's quite unheard of. Especially at your age. And what was Mrs. Harding saying to Mrs. Simmons? Do you remember? Was she deploring the fashion of a young woman's dress?"

Cettie felt a shadow on her heart. "No. She was talking about you and how you rescued Lady Maren's reputation. Back when she was shunned from society."

Fitzroy was taken aback. "Was she indeed?"

"They said something about a man she used to love. Before she loved you."

She saw the look of pain in his eyes, the subtle crinkling of his brow. There was still a partially healed wound there. She instantly regretted sharing the gossip.

"I'm sorry," she apologized.

He waved aside her discomfort. "It pains me that she still talks about it," he said softly. "Not that it happened. It was a long time ago, Cettie. Well, did you hear anything else of interest?"

She swallowed, feeling conflicted. There was more.

"Go ahead," he said encouragingly. "There is nothing you can say that I wouldn't want to hear. And I'd prefer to set the record straight with you. The stately Mrs. Harding knows a great deal. But she does not know all of it."

She yearned to tell him about Mrs. Pullman. But that was impossible. Mrs. Pullman had made it so.

"Mrs. Harding thinks that *I* may be the daughter of your lost love."

If her previous comment had caused him to flinch, this one made him writhe. The expression on his face changed markedly, and she could see the hurt and wretchedness on his countenance. He leaned forward, hunching his shoulders, letting his head sag. His lips quivered with suppressed emotion.

"Ah, so they *are* still talking about her," he said with pain lacing his voice.

"Who was she?" Cettie asked sympathetically, touching his arm.

Fitzroy shook his head, trying to master his emotions. The pain was still raw, still buried like a thorn beneath the skin. It was festering and sore.

She was trying to comfort him. It made her so sad to see him suffering.

He glanced down at her hand and sighed. "I don't tell this story very often, Cettie. Not even to my children. I prefer to keep my privacy. But since you only know part of the tale, I will provide a few more details."

"I won't tell anyone," she promised.

He patted her hand. "I know you wouldn't. I trust you." He turned away, his voice changing. He tried to keep his tone lighthearted, but there were cracks. "When I was a young man, my parents took in a ward, a young woman who had been abandoned by her parents. They'd signed away a deed for the rest of her life for a modest sum. I was away at school when they brought her home. Her name was Christina." A little sigh escaped his mouth. "My father bought her deed with the intent of her becoming a lady's maid for my mother. Nothing more. She was sixteen. Although I was younger, I was far more knowledgeable about the world than her. Or so I thought." He chuckled darkly. "Music has always fascinated me, and back then I used to play the clavicembalo with much vigor. Sometimes, she would neglect her duties and listen to me play, either my own songs or some of the popular music of the day. They were modest accomplishments. I'm not trying to boast. But I would often catch her staring at me, showing interest in the music. I offered to teach her in secret, because I knew my parents would not approve. Then I went back to school, but I kept thinking about her and wondering about her progress. When I came back to Fog Willows, I saw that she'd improved quite a bit. It made me so proud of her." He cleared his throat. "I was very young, but I began to have a bit of a fancy for her."

Cettie continued to gaze at him, deeply interested in his story. It was difficult imagining Fitzroy as young as Stephen. His graying hair prevented such a vision. But she felt a pang of sadness already, knowing the story would end badly. "Was she kind to you?"

"Indeed," Fitzroy added, looking at her. "She didn't have airs. She worked hard to please my mother and didn't aspire for anything beyond my friendship. I taught her several duets, pieces that we could play together. She was eager to learn them, eager to listen to my stories from school. I could see a hunger for learning in her eyes." He shrugged. "We became close friends. Companions, really. And then I went back to school again. My parents wanted me to distinguish myself in the Law or War. But I had always been more drawn to the Wind. I thought I might be a musician. When I returned the next summer, she had grown so beautiful that I thought my aching heart would be wrenched apart. It became impossible to keep my feelings a secret. I told her honestly how I felt. That I was drawn to her, and if it were up to me, she would study at the same school and master the same talents that I had." He scratched the side of his head, looking quite uncomfortable. Then a little smile played on his mouth. "She took my hand and kissed my fingers and said that her heart would always be mine, whether or not circumstances prevented us from being together."

He sighed forlornly. "She was a harbinger. They did. When I told my father about my intention to court her, he flew into a rage. I'd never seen him so angry, neither before nor after. I was his only son, and he threatened to bequeath Fog Willows to his younger brother if I defied him. He said music had made me too passionate, and he forbade me to play the cembalo. He compelled me to join the Ministry of War and paid for a commission. Even so, I was determined to keep faith with Christina. I'd give up the estate and make my fortunes in the military. I promised to come back for her." He heaved another ragged sigh. "Knowing my determination to defy him, my father preempted me. Before I finished school, he sold her deed and sent her to the Fells. I searched and searched for her, but my father refused to disclose what had been done to her. And then I was deployed on a hurricane to a distant part of the empire. By the time I returned and could search for her in earnest, it'd become an impossible quest. I hired advocates with my midshipman's wages to conduct the search in my absence. The same advocates that you met in the Fells."

He folded his arms and stared into the distance. "Would it not be a twist of fate, my dear Cettie, if the woman I am seeking, the woman who gave birth to you, is, in fact, Christina? I don't know the truth. I do know that when I first met you, I was struck by the force of your presence. I felt compelled to help you. Did that come from your desire to leave the Fells? Your ability to see the ghosts? Or was it something even more powerful? Sometimes I think Christina is nothing more than a ghost now. I've tried everything to find her. But still she eludes me."

He began to pace slowly, his seething feelings apparent beneath his calm exterior. "When I met Lady Maren, her mother had been disinherited and was on the verge of the extreme measure of signing a deed for one of her daughters. Sir Jordan, a distant cousin, took them all in and gave her a reduced rent in light of her reduced circumstances. Maren shared my passion for music . . . for *life*. I'd been a bachelor for a long time by then, hoping against hope to somehow fulfill my promise. In time, and it was gradual, I came to have feelings for Maren. She did not care very much for me back then." A wry smile lit his face. "But through persistence and kindness, I won her heart." He paused for a long moment, and then added, "I've always harbored sympathy for those trapped in the Fells. If I could change their circumstances, I would. And I cannot deny that something powerful drew me to *you* that night at Miss Charlotte's. I am grateful that our paths crossed. More grateful than I can express." He gave her a warm smile. "I've come to care for you quite strongly, Cettie. I want you to have a happier life than you've known."

Cettie's respect for him had deepened with the tale. She stared into his eyes, willing him to ask her a question that would reveal the truth about his household—and the poison that was infecting it from within. *Ask me about Mrs. Pullman,* she thought. *Please, you must ask me. If you ask me, then maybe I will be able to tell you.*

His eyebrows narrowed. "Is everything all right, Cettie?"

She shook her head slowly.

"Is there something you wish to tell me? Something you know?"

She felt her tongue already swelling. But she defied it, nodding yes.

"What is it?" he asked.

And, once again, she couldn't speak. Almost at that very moment, Kinross entered the study. "Sir, I just received word that the prime minister wishes you to attend him at the City. The weather portends to be clear. I don't know the reasons for this summons, but this may be the opportunity we've all been waiting for."

The butler smiled broadly. Cettie's heart fell.

CHAPTER THIRTY–TWO

REVENGE

It was time for Fitzroy to leave for Lockhaven. His tempest hovered over the landing dock. The air contained the shiver of autumn, and every day, the manor in the clouds was a little colder. Fitzroy was going with Raj Sarin, so Cettie's training with him would be interrupted. A deep sense of foreboding weighed on her. She desperately longed to talk to Fitzroy before he left, to confess her fears and to warn him about Mrs. Pullman. But the older woman's power kept her silent. And he was so interested in leaving for the City and talking to the prime minister that he hadn't noticed her change in mood.

Lady Maren was wrapped in a cloak as she walked, arm in arm, with Fitzroy from the manor. Anna and Cettie trailed behind. Raj Sarin waited by the tempest, and he gave Cettie a respectful nod as she approached.

"Good morning, Cettie Saeed," he greeted.

"Good morning, Raj Sarin," she replied.

"I want you to keep practicing the Way while I am gone with the master. Will you do that?"

"Of course I will," she replied with a smile. "I will miss our lessons."

"Is everything all right, Cettie Saeed? You look troubled."

Her heart was sick with worry, but there was no way to tell him that, so she merely nodded and shrugged. Her throat instantly began to swell.

"I don't know how long I will remain in Lockhaven," Fitzroy said to Lady Maren. He gripped her shoulders and kissed her forehead. "The prime minister will likely ask for demonstrations, which will require a storm. It's possible I'll be gone for several weeks. It is not uncommon for storms to strike this time of year, and that would prevent a return home. But I will come as soon as I can."

"I don't like it when you leave us," Lady Maren said, pressing her cheek against his chest while he held her. "Anna did not do so well the last time you were gone."

"I'm worried about her, too," Fitzroy said. "Send word if anything changes. I'll respond as quickly as I can."

"Travel safely, my love," Lady Maren said, leaning up and kissing him on the mouth. "I am worried this time. I know I shouldn't be, but I have a feeling of dread."

Lady Maren's words only heightened Cettie's sense of gloom. She wished that Fitzroy would take her. But she'd already caused him enough trouble with his political peers, and he was going to see the prime minister. It wouldn't do for her to come.

Fitzroy looked at his wife in concern. "If anything happens, send for me at once."

"But the prime minister . . . ?" Lady Maren said. "He is such a greedy man. All the ministers are. Will the prime minister attempt to claim your invention for himself?"

Fitzroy shook his head. "I have known him for a good many years, love. I'm fully aware of his character. I have no intention of revealing all that I know, not until I've secured the rights through the Ministry of Law."

"You are wise, Husband. And I'm comforted that Raj Sarin is going with you."

After giving her a final embrace, he knelt before Anna and hugged her fiercely. "Be brave, Felicianna."

"I'll try, Papa," she answered, her voice quavering. She wrapped her arms around his neck, squeezing hard, and kissed him. "I love you!"

"And I love you, child. Sweet Anna. It hurts to leave you all."

"Be brave, Papa," she said, smiling through her tears.

He turned, still kneeling, and beckoned Cettie to him. She rushed forward and hugged him just as hard as Anna had, feeling comforted by the embrace.

"And I love *you*, Cettie Saeed," he said, giving her a tight squeeze. "As if you were my own."

Cettie closed her eyes, relishing the delicious feelings that swept into her heart at the words. "I love you, Fitzroy," she whispered, kissing his cheek.

As he rose and brushed a tear from his eye, he gave her a quavering smile. "Now you, young lady, have an especially important duty while I am gone. You must record the readings here at Fog Willows and report them to Kinross. He will make sure that I get them. This is an important responsibility, Cettie. Can I count on you?"

She nodded vigorously. "You can, sir."

"That is good. Discipline must be maintained." He gave her a smart salute. He gazed at each of them in turn, his gentle smile a balm to Cettie's troubled heart. "You are all precious to me. I cannot return soon enough. But duty to the empire calls, and I must obey."

He then turned and climbed up the rope ladder to the tempest. Raj Sarin still waited below. Giving Cettie another scrutinizing glance, he then took a deep breath and began to float up to the tempest, arriving just after Fitzroy.

Even though she shivered from the cool air, Cettie watched until the tempest faded out of sight, long after Lady Maren and Anna had gone inside.

The bell awoke Cettie from the middle of a terrible dream. Her eyes blinked open in the darkness, and she found herself cold and cramped on the floor of the garret. It had been a miserable night of lying awake in fear, dreading the tall ghost's arrival. Its touch chilled her heart, made her feelings numb with cold. Now that the children weren't around to keep her safe, she finally knew what it wanted, because she could sense its thoughts. It wanted to engulf her, to steal her life and energy for itself, but somehow it couldn't. Perhaps her hope and the love she felt for Fitzroy and his family kept it from totally engulfing her. But her dreams had been of the Fells that night, and she felt disoriented and sick inside. The bell sounded again, and Cettie scrambled to the trapdoor and opened it, hugging her blanket close.

She scurried down the ladder into Mrs. Pullman's room and found the stern woman standing there with a lantern. The sun had not yet risen, and it was very dark outside. Cettie shivered beneath her nightdress and blanket, rubbing the sleep from her eyes.

"Don't just stand there. Put your dress on."

Cettie looked for her chest, but it was gone. In its place was something else. She gasped in surprise and sudden fear. It was her old, ragged dress, the one she had been wearing upon her arrival to Fog Willows.

She looked at Mrs. Pullman, dread threading inside her stomach.

Mrs. Pullman smiled archly. "Put it on, child."

"What's happening?" Cettie demanded.

Mrs. Pullman shrugged. "You are going back where you belong."

Cettie's breath became faster. "You can't make me go," she said, backing away.

The wrinkles on Mrs. Pullman's face quivered. "Insolent child," she said sharply. "I cannot make you go? I've been planning this a good long while, little miss. You have never belonged here. You will *never*

293

belong here. And at the master's moment of triumph, you would steal his glory for yourself. Oh, this has been long overdue."

Cettie backed away from her.

"You can't leave this room without the key," Mrs. Pullman said. "And if you won't put on the dress willingly, then you will go back to the Fells wearing nothing but that shift."

"I won't go back," Cettie said, shaking her head.

"You *will*. Because I said you will. It seems your parents are tired of negotiating with that fool advocate Mr. Sloan. They will get more from the master if they first have you in their possession. Each deed contains a recapture clause for the child's parents that is viable even if the deed has been paid off. Not even Sloan and Teitelbaum can deny them their right." She gave Cettie a savage grin. "Your *mother's* right is the strongest."

Cettie gazed at Mrs. Pullman. "You know where my mother is?"

"Of course I do," Mrs. Pullman said. "I'm the one who sent *her* away, too. To a place she was never found. Where she will *never* be found." The hatred in Mrs. Pullman's eyes made Cettie quake with dread. "I have many connections down below, child. People with power. People who owe me favors for bringing their friends or family to work here. A zephyr is coming. Lieutenant Staunton is fulfilling his final duty before his *promotion*. When I come back to fetch you, you will come peacefully. Or there will be bruises. It makes no difference to me."

Mrs. Pullman carried her lantern to the door. She withdrew her set of keys and unlocked it. She gave Cettie a cunning look before shutting and locking the door again.

There was no doubt in Cettie's mind that Mrs. Pullman would fulfill her threats. She'd clearly been planning this for some time. Fitzroy was already far away, still bound for Lockhaven, and it could take days for news to reach him. Lady Maren and Anna were likely fast asleep; they wouldn't notice she'd been taken until it was much too late for them to intervene. She shook like a leaf in a storm and felt like dissolving into tears. But tears wouldn't help her solve her problem.

She had to do it on her own.

As she stood trembling, she calmed her breathing using the techniques Raj Sarin had taught her. She needed to calm her frenzied mind. After a few minutes of practice, she felt her wits beginning to return. What should she do?

First, she decided to change into the dress. If she wandered the streets and alleys of the Fells in one of the gowns from the manor, she would stand out as an easy victim. Wearing her shift, she'd be even more vulnerable. So she snatched the tattered dress and hastily put it on. She remembered how loose it had been on her thin frame when she'd last worn it. Now the sleeves squeezed her arms and shoulders, and the hem exposed too much leg for anyone's sense of propriety. Had she really grown so much since coming to Fog Willows? She could hardly believe it.

There was a hole in the elbow, and many of the seams were stretching to the bursting point. The shoes were falling apart and felt tight and jagged against her feet. They'd once belonged to her, but now they felt like a stranger's. Cettie parted the curtain that faced the landing yard and saw her own reflection. It brought back painful memories, and again her mind started to take flight into reckless panic. But she breathed deeply and calmed herself. She saw the zephyr had positioned itself below the landing platform instead of above it. Mrs. Pullman probably intended to shove her off the edge.

Cettie bit her lip, trying to think. The door was locked. The garret held no exit. But what about the windows? Mrs. Pullman's room was full of windows that faced every direction. She hurried to the one opposite the landing yard and tugged on the lever. She heard the noise of footsteps coming up the stairs and recognized Mrs. Pullman's heavy, deliberate step. The handle was difficult to move, but she put all her strength to it and tugged it loose. She pushed open the window, and a gust of icy wind struck her.

Even though the wind stung her eyes, she squinted and gazed out. The tower housing Mrs. Pullman's room was at one end of a long ridged roofline leading back to the main house. The roof's stone shingles were very steep and likely slippery. Leaving the tower, she'd be on a sharp angle and have to climb up to the ridgeline leading to the main house. That was flat and narrow and would be easier to traverse. If she could make it to the main house, she could try to wake a servant by hitting one of the upper windows, or maybe she could break it with her shoe.

She glanced back at the door. In her mind, she made the decision that she wouldn't willingly go back to the Fells. She didn't want to be swallowed up like Christina.

Cettie climbed out the window. The wind blew sharply against her, making her suddenly dizzy and fearful. The shingles were damp and slick. She doubted herself. Now that she was outside, the cold began to suck at her, making her fingers and cheeks numb. And she had always been somewhat afraid of heights, so her precarious position was terrifying. Clinging to the window frame, she edged her way along the roof to the next one. Fear stabbed her again; there wasn't much to grab on to, and the wind was blowing at her, making her unsure of her balance. But she made it past the second window and then the third. The ridgeline of the roof was just ahead. The spine looked very narrow upon closer examination. If she ran toward it, she thought her momentum might carry her to it. Then she could dash along the spine.

The wind whistled in her ears. She gazed at the dim horizon and saw just a strip of yellow from the rising sun. It was barely visible against a backdrop of clouds. Had another storm been brewing during the night since she had last taken a reading on the storm glass?

Cettie judged the distance to the roofline and made her decision. She could be there in three steps. If she kept herself light on her feet, she would make it.

Cettie took a deep breath, wishing she had Raj Sarin's abilities, and started a dash for the ridge. The shoes she wore were too smooth and slipped on the shingles. She crashed onto the roof, clawing for the roofline with her fingers as she began to slide down. Her stomach lurched as her speed increased. She tried to grab anything, but there was nothing to grip. She was sliding toward the edge, scraping her palms and shins as she went.

She spread her arms wide, trying to hug the roof, and the descent slowed. She was sprawled halfway down the roof, and her body was still sliding. She gasped for breath and realized each spasm was tugging her lower. The only way she could manage to stop the downward slide was to calm her breathing.

Pure panic erupted inside of her. Her fingertips struggled to grip the shingles. Her elbows throbbed. She didn't know how long she waited there, breathing shallowly, silently hoping she wouldn't fall off the roof and plummet off the estate. The wind lashed around her, making her colder and colder.

Hearing a noise, she looked up and saw Mrs. Pullman leaning out the window with confusion. Then, looking down, she spied Cettie on the roof. A look of exasperated anger wrinkled her features even more.

"Go ahead and fall, child!" Mrs. Pullman sneered. "Is that what you want? To kill yourself?"

Cettie shook her head no and felt herself slide even farther. She was terrified and pressed herself against the roof. Now she wished she'd tried another way.

As she hung there, too afraid to move, the wind picked up its viciousness. Mrs. Pullman stood at the window, muttering to herself, no doubt about Cettie's stupidity. She wasn't sure how much time passed like that, with her clinging to the roof with aching fingers.

The sky was getting brighter and brighter, revealing the details of this place that had become her home. She saw Mrs. Pullman waving, and then a shadow fell over her. It was the zephyr.

The creak of ropes sounded. She heard a man grunting as he climbed down. Then a sturdy pair of boots landed next to her on the roof.

"Come on, lass. Enough trouble." She recognized Lieutenant Staunton's voice. His strong hands gripped her waist and hoisted her off the roof and slung her over his shoulder.

"Hold tight. I don't want to drop you. It's a long way down."

She looked into his face, her mind full of anger and helplessness. She opened her mouth to accuse him of betrayal.

But her throat tightened, and no words at all came out. Just like Lady Admiral, Cettie's voice had been taken away.

CHAPTER THIRTY-THREE

CETTIE OF THE FELLS

With anguish pounding against her heart like thunder, Cettie watched the Fells come into view beneath the sleek zephyr. She was sick inside and not because the sky ship lowered at a precipitous rate. Gripping the edge of the railing and shivering because of the wind whipping through her threadbare dress, she saw the dismal tenements loom closer, the pocked gray walls stained with chimney smoke. Even worse, she remembered the persistent tenement ghosts. What little protection Mrs. Pullman had allowed her in Fog Willows would be stripped away.

And, to make matters worse, she had no voice.

Lieutenant Staunton paced, his expression betraying the agitation of his mind. He was pursuing his own interests, of course, getting the captain's post he had always wanted. But Cettie could feel something raking against his mind. An inner part of her whispered that his actions were tormenting him.

"More to the starboard," Staunton barked in command. The pilot obeyed, and the zephyr lurched to the right.

"Aye, sir," he replied.

How much had the pilot been told? Probably nothing. He was just following the commands of his superior. He may have felt some pity for

Cettie's fate, but he likely did not know what had been arranged. The zephyr was not approaching the business district of the Fells, where the factories and government buildings and law offices were located. No, they were headed into the tenements. If she was being brought to her father and stepmother, as the old keeper had implied, she imagined they would be easier for Fitzroy to find. People changed dwellings often, and there was no way to follow a trail without effort. Besides, if they were truly taking her to her mother, Fitzroy would have little hope of finding her. After months of searching, he still didn't have a lead on the woman. By the time he learned of Cettie's disappearance, she might be locked in a cesspit cellar, unable to cry out if he searched for her.

She had to take action. Even without words, she could still communicate.

Walking up to Staunton, she tugged at his sleeve. He flinched and turned, looking down at her with a clenched jaw. She gave him an accusing look and shook her head no. Then she pointed back to the sky, back toward Fog Willows.

Her demand made him wince. "I *can't*, lass," he whispered, scraping his nails through his hair.

She stomped her foot and pointed again, staring at him with mingled fury and determination.

The zephyr shuddered and jolted up suddenly, making her stomach thrill. She felt a growing awareness of the craft. Something told her it had felt her thought of command . . . and it had responded to it.

"Jaggers!" Staunton yelled.

"The controls are fighting me," the man called back. The zephyr shuddered again but continued its descent.

Cettie leaned into the thought, into the *demand*, that they return to Fog Willows. The zephyr started rattling.

"What's going on, man!" Staunton said, whirling around and striding to the helm.

"She's kicking against me," the pilot said in confusion.

"It's the girl," Staunton muttered. He turned and gave Cettie a sharp look. "Stop it!"

Cettie had no intention of stopping it. She felt the core of the zephyr, an inner intelligence that directed its motion, direction, and speed. It was receiving conflicting orders, growing confused by the wills pressing at it.

The zephyr bucked, knocking Staunton and Cettie off their feet. The pilot groaned, cursing under his breath.

"I'm warning you, lass," Staunton said angrily, struggling to grip the railing. Cettie felt the weight of his thoughts join the pilot's, and the descent became controlled once more.

"Sir, what is going on?" demanded the frightened pilot.

"Hold fast, Jaggers. Fix your purpose."

Cettie stared at the pilot and pushed her thoughts past him into the middle of the zephyr. Closer to the rooftops. Closer.

The ship began to buck again, more violently this time, and both men groaned as it dipped furiously. The motion shoved Cettie against the side of the railing. She glanced down, seeing the peaked rooftops and broken shingles.

"We're going to crash, sir!" Jaggers yelled. "I'm losing control of her!"

Staunton's eyes blazed with fury. He struggled to his feet, swaying from the bucking of the zephyr, and pulled himself hand over hand along the railing ropes toward her.

"Enough!" Staunton shouted, striking Cettie across the face so hard it made her vision black out for a moment. She collapsed onto the deck boards, dizzy with nausea and confusion. The world was spinning around her, and she fought to stay conscious. If she failed, she'd have no idea where they landed, no idea how close she was to the city center.

Her cheek stung and her cheekbone throbbed. Looking up, she saw Lieutenant Staunton towering over her, his face full of fury and fear. The zephyr was rising again. The pilot had regained control.

"If you try that again," he warned her savagely, looking ready to kick her while she lay crumpled on the floor.

Cettie closed her fist and drew in a calming breath as Raj Sarin had taught her. There was no way she could fight two grown men and win. She had no illusion about that. But she refused to accept her fate, refused to go along docilely. She would do all that she could to free herself. She would not be lost to the Fells like Christina. Cettie was determined to be *found*.

She slowly got to her knees, preparing herself. The zephyr was rising again. She didn't have a moment to lose. Cettie struck Lieutenant Staunton in the groin as hard as she could. His eyes widened with shock and instant agony, and he bowled over, issuing a hissing gasp. She slapped him across the face with a blow that stung her hand and then raced down the back of the sky ship.

She didn't pause as she reached the edge of the railing. Clambering up the back, she saw the nest of roofs below, sinking farther and farther down. Her mind went black with terror at the thought of jumping. Many of the roofs below had skylights . . .

"No!" Staunton moaned, gazing at her in horror.

Jaggers shouted in shock. "Lieutenant, she's going to—!"

His words were cut off as she jumped.

⚊⚊

Cettie watched the roof rush up to meet her. The thrill of falling lasted only moments. She feared she might miss the edge of the roof entirely and plummet down five stories to shatter on the street below. But she struck the wooden shingles with her knees and elbows, just a few feet from the dirty glass of a skylight.

The bone-jarring crash of the wood exploded in her ears, and suddenly everything was dark. The roof caved in on impact, and she plunged into the attic of the tenement, landing in a heap of broken wood and splinters. The attic was dusty and full of rats, which squealed and scattered upon her intrusion. The wind had been knocked out of her, and she lay writhing and struggling to breathe. Looking up, she saw the huge hole in the roof and was amazed she hadn't shattered all her bones. The pain and shock of her abrupt landing began to lose its sharpness, and her breathing returned. Slow and calm, slow and calm, just as Raj Sarin had taught her.

No doubt Staunton would circle back and leap down into the hole after her. No doubt his reward depended on delivering her into her "parents'" hands.

Scrambling to her feet, ignoring the pain, Cettie searched for the attic trapdoor and found it. As soon as she yanked it open, she could hear the commotion coming from below.

People called out in concerned shouts. There was a woman in the room just below, gazing up at the ladder as Cettie hurried down it.

"And jus' who in the Fells are you!" the woman demanded in her thick accent.

Cettie couldn't have responded if she'd wanted to; her tongue was still blocked from speech. The woman grabbed at her arm, and Cettie jumped down the rest of the way to avoid the reach. She ran to the door and opened it, trying to plunge into the dark corridor. Trying to get out. The woman managed to grab Cettie's hair and yank her back. Cettie whirled and kicked the woman's knee. The woman bellowed in anger as her hand slipped out of Cettie's hair, and Cettie fled down the hall, shouts and cries following her. A few doors opened, confused dwellers poking out their heads.

"Stop her! Stop her!" the woman bawled.

Cettie reached the narrow stairwell before anyone could try, and soon she was flying down the steps. Sounds and yells erupted all around her, but she kept her breathing focused and quickly reached the lower levels.

A man in a dirty cap was coming up from below. "Oy, there, what's all the ruckus?"

Cettie pointed back up the stairs and pressed against the wall to let him pass, giving him a fearful look as if she were running away from something terrible. The man grunted and started to jog up the stairs, nodding to her as he passed. To him she was just another waif with a bruised cheek. In the tenements, people minded their own business. They didn't trust one another. They stole from one another.

She *hated* the Fells. And now she was back there. Maybe forever.

After reaching the ground floor, she walked hastily to the main door and hurried out into the street. A crowd had gathered, a mixture of tradesmen and starving beggars, but most were pointing at the sky. Looming in the gap above them was the shadow of the zephyr.

A man grabbed Cettie by the arm, and she nearly brought the heel of her hand into his nose, but he was looking at her in concern.

"Are you all right, miss? You're bleeding something awful."

The fabric of her dress had been slashed at the elbows and forearms, and streaks of blood were coming down her arms. Her chin stung as well, and when she dabbed her wrist against it, she saw the red smear. Her knees and shins throbbed as well. But she couldn't stop here, not so close to where Staunton would come looking.

She shook her head no and wrested her arm out of his grip.

"Did someone hurt you?" he asked her. "Can I bring you to a doctor?"

His sympathy made her long to trust him. But she dared not trust anyone, not even a potbellied old man with stubble for hair beneath his soiled cap. She thought of Adam Creigh, who wanted to be a doctor so he could improve life for people in the Fells. The thought of never seeing him again drove a spike of pain through her chest.

She shook her head no and started to back away.

He looked at her sadly, hand outstretched. But it couldn't be helped. She couldn't go with him. Folding her arms to hide the blood, she began to walk briskly away down the alley, letting her hair dangle in front of her face. She remembered the warmth of sleeping in Anna's bed. The dances they'd all practiced together, like "Genny's Market" and "Sky Ship's Cook." A sob threatened to break loose, but she stilled it. She grasped the memories in her mind as she walked, going down alley after alley, not daring to lose herself in the maze. If Fitzroy came after her—and she believed he eventually would—she would need to find him before the officers of the law found her.

She had no shelter. She had no money. She had no voice.

Tears welled up in her eyes, and she rubbed them away with the heel of her hand. Crying wouldn't solve her problem. Thinking would.

She needed to go to a place where Fitzroy would end up. Her first thought was the law office of Sloan and Teitelbaum. If she could find that place, near the square, she could wait for Fitzroy to arrive.

If she didn't starve or freeze to death first.

SERA

Most speculations end badly. All are masked in the guise of legitimacy. Early success can lead to frenzied participation. But often that early success is itself a clue that the idea behind the scheme is shallow at best. Men hope for riches without working to attain them. They will barter their very souls to advance another rung on the ladder, even though they risk falling from the ladder completely. But every so often there comes an idea—a genuine one—that will change the world. New ideas are delicate. The wise see these opportunities and get involved early. They are the ones to claim the rewards, often before their creators even glimpse them.

—Lady Corinne of Pavenham Sky

CHAPTER THIRTY–FOUR
Her Majesty or No

Sera felt as if her life were dangling from giant hooks. She had never understood the world in which she was living. No one other than Mr. Durrant had ever bothered to explain it to her. Now, for the first time in her life, she understood the importance of the Mysteries in her society. And how woefully ignorant her parents had kept her of them. She understood how the estates and even the City itself floated. She understood the precarious balance of this awe-worthy magic and how people holding certain keys held it all together.

Sera's daydreams had ended. With an almost frenzied pace, she gobbled up every book on the subject of the Mysteries that she could lay her hands on—until Father found out and banished her from the library, ordering the keeper to lock the door. Rather than allow this obstacle to prevent her from her course, she improvised. In her mind, she went through every lecture she had received on all the facets of the Mysteries. She forced her mind to recall information, and she tried to write down notes from the snippets she remembered so that she could study them later. She wrote constantly, trying to conjure the studies that she had taken so casually, and she felt sick to her stomach that she had given them so little attention. She understood the *why* of the Mysteries now, which gave her the missing context that all the dry lectures had lacked. And it revealed her role, as a Fitzempress, in maintaining them.

Mr. Durrant was a capable mentor, and he brought her books with each visit, mostly related to the Mysteries of Law, but he had dabbled in the other Mysteries. Just as she'd long suspected, she found herself most drawn to the Mysteries of Thought. She craved every scrap she could find and experienced an almost voracious appetite for learning. Her father was trying to forbid her access, and it only stoked the frenzy more. If she hadn't known better, she would have imagined this was her father's ploy to entice her into learning. But that no longer seemed feasible. Father no longer treated her like a daughter. He was convinced that she wasn't his child at all, that Mother had committed adultery and she had been the result. It was utter nonsense. Her mother had angrily denied it and said it was a ploy Father was using to disinherit his own daughter.

The breakup of her parents' marriage had become a very public spectacle. Mr. Durrant did what he could to protect her rights, but he assured her that talk of it had spread throughout Lockhaven and then down into the City and across the empire. Sympathy for her was growing among the people, who saw this as a contemptible ploy by her father to strip Sera of her power as a Fitzempress and as a rival for her grandfather's throne. The populace grew restless, he said, and demanded to see her. The pressure from the public was only making the prince regent more belligerent. Again, it felt as if she had two hooks in her, each one tugging her a different way, both agonizingly painful.

She was in the middle of reviewing her notes when a knock sounded on the door. For a moment, she let herself imagine Baroness Hugilde was still with her. That *she* would answer the door. She so missed her friend's companionship. With sorrow, Sera put aside the papers and answered the door. Mr. Durrant bowed to her, and she stood aside to let him enter.

"I brought this for you," he said, handing over a small black book. "I saw it in my library this morning and thought you might enjoy reading it. It's very old, very dusty, and it will probably bore you to tears, but it is one of the earlier works on the Mysteries of Thought—"

She snatched it from his hand before he finished his little speech, earning a chuckle from the man.

"Well, maybe you will like it after all," he said with a genuine smile. "It was required reading when I went to school, but they offer more modern interpretations these days."

"Which school did you study at, Master Durrant?" she asked, holding the precious volume in her hands. She was eager to begin reading it right away.

"One of the eastern ones. Not the most famous, of course, but it suited my tendency to walk and brood by the sea."

"Thank you." Sera squeezed the book in her hands and resisted the temptation to start reading it right then and there. She set it down on the table. "Is there any news regarding my case?" she asked him.

He shrugged. "I was summoned here today to meet with the prince regent's advocate to review some contracts and papers. Every week he has attempted to extort your mother into signing something or other, and we refuse to cooperate until your rights are addressed. Which, of course, your father refuses to do. It's a vicious game of *tug and war*. Do you know it?"

Sera shook her head.

"It's popular down below. Two teams of equal size grip a rope from the dockyard and try to pull the other side across the pier into the water. Obviously the losers get wet. It's rather barbaric, but intriguing to watch. My offices are near the docks, so I see such matches play out on occasion. I wonder what nonsense your father will attempt today."

Sera clenched her teeth and fumed. "I wish he would catch ill and stop all this nonsense."

"They are only ploys, Sera. You are made of tougher stuff than this. The people are worried about you because they see you as a potential champion of the poor." He smirked. "It only took some whispers in the right ears. Now I hear it every day as I walk the streets below the City.

You are loved by a populace that scarcely knows you. They are beginning to clamor loudly on your behalf, and your father's rejection of you is only heightening their animosity toward him."

"But I hear nothing up in Lockhaven," Sera said, starting to pace and wringing her hands with anxiety.

"It's probably better that you don't," he said wryly. "It's very noisy down below."

"Is there any other news of interest, Mr. Durrant?" she asked, trying to change the subject.

"Indeed, there is," he replied, scratching his sideburns. "The prime minister has called for Lord Fitzroy. Actually, he's a *vice admiral*, but I tend not to use ranks when one has left the military. The Ministry of War has caught wind, if you'll pardon an intentional pun, that he has made a major discovery. Something rather impressive, I hear. I do not know what it is, but, apparently, he's been hunkering down—or *up*, I should say—at his estate, Fog Willows, and may have unraveled a new Mystery. He's not a man prone to exaggeration, and his reputation for integrity . . . well, I need not repeat it. There are investors aplenty who wish to get in on a scheme, if he has one." He sighed and rubbed the single lock on his forehead. "I fear the man has so many scruples that he may be taken in by those with few. You may even see his tempest approaching from the northwest if you watch your window."

"Is he coming here?" Sera asked.

"I believe the prime minister will be meeting him here, yes," Durrant said. "On the morrow, I think."

Sera shook her head. "I feel sorry for him, then. My father will try and ruin him and steal whatever he's discovered."

Mr. Durrant shrugged but didn't argue the point.

There was another rap on the door. Mr. Durrant obliged her by answering it himself, and there was her father's new advocate, Mr. Swan. He was younger than Mr. Durrant, with a charming smile and the look of a man who had won a fortune in a speculation. He wore the latest fashions and an elegant golden cravat with a jewel pinned to it.

"Ah, Durrant. I had heard you'd arrived." He flashed his teeth. "The prince regent is waiting in the parlor with the girl's mother. Shall we?"

The deliberate reference to her as her mother's child made Sera boil with anger. She caught a disapproving look from Mr. Durrant, who had reminded her on multiple occasions not to be goaded by the ill manners of others. Sera held her head erect and took the book from the table to bring it along. The meetings—arguments, really—between her parents could be dull, and she was craving a chance to start reading. Since the book didn't belong to Father, he couldn't take it away from her.

They walked down the corridor and entered the parlor, which had become the agreed-upon meeting place for their respective advocates. Mother was sitting in stony silence. When Sera entered, her look did not change in the least. Her skin was ashen from the constant worry and festering anger in her heart. The hatred between her parents was palpable to all in the room.

Father, on the other hand, was trying to conceal a self-satisfied look, and that immediately put Sera on her guard.

"Let's begin, Swan," he said with agitation.

Mr. Durrant's brow creased—a sign that he, too, had noticed her father's mood—but he paid his respects to Sera's mother and even kissed her hand. Then he turned and subtly motioned for Sera to take a seat near where he stood.

"Yes, we shall begin and end if all goes well," Mr. Swan said. He smiled pleasantly, although it wasn't a pleasant occasion, and produced a leather folder from his jacket pocket. Opening it, he said, "You will find . . . madame . . . a deed signed by yourself and your lawful husband one year ago, on this precise day. It is a deed with an option to be exercised, and the prince regent would like to exercise that option. Today. The deed is in the name of Seraphin Fitzempress."

The advocate then turned his charming smile to Sera as she felt her world lurch and begin to spin.

Sera's mother began to speak fast and breathe even faster. "What is this . . . What are you saying? Mr. Durrant, what is he saying?"

"May I see it?" Mr. Durrant demanded, stepping forward.

"Gladly," Mr. Swan said with a triumphant tone. "It was witnessed by Eakett and Baggles. They have a copy in their offices, duly stamped and signed, which you may, at your upcoming leisure, peruse for yourself. This is the original and has been authenticated by the Ministry of Law." He puffed out his chest and handed over the document. "All is in order, Durrant. You lost."

"I never signed a deed," Sera's mother said accusingly.

"Ah, but you did, madame," Mr. Swan said with his oily smile. "I have ample samples of your signature to verify it, and it was done in the presence of two advocates, not just one. The Mysteries prevent the forgery of such a document. See for yourself."

Sera's heart was racing with terror. "Am I to be sold, then?" she asked with growing dread.

"Indeed you are, young lady," Mr. Swan said succinctly. "For the rights and terms according to the deed. I believe the prince regent has been making some discreet overtures to possible buyers."

"I have," her father said coldly, not even looking at her, but gazing contemptuously at her mother.

"Mr. Durrant, do something!" her mother begged.

Mr. Durrant was reading the document quickly, his face growing white. Sera could see already that it was a binding document. Never had she imagined her father would stoop to such an action. Deeds were signed by the poor, never for the wealthy. Never for a princess. She gripped the edges of her chair, afraid she might leap up and start striking her father with her fists.

"It appears to be in order," Mr. Durrant said in a choking voice. "Surely my client was unaware of what she was signing. You can see by her expression this was not done willingly."

Mr. Swan looked unconcerned. "But she *did* sign it. It is not my fault that my client had more wisdom and foresight. The lord high chancellor has reviewed it, Durrant. He cannot go against the law."

"But the people may revolt," Durrant said passionately. "They do not understand the intricacies of the Mysteries. It could lead to another uprising."

"They're ignorant ruffians. Dogs. They will come to heel when the master lifts his cane. Come now, man. Have the good grace to concede defeat. You cannot protect your client from this. It's her mother's fault, after all. It's all . . . her . . . fault."

At his cruel, barbed words, Sera's mother began sobbing with despair. Her father, the prince regent, had a look of vindication on his face. She could see that he was relishing seeing his wife suffer. Inside Sera's heart, the remnants of the love she had once held for him withered away, replaced by fury and hatred. She had always wished to leave her confinement. But not like this. Not as a bond servant.

Her voice was trembling, but she spoke up anyway. "How l-long?" she asked, trying not to stammer. She knew from her studies with Eakett and Baggles that deeds were for fixed periods of time. The life of a child in the Fells was drastically short, so a deed might only last a few years.

"Excuse me?" Mr. Swan asked, showing some annoyance.

"How long is the deed for?" Sera asked again, more firmly this time.

Durrant was holding the document. "Seven years. A veritable lifetime." He smacked the paper down on his hand. "This prevents her from studying the Mysteries. Prevents her from *ever* inheriting the throne."

"Indeed it does," Mr. Swan said. He gave a passive shrug.

"This is what you want?" her mother accused with a hysterical sob. "Because you were jealous of her rights? Because you couldn't bend her to your will?"

"I have nothing further to say," the prince regent said. "I do not owe you or anyone anything."

"Father," Sera pleaded in anguish.

The word jolted him. He stiffened with physical pain and shook his head, shuddering. He was still suffering from the pain of his belief that she wasn't his true daughter. Whatever information he had been told had convinced him utterly. Even if it had been a lie.

An idea blossomed in her mind. She blinked quickly, watching her father knead his brow with his thumb and middle finger. Mr. Swan put his hand on her father's shoulder and whispered to him. Mr. Durrant looked impotent. But Sera felt a calm sense of self-assurance. It was just a little thing. The tiniest of whispers, but maybe this was the power that Mr. Durrant had explained to her, the one behind all the Mysteries. The one that could enlighten a mind and pierce a heart. The one that could make thoughts into a command. She had never felt its influence before. Maybe it had finally come to her in her hour of need.

Sera held herself erect. "And what if he is *not* my father, Mr. Swan?"

Her words landed like thunder.

Mr. Durrant leaped on them, his eyes widening with surprise. "Has not the prince regent begun an investigation as to the facts behind the *purported* adultery of his wife? What Princess Seraphin has said is very relevant to the point. Only the child's *father* can rightfully sign the deed. Until the investigation is complete, this deed cannot be enforced." He smacked the paper down on his hand again, a look of triumph blazing on his face.

Her father's look of victory trembled and then, with a great shudder, collapsed into acrimony.

"You said it couldn't be broken!" the prince regent shouted at Mr. Swan in anger. "There was nothing that could stop it!"

Mr. Swan was flummoxed. His cheeks were blotchy and red.

"Clearly your advocate underestimated the intellectual acuity of a *child*," Mr. Durrant said with particularly spiteful emphasis to the word. "As did I," he added, chuckling to himself and turning to give Sera a proud look. "As did I."

CETTIE

CHAPTER THIRTY-FIVE

LOST

Cettie hurt all over. Not just from the walking, but from the cuts and scrapes that she had suffered so far that day. She was hungry, tired, voiceless, and lost in a sea of angry faces. She stopped at a circular fountain in a court where washerwomen were attempting to clean clothes. She sat on the far side from them. Although she was thirsty, the water looked dirty and uninviting. Still, she might have tried to scoop up a handful and drink it if not for the sight of the soiled clothes being cleaned in it.

Dipping her hand into the water, she started to wipe away the dried blood from her arms and legs and was almost immediately accosted by one of the washerwomen.

"Oy there, be gone with you, waif!" one of them said, scowling. Rising from her work, she stalked over and lifted her hand. The threat was clear. "Don't be getting your filth in the waters now. Off! Off!"

Cettie sighed at the lack of reprieve and her inability to answer. The waters were already disgusting; she was hardly making them worse. If she'd had her voice, she could have tried reasoning with them. But she'd already earned a bruised cheek from Staunton, and she knew the woman was ready to cuff her if she didn't obey. Cettie abandoned the fountain and slunk off.

"Don't mind her," one of the other women said as Cettie left. "Poor thing. She's run off."

"That's not my problem," said the washerwoman. "Forsook her deed by the looks. Them kind is nothing but trouble."

So Cettie continued to wander the streets, walking with a fierce determination. She knew that by wandering aimlessly, she would catch unwanted attention from one of the many street gangs in the Fells. Her ill-fitting, torn dress and her injuries had already garnered plenty of looks. She had no money to steal, so the pickpockets would likely leave her alone, but she needed to find shelter. The skies overhead were thick with clouds from the storm she'd seen approaching earlier. Another part of her mind, one she barely allowed to hope, was still intent on finding the law offices of Sloan and Teitelbaum. It didn't seem possible, but she'd not stop looking until she found it.

Hunger began to torment her. It was a familiar feeling, a ghost friend she'd not met up with in a long, long time. *Remember me?* it seemed to say. And she did remember. She remembered Miss Charlotte spending all the living she received from the deeds on drink. How the children had gone to bed hungry each night. How Cettie had sometimes given her portion to the others because their sobs were more needful than hers. Cettie had grown a lot since coming to Fog Willows. Properly nourished and cared for, she had already begun to blossom into a young woman. As her ankles throbbed on the hard cobbles, she felt a pang of longing for Anna, for her companionship and comfort. For anyone. Instead, her only companion was the hunger, its skeletal clawing against her ribs. She did not cry. It was not so bad as that yet.

Eventually the sun began to fade, and Cettie knew she would need to find a place to rest and wait out the night. Walking the streets at night was a sure way of getting attacked. But she wanted to find a safe, secluded place. She remembered passing a kirkyard a few streets back.

It was small and crowded with thin stone grave markers, but she'd spied a tree and maybe a little patch of grass. It might be her best option. In the Fells, people stayed away from kirkyards, especially at night, for fear of the ghosts. She didn't imagine she'd have much competition in such a place, though there was the possibility ghosts would assail her sleep. She decided to give it another look and turned and went back in that direction.

Just as the sun was setting, a loud factory whistle blew, and she knew the streets would soon be full of workers trudging their way back to the tenements. These men and women worked in the factories all day, from sunup to sunset, and they'd be angry and irritable. She hastened her step. Just when she was beginning to despair that she had lost her way again, she spied the kirkyard with weeds choking the bottom of the metal gate. The gate was closed. Cettie stopped to stare at it. There was indeed a singular tree; the bark of the trunk had been scored away with knife marks from where people had cut into it. Around the tree was the sight that had drawn her eyes earlier that day. Headstones surrounded it on all sides, stacked up against each other. It was a curious sight.

The noise of marching men filled the streets, giving her impetus to act. She squeezed through the bars of the gate, which were spaced just barely wide enough to admit her. She really had to push to get through and feared for a moment that she'd get stuck there. But she managed it and then stole into the kirkyard and hid behind the moldering heap of stones. The earth was soft, and she was grateful for the chance to rest. Leaning her back against the stone, she listened to the noise of the marching workers, their coughs and grumbles, the thrumming of their feet against the ground. Cettie lay down, her cheek pressing against the earth, and she listened, and listened, wanting to wait until the workers were all gone. Maybe she could find another place. Another shelter. But she was so exhausted she fell asleep.

She awoke in the dark to the overpowering feeling of invisible hands groping her arms and legs. It felt as if the dead in the graves arrayed below her were sucking her down to join them. The feeling of combined violation, greed, and suffocation was overpowering. Cettie wrenched her way loose and quickly stood, only to realize she was surrounded by ghosts. The desire to lie down and die slammed into her. She had no friends, no rescuer, no guardian. She would perish in the Fells before Fitzroy ever found her. Why not sleep in the kirkyard forever, her bones mixing with the slabs of stone?

The thoughts pounding in her skull were not hers. She pressed her fingers to her ears and started to walk away, tripping against the crush of headstones.

She started to squeeze herself through the gate bars again, and this time it was more of a struggle—it felt like hands were gripping her limbs and trying to keep her inside.

Be gone! she shouted at them in her mind, and the ghosts recoiled from her. But they only receded for a moment before renewing their attack. She finally managed to squeeze through the bars, her arms and legs wooden with cold. To her relief, the ghosts remained penned in the courtyard as she walked away. She could feel the writhing mass of them behind her. Could feel their hatefulness, their desire for revenge against her, one of the living. Some warding had been set to hold them in. A warding that she had violated. Cettie shuddered and knelt by the gate, leaning against the dilapidated wall of the building nearby. The night was so bitingly cold. She blew on her hands and rubbed them together, shivering beneath her torn dress.

She lay against the wall of the building and fell into another fitful sleep.

She was awakened again, this time by a stiff finger jabbing her in the arm. She heard a sharp intake of breath.

"Blimey! She's alive!"

It was a boy, probably eight years old, with a dirty cap askew and scraps for clothes. The small face was so smudged and dirty it was impossible to make out his features. It was early morning now, with just enough light for her to see the lad.

"Oy, Renn! It's a girl! She the one?"

Cettie hurried to her feet, her knees aching and her whole body trembling with cold. She became aware of the sound of others approaching. Not the marching of workers, but the stealthy sound of children. She realized she'd been found by a street gang. The numbness in her mind began to flare with worry.

The boy who had poked her was backing away, but his eyes sparkled with greediness and hunger.

"Oy," said a deeper voice. As Cettie saw the other children approach out of the gloom, she knew she was in trouble. This lad was sixteen, and, by the looks of him, the best fed of the bunch. He was chewing on an apple core as he approached. "You're the lass the law is out searching for. Been lookin' all night long. We found you first." He gave her a gap-toothed grin and a chuckle.

Cettie backed away from him, preparing to flee. The boy-man, Renn, gave a curt nod, and suddenly his gang pounced on her. One grabbed her arm; another grabbed her around the middle. Then Renn was there, grabbing her by the jaw with his fingers and looking into her eyes.

"Come on, lass. We'll get that reward."

She was ushered forward by the gang, trying to think of what she could do to escape. There were six in all, most as young as her. Gangs usually worked for older men, anyone who would provide shelter in a crumbling building.

As they reached a side corner, there was someone else blocking the way.

"Oy, Renn. Let her go."

Cettie recognized the voice. She'd not heard it in a while, but she knew it well. It was Joses, her friend from Miss Charlotte's. The despair from a moment before turned to hope.

Renn stopped, visibly angered by the intruder.

"We found her first, Joses," he growled.

"Do you think Clayton will care a rat's whisker about that?" Joses shot back. "He sent me to warn you. Hand her over, or he'll stick you in the ribs. You know he will."

"This ain't fair, Joses," Renn said with fury. "We found her first!"

"What's fair in the Fells?" Joses said with open palms and a look of exasperation. "I'm just the messenger. You want Clayton as an enemy?"

"No," Renn muttered.

"Smart one. Let her go."

Cettie felt the hands on her loosening. Joses stared down the much-bigger boy.

But in the end, the threat of Clayton prevailed, and Cettie found herself walking alongside Joses as he led her down the street.

"Blimey, Cettie," he said, shaking his head. "I told you to be careful. Is it true you can't talk?"

She looked at him in surprise and nodded vigorously.

"Blimey," he said again. "Everyone is looking for you. They want to keep you away from Fitzroy. But you want to go back to him, eh? Right?"

She nodded again, squeezing his arm.

He gave her a crooked smile. "I figured. Been up all night looking for you. The law wants you. But I don't trust that Staunton. Never have." He coughed against his forearm, a huge hacking cough. Cettie noticed the pallor of his cheeks, the feverish look in his eyes. Joses was sick. She'd heard that kind of cough many times, and it usually ended badly. A flicker of worry shot through her.

He noticed her looking at him in concern and gave her a shrug. "I'm all right, Cettie. Better than most. Look at you now. Like one of us again."

A loud whistle blew just overhead, startling them both. Then Joses began to laugh. In a moment, the streets were thronged with people preparing for the labors of the day. They were just two in a crowd, lost in a sea of bodies and desperation. But she felt comforted that her friend had found her.

"Hungry?" he asked her in a low voice as they walked.

She nodded, her stomach desperate for food.

"Just keep walking," he said. With that, he disappeared into the crowd, weaving through it deftly. She worried about him. He'd been caught stealing before, but he was back at her side in a trice with some bread, a small, hard loaf. Cettie gave him a scolding look, but he didn't seem chagrined.

"I'll not let you starve," he said, offering the bread. "Not after all you did for us."

She took it and tore it in half, giving the second portion to him.

"You eat the whole thing," he said, shaking his head.

She held it out to him again, giving him a forceful look.

"All right," he said begrudgingly. He hadn't grown since they'd last seen each other. If anything, he looked even weaker than he had before, wasted away by illness. He took a few nibbles on the bread, obviously intending to savor it. Cettie did the same.

"When I last saw you," he said above the noise of the crowd, "I warned you about the sham. The trick."

She nodded eagerly.

"Lots of folk have been talking about you. That you belong down in the Fells, not up in the clouds. Fitzroy's advocate has been hunting for your records. But he's not the only one. There are others who will pay more than what Fitzroy is offering. Pay more for *you*. It's a scam, Cettie. They want to shackle Fitzroy through you. He's kind of a hero cuz of what he did for you. They say if he's the prime minister, things will finally change. But others don't want them to change. They'll pay to keep you lost, to keep him distracted, searching for you." Joses shook his head angrily. "I don't know who to believe. But I won't let nothing happen to you, Cettie. I don't care what Clayton does to me. I'm getting you back to a real home."

She felt her throat tighten at his show of loyalty. They walked for a long way. Many of the workers had already started their shifts, but the streets were still crowded. As Joses led her, she began to notice that the clothes were growing finer, the smell not as putrid. They were entering the business district. The structures were better kept, and she saw street sweepers pushing their brooms. There was something vaguely familiar about it.

Then she saw the streets open to a giant square, and she recognized it instantly. She had come there with Fitzroy. She even saw zephyrs flying overhead. Excitement built inside her.

As they reached the opening to the square, she saw the law offices she had visited with her guardian. She nearly broke free and ran to them, but Joses gripped her arm and pushed her against the wall.

"Hold up," he said, eyeing the square and the crowds. "That's Staunton's ship," he said, nodding toward one of the zephyrs. "The square is crawling with the law. I recognize one of the men in the square. He's not even wearing a uniform, but I know him. They're waiting for you. They'll have us before we reach the fountain." He uttered a foulmouthed curse and then, "Let's go around the other way."

Still gripping her arm, he turned and led her back down the street. Then Joses stopped in his tracks, his fingers digging into her flesh.

"Clayton," he whispered in fear.

CHAPTER THIRTY-SIX

BEHIND THE DOOR

Cettie had never seen the gang leader before, but she had no trouble picking him out of the crowd. He was well fed and had lank dark hair that went down to his shoulders and a new cap on his head. Mostly, though, she recognized him by the look he was giving Joses. He knew he'd been betrayed, that Joses had taken Cettie away. In his clenched fist, Cettie saw a cutting tool. The blade looked rusted—or maybe it was covered in dried blood.

"We have to run for it," Joses whispered to Cettie. "I know an abandoned house. I stay there sometimes. You have to keep up with me."

She clutched his arm and nodded, her mouth dry, her body tensing.

Clayton's gang charged first, rushing toward them through the gaps in the street. Joses gripped Cettie's hand, and they plunged into the square. There were so many passersby that they had to cut and dodge to avoid running into them. Urchins abounded in the public places and were an annoyance to everyone, and soon Joses and Cettie were followed by angry shouts as well as Clayton's gang. Her heart pumped wildly in her chest.

Joses led her to another alley, and a man in uniform stepped forward to block the way. He had a thick mustache and sandy-colored hair.

"Hold there!" he barked in command, but Joses let go of Cettie's hand, and they dodged around him on either side. He reached to try to snatch one of them, but couldn't get a hold of either. A ministry whistle began to sound shrilly in the court, adding to the mayhem and confusion. Joses grinned in triumph as they dodged the officer, and they plunged into the narrow street, dodging carts and slower pedestrians. Soot smudges smeared the walls, and litter and refuse required them to be constantly alert to avoid tripping. Almost as soon as they had entered the street, Joses grabbed her hand again and pulled her down another alley. It was so narrow they had to run one at a time, leaping over the sleeping forms of drunkards and those who had no shelter.

Behind her, Cettie heard the noise of the chase. Some of Clayton's boys were still on their heels.

"Turn!" Joses called and abruptly fled down an even narrower street. Cettie almost missed it but rushed after him. The sound of pursuers was drawing closer. They were faster and very motivated to catch up.

The shadows were deeper now, and it was getting harder and harder to see. She was afraid she'd fall and ruin the escape, but somehow she managed to keep her feet. Her chest burned with the need for more air, and her limbs were tiring quickly.

A hand brushed against her hair, the fingers trying to grip her, and she bent forward, spurred to greater speed.

"Turn!" Joses shouted again, and disappeared around the next corner.

Cettie followed, only to realize that Joses had stopped at the edge. As their pursuer came around the corner, Joses swung out his leg and tripped the fellow, causing him to crash painfully onto the cobbles. Joses then kicked him hard in the ribs and motioned for Cettie to keep running. Only she couldn't—a stone wall at the end of the alley blocked the way. Her heart went into her throat with fear.

Joses increased his sprint, heading right for it. He didn't stop as he ran, jumped, and caught the high part of the wall. Swinging his legs up onto it, he beckoned to her again.

"Hurry, Cettie!" he called.

Heart pounding, she leaped up the wall and grabbed his hand. Her feet scrabbled to find footing, but he held her and kept her from dropping. Footfalls approached, and she tried not to panic, fearful one of the gang would grab her legs and pull her back down. But Joses hoisted her up onto the wall.

Clayton and the other boys now filled the small alley, their faces dripping with sweat and grime.

"You traitor!" Clayton bellowed.

"Jump!" Joses said, grabbing her hand.

Out of the corner of her eye, Cettie saw Clayton pull back his hand and throw something. Joses stiffened with pain as the blade struck him in the back, sinking all the way to the hilt. They were already coiled to spring, and she leaped, but Joses fell, landing in a heap of broken crates at the base of the other side of the wall. The jolt of the landing jarred her knees and made her fall on her hands. But her own pain didn't matter. When she turned to find him, frantic, Joses was struggling to exit the debris. His face was tight with pain, but his blue eyes burned with determination. He looked at the hilt sticking out of his back and shook his head.

"Pull it out," he gasped.

She stared at it in horror, watching the blood stain his clothes. She heard the noise of youths running at the wall and knew they didn't have much time. Gripping the small handle of the dirk, she pulled it out of him. Blood began to flow down his skin, making her blanch. He pressed the heel of his hand against it and started to jog down the alley. His hiss of pain made her heart cringe with anguish. She held his arm with one hand, trying to help him away, and gripped the blade with the other to defend them both.

"That way," Joses said, jerking his head. They went down another alley and then another, but they could hear their pursuers.

"See that . . . broken crate?" he whispered, gasping. "Hide . . . under it. They don't know which way we went. I need . . . to rest."

She rushed over to the dilapidated crate and lifted it. Rodents scurried away from the disruption, and Cettie helped Joses curl up and then crouched down next to him and covered them both with the crate. The gaps were huge. It didn't provide much cover.

The noise of the approaching gang reached the alley. "Oy! Where'd they go!"

"I dunno, Clayton."

Clayton let out a curse. "They can't be far."

"No. Did they go through one of the back doors?"

"I dunno. Joses is clever as a rat. But I stuck him. He won't make it far. You two, that way. You two, this way. I'll take this one. Holler if you see them. We'll be rich as the prince regent if we catch her."

They went different ways, but it was Clayton who walked toward where they were hiding. Cettie needed desperately to breathe, but she held her breath and tried to hold completely still. Joses writhed in pain and started to groan, but she covered his mouth and tried to calm him.

The slap, slap of Clayton's shoes stopped right next to them. Cettie froze, willing him to look anywhere else, but a quick glance upward revealed that he was standing right by the crate.

"I'll kill him," Clayton grunted savagely.

Cettie closed her eyes, squeezing the dirk's handle in her hand. Suddenly the crate flew off of them, cracking into splinters. Had he seen them, or was he just venting his anger? It didn't matter. With the sudden rush of air, she heard Clayton's surprised gasp. He saw them now. She flung herself at him and stabbed him in the meat of the leg as hard as she could, letting go of the knife only when she felt it jar into bone.

Clayton howled with pain, dropping down to squeeze his knee. Cettie did the technique of butterfly hands Raj Sarin had taught her and hit him in the chest. He stumbled backward and toppled, yelling and cursing in pain. Cettie kicked him in the jaw, and his eyes rolled back in his head, and he lay limp and unconscious. She saw Joses trying to stand, his hand still pressed against his bleeding back, and, despite the obvious pain he was suffering, he grinned at her and nodded in respect.

She helped him rise, and they hurried away as quickly as they could.

⌒

Joses's strength was failing. He walked hunched over, grunting with pain, and his coughs grew more severe. They were in the depths of the Fells now, not the tenements but a neighborhood. Children poked their heads out of windows to look down at them. At least they were no longer being chased. Cettie was hungry again—no, famished. But she didn't know how to steal, and she didn't dare try lest it bring the officers down on them in moments. Joses needed a doctor, but he refused to consider it, insisting instead that he bring her to the abandoned house. All the windows were broken, and no one had lived there in years. It had become his private refuge, a place to escape the gangs and life on the street. He said there wasn't any food there, but it would provide shelter.

It was hidden in a backstreet, split by a narrow alley. One could have reached out from the broken window and touched the window on the other side with a small pole. The exterior was falling apart. The cracked windowsills gaped emptily. Not a single pane of glass was left. The front was on the other side, but Joses led her to the back.

"Open the trapdoor," he whispered, gazing up at the roofline high above. "It's for the cesspit, but it's not used anymore. It doesn't smell so bad, and no one will see us enter this way."

She dreaded cesspits, but there wasn't another choice, so she nodded and gripped the handle of the trapdoor and pulled. The stench was bad but not overpowering. She carefully set the lid down and then helped Joses to the edge.

"I can make it," he said with a dreamlike voice. With one hand guiding him, he descended the narrow steps leading into the cesspit. Cettie followed, and she heard him call behind him to shut the door.

It was as black as a well.

"Come closer. Hold my arm. I'll guide you."

The passage was narrow and foul smelling. She put her hand on his shoulder, and he led her deeper into the cesspit. Fear crept up her spine—what would she do if a ghost attacked them in the dark?—but she kept moving. It felt like they'd been walking forever when she suddenly felt him stop. They'd reached the stairs at last. As they went up, the black turned into gray, and she could begin to see again. Still, she could not help but worry some hand would grab her from the dark.

The home had long been abandoned. Even the rugs had been torn up, leaving stubs of nails beneath. They walked carefully, their shoes echoing on the planks. It was a narrow, little home, nothing like Fog Willows, but it wasn't as bleak as the tenements. The walls were discolored from where pictures had hung in frames. The baseboards were nicked and scarred. She could almost hear, in her mind, the sound of laborers carting off the things as the family had to abandon it. There was a sadness to the house, a sense of loss.

But there was also something else. As they walked down the corridor on the main floor, she sensed something speaking to her mind. It was the source of the memories that haunted the halls. Not a ghost, but an awareness. A knowing thing. It had gradually become aware of her as she'd mounted the steps from the cesspit.

She saw the narrow door halfway down the hall and knew by instinct that the source of the feeling was hidden inside. It felt similar to the locked door at Fog Willows, except it wasn't polluted.

"I have a place set up upstairs," he whispered. "By the skylight. There's a blanket. Some old shoes. A knife and spoon. Not much, but it's my own. You can stay with me, Cettie. As long as you need to. Then we'll sneak back another way to the square. I just need . . . just need to rest a bit."

She had let go of his shoulder after reaching the top of the stairs but now squeezed him again. She pointed to the door with a questioning look.

"Oh that," he said, a crooked smile on his face. "That's where they hide the Mysteries. Have you ever been in one of these?"

She shook her head no.

He gave her a smug look. "I picked the lock. Come and see. Then we can—*nngghh*—go upstairs."

As they approached it, she felt drawn to it, filled with an eager curiosity to learn the secrets of the room. Joses limped forward, twisted the handle, and pulled the door open. It creaked.

Cettie peered inside. It was a small closet that contained another door. She felt the sense of awareness coming from behind that one.

"It's not locked," Joses assured her, and motioned for her to go in. He leaned against the wall, wincing. "I don't go in very often. Makes me feel strange."

Cettie stepped into the closet and put her hand on the inner door handle. As soon as she touched it, she felt her mind begin to unwrap layers. She'd experienced something similar in Gimmerton Sough and the day she had confronted Mrs. Pullman's thoughts. More memories began to come alive in her mind, memories that weren't hers. She could see the father of the household sitting in a small den crowded with bookshelves. She could see a mother and three little girls. Cettie saw affection, hard work, and caring. These were the memories of someone else, hidden and buried within the house itself. She squeezed the handle and twisted it, and the door yielded.

When it opened, she saw two glowing lights in the dark. The lights were not very bright, but they were bright enough to drive the shadows back. The lights came from a hunk of stone, about as high as her waist, sitting on a carved stone pedestal. A face was carved into the hunk of stone, and the eyes of the face were glowing. A sense of peace and serenity came from it, as if it were welcoming her back home.

It was the most beautiful thing she had ever seen. As she stepped deeper into the shadowy alcove, the light in the eyes began to grow brighter, bright enough to illuminate her ragged dress and the scrapes in her hands. Reaching out her hand, she gently touched the rock.

It wasn't exactly a voice that spoke to her. It was more like a whisper, a soft kiss against her mind.

Are you the keeper?

Cettie stared at the face. It was a woman's face, carved and sculpted with the elegance of a statue. She could see in her mind the image of the previous keeper, a woman who had been loyal to the family and its children, who had nurtured and cared for them and the dwelling. A position of trust and authority.

Yes, Cettie thought in her mind. She knew the stone could hear her thoughts, even though she could not speak.

I've been waiting for you.

And then Cettie heard music fill the house, the same beautiful strains she had enjoyed at Fog Willows. The lights all began to shine, coming from apertures fixed into the walls, which she suddenly realized were also made of carved stone, only smaller. Every aspect of the house was commanded by this central stone, which had decided to obey *her*. Memories gushed inside her, knowledge of the previous inhabitants, the families who had lived there for generations. Her mind was engulfed by the information and names and history extending for hundreds of years.

Suddenly her contact was broken. She felt Joses's fingers digging into her arm as he yanked her away from the stone obelisk.

"What are you doing?" he shouted at her. "Turn it off! Turn it off! The music—they'll hear it!"

CHAPTER THIRTY-SEVEN

Reversed

Cettie did not know *how* to turn it off. Everything within the house was coming alive at once. Even the smell of flowers that suddenly wafted into the stagnant hall. Music swelled in the corridor, a tinkling melody that belied the ruined look. Joses bent over, groaning with pain. He was pale—too pale—and slouched against the wall again, looking on the verge of collapse. She tried to silence the music, to return the house to its former quietude, but it wouldn't listen to her.

"We can't stay here now," Joses wheezed, shaking his head. "The whole street will know we're here. Clayton will find us."

Cettie held his arm and tried to help him walk away from the room of Mysteries. He leaned heavily against her, and she noticed the red smear he had left on the wall. Together, they continued down the main corridor, which was now brightly illuminated. The front door was across from them, a little crooked on its hinges, and a loud thumping sounded on it, startling her.

Intruders are coming into the basement.

She heard the whispered premonition, and suddenly she could see into the cesspit through a set of eyes that were not her own. It was glowing now, flooded with light, and she saw the boys of Clayton's gang descending into the pit. Clayton had a strip of leather tied around his leg, but he hobbled forward with determination. Sickening fear shot through Cettie's heart.

Can you stop them? she thought to the house's magic.

Yes.

She felt a throb in her mind, and suddenly the stone carving in the cesspit took on a menacing air. It radiated fear and danger, triggering unthinkable terror in the boys' minds. She watched in joy as the boys turned around and fled in panic, nearly trampling one another to escape. As soon as the last one had fled, the trapdoor lurched over and shut all by itself, and the image in her mind cooled and faded.

Her relief was short-lived. The door handle jiggled, and suddenly Cettie could see the man standing outside, through another set of eyes. He had a fashionable hat and coat and looked concerned at the noise and commotion he heard within the house. The lock held because the man did not have a key. No matter how fiercely he struggled against it, it would not open.

Joses crumpled to the floor.

Cettie instantly knelt by him, worried for her friend, but she could not rouse him. The pounding on the door continued awhile longer and then went silent. Still the music played on.

Cettie lifted Joses beneath his arms and began to pull him up the stairs. She wanted to find a place to hide, for she knew that the officers would be called to respond. The dwelling was very narrow and tall, each floor holding a different room. With all her strength, she heaved and pulled him up the stairs. It was a slow and grueling process, but she managed to find the floor where he had made his little shelter. She wrapped him up in his blanket, hoping to at least warm his cool skin. There was nothing she could give him. No food, no drink. She couldn't even speak to him, and the helplessness of that was overpowering. Overhead the skylight shone down on her. Time stretched and faded. The shadows on the floor moved.

"Cettie?" Joses mumbled, coming awake at last.

She rushed to him and knelt, smoothing his hair from his brow. Down below, she heard more pounding on the door. She summoned the power to her and could see who was on the front steps. When the vision opened, she saw the same man as before and Lieutenant Staunton as well.

"You're sure this is the one?" Staunton asked the man.

"Yes, and you can still hear the music playing. This house has been abandoned for years. The deeds are all tangled up in the courts. Something has awoken the house. Someone's inside. I don't know how."

"Thank you for calling the ministry," Staunton said. "You did the right thing. My men and I will investigate. Return to your home."

"It's unnerving hearing that music from an abandoned dwelling. Do you think the house is haunted?"

"Don't be superstitious. I'll see that it stops. Good day, sir."

It was as if Cettie were standing on the porch with them, the same experience she'd had at Gimmerton Sough. She could see and hear through these strange stones placed throughout the house, all of them connected to the master boulder in the keeper's room.

"I'm cold," Joses said with a shiver. She gazed down at him, her heart twisting with sadness. She was watching his life ebb away, helpless to save him. Anxious tears stung her eyes. She leaned down and kissed his cheek, kissed his forehead, trying to offer him comfort in a way other than words.

She heard Staunton say something, a word she didn't recognize, and suddenly the doorknob turned. She saw officers, about six, enter the dwelling.

Keep them out! Cettie ordered the magic in her mind.

I cannot. They are officers of Law.

She felt the defenses of the dwelling start to fade. The combined will of the six men was enough to overwhelm them. The music went quiet. The lights dimmed. She stared down at Joses's face, saw the pallor deepen.

"It's growing dark," he said worriedly, his lip trembling.

Cettie wanted to tell him it was only the lights in the house. But she could say nothing. She stroked the side of his face, listening to the noise of boots marching up the steps. Staunton wouldn't help her friend. To those men, Joses was just another dying street urchin. A flickering candle. So what if another one blew out?

Well, to her he was so much more. She gripped his hand and squeezed it hard. His eyelashes fluttered. He gazed at her, looking worried.

"I'm afraid," he whispered. "I'm afraid of becoming a ghost."

The grip of his hand was getting weaker. She squeezed even harder, feeling tears drip down her nose.

"You always looked after us," he croaked. "You sang little songs when we were frightened in the dark. It's so dark now. I wish you could sing again, Cettie. I'll miss that."

Stay with me, she thought toward him. She could sense his life spark quivering, dandelion fluff about to be blown away by a breeze.

The noise of boots came down the hall. She turned and saw Staunton in the doorway.

The officer gazed down at them, his face impassive, and she glared back. "That was quite a chase, Cettie of the Fells. In the end, his blood led us to you. You should have abandoned him in the street."

Cettie let go of Joses's hand, and it fell limp to the floor. She rose, feeling her insides boiling with anger, with the desire for revenge.

Attack him, she thought to the stone face down below.

I cannot. He is an officer of Law.

She clenched her fists with fury. *Attack him!*

Cettie felt the room begin to brighten with light. Her thoughts were overpowering the magic. Staunton's eyes widened.

"There are six of us and only one of you," he said angrily. "I don't care how strong you are. You cannot overpower us. Now come with us right now. He's gone. There's nothing more you can do."

She shook her head no and backed away from him. She would fight them all if she had to.

Staunton scowled. "Very well. Then I will drag you back to the zephyr in bonds." Three more officers crowded around the doorway.

Cettie increased the pressure on the stone, commanding it to obey her. In her heart, she knew she could summon fire from it and burn the entire house down. She would do it if necessary. She would *not* go with them. She would not be used as a tool against Fitzroy.

"She's *strong*," one of the officers said worriedly.

"Take her!" Staunton said.

Suddenly there was a ping of broken glass, and something struck Staunton in the chest, knocking him backward. The glass from the skylight shattered down, raining in fragments. The pool of glass lay between Cettie and the officers. A shadow blotted the light from above, and then Raj Sarin descended into the room, gliding down like a leaf.

Her heart thrilled with recognition as he landed amidst the crushed glass.

Staunton had staggered back, holding his chest. He dropped his hand and looked at the small gray ball that had struck him. There was no blood, but his face was a mask of pain.

"I think, gentlemen," Raj Sarin said, "that you have forgotten how to count." Then he leaped forward, taking in a gulp of air, and crashed down in the midst of the officers. Cettie watched in transfixed joy as he struck each man, bringing them down one by one with a series of sharp blows. She recognized his forms, saw how all the moves he had been teaching her could be used in practice. The officers quailed before the Bhikhu. One took an elbow in the mouth, another a foot in the stomach. One tried to fight back, but his arm was broken when Raj

Sarin scissored his arms across his elbow and forearm. He howled in pain before being silenced by a well-placed punch to the throat.

Then Fitzroy landed in the heap of glass. He held a weapon like the one Cettie had seen him use at Dolcoath—an arquebus. It was partly made of wood, partly of metal, like a half staff. She realized that Fitzroy was the one who had shot Staunton through the glass.

That he was even there, in the room, filled her with wonder and gratitude. His face had become a mask of controlled rage battling with intense relief. When he saw her, staring at him in wonder, he smiled and sighed. Then he marched over to where Lieutenant Staunton was trying to recover.

"V-vice Admiral!" Staunton stammered.

Fitzroy jerked the butt of the arquebus and slammed it into Staunton's stomach, knocking the wind out of him. "I know *all*, Staunton," Fitzroy said with fury. "I've been chasing you down like a stag in the hunt all day. Your alliance with Mrs. Pullman is over. She's been dismissed from my household, permanently. If you had come to me or tried to warn me, this would have turned out very different for you. But your ambition blinded you to the risks. How *dare* you." Fitzroy shook his head, looking as if he was only barely restraining himself from striking the man again with the arquebus. "Pray the Law saves you. I will be prosecuting you myself."

Staunton's eyes were wide, and he trembled with misery and buried his face in his hands.

"Raj Sarin, take them out of my sight," Fitzroy said gruffly.

"With pleasure," the Bhikhu replied, and began corralling the officers away.

Cettie ran up to Fitzroy and hugged him fiercely, pressing her tears against his familiar coat. She sobbed without words, squeezing him harder and harder.

"How is your friend?" Fitzroy asked, tousling her hair. She pulled away, looking up at him with newfound misery. He handed the arquebus to her and stooped over Joses. He leaned down and put his ear against the boy's mouth.

"Well, he lives . . . if barely," he said after a moment's concentration. "His name is Joses, is it not?"

Cettie nodded quickly, staring at him. Fitzroy wasn't a doctor. What could he do?

"Close your eyes, please," Fitzroy said. "This is one of the Mysteries."

She obeyed without hesitation. After a moment, she heard Fitzroy say in a clear, calm voice, "Joses of the Fells, I *gift* you with healing. Your wound is severe, but I grant you your life. Blood and sinew, mend as one. Make it so."

The feeling that came into the small upstairs room was one of peace and gentle power. Cettie felt the throb against her mind again, but there was no stone channeling it this time. A queer sensation that all would be well filled her bosom. Of course it would all be well.

Fitzroy had found her.

Again.

⸎

The wind blew through Cettie's hair as the zephyr streaked through the sky. She would never grow tired of that feeling. Joses was wrapped in his blanket, a silly grin spread on his mouth. He was weak still, but he was awake again and improving. For the first time in his life, his belly was full.

Fitzroy finished consulting with the pilot, nodding and clapping the man on the back, before he returned to where Cettie and Joses were sitting near the prow.

"We should be at Fog Willows soon," Fitzroy said with a smile. Cettie looked eagerly at him, but he shook his head. "We will not be there long, however. Just long enough to set Joses in a bed to rest and to collect some things. You cannot stay at Fog Willows."

Cettie stared at him in horror, her heart beginning to ache. Tears sprang into her eyes, but she struggled to hold them back. Perhaps she *deserved* to be sent away. She had brought evil to Fitzroy's house.

He put his hand on her shoulder. "No, Cettie. I'm not sending you away. You must start school to learn the Mysteries. I thought we could wait two more years, that you would be safe at Fog Willows until then." He shook his head. "But you need to learn how to protect yourself from the beings that haunt you. To be given power *over* them. And I need to take you there to remove the binding that afflicts your tongue."

She felt such a surge of relief that she wrapped her arms around him and pressed her face against his chest.

He hugged her back and then pulled slightly away. "I must give the credit to Raj Sarin," Fitzroy said, gazing back at the dozing Bhikhu. "Before we left for Lockhaven, he was concerned that something was wrong. You had not been yourself. Neither had Anna. He was concerned that both of you were being mistreated by Mrs. Pullman. I've come to rely on Raj Sarin's wisdom." He gave the other man a kindly look. "I also harbored concerns that the prime minister might have a hand in this, that he might try some trickery to win our invention for himself. So I made it appear to everyone that I was obeying his summons. But we returned shortly after leaving Fog Willows. That was when I discovered the full extent of Mrs. Pullman's treachery. I reclaimed the keys from her, and the manor revealed to me the things she has kept hidden from me these past years. Not only has she tortured you and Anna and my servants, but she is also responsible for my wife's malaise." His face hardened with disapproval. "She will be there when we land but has been relieved of her duties. I've summoned Sir Jordan's wife to fill the role of keeper of the house. Lady Maren was given the keys while I set off to look for you, young lady. Without them, Mrs. Pullman has no power at Fog Willows. I was never far behind you, yet it would have been enough time for you to disappear. It's a miracle I found you at all."

She sighed with relief—Fitzroy finally knew the truth, and Mrs. Pullman could no longer control her. How dearly she wished she could speak to him and ask him questions.

"I thought to go after the one who had taken you away," Fitzroy continued. "I followed Staunton's zephyr from a distance. I wanted to search for you myself, but I felt I'd find you faster if I kept my eye trained on him."

"Sir?" Joses asked, then coughed into his hand.

"Yes, lad?"

"Why is it that Cettie can't speak? What did they do to her?"

"It's not an easy question to answer. And I cannot tell you in full because it is part of the Mysteries. Apparently, Mrs. Pullman is more adept at the Mysteries of Thought than I was ever aware. I don't know how it is done, but information can be recorded and sealed in such a way that it prevents someone else from uttering it. The power is even strong enough to remove someone's voice, which is quite remarkable for anyone to accomplish. It's a dangerous thing and prohibited under normal circumstances. What Mrs. Pullman practiced on the servants of Fog Willows . . . and on Cettie . . . is not an approved use of the Mysteries. And she did it under my authority, which heightens the crime. While she claims her motives were honorable, her means to that end were not. Thankfully, the master of the school Stephen and Phinia attend is knowledgeable about these matters and can remove such a binding. She will speak again soon."

He rested his hand on Cettie's shoulder. "The school I'm taking you to is an ancient one. It is also a well-guarded secret. There are no roads that lead there. One can only arrive by sky ship and . . . well, another means. It is the place where the first empress, Maia, was taught after her father disinherited her. That was before the empire, before she set up the current system of government. Before there were flying manors. It is where I studied, and it is where *you* will be studying. The school is called Muirwood Abbey, and we will go there this evening."

"Approaching Fog Willows," said the pilot from his perch.

"I think Cettie would want you to see this, Joses," Fitzroy said. The young man clutched the blanket to his chest and winced as he rose. Cettie saw the look of wonder on his face as they descended toward the glowing manor still shining from the various stone faces hidden behind opaque glass. She felt that same emotion as she looked down at it . . . at her home. Joses would be fully healed there. She trusted Fitzroy to see to his protection.

As they came to the landing platform, Cettie saw Lady Maren and Anna waiting down below, waving frantically. Behind them, she saw Mrs. Pullman surrounded by two officers of Law and Mr. Sloan, the advocate. The old woman's face was a mask, but Cettie could sense the depths of her suffering as the zephyr hovered lower. Mrs. Pullman was in anguish as she watched her master return to the manor with the child she hated.

Finally, after sending so many servants down to meet their fate in the Fells, she herself would be sent there in disgrace to face a magistrate for her crimes.

Cettie gazed at her, feeling just a little glimmer of pity. For all the harm she had done, Mrs. Pullman had been her own worst enemy. Then she looked up to the keeper's tower and saw that all the lights were out.

SERA

CHAPTER THIRTY-EIGHT

SERAPHIN FITZEMPRESS

The sunrise over Muirwood Abbey was spectacular. The sky was full of clouds, and the sun made them shine in a brilliant array of color. Ever since Sera had arrived, her world had expanded, and she thrilled at the possibility of studying the Mysteries and earning her right to become the empress. Her parents had kept so much from her; her world had been so limited.

"Oh, look, that is Fitzroy's tempest moored over there," Durrant said as he walked side by side with her. "I thought he was at Lockhaven?"

Sera did indeed recognize the ship from its long-ago visit to her manor. Excitement shot through her. She had always longed to meet Lord Fitzroy and his young ward.

"He must have arrived last night, for I don't recall seeing it yesterday," Sera said.

"Those of the ministries rarely come here anymore. Perhaps the Aldermaston of Muirwood invited Fitzroy to celebrate his new invention. He is going to be a *very* rich man, Sera. Or so I've been told. You should seek his goodwill."

"He is also a very honorable man," Sera said.

"He is that, of course," said Durrant wryly. "But it was the 'very rich' part I was referring to." He pursed his lips. "No one has rivaled Pavenham Sky in a long time. The winds are changing, Sera. I can smell it in the air."

"Somehow, I don't think you mean the smell of the lavender bushes," Sera said with a smile.

"They make me sneeze, unfortunately," he quipped. "No, things are changing. Your father's attempts to delegitimize you have been put to an end by the privy council."

And Sera was relieved that they had finally intervened. They had warned her father that if he tried to exercise the deed on her, they would remove him from power as prince regent and appoint one of his brothers instead. That threat had cowed him in short order. On the council's command, she had been sent to Muirwood to begin studying the Mysteries so that she could at least have an opportunity of fulfilling her destiny.

"I'm grateful they did," Sera said. "And grateful for your help on my behalf."

"You can thank me when you become empress, I'm sure," he drawled. "Oh, look, the family is leaving the Aldermaston's manor. That building has stood there for generations. I've heard the kitchen itself is five hundred years old!"

"It's a quaint little building. But I like all the dormitories in the village that lead up to the abbey. The small stone houses and chimneys. Where all the students live."

"Yes, the dormitories—Vicar's Close," said Durrant. "But you won't be staying there, naturally. You will be staying at the *Aldermaston's* manor. You are, after all, royalty."

Sera pursed her lips. "But I don't want to be set apart. I want to live at Muirwood like all the other learners."

Durrant winced. "You are rather *young* still, Princess."

"I'm not asking for your permission, Mr. Durrant," Sera said, adopting her authoritative voice. "I'm telling you what to do. I want to live in Vicar's Close. Make it happen."

He gave her an arch look. "So you *have* been listening to me. I'm astonished. Whatever will happen next? Ah, as I see the Aldermaston just ahead, I will broach the subject with him. And, of course, introduce you to Vice Admiral—"

"Brant Fitzroy," Sera said, interrupting him. "I know his name already, Durrant. Don't be tedious."

"I try never to be tedious, Your Highness," he replied, and gave her an approving look.

As they approached the family, Sera felt a little strange intruding on the scene. It was the kind of moment she had never experienced with her own parents. Fitzroy and his wife, Lady Maren, were holding hands and smiling as they watched their children. Their son was rather handsome, Sera admitted to herself, but he lacked Will's warmth, his drive to rise above his father's fall. The eldest sister was talking fast and playfully swatting at her brother's arm. There was another young man beside Fitzroy's eldest who was plain and stood slightly to the side of the gathering. He wasn't family. But her interest was more focused on the youngest two . . . one of whom was Cettie of the Fells. She was the darker-haired girl, the one who appeared more calm and tranquil. She had a bruise on her cheek. She was hugging her sister, the small, blond-haired one, with loving tenderness. Sera couldn't remember the girl's name, but she felt a pang of jealousy for being deprived of siblings.

The Aldermaston was a wizened man with a frizzy gray beard, which was the size of a small wolf, and a crown of equally gray hair on each side. He wore a set of spectacles high on his nose and a dark gray vest that buttoned up to his throat beneath his coat. Sera would never want someone like him to kiss her on the cheek because that beard would tickle her half to death. It was positively enormous. It was a disrespectful thought, and she internally chided herself for it, but she was prone to disrespectful thoughts.

"Aldermaston," Durrant said, waving as they approached. "Pardon the intrusion."

The Aldermaston had bushy dark eyebrows joined in the middle by three equal-sized furrows that lent him an austere appearance. Sera had already found him to be a very alert listener. He never said anything that showed disapproval, but he was stern and quiet.

Sera felt his gaze on her, and her bravado began to melt. It was difficult being in his presence when his look was so piercing.

"Yes, Mr. Durrant?" the Aldermaston said in a deep voice.

"Again, pardon the intrusion," Durrant said. "Greetings, Vice Admiral. All the Fitzroys are here. How wonderful. Plus two additions? The young man and the young lady?"

Fitzroy had an amiable voice. He didn't seem offended at all. "This is my ward, Adam Creigh. He's studying to become a doctor."

Sera thought the ward somewhat handsome upon closer inspection, but not in a brooding way like Fitzroy's son. No, the ward was smiling too pleasantly. And why was he standing so close to Cettie?

Well, it hardly mattered; she still preferred Will Russell above all others.

"And this is Cettie," Fitzroy continued, gesturing to the person Sera had long wanted to meet. "A young woman that I'm still trying to adopt."

Cettie gave a small curtsy. "A pleasure to meet you," she said in a clear, charming voice.

"Cettie, this is Seraphin Fitzempress. If I'm not mistaken."

The look that came over them all nearly made Sera giggle. They seemed flummoxed—all except for Cettie, who gave her an intrigued look.

"She'll do," Sera whispered to Durrant, and gave him a knowing look.

Durrant sighed. "Aldermaston, I hate to impose on you. It is manifestly clear that your authority on these grounds supersedes even that of the prince regent himself. The charter of that authority is an ancient one. But the princess would like to stay in Vicar's Close instead of your manor, and she will need a companion, as is the custom. Would you consider allowing Miss Cettie to be her companion? They seem of an age, and Lord Fitzroy has an impeccable reputation."

The Aldermaston had not reacted at all to the request. It was almost as if he had expected it. "I think something suitable can be arranged," he said. "This young lady is also in need of a companion, as it happens. It seems rather . . . fortuitous that both of you arrived simultaneously. I will consider it."

"Thank you," Durrant said.

Sera didn't bother waiting. She had spent her whole life waiting, confined to Lockhaven. Now she was at Muirwood, and she finally felt free. There wouldn't be much time for her to study the Mysteries, however. She would need to master them quickly and efficiently if she wanted the privy council to consider her claim above her father's . . . if she wanted to save her people. With the emperor's frail health, he could pass at any time. But that was a problem that lay ahead of her. She was finally about to meet Cettie of the Fells, after months and months of wishing. And so she approached the other girl and took her hand.

"I think we are going to be great friends," Sera said.

Even the ancient believers of the Mysteries were called the mastons. They recognized that when certain eternal laws are obeyed, the results come promptly. A wise Aldermaston once said that when riches begin to come, they come so quickly, and in such abundance, that one wonders where they hid during the lean years. Yes, riches do come suddenly, as I can attest to in my own life. But they flee just as quickly. Now that Fitzroy has begun to summon his fortune, will he be able to hold on to it? I've not known many men, my husband excluded, who did not let their riches ruin their good judgment. The mastons have withstood murders, poverty, war, and all manner of persecution, and remained true to their beliefs. But can they withstand wealth? They have been tried with riches. And when you count the number of the poor, they are already failing.

—*Lady Corinne of Pavenham Sky*

AUTHOR'S NOTE

When I was in high school, I loved my British Lit class. I first read Charles Dickens's *Great Expectations* then, and I've read it multiple times since. It's always been my favorite of his, followed by *Bleak House*. I'm also a huge fan of Jane Austen, Elizabeth Gaskell, Anthony Trollope, the Brontë sisters, and many other period novels, and I've watched the various films since *Sense and Sensibility* was first made into a movie.

So for *years* I have wanted to write a period novel based on that era. I hesitated because switching genres from fantasy to historical would be a really big jump, and I knew I'd possibly lose many readers. I kept the ideas bubbling in the back of my head while working on other novels. It was finishing the Kingfountain Series that gave me the idea that instead of using Regency England, I could *invent* that kind of setting in one of my own worlds. And not just one world. The barriers that separate my worlds can be crossed, as some of you have seen in the final Kingfountain books.

An epic story arc began to take shape in my mind, not a trilogy, but a five-book series. I began to envision the flying cities (don't you just love little Cosette singing "Castle on a Cloud" from *Les Mis*?), which I'd already invented in my Landmoor series. Floating boulders also appeared in *The Wretched of Muirwood*. And, of course, the Bhikhu are from my Mirrowen series. I didn't want to write a steampunk novel and use machinery and zeppelins to approximate technology. Instead, all the wonders of this world have their basis in the magic system of my Muirwood books. *Storm Glass* is set hundreds of years after the Covenant of Muirwood series. I used the name *Fitzempress* to denote the direct descendants of Maia and Collier and *Fitzroy* to denote descendants of the other kings.

This is not a continuation of the Muirwood stories, however. It's something altogether new, which is why I gave it a new name: the Harbinger Series. You don't need to have read the other series to understand this one. It will be a great entry point to my fiction for new readers.

I've never tried writing a series on such an epic scale before. As all these delicious ideas began to flow in my mind, I began to mix some more historical elements into it, as I usually do. For example, the term "storm glass" and its use by the historical Admiral Fitzroy were teased in with the invention of the barometer. I also invented Cettie, who represents one edge of society, and Sera, who comes from another hierarchy. I wanted both protagonists. They'll both be featured throughout the series, but in some books one will get more focus than the other.

So please indulge me in my journey into a period of history I've come to love so much. I've tried to take something old and remake it into something new. My world isn't as pleasant as Austen's England. Social ruin isn't the only risk, and failure can have terrible consequences. And when different worlds collide, many unexpected things will happen.

I hope you love experiencing this new world.

ACKNOWLEDGMENTS

Most of the time, these acknowledgment blurbs rarely get read as the author thanks the team who helped make this book happen. But in this case, I need to call special attention to services rendered above and beyond. There is a great quote in the first Harry Potter book that I love where Dumbledore says, "It takes a great deal of bravery to stand up to our enemies, but just as much to stand up to our friends." After turning in the first version of *Storm Glass* to my editors, Jason Kirk and Angela Polidoro, both had the courage and candor to speak up and tell me that the book could be much better than it was. It has been a long time since I have had to so thoroughly rework a manuscript. Their instincts were spot-on and helped make the characters richer, the setting more stunning, and this story the best it could be . . . and the version you've just read. So thank you, Jason and Angela, for your mighty editorial chops, your relentlessly helpful suggestions, and for being a critical part in making my books so successful.

I'd also like to thank Wanda, my excellent copyeditor, and my early readers who help motivate me and continue to support my work: Robin, Shannon, Emily, Isabelle, Sunil, Travis, and Dan. I hope you continue to enjoy the magic of this world!

ABOUT THE AUTHOR

Photo © 2016 Mica Sloan

Jeff Wheeler is the *Wall Street Journal* bestselling author of the Kingfountain Series, as well as the Muirwood and Mirrowen novels. He took an early retirement from his career at Intel in 2014 to write full-time. He is a husband, father of five, and devout member of his church. He lives in the Rocky Mountains and is the founder of *Deep Magic: The E-zine of Clean Fantasy and Science Fiction*. Find out more about Deep Magic at www.deepmagic.co, and visit Jeff's many worlds at jeff-wheeler.com.